R

TEXAS HORROR
by
TEXAS WRITERS
Vol. 9

curated by

Bret McCormick

A HellBound Books® LLC Publication

Cover design by E. R. Bills & Robert Elrod for
HellBound Books® Publishing LLC

www.hellboundbookspublishing.com

Printed in the United States of America

PRAISE FOR PREVIOUS EDITIONS . . .

I knew Texas had some good authors, but I didn't know just how many until I read *Road Kill Vol. 3*. This anthology is edited by E.R. Bills and published by HellBound Books. I found some new authors to read. If these short stories are any indicator, they have bright futures ahead of them.
—***Cedar Hollow Horror Reviews***, December 18, 2018

Road Kill: Texas Horror by Texas Writers 4 is an impressive addition to an already great series. There is something for every horror afficionado here. Texans reading will also appreciate the eerie familiarity of the environment the stories take place in. Finally, one will be hard-pressed to find another volume which presents such an original take on horror. It's truly a slice of Texas life: perhaps an actual slice of pecan pie and sweet tea, with a side of gut-wrenching, gag-inducing, page-turning terror. Boo y'all.
—***Texas Books in Review***, Spring 2020.

Genre readers get their fill of monsters, ghosts and the undead, the subhuman, perversity of all kinds, and murder. And the plotlines and climactic denouements brim with satisfying wit, satire, irony, social commentary, and sometimes just plain fun, even in the face of several strains of darkness.
—***Fort Worth Weekly***, January 15, 2020

Road Kill: Texas Horror by Texas Writers, Volume 5 is an immersive, haunting collection of short stories that are as thought-provoking as they are frightening. The world building will pull readers in, holding their attention until the last word. Every piece carries a strong sense of place, many of them masterfully steeped in Lone Star detail, grounding the reader in

hometown familiarity before unleashing inevitable Texas-sized chaos.
—***Fort Worth Weekly***, January 13, 2021

Monsters, ghosts, and relentless dread inhabit this anthology of Texas-based horror short stories . . . Gleefully unnerving and often profound scary tales.
—***Kirkus Reviews***, December 9, 2022

CONTENTS

So do we pass the ghosts that haunt us later in our lives; they sit undramatically by the roadside like poor beggars, and we see them only from the corners of our eyes, if we see them at all. The idea that they have been waiting there for us rarely if ever crosses our minds.

Stephen King

Foreword

Road Kill 9 features a killer line-up (pardon the pun).

New York Times bestselling author Kathleen Kent writes the final chapter on a hellish early 20th century catastrophe that killed hundreds of Texas children. *Road Kill* regular Mario E. Martinez fixes his gaze on a morbid, modern-day Romeo wondering *O Juliet, Juliet, wherefore art thou Juliet*? Repeat *Road Kill* contributor Jae Mazer fiendishly plies the sometime grave tug and to and fro of early motherhood. And *Road Kill 7* editor William Jensen braves one of the scariest trunks in our cultural attic.

"Toadflax" by talented newcomer Lucas Strough is a discombobulating omen that mimics reports from Newsmax. Indigenous veteran Juan Perez's poetic incarnation "Noche De El Chupacabras" hails an aboriginal creature from the darkest corners of our land. And, finally—or infinitely   the ghostly sage of a late 19th century Black "Robin Hood" haunts a traveler in "Railroad Bill Rides the Bus."

Grim depredations, manifestations and implications. That and so much more. Saying *Road Kill: Texas Horror by Texas Writers* is just a regional horror anthology is like insisting Frankenstein's monster was just a misstep in medical technology. *Road Kill* is no longer just an annual anthology of horror stories. It's a serial collection of serious voices in Lone Star literature. It's a chronicle of Texas terror, and *Vol. 9* is eerie, edgy and feral. It will haunt you long after its first reading.

Road Kill Vol. 9 is as fine a collection of horror fiction as you'll find today. *It's alive.*

E. R. Bills
August 25, 2024

Introduction

Are you the same person you were nine years ago? If so, congratulations, you are a rare commodity, a personality as stable as the Rock of Gibraltar. I am not the same person I was in 2016 when my new friend and eager would-be anthologist convinced me that an anthology of horror stories set in Texas, written by Texans, was a good idea. That new friend was E.R. Bills, and in the ensuing years he has become one of my closest friends, confidants, and sometime adversary in spontaneous debates.

How was I different in 2016? I was new to writing fiction. Relatively new, I'd only been pursuing the craft seriously for a couple of years. And I was new to sobriety. I had given up intoxicants of all forms about the time I got busy writing. Two aspects of my personality that are now deeply rooted, were uncertain fledgling aspirations when the first *Road Kill* anthology became a reality. Anyone who has not suffered from addiction cannot imagine the uncertainty, the timid clarity a recovering individual experiences as the years of blurred thinking, poor choices, and daily intoxication fade from the mind and a new person emerges.

In 2016 I was committed to writing, and doing a lot of it, but I was uncertain in my social life and I had not quite found my voice as a writer or the confidence that comes from knowing who you are and a commitment to the set of values in your heart and mind. I co-edited *Road Kill Vol. 1* and I think I played a part in selecting some good stories and setting the tone for the future of this literary endeavor. But I was not the person then that I am now. I let things slide on that first volume I would not let slide today. My friendship with E.R. was new and I never pushed too hard on any disagreement for fear of alienating another friend, after a lifetime of burning bridges and disrupting other people's lives.

E.R. Bills was the originator of *Road Kill*. The germ of the idea first appeared in his mind and he was persistent in convincing me to collaborate with him. I'm glad he did. Over the years, we've each taken turns curating the series and we have had some great guest editors step in to expand and diversify *Road Kill*, lest our brainchild become as stale as an actual piece of road kill on a sunbaked Texas highway. E.R. has often consulted me regarding specifics of how to proceed with our anthology but he has also allowed me to step away for years at a time to pursue filmmaking, screenwriting, and other fiction pursuits. He never made me feel weird about taking time away.

I want to thank E.R. for maintaining a constant and steady hand at the helm of this enterprise. Without him, *Road Kill* might have vanished from the literary landscape after a handful of years. Instead, it has become a milestone in contemporary regional literature. The anthology gains more respect every year among the people who really matter: you, the readers. Thanks for hanging in there as we found our way, sometimes in dark tangled woods and sometimes in the open prairie navigating by the North Star. It's been a process. A process for which I am infinitely grateful.

This year I have had a truly positive experience assembling Vol. 9 of *Road Kill*. We got lots of great stories from writers we had never heard of before and, of course, some fine tales from returning authors. The tone of this volume may be somewhat more subtle than usual, the horrors thoughtful and menaces internal, execution a tad more literary. It seems that way to me, anyhow. Not by design. These are just the stories that showed up on my doorstep.

It's common in these intros for the curator to run down the list of titles and give a brief pat on the back to each. I'll pass on doing that this time. All of the stories in *Road Kill Vol. 9* are good, solid stories with a thoughtfully disturbing angle. I'm going to let you discover them for yourself. My favorite way of finding new stories is to stumble onto them serendipitously, with no foreknowledge. I'll wager you find more than a few horror tales herein that float your boat, light your fire, turn your head or tingle your spine.

I hope you enjoy reading this book as much as I enjoyed putting it together. Thanks for taking this journey with us and allowing me to exercise my mind in ways I find truly gratifying. All the best!

Bret McCormick
May 2024

Promises, Promises
Mario E. Martinez

I.

It was beautiful, at first. Alicia and Joaquin made all the preparations. They'd written their notes and put post-its on everything so there'd be no confusion or fighting over their stuff. They tidied the house, mowed the lawn, and even fertilized it so when people came they wouldn't make assumptions about their decision. They even turned their cupboards over to a local food bank.

Together, they drove to the ranch outside of Dodd and up to Joaquin's family house. It was a cabin with big windows overlooking a pond. On the cement porch they often watched the sunset play at colors on the cloud smears above. On that porch, months ago, Joaquin first proposed the idea.

After they arrived, they went out to a little shed to collect a pick and shovel. Joaquin thought it was funny that Alicia kept stomping and kicking the walls to scare away spiders. "Well, I don't want to die in here," she said.

The spot they chose was in the back pasture, near the banks of what his family called Ghost Lake, because sometimes it was there and other times it wasn't. When they unloaded their tools, the waterline was high enough to cover the roots of nearby willows and a siege of herons waded through the mud on the opposite bank.

Alicia stood looking at the wind-rippled water, and inhaled the scent kicked up by the warm breeze. She thought she could look at the lake forever and smiled, knowing that, in a way, she would.

Joaquin came up behind her, wrapped one arm around her waist, and kissed her neck. Goosebumps rose on her arms. She giggled. "Perfect, isn't it?" he asked.

"Just like you promised," said Alicia.

Joaquin brought his other arm around and drove the tip of a shovel into the ground.

Alicia playfully frowned and squeezed his arm. "Just a little longer," she said.

He kissed her. "OK. I'll start but don't dawdle. A promise is a promise. It's getting hotter and we've got to finish before dinner."

Joaquin left the shovel with Alicia and got the pick from the ground and started breaking the hard earth.

II.

Digging their graves was tough business. The first foot of earth was mostly roots and the pick and shovel couldn't get more than an inch into the ground before the little hair-like roots banded together to stop them. The next layer was worse.

Seeing all the greenery around the lake gave them the illusion of soft dirt that could be cut like cake. But it was south Texas and the soil beneath that first layer was mostly clay and pebbles which slowed them further.

Once one grave was deep enough, Joaquin laid down in it to see where it had to be widened.

They were slower digging the second grave because their limbs were heavy from digging the first. They almost missed that last sunset, and the little they saw of it was from inside Alicia's grave.

Dinner was rushed. The steaks were too rare for Alicia and the wine too warm. She didn't say anything because Joaquin was so happy. It was close now and that seemed to make him appreciate the myoglobin leaking from his steak and the bitter char on the spears of asparagus. He kept toasting to things because he knew that, after tomorrow, there'd be nothing left to toast to.

Joaquin drank to the sun, to the air, to time and the stars, to finding someone to walk through oblivion with and have their souls meld into the universe together. The way he talked about dying, Alicia felt as if tomorrow wasn't going to be the end of anything. It was just going to be stepping through a doorway into a new phase of their lives.

That night, they made love like it was the last time—because it was. Joaquin finished. Alicia didn't.

At sunrise, they dressed for the grave. They shared the bathroom, alternating at the lone mirror, adjusting one another's clothing. Joaquin tied the ribbons on the back of Alicia's dress and Alicia fixed Joaquin's tie.

He placed the .38 between them in the truck cab like it was a child.

The day was bright and warm and a sedge of sandhill cranes made throaty calls as they glided across the sky. At the site, in the shade of trees, Alicia spotted butterflies lighting onto dewy flowers. She held Joaquin's hand and he squeezed it.

Joaquin got out of the truck with the revolver in his hand. He hopped eagerly into his grave and handed the gun to Alicia. They'd decided the order weeks ago and, at the time, Alicia had thought it romantic Joaquin wanted to go first. "I don't want to live a single solitary second without you," he'd said.

But, holding the gun and feeling its weight, Alicia stared at it.

Seeing her hesitation, Joaquin beckoned her with both hands, almost like a child asking to be picked up by his mother.

Alicia went to him and knelt.

Joaquin took her hands and kissed them.

"It's time," he said. "I know you're nervous. Lots of people are afraid of where we're going. But that's because they're going alone. Us, we decided this. And as scary as the next place seems, we're going together."

Joaquin's eyes were so earnest, his smile so sincere, that Alicia nodded and so did he.

"They'll call us cowards," he said, placing her hands around the gun handle. He pushed the hammer back for her and kissed her hands again. "But you're doing a brave thing, sweetheart."

He guided her hands and rested the gun barrel to his forehead. A sudden idea popped into his head. He readjusted himself in the grave and tried to work out the trajectory of his fall. Satisfied, he put his forehead to the muzzle again.

"Ready?" he asked.

Alicia nodded.

Joaquin took a deep breath, scanned the sky, and looked at Alicia's face. "I'll be waiting on the other side," he said, closing his eyes.

He nodded.

He was ready.

But, as Alicia steadied herself to pull the trigger, Joaquin's eyes shot open. He managed to say, "Oh, wait–" but the bullet screaming out of the barrel deafened Alicia and punched the thought right out the back of Joaquin's head.

The instant the .38 went off, Alicia saw a nimbus of blood mist out of Joaquin and he went cross-eyed before his body dropped. He didn't fall backward as he'd thought, but instead collapsed like a demolished building until his frame accordioned and he lengthened like a worm on the grave-floor.

Deaf, Alicia knelt there for a long time.

Joaquin's eyes were open. The gore leaking from his head soaked into the ground. Alicia was amazed the flies already smelled death and danced above the grave.

She cried. Her tears were complicated. She loved Joaquin and death hadn't changed that. And though she was repulsed at killing him, Alicia understood Joaquin had been unfit for this world. Others might call it murder but Joaquin would call it setting him free. He was sure to put that in his note.

Alicia let her tears finish. She got into her grave and chuckled in a helpless way because she was careful not to get hurt or soil her dress when she would shoot herself in a few moments.

Like Joaquin, she took a last look at the sky and the land, took in its aroma. She even ran her hand over the pebbly sides of the grave. She listened to the cranes.

Unlike Joaquin, Alicia knew she wasn't going to fall back like a man shot in a western and sat at the bottom of her grave and tried to think of how to shoot herself.

Holding the gun to her forehead was awkward and made her afraid she'd do it wrong and die slow—a vegetable that planted itself. She decided the best way would be to put the gun in her mouth.

Alicia had no last words because, even if she did, no one was around to hear them.

She closed her eyes. Her finger rested on the trigger and Alicia put the slightest pressure on it.

Something tickled her nose and her eyes opened, spooking a fly. It went off and returned and Alicia swatted it away. She put the gun in her mouth again, but the fly returned to kiss her.

Alicia stood, cursing, and chased the fly away. "Give me a second and then do your worst," she said, looking around for more. There were a bunch bouncing around Joaquin's grave and Alicia looked beyond their graves to the nearby trees.

A committee of vultures waited in the branches. They exchanged glances and, as if struck by lightning, Alicia realized that for all their romantic talk and all their planning, they hadn't thought of who would bury them.

She looked at the vultures, at their beaks, and imagined them tearing through her dress to dot her body with stink and oily birdshit.

"Goddamn it," she said, getting out of the hole, and retrieved the shovel to bury Joaquin.

III.

Alicia thought burying Joaquin would be easy but, first, she had to get in his grave with him and lay him out properly. His dead weight was cumbersome. By the time Alicia laid him out and crossed his arms over his chest, her hands were caked with bloody dirt, one of her heels had broken off, and her hair was slick-stuck to her forehead.

Getting out of his grave was difficult because Alicia convinced herself using Joaquin as a stepstool would be disrespectful.

And then there were the flies. Where the vultures waited in the trees, the flies were bold and clumped onto Joaquin and the gore beneath him. Alicia tried to kill them but they were too fast.

Alicia got the shovel and sunk it into the dirt. She hefted a quantity of earth and gently dropped it into the grave. The flies got spooked and fled to her and she swatted them away until they settled on Joaquin again.

Learning their habits, Alicia almost made a game of it. She waited for the flies to settle and then threw dirt on them quick. Going to the dirt pile and back as fast as she could, each time she found a sick joy that less and less flies escaped the hole.

Before long, Alicia took the shovel to the shade of the willow and let her breathing settle. The lake was fragrant and faint ripples lapped at the shore. The calls of the sandhill cranes sounded otherworldly, deep and resonant like dragon snores, and when Alicia looked for the sedge, she saw Joaquin standing on the lake.

He was dressed in his death clothes and a pinprick of light shined through the hole in the center of his forehead. There was no anger in his expression, just languid excitement. He beckoned her with one hand, as if inviting her into a ferris wheel gondola. He mouthed her name.

Taking up the shovel, she said, "OK," and got back to it.

After the better part of an hour, Joaquin was buried and Alicia had found some rocks to mark the grave.

Alicia looked back out to the lake.

Joaquin stood there like a mirage.

She nodded to him and he to her.

She got into her grave again and took a moment to prepare. There was no place to dry her sweaty hair or her slick hands so she did so on the back of her dress which she then slap-dusted and straightened. Alicia got the .38 again and sat on her grave-bottom and stretched out her legs and then quickly retracted them.

Her legs were tight and uncomfortable and the dust sticking to the backs of her knees didn't help. She bent her legs and pulled the hammer back.

As before, she looked at the blue of the sky and a single cloud drifting past her tomb's mouth and took a long inhale of air, savoring it, before picking up the pistol and sticking the muzzle into her mouth.

Joaquin peeked into the grave. The sky behind him rendered him a silhouette, the hole in his head like a bindi of light.

"I'm right behind you," she mumbled against the muzzle, resting her finger on the trigger.

The gun trembled. The digging yesterday and all the burying had made her arms weak, her shoulders sore, and conjured a deep rumble in her stomach. She laughed at how loud it was. "I'm going to leave that behind," she thought. "No hunger, no thirst, no nothing." She closed her eyes and the deep emptiness in her stomach grew sharp, painful.

Her eyes opened and she took the pistol out of her mouth. She sighed. The grave was already dug and, to the dead, what was another few hours?

She climbed out of the grave and dusted herself off. "If today's my last day, I don't have to be hungry for it," she said, turning to the truck.

Joaquin stood between it and Alicia. His forehead was creased, puckering his wound.

"I'll be right back," she explained, and went to the truck. "We've got eternity and it's only a couple of miles to town. We'll be together by sunset."

She put the gun in the glove compartment and found the keys in the cup holder. Alicia turned on the truck and set the a/c to high. It was blow-dryer hot at first, but she still pointed all the vents at her face and let the air dry her skin.

Alicia turned on the radio and found a local station. She'd never really cared for cumbia but the song had her keeping time on the steering wheel anyway. She put the truck in gear and looked out the window at Joaquin.

He pointed at her grave.

"A promise is a promise," she told him. "I'm just getting something to eat. No sense meeting eternity cranky."

Joaquin called after her to come back, but she couldn't hear him. The a/c was roaring, the tires crunched the road, and Alicia had turned the music up as loud as it would go.

IV.

Alicia stopped at a diner called Jeane's Feed Barn and got a window booth. She ignored all the stares from the townies. Alicia knew she was in a soiled dress and Joaquin's discarded sneakers.

When the waitress came to give her a menu, Alicia didn't even look at it.

"Y'all got cheeseburgers?" she asked.

"This is America," the waitress said.

Alicia nodded. "A cheeseburger. And, uh, the bacon you put on it?"

"Two pieces. Thick cut."

"That'll be great," Alicia said, smiling.

"How do you want it cooked?"

"A little blood's fine. I just don't want it kicking. Give me some onion rings, too," Alicia said.

"Instead of fries?"

"In addition to," Alicia corrected her.

"Drink?"

"Zap Cola. Extra ice," Alicia said. "It's hot out there."

"It's hot in here, too," the waitress said, going to the back.

Alicia wasn't sure what that meant but she paid the words little attention. She looked around. The register sat on a display counter full of candy and behind it was a corkboard decorated with town notices and old calendars. Beside it was a tall cake display with pieces of pie and cake revolving on little platforms.

She watched it and tried to decide which one she wanted.

Alicia was met with a familiar face when she turned back around.

Joaquin sat with a little of the diner showing through the hole in his head.

Alicia grinned at him and said, "Hey, darling."

A man seated in the next booth looked over his shoulder.

Alicia waved at him in apology. "Not you, sorry."

"You don't seem like you're in much of a hurry," Joaquin told her.

Alicia looked at the reflection in the window in hopes of seeing the back of Joaquin's head, but, dead, he cast no reflection. His eyebrows went up as they had in life when he scolded her without words.

Shrugging, she said, "I just ordered. I can't go to the window and demand they make it snappy because I've got dying to do, now can I? They'd commit me and you'd just have to wait longer."

"I suppose you're right," Joaquin said. "Are you getting dessert?"

"For my last meal?" Alicia asked, scoffing. "Hell, yes." She caught an old couple looking at her and she winked at them.

The waitress returned with Alicia's Zap Cola.

The glass barely tapped the table before Alicia picked it up and drank three hearty gulps. She let out a satisfied exhalation at the cold fizz and jolt of caffeine.

"That's good," she told the waitress. "Hey, which is better?" She pointed at the dessert case with her thumb. "It's between the cherry and the pecan."

"Pecan's the best seller."

Alicia hummed in thought. "You know what? I'll get a slice of both. Could you bring them once I'm all done?"

Writing, the waitress nodded. "Want ice cream on those?"

Alicia looked at Joaquin and said, "Oh, you know . . . to hell with it. Let's do it. Life's short."

Walking off, the waitress said, "Attagirl."

Alicia waited for the waitress to leave before speaking again. She ran her knuckles up and down the sides of her sweating glass, drawing scribbled nothings that the cold drink made vanish like invisible ink. She said, "Don't be mad."

Joaquin sighed. "I'm not mad. I'm dead."

"What's it like?"

"Lonely," Joaquin said, narrowing his eyes.

"Not for long," Alicia said. "I told you, I'm right behind— oh! The food's coming."

The waitress came and placed two paper-lined baskets of food on the table. One held a hearty burger with curled tongues of bacon lolling out from under the bun, all atop a bed of crinkle-cut fries. The other almost overflowed with onion rings. The waitress took a ketchup bottle from her apron pocket, placed it on the table, and was gone.

Alicia reached for the ketchup but stopped herself. "Let's see how the chef wanted it to taste," she said, hefting the burger with both hands.

Even dead, Joaquin's expression changed when Alicia took the biggest bite she could and worked the food around her mouth and chewed until she could finally swallow. "Now, this is what I was waiting for," she said, placing the burger upside down on the wax paper.

She ate a fry and stuck the next in her mouth like a cigarette as she worked the top off the ketchup bottle before pounding out a few dollops. Her bites alternated between burger and fries and onion rings and each gulp of her soda had her saying, "Man, oh man," before she went back to eating.

As she ate, a fly landed on the table and went about kissing it in patterns that only its sand-grain brain could detect.

Alicia tried to wave it away but the fly was used to people and went on kissing the table. Alicia watched it like dinner theater. Someone passed her table and still the fly did no more than taste the Formica.

"Watching flies now, are we?" Joaquin asked.

Alicia made a face at him. "It's interesting," she said. "It doesn't fly away

"And that's interesting to you?"

Alicia munched on her fries. "It's not to you?"

"At the moment, I've got other things to think about," he said. "Like being dead and alone and the woman I love–who swore she'd be here with me–is stalling for time with a cheeseburger and philosophical musings about a podunk fly with people-skills."

"Don't forget about the pie," Alicia reminded him.

"How could I? Maybe it's the hole in my head. The one you put there–"

"At your request," she cut in.

"At our agreement," he corrected.

After a few seconds, Alicia said, "I can't believe we didn't think about who'd bury us. Seems like an important part, right?"

"Yes, it was a bit of an oversight," he admitted. "Our bodies were the problem. I didn't care much about our remains."

Joaquin frowned because it seemed like Alicia had stopped listening. She held her burger away from her face and watched the fly walk across the table, tasting and testing and moving on.

"I know I've got the food but . . . I think it'll go to you first," she said. Seeing his face, she went on. "It's just, if we were outside, then I'd say me because flies smell the food but, in here, everything smells like this so maybe he goes to you–"

"Because I'm dead," he said.

Alicia sighed and opened her mouth to speak but the waitress returned with an unprompted refill.

She asked, "You ready for those pies?"

"Yes, ma'am," Alicia replied.

The waitress stopped mid-turn to the dessert case. "Um, who've you been talking to?"

Alicia looked at Joaquin and said, "My dead boyfriend."

"Didn't make it to husband, huh?"

Joaquin glared at the waitress.

Alicia raised her eyebrows at Joaquin. "No, we didn't get there."

"When'd he pass?"

Alicia chuckled. "This morning. I shot him in the head and buried him out on a ranch," she said.

The waitress laughed. "Well, if he wants some company, I've got a prime candidate getting drunk on my couch." She wrote out the ticket, tore it from the pad, and put it on the table, saying, "My condolences. The pies are on the house."

The fly didn't move.

Alicia watched the woman walk away and set to finishing her onion rings. They were soggy with grease to her delight.

"You're not going to do it, are you?" Joaquin asked.

Alicia's face softened. She put out her hand for his but it just passed through Joaquin's. "Of course, I am. I'm just waiting on two pieces of pie."

"With ice cream," he said.

"With ice cream."

V.

Joaquin remained even after his body was nothing but dusty bones in the earth. Ghost Lake had filled and dried and filled again, in cycles, for more years than Joaquin could recall because time and its nuances meant very little to the dead. The sandhill cranes were back, croaking and circling the lake with necks outstretched. Joaquin's gaze followed them across the sky and would've done so for the rest of their flight if not for the dust cloud.

He watched the dust go from the main road, deeper into the ranch until, up the path to the lake, a truck came into view. It stopped a few yards away.

The driver was in his late thirties. Joaquin grinned at him in a lazy way. He'd seen this man grow from a child, after all. The driver went to the other side of the truck and opened the door for an old woman. He helped her out, surveyed the land, and told her something before getting back in the truck.

The old woman carried flowers and hobbled to Joaquin's grave. Even with decades on her old frame, Joaquin recognized glimmers of his Alicia—the shape of her eyes, the gentle turn of her smile—and waved at her. He'd long since given up anger.

"Do I see some gray on the boy?" Joaquin asked.

Alicia knelt as best she could to put the flowers on a dusty pile of rocks. "He's getting old. We all are," she said.

"Well, some of us," Joaquin said, grinning.

Alicia nodded. "This place still scares him, though. I thought it would clear up with age, but he thinks it's creepy. Like there's someone he can't see watching him."

"I could go whisper in his ear," Joaquin offered.

Alicia giggled at the thought. "Then I'd have two people to visit out here."

She stood beside Joaquin and together they looked at the lake and the cranes gathered there. "I'm traveling next month. Asia. First Japan, then Hong Kong, and last Korea. I've never been so . . ."

Joaquin looked at her warmly. "We will have so much to talk about when you join me . . . whenever that is. A whole lifetime of things."

"You hoping for sooner or later?" she asked.

"Time doesn't really mean anything anymore," he replied.

"Well, it's probably sooner," she said. "No bullets, just old age . . . I wonder what I'll look like to you then. A young woman or an old maid."

"You'll look like Alicia," Joaquin replied meaningfully. "Always."

She didn't disagree. They stood side by side, each to their worlds, and watched the cranes doze in the sun or lightly step across the muddy banks. After a while, Alicia's son called her. It was hot and she had no hat.

"I'll see you sooner than you think," she told Joaquin.

He smiled. "Promises, promises."

To Cimmaron City and Points Beyond

L. H. Phillips

"All off for Tombstone!" Lily yelled and pumped the porch swing higher. "Next stop, Dodge City!" The chains on the swing creaked in protest.

"Lily, don't swing so high." Lily's grandmother came out on the porch, a cold Coke in one hand and a napkin folded over two sugar cookies in the other. "I brought you a snack. You sure you don't want to come in and watch my afternoon stories with me?"

"No, ma'am," Lily muttered, taking the offered Coke and cookies. She had been left behind with her grandma this hot July day by, well, everybody. Her big sister had gone with her friends to the public swimming pool in their little East Texas town, and had declined to be burdened with eight-year-old Lily. Her brother was gone, too, helping their granddad on a house painting job. Lily's parents were the only ones with a real excuse in her eyes, since they obviously had to work on a weekday.

"All right, little monkey, stay on the porch or in the backyard, and quit swinging so high. Someday those chains are going to break with you kids." Lily's grandmother retreated into the relative cool of the living room to watch her soap operas and rest from cleaning up after lunch.

Lily ate the excellent homemade cookies and sulked, bitter as only a young child can be. It was not fair at all. Margaret had called her a baby when she had begged to go with her to the pool, like being fifteen made her and her friends so superior. Her twelve-year old brother Paul was still a willing playmate, but he was saving up to buy a guitar and the lure of being paid for helping Grandpa was too great. There was nothing, nothing to do this scorching day. Even the kittens her Grandma's cat had given birth to in June were all sleeping in the cool dirt beneath the porch.

Lily had been trying to amuse herself by playing Stagecoach, a game of Margaret's invention, but it was a stupid game for only one person. The whole point was for the driver of the stagecoach (that is, the porch swing) to make it as difficult as possible for the passengers to board or leave the stagecoach by pumping the swing as high as they could. When the driver yelled out your destination—Tombstone, Dodge City, or farthest out, Cimarron City—you had to bail out of the swing and go stand by one of the porch columns, the columns being discretely labeled in pencil with the different towns. Likewise, to re-board for a new destination, you had to try and get on the swing as it was arcing wildly between the porch floor and ceiling. It was not an approved game in the grownups' eyes, but Lily and her siblings loved it. With no one to play with this afternoon, Lily could only shout out town names to imaginary riders, or bail out herself, effectively ending the game. Boring.

Lily finished her soda, finally tiring of her self-pity. An idea came to her, probably a bad one, but totally in tune with her restless mood. She could sneak off and go down to the canyon.

The canyon was a place of glamorous mystery to Lily. Her grandparents owned half an acre beyond the backyard proper that her granddad kept planted in a vegetable garden. Corn, beans, tomatoes and bell peppers all flourished in tidy rows. Beyond the garden were open fields of uncertain ownership, filled with dewberry brambles, full of juicy, purple berries in the spring. All of this was very familiar to Lily, but somewhere farther out, where Lily had never been permitted to go, was the canyon. Her brother and sister had been there, and regaled Lily with tales of what went on in its walls: A suspicious vagrant was camping in it. A wild horse was spotted galloping in its bottom. College kids went down there in a group and did—Margaret and Paul weren't sure what. And so on. Lily had always been considered too young to go on any of these exploratory missions.

Lily peeked into the living room. Her grandma was dead asleep, tired out from the heat of the day. Lily had been quite clearly told not to leave the immediate vicinity of the house. She was not usually disobedient or adventurous, but she had worked herself up into a state of aggrieved defiance. She would go to the canyon and see some amazing sight. Later, after supper, she would nonchalantly mention it to Margaret and Paul, and they would be impressed and jealous they had missed it.

Lily walked through the backyard, past the mustang grape vines that divided it from the vegetable garden, past the rustling cornstalks drying in the July sun, and out into the no-man's land of the unused fields. She went carefully, as the fields were full of thorny vines and bull nettles that would punish an unwary walker. The afternoon sun was stupefyingly hot and the weeds buzzed with little red and black grasshoppers.

Lily turned and looked back at her grandparents' white frame house. There were more cold Cokes in the refrigerator in that kitchen. She almost abandoned her plan, but a certain angry stubbornness drove her on. Lily wasn't sure exactly how much farther the canyon was. There was a line of chinaberry trees in the distance, and she made a bargain with herself that she would keep walking at least until she reached that landmark.

By the time she made it to the little group of trees, she was more than ready to stand in their shade and catch her breath. The error of not bringing any water with her had been driven home exceedingly well. She was hot and itchy, but, moving a little past the trees, she suddenly forgot all about that. Before her was what must be the legendary canyon. It was really just a large, steep ravine with rocks and sad, scrubby little bushes going down to a sandy bottom. It was deeper and wider than the highway cuts running through the surrounding East Texas hills, but just as ordinary.

Lily was happy to have made it to her goal, but couldn't deny her sense of disappointment. The "canyon" was a glorified ditch. Neither mysterious wanderers nor mystical horses were apparent in it. Not even a stray college freshman. There was a flat rock in the shade of the trees at the edge of the incline, and she sat down on it to rest.

Lily pushed her sweaty bangs out of her eyes and thought about the stories her brother and sister had told. Were they even true? Lily was the kind of kid who looked at the treetops peeking over a neighbor's house and imagined they were fairy-tale mountains rising in the distance. She had thought her older siblings led less boring lives than she, and didn't need to imagine places of enchantment and romance the way she did. Maybe she was wrong.

Lily stood up, debating whether to head back to the house right away or wait a while and see if anything happened. She felt uneasy all of a sudden, without being sure why. The afternoon had gone completely silent. The background hum of the grasshoppers was gone; no birds rustled and twittered in the trees. The air, already oppressively hot, seemed to press down on her with an actual weight, as if she were trapped beneath an immense, smothering beast. Gasping a little, Lily looked down into the gully.

Some kind of distortion in the air was occurring down there, like heat waves coming off of asphalt. At the center of the distortion, Lily saw what appeared to be a large slab of granite. Had that been there before? She leaned forward and rubbed her eyes to try to remedy the odd blurriness. Was it actually rectangular? She couldn't understand how she could have missed seeing it before. It looked at least six feet long and maybe four feet wide. The thing was somehow elevated above the sandy ground, although Lily's eyes kept refusing to focus on it properly. A dull pounding started at the base of her skull.

The harder she stared at it, the harder it seemed to make out any details. Almost without thinking, Lily started picking her way down the slope. Her tennis shoes slipped on the crumbly ground. Once she ended up on her rear end, skinning both hands as she caught herself from sliding all the way down. She was too engrossed to notice. She could hardly take her eyes off of the stone. She needed to get to it and see it properly and relieve the strange anxiety she felt about its exact nature. Probably just a make-shift picnic table or something, Lily told herself.

Lily finally reached the bottom of the gully, accompanied by a small cloud of dust. She approached the slab slowly. It was ancient looking, gray and weathered as an old tombstone. Here and there on its surface were faint grooves, forming swirls and angles whose pattern seem to subtly shift every time Lily glanced away.

Lily bent and looked underneath it and circled all around, hunched over like a pale little crab. There were no supporting columns or legs. The thing was floating. Lily laughed in amazement. She was seeing something impossible. Lily walked around it again to make sure she wasn't mistaken. She started to pass her hand beneath it, like a magician demonstrating a trick, but a sharp pang of fear stopped her. She backed away and watched it with a sudden wariness, as if the stone was a rabid animal that might attack.

"This is dumb," Lily muttered to herself. "It's just a rock." Yeah, a deeply concerned inner voice replied, a rock that's floating in the field behind my grandma's house.

"Right," Lily said with a giggle, and then was further unnerved by how loony she sounded.

Lily crept up close to the slab again and reached out a shaky hand. She expected the stone to be hot—it was situated in direct sunlight—but a numbing cold shot through her fingers and up her arm as soon as her fingertips brushed its gray surface. The world around her seemed to blink out and Lily was thrown back several feet, as though hit by a cresting wave. She landed with her butt in the sand and a growing panic in her mind. The world re-asserted itself, but weakly, like a bad TV transmission.

She turned and scrambled up the side of the gully on her hands and knees, oblivious to the damage to her palms and kneecaps. She grabbed a straggly bush at the top of the incline and hauled herself completely out of the gully. Lily hardly paused to catch her breath but started across the field in a staggering run.

Chaotic images flashed through her mind, defying description and leaving her disoriented. She wasn't sure if she was really headed back to the house at all. There weren't supposed to be any buildings in the fields she had crossed to the canyon, but now there was some kind of broken down barn off to her right. Lily paused in confusion to look at this problematic structure. The barn, or whatever it was, was black with age. Its walls and roof did not seem to meet at quite the proper angle and, as Lily watched, the walls folded in and then heaved out, as if the building were breathing.

Lily fell to her skinned knees and retched violently, her vision graying out at this insult to reality. After a moment, her stomach settled and she cautiously looked up, wiping tears from her clammy face. To her immense relief, the heaving barn was gone. The only building she could see was her grandparents' white frame house in the distance.

"Don't go away, don't go away," Lily chanted, and began shakily traversing the field again. She stared fixedly at the distant house, afraid it might vanish or turn into something else. When she stumbled into a dewberry bramble (and the red wasp nest concealed within it), it took her a few seconds to realize what she had done. The annoyed wasps swarmed over her ankles, buzzing and stinging, and the world snapped back into a painful, sharp focus.

Lily gave a strangled scream and bolted for the house, crossing the remaining distance in record time. She hit the screen door of the kitchen and fell inside, sobbing. The wasps had abandoned her a number of yards back, deeming sufficient punishment had been doled out to the interloper.

Her grandmother and mother came running from the living room. "Oh, Lily, honey!" her mom exclaimed, seeing her red, swollen ankles and scratched up legs and hands. They sat her down at the kitchen table and put her fiery ankles and feet into a basin of cold water, and began tending to her other scrapes and cuts, wiping her face with a cool washcloth and murmuring consolingly.

"Whatever were you doing? Your grandma said you were out back playing with the kittens," her mom said finally, when Lily had calmed down and quit crying.

Lily looked at the kitchen clock. It must be past three o'clock for her mom to already be off work. Sure enough, the clock hands read three-thirty. It didn't seem as though she should have been gone quite that long. Maybe she had stood there gaping at that stupid rock longer than she had thought.

"I was out in the fields a bit, exploring," Lily said. She felt surprisingly secretive about the floating stone. It was her discovery, only for her.

"Didn't your grandma tell you to stay close to the house? You shouldn't have been out there without Margaret or Paul." Lily felt tears starting up again at the mild scolding.

"Ah, never mind, never mind," her mom said. "I guess you'll know not to do it again." She kissed Lily's forehead, and presently they walked the block home together.

Lily was very quiet that night at supper. She kept pushing her food around her plate with her fork, but it never seemed to achieve an appetizing configuration. Elusive little flashes of light kept playing at the corner of her eye, causing her to jerk her head in their direction, but she could never catch them in full sight. Margaret and Paul paid her more attention than usual—red wasp stings demanded even sibling sympathy—but Lily couldn't muster up much response. She couldn't talk about her experience at the canyon for some reason, or even think about it very coherently. There was such a loud buzzing in her head it seemed the wasps had taken up residence between her ears. At last, her mother exchanged a worried look with her father and picked up her mostly uneaten plate of food.

"Maybe you should go on to bed early tonight, Lily. You'll feel better in the morning."

Lily went without protest, even though her favorite show, *Bonanza*, was on and she would miss seeing her secret crush, Little Joe Cartwright. Lying in the dark of her room was soothing and Lily dropped off to sleep quickly, the muffled sound of the TV in the living room acting as a lullaby.

Sometime later in the night, Lily awoke with a start. The house was very still. In her dresser mirror, across from the foot of her bed, she could see a tiny pinpoint of light. As she watched, the pinpoint grew into a luminous, swirling blue cloud. Lily found herself sliding feet first toward this improbable storm, like a nail to a magnet. She clutched ineffectually at the bedclothes in an effort to stop her motion. Her feet and legs went off the end of the bed, pulled as straight as a ruler toward the center of the light. Lily grabbed one of the bedposts as her shoulders drew even with it and let out a scream. Her body was pulling painfully toward the mirror, and her fingers were losing their grip on the bedpost. The buzzing in her head was now a roar, the roar a somehow hungry voice that seemed to say 'come to me'. Lily's fingers slipped from the post.

"Lily! What's the matter?" The bedroom light snapped on. Lily found herself on the floor, a parent on either side, helping her sit up.

"She must have rolled out of bed," her dad said.

"Rolled over the footboard? She must really have gotten twisted around," her mother said, and pressed her hand to Lily's forehead. "She's burning up. I think she needs to see Dr. Thomas tomorrow. Maybe she's having a reaction to the wasps." Lily's mother brought her a baby aspirin and tucked her back into bed.

The next day, Lily found herself sitting on Dr. Thomas's paper-covered table. Her fever had broken with the morning light but her mom still insisted upon seeing the pediatrician. He peered at her with his tiny lights and prodded her neck and abdomen.

"I don't see that she is having an allergic reaction of any kind," the doctor said. "Perhaps it was just the emotional upset putting her off kilter. Keep an eye on her the next few days, but I'm sure she'll be fine." He patted Lily's back and gave her a green sucker.

Lily trailed after her mom to the car. The sucker dropped from her fingers in the parking lot. The candy was no more appealing than last night's supper had been.

Lily spent the next few days in a distracted haze. She could barely eat the food put before her, the texture and smell of it being at best bland and at worst repulsive. Everything seemed false, the colors too bright and the sounds too shrill. She had seen beneath the ordinary skin of the world, and now that knowledge was beneath her skin, working to change her. She spent more and more of her time sleeping, lost in dreams of dark water and submerged ruins. The incident with the mirror did not repeat itself, and Lily began to feel an anxious regret that whatever had tried to reach her had been interrupted. She was frightened, but there was an unbearable itch in her mind that needed to be soothed, could only be soothed by whatever had been beyond that maelstrom of light. She felt an attraction that was almost a command to begin a different existence. Lily wanted to visit the canyon again, but everyone seemed to be watching her very carefully.

A week after Lily had made her trip to the canyon, she awoke no longer anxious and with her thoughts sharply focused for the first time in days.

"Can we go over to Grandma's?" Lily asked Margaret.

"Sure," Margaret said, and exchanged a look with their mother that seemed to communicate a certainty that she would not be left alone.

Lily and Margaret walked the block to the little white house. Grandma fussed over them and gave them ice-pops, even though it was barely nine in the morning.

"I want to swing on the porch some," Lily said. She picked up a pencil from the living room coffee table on her way out.

"Okay," said Margaret. She and Grandma sat down in the living room, positioning themselves so they could watch her through the screen door, Lily noted.

It didn't matter. Lily had had a different sort of dream last night, one that explained exactly what she needed to do.

Lily went to the porch column beyond the one marked "Cimarron City", the one they had decided was a little too far out for the Stagecoach game. She drew a series of triangles and whorls on its base, much like the symbols she had seen on what she now thought of as the stone *door*. When she was satisfied with the inscription, she threw both the pencil and her ice-pop over into the flower bed.

Lily got into the porch swing. She could see her writing on the column starting to glow. Lily pumped the swing vigorously. She could hear Margaret and Grandma talking quietly in the house, and she felt a growing sadness she that could no longer be with them.

The glow at the end of the porch increased and spread toward the swing, forming a tunnel, a passageway. Lily pumped the swing even higher. "R'yleh!" she screamed out, and leapt into the bright and expanding air.

Toadflax
Lucas Strough

If I close my eyes and breathe deep, I can smell it: the room reeked of teenage boy sweat and the cheapest, dirtiest pot that crumpled dollar bills could buy.

Back then, we spent days killing time in Duke's double-wide trailer, way out in the sticks in Hallsville. I lived in a single-wide, so his place felt like the lap of luxury.

In the far eastern part of the state, only a short drive from the Louisiana border, Texas is a lot like a jungle. The air gets so hot and damp in the summer, it steals your breath whenever you step outside.

At the time, we were kicking around with this other kid who we called Zed, and I don't remember now if that was his Christian name or if we just stuck it on him one day. Zed was younger, or at least smaller than us, but he was funny and easy to get along with. As a bonus, he always seemed to have something cool for us to mess around with: a butterfly knife, a taxidermed coyote head, or half-full cans of Copenhagen he snaked from his dad's work bag.

"Let's burn something," Zed said on a day when the East Texas sun was an overhead broiler, roasting us all in our skins. We were laid up, silent and panting in Duke's bedroom, fighting for the perfect vantage point between the overworked window unit air conditioner and the one oscillating fan in the trailer plugged into an extension cord running all the way from the kitchen.

"Yeah," Duke said around a wad of Copenhagen.

"Let's burn something."

Next thing you know, we're out in the front yard, spitting brown streams at fire ants marching through the scorched brown grass.

"Find something to burn," Duke told us, never lifting his eyes from his targets, the bumbling lines of ants with their searing bite, blasting them with laser-focused torrents of Copenhagen juice.

We did as we were told.

Watching for fire ant hills and water moccasins who might've wandered away from the dried-up creek bed, Zed and I stalked through the back portion of the dead and dying plot on which Duke's double-wide sat.

The pickings were plenty. The drought had killed many trees and they'd dropped their dead, dry branches. There were sticks, logs and scraps of pallets scattered all over, from the back of the double-wide across the 100-foot stretch of dead grass and red clay which separated the trailer from the woods.

I was in no hurry and only secured a single armload of good-sized sticks and branches. I kept my left arm free to brush the bullets of sweat out of my eyes each time I bent to pick up another bit of wood.

Zed paid no such heed. He ran from spot to spot, hyena-shrieking each time he found another half of a yellow pine bough or a pile of twigs and pine bark, even dried out pine straw.

We deposited our hauls at Duke's feet, like peasants offering up the first and best pickings of our harvest.

These he surveyed, judging them in some inscrutable way. What he judged acceptable, he nudged into a pile with the big toe of his right foot, black with dirt inside a Dollar Store flip-flop. What he deemed unworthy he ignored or spat brown streams of dip juice upon.

Thankfully, he wasn't too picky. We wouldn't have lasted long in the heat.

Duke gathered up a pile of the dry branches and sticks, snapping some over his thigh to size them down to burn better. Zed and I watched, sweating, too hot to speak or move.

"Lighter," Duke said, snapping his fingers at Zed.

Little Zed, purveyor of so many pilfered treasures from his dad's work bag or recliner or pickup truck, quickly snapped out a shiny brushed chrome Zippo from the pocket of his threadbare Wal-Mart blue jeans. It really was a thing of beauty. Always shining and always sending up a big jet of flame when you flicked the wheel. It bore an engraving on the front side of a naked woman wrapped around a grinning, burning skull with dice for eyes.

Zed hucked it over to Duke, who caught it one-handed without looking up. He flicked it and knelt, putting the high flame to the pile of shredded pine bark, dead pine straw and small twigs in the belly of the triangle of sticks he'd assembled.

It roared to life in no time. Three weeks of July sun had sucked out every molecule of moisture from the wood, which kindled and caught and sputtered upward with the strange, heady orange of a flame burning at midday.

Duke slowly stepped backward, away from the flames, and we followed. Each of us were already soaked through with sweat and the fire was hot enough to make you feel sick in the midst of the summertime swelter.

We were transfixed so tightly, hypnotized by the blaze, that we didn't notice the sparks sent flying as the flames ate through the bigger pieces of wood and found sap-soaked knots in the pine. These cooked—popping and sizzling and sparking like bacon in a pan, sending tiny orange devils shooting out of the fire and into the grass and dead twigs scattered all around.

Just like that, before we could say or do anything, there was fire in the grass, spreading so fast it made your head spin.

"Get it out!" Duke shrieked. I'd never heard his voice sound so strained, so frightened. He hardly ever spoke much above a dissatisfied grumble. The sound of it shook us, Zed and I, so we snapped to attention.

We both dashed to the flames nearest us and began stamping and spitting. Zed even shimmied out of his jeans and started trying to piss the conflagration out until Duke slapped him on the back of the head and barked at him to fetch some water.

He came back bearing a glass from the kitchen, filled at the sink, and tipped it over, extinguishing one tiny patch of flames. Duke hollered again for him to bring the hose.

Duke and Zed manned the hose while I ran around like a headless chicken, still trying to stamp out the flames. I pulled off my sweat-soaked shirt and used it like a towel to splat out whole sections of the fire at once, but I scalded my hands. I could smell the hair on my arms burning.

Our efforts were valiant for twelve-year-olds, but it wasn't enough. We saw the flames spread and grow, overtaking the boundaries of Duke's property and leaping into the neighbors' yard, the Miltons.

By then we began to hear shouts from the trailers nearby, grown-ups screaming about the blaze and calling the fire department. Any second the yard would be flooded with adults looking for asses to kick and we'd be there with our narrow asses all lined up in a row, ready for their boots.

"Run!" Duke hissed.

In my memory I can see little devils of dust kicking up from our feet when we bolted—the kind of thing you'd see in a cartoon. But the memory can't be right. There's no way I could've seen the dust kicking up under our heels. We were all laser-sighted onto the treeline at the far edge of the property and none of us stopped or turned to look back.

In my mad break for the treeline, I hurtled through a stand of spiky green stems. On top of each stem were flowers, yellow like the late summer sun sinking through a hazy scud of thin clouds. I recognized them without thinking. This was only because I had pulled so many of them out of the ground by the roots with my bare hands.

I knew them from my mom, who kept a piss-poor patch of dirt she called a garden, which only bore a few tomatoes each year. She was always too busy running around to keep up with the garden so she had me do it.

Mostly she made me pull weeds. I learned at a young age to never complain of boredom because one whisper of that and she'd be all over me, whooping me and kicking me out of the house and locking the door, saying I couldn't come back in until I'd filled up a plastic five-gallon bucket with weeds. I had to show her the bucket to get back in the house and, if it wasn't to her satisfaction, she'd dump the bucket and make me start over.

It was her who taught me the name of those yellow flowers. She called them butter-and-eggs or toadflax. She said they were weeds and she detested them. I must've pulled up pounds of the stuff over the years.

I flew through the patch of toadflax, knocking stems over as I sprinted, sending lazy yellow petals circling down into the dirt.

We may have been spotted that day but not recognized. I can't say for certain. But it doesn't really matter now. The only thing that matters is that we made it to the forest and that we found the box there.

We didn't stop sprinting until we were a good twenty or thirty feet inside the tree line and under the shade of the evergreens. Many trees were dead from the heat but just as many were ancient and gigantic and deep-rooted—and had seen many summers. These were our savior, as they cast shadows for us to hide ourselves in as we squiggled and squirmed into spots behind stumps or branches and stared back at what we'd fled.

There were a good lot of them fighting the blaze by then. Grannies and no-neck kids and shirtless tough guys who didn't work but always had cash—rednecks all. They had gathered from every far-flung corner of the surrounding trailer lots to the site of the blaze, like roaches on Cheez Whiz.

They were whooping and hollering and fetching bowls of water and hauling garden hoses and stamping at the flames, beating them back with towels, feet, and shovelfuls of yard dirt.

We watched them for a long while. It must have been more than an hour, maybe two. The dome of heat in place above us broke its back as time rolled on and dusk slowly came, bringing a small, slight breeze.

They beat the fire eventually, stamped and shoveled it out and were mostly now milling around, firing up cigarettes, cracking beers, and pulling up lawn chairs. One kid ran away and came back pulling a small grill and a big bag of Kingsford. The scene of our crime was turning into a barbecue, our bright flames replaced with the gentle smolder of briquettes.

I don't remember if any of us spoke during that whole time. I do recall that, as soon as it was clear, all of the gathered were not immediately going out in search of our blood and hides. Zed and I glanced at each other just in time to see Duke slinking away farther into the trees, beckoning us with one finger to follow.

We reached a spot where the forest floor fell away in a sharp dip and down below us was bottomland, with bald cypress trees and their knobbly knee-roots gawping up at us from down the slope.

When we stopped panting, Duke spoke.

"No way they saw us," he said. His voice was small but firm, clear.

"No way. Even if they did, they'll forget all about it when they stuff their fat faces with beer and weenies."

Zed and I laughed.

"We should wait, though, right? I mean . . . wait around out here until it's dark and then sneak back? When's your mom get home, Duke?"

Duke opened his mouth as if to speak and began to nod in agreement, seeming to say "yes" to the plan of waiting around until dark—only something caught his tongue and trapped his words in his throat.

Looking back, that very moment, when Duke was talking to us in the woods, is the only time I can recall his face looking just that way: frozen solid and, more than that, spooked. Then, his eyes bugged wide and his mouth hung open for just a moment. Both Zed and I remained quiet. I felt something like ice water churning in my guts.

We both turned, acting on instinct, to look in the direction Duke's bugged-out eyes were staring.

And then we saw it.

The box.

Down at the bottom of the slope, the ground was churned up and broken, uneven. In cooler months, when rain had fallen, this had clearly been a spot where water stood and went rank and stagnant. Deer and coyotes and other critters must have come here to drink, hunt for food, piss on a tree to mark their territory. Summer heat had sucked up all the water from the low spot and the ridges and depressions made by the water and passing animals had been frozen in space and time, made into miniature red clay pottery projects by time and heat.

The box sat in the very middle of the spot, equidistant on all sides from the edges of the hollow.

One glance was all we needed to understand why Duke was so shocked. It wasn't uncommon to find trash and cast-off crap and dumped trash way off in the woods. We found stuff like that all the time. If this thing was like any of those items, we wouldn't have thought much of it. Maybe poked around a junk pile with a stick to see if anything cool or shiny was hidden inside, but not much more than that.

But this wasn't an old, rain-logged cardboard box or busted up chest-of-drawers or even a pile of old dirty magazines.

The box was spotless. Even sitting in the dried-up bed of a stagnant pond, it didn't have a speck of dirt or dust on it. It even seemed to shine in the sunlight filtering through the pine trees.

It was ornate. All dark wood and golden hinges and spit and polish.

It looked heavy. It looked expensive. It looked dangerous.

"What the hell—?" Zed squeaked. His voice trailed off into a chipmunk sound but Duke and I were too entranced to laugh at him for it.

Slowly, and without speaking, Duke began to gingerly pick his way down the slope toward the deepest part of the hollow and Zed and I, not knowing what else to do, followed him.

Dry, red pond mud cracked and crunched under our sneakers. The pond bed was as desiccated as an old bone.

Duke reached the box and put one hand softly down on top of the lid. All around us the woods were a cacophony of silence. No birds calling and no squirrels digging in the pine straw or leaves, only the heavy thumps of our heartbeats.

He lifted the lid and I'm not sure now whether it squeaked as it creaked open or if I moaned, dreading what might be inside.

Duke saw what was in there. He didn't speak. He only motioned to us, raising one crooked finger again to beckon us to his side.

We joined him, softly crunching the dry mud under our feet. We stood beside him, looking down into the box. It sent up a smell like cedar, cool and clear and clean, but the smell was masking something else. It covered something old and ripe and raw and wrong. It was the smell of something in a place where it didn't belong—like the stinking tang of rot in the living room when a mouse died behind the wall.

Inside the box there were a dozen or more wooden cubbyholes. Thin boards had been cut down and slid into place, forming small spaces just about big enough to sink our fists into. They reminded me of the chunks of honeycomb that you could find in the jars of honey Mrs. Alvin sold in her stall at the farmers' market, only they were straight across and up and down, instead of the hexagons in a honeycomb.

Inside each little cubbyhole was something dark. I thought at first that each weird, dark thing was a dead mouse, or maybe a dead squirrel that had dried up and blackened.

Zed, who had been frozen in fear and shock like me, slid right up to the edge of the box and nudged past Duke. Before Duke could even act surprised, Zed stuck his little dirty hand inside one of the cubbyholes and yanked out the thing inside.

He held it up in the light and peered at, squinting his eyes to try to make sense of what he held in his grip.

It wasn't until the thing twitched and wriggled to life in Zed's hand that I saw that it was a human tongue.

Zed opened his mouth as if he was going to shriek but the only sound that came out was a strange, dry creaky maunder. His tongue wiggled and flopped about like a caught fish fighting against a hook and line gored through its lip and gills.

All three of us shirked backwards, making a loose, lopsided circle around the box and the wriggling thing pitching back and forth on the forest floor.

We all watched as it spasmed and leapt up from the ground. Small as it was, it couldn't jerk itself more than an inch off the ground at a time. It was soon covered in dirt and broken bits of pine straw and I guessed that the thing must have been somehow wet, though it had looked shriveled and dry.

At the base, where the tongue would have hooked into a throat, there was only a raggedy shred of meat. This thing had not been sliced out. It had pulled. It had been ripped free.

I had seen tongues before, beef tongues. You could find them at the Piggly-Wiggly or at the Wal-Mart, three or four of the hulking huge things wrapped up in styrofoam and cellophane at the far end of the meat case. They kept the tongues near the tripe and the pork neckbones and the knuckles. All the bits that the Mexican folks and the poorest, cracker-ass rednecks liked to eat.

"Guys?" Duke said. It may have been the only time I ever heard a quiver in his voice. It was so slight that it made me think of a fine crack in pond ice.

"Guys, what do y'all think we're looking at here?"

Zed didn't speak.

"I . . . I think it's a tongue, Duke," I said. While Duke's voice betrayed only a slight tremor, my own was jiggling back and forth like Jell-O dropped on the linoleum.

"A tongue from what?" he replied, never lifting his eyes from the thing on the ground between us. Its spasmodic jerks and wriggles had slowed to only an occasional twitch.

"Well . . . way too small to be a cow tongue," I said.

"Man, I think this came out of a person."

Zed made a funny sound at the edge of my vision. By the time I looked up at him he was horking up both his lunch and his breakfast beside a pine tree, leaning against the trunk for support.

Duke narrowed his eyes and I suddenly noticed sharp and deep shadows on his face. Night was coming, I guessed. Out under the trees, sometimes you don't notice nightfall right away. I could feel the heat of the day beginning to break and a coolness slickened the air, slipping between my ribs to put a knife in my heart.

Without a word, Duke squatted low and swiped up the tongue. The way he moved put me in mind of a hawk going after a field mouse or a garden snake.

He brought the grisly thing up close to his face, peering at it through the slits of his eyelids, turning it over and over in his hands. His fingers were still stained and streaked with black from fighting the fire and scrabbling through the woods. I could see the overgrown edges of his fingernails, jet black half-rings of dirt at the ends of his long fingers.

He sniffed it. Listened to it. For a gut-jolting second I thought he was gonna lick it.

"Duke, put it down, man. Put the damn thing down and let's go. Let's get outta here, man."

I was aware of the pitch of my voice rising, keening, pleading. I walked over to Zed and hauled him to his feet with a quick jerk of his bony arm. He weighed next to nothing and floated up beside me with scarcely an effort on my part.

On his feet, Zed wobbled and rocked back and forth. He looked as if was just waking up, just coming back from the far side of a terrible dream.

I remember watching over Zed, keeping one hand on his bony shoulder to keep him from teetering all the way over and collapsing into a puddle of his own vomit.

I remember looking up once I felt he'd steadied and could stand, for a moment or two at least, on his own two chicken-thin legs.

I remember my eyes falling on Duke, who still held the dark and foul thing in his dirty paw, holding it up close to his face like he was trying to light a cigar in a stiff wind.

I remember seeing the thing wiggle.

Just like that, the tongue came to life in his hand. At first, for just half a moment, it seemed to shimmer, the way the air over asphalt does when it's baking in August. Then, with a spurt of frenetic energy, the thing jolted in Duke's hand.

I once saw the body of a squirrel, its head crushed by a passing car, wriggle in much the same way as its body struggled to escape the reality its mashed brains had already accepted.

I don't believe that Duke saw it move at the same time as I did. It was as if he was transfixed on it so completely that he didn't, or couldn't, see it jump in his hand like a fresh-caught crappie.

But he felt it, I could sense that much, and I saw his eyes light up as he sensed the thing pulsing whatever rotted muscles remained inside it.

As his eyes flashed, his face changed. It tensed up, like pulling all the slack out of a rope and making it taut. Before I could say anything or reach out to stop him, Duke opened his mouth wide, like he was readying himself for a bite through all the layers of a deluxe double cheeseburger with all the fixings. He held the tongue up to his open mouth and—it still makes me feel ill to think of it—the thing slithered into his mouth like a snake into a hole in the wall.

I don't recall hearing any sound, but the way the tongue slithered and moved makes me think of the sound of wet ground beef hitting the inside of a mixing bowl as you prepare meatloaf.

Duke's head rocked back and I saw a bulge in his throat, as if his neck had been invaded by a small creature. Veins pulsed and popped up from the skin of his neck and face.

Then, in only a moment, it was over. Duke was just standing there looking at Zed and me.

He looked deeply into my eyes, then languidly turned his head to Zed and did the same to him: looking steadily and far into his eyes.

"Punch each other," he said, in a voice I'd never heard come from his mouth before.

I wanted to fight him for even saying such a thing. I wanted to knock some sense into his head. I wanted to kick that damn box over and stomp the tongues under my sneakers until they were muddy pulp pressed into the dirt and the pine straw. I wanted to grab Zed and run.

But I didn't do those things. Instead, I felt a pricking sensation all along my arms, just below my skin. It was something like the feeling when the nicotine hits after you tuck a load of Copenhagen Long Cut into your lip.

It was warm and golden, like sunshine.

I felt my mind go slack. There was suddenly no fight left in me and somehow that was all right. I turned to face Zed, raised my hand, and balled my fist. I cocked my arm back and smashed my fist into his jaw, noticing for the first time how small and elfin his head was. Inside my own head, my thoughts ran out of me, like rainwater through a storm drain.

I looked over at Zed and saw him doing the same. His face was blank as a brand-new chalkboard but he squared up and lunged, sinking his small fist into my gut and knocking all my breath out through my nose.

We three, brothers only in thought up to that point, were now brothers in some other, darker, way.

Duke smiled, then turned and once again raised his hand to beckon us to follow him.

Somehow, we just knew; there were things to do.

I don't remember much about the rest of that day. It may have been something to do with that tongue stuck up inside Duke's head. It may have scrambled my brain or wiped my memory.

I remember being covered head to toe in cuts, scrapes, and bruises. Duke had made us throw down again and again. He willed us into all-out battles with one another until we were too exhausted to raise our fists anymore. That much I can piece together.

I know we went walking for a long time, long after the sun had set. We stumbled across two grizzled, rail-thin men camping under garbage bags and old newspapers in the woods. Duke made them fight each other, with that new voice of his. At some point I realized that voice was the voice of the tongue he'd pulled from the box. It was the voice of a man or a woman who had been dead for a long, long time.

Maybe they had been a witch or a sorcerer. Maybe they had been a hypnotist. Maybe it was the tongue of the Devil himself. I don't know. But he used that new voice to make those two hobos beat the living hell out of one another. While they were tearing each other apart, Duke leisurely dug through their scattered belongings until he found a small bottle of Evan Williams whiskey. This he kept for himself, nipping at it as he beckoned us once more to follow him.

After a while the bottle was empty. He hucked it into the woods as far as he could and we saw it bounce off a live oak tree.

"What now, guys?" he said, that funny new voice dripping into our ears like dirty motor oil from an old car.

He was smiling. I can recall that he'd not stopped smiling once, ever since that thing slithered up inside his skull.

"I wanna go home," Zed said. He sniffled and I looked over to see tears making clean tracks on his grimy cheeks.

"Yeah, Duke. We're tired. Just let us go, man," I said. I hardly had the strength to speak. I remember wobbling on shaky legs, swaying back and forth, and feeling numb. My stomach was empty and growling at me.

"I oughta make you fight some more," Duke spat.

Tough as he was, he was still a kid, and the whiskey had done a number on him. None of us were strangers to booze at that stage of our lives but the most we'd managed was pilfering a beer or two out of the fridge when our folks weren't looking, or taking a quick swig of vodka out of Zed's mom's bottles of Heaven Hill or Taaka then refilling them with water so she couldn't see that the level of liquid was lowered.

"Please, man. We're tired. We're filthy. Our folks are gonna beat us to hell when we get back. Just let us go. Please," I pleaded. My voice had become thin and small.

Duke looked angry but his weariness won over.

"Fine," he said.

"Empty out your pockets. Gimme whatever money you got."

We did. We couldn't have resisted even if we wanted to.

There was scarcely two dollars and change in crumpled bills and greasy coins between us. I don't know what he aimed to do with it. I never would find out, either.

"Awright," Duke said. "Get home. I'll come find you when I need you."

The way he said that chilled my guts. I knew he meant it. I just didn't know what he'd want us for, or what he'd want us to do for him. Just earlier that day, only hours before, the most he'd want of us would be to help him steal firecrackers and set them off in a big pile of dead leaves or maybe have us distract the cashier girl at the Rite-Aid while he stuffed candy in his pants that we could later divvy up in the bare lot behind the store.

Now, maybe he'd have us fight again, but worse. Maybe he'd make us kill each other.

"Go!" he shouted, when we didn't move quickly enough. We both spun on our heels and I put one arm around Zed's thin and bony shoulders, hustling him along as we made our way back through the pitch-dark woods.

I'm still not sure how we made it home, but we did. Standing outside his trailer after I dropped him off and said good night, I could hear Zed's mom shouting at him and likely knocking him around for being out so late and coming home so filthy. I knew my fate would be much the same.

But I wasn't going home just yet.

Tired as I was, I had more to do. I was going back to find that damn box.

When I walked Zed home and sent him off to bed and a royal ass-whooping, I pilfered the shiny chrome Zippo from his pocket. I could've asked him for it and he likely would have handed it over without any protest, but I was too weary to ask and he was too weary to listen.

I'd slipped into the tool shed out back of my own trailer and found a can of Ronsonol and a mostly-empty canister of charcoal starter. These I hauled with me as I trudged back into the open jaws of the woods, plodding down into the throat and belly of the pines.

Something inside of me led the way. Tired as I was, my thoughts were somewhere in that dim place between waking and dreaming, between hope and giving up. Maybe that's what helped me find the box again, in the end. To tell the truth, I don't know to this day how I found it again and I doubt I'll ever know.

I remember walking and walking and walking, very near to collapse, and then, there it was. I walked up to it, holding my breath. I was afraid one of those damn tongues would leap up and squirm its way down my gullet and take me over, making me a slave to Duke.

But they just lay there. I could see them, brown and black and purple, lifeless in their dank little cubbyholes.

I raised the can of Ronsonol and the container of charcoal starter above my head like some mad wizard readying himself to chant above a bubbling cauldron and call forth something from an unknowable faraway place.

I would drown them and then I would burn them.

I poured the stinking liquids out, mixing the two streams together as they fell, making sure to get a good pour into each cubby. I half-expected the meaty things to squirm or shirk or hiss at me in anger or pain or fear or whatever things they could feel. But they only lay there, dumb and silent, soaking up the acrid stuff I poured over them.

Zed's Zippo sparked up good and true, as it always did.

In the faint orange glow, I saw something I hadn't noticed before. There was a small brass oval on the lip of the box.

I knelt close and peered at it through the darkness, squeezing my eyes to slits.

There was an inscription in a dark, faded script. It was old. How old, I couldn't guess, but it was nothing from this century:

Truth Ramsey & K.S. Blood
Sole Proprietors
Doctors of Physick, Men of Renown

To tell the truth, I didn't understand what several of those words meant at the time. I was just a dumb kid.

But I was a dumb kid with a head full of hate and a fistful of fire.

"Well, Mr. Ramsey, Mr. Blood. My name is Alden White. I'm here to send your box back to hell."

My own voice surprised me. It sounded much taller than the four and a half feet I stood up to when they checked my height at the school nurse's office.

I touched the flame of Zed's Zippo to a corner of the box that was soaked and stinking with the accelerants.

The sound of the thing going up was a great *WHOOMP*.

I toppled over backwards. My eyebrows didn't grow back for a few weeks. I got teased by other kids for looking funny and I stank like burnt hair for a while. I only smiled to myself.

I felt like a hero.

I watched the box burn for a time. After a bit, it started to break down and fall in on itself. That's when I turned on my heels and left. I went home to a grand ass-whooping of my own, and then into a still and dreamless sleep.

I woke early the next morning, snagged a couple of slices of Wonder bread for breakfast, and slunk out the back door unnoticed. I wanted to make sure the box was gone.

Sure, enough, all that remained of the box was a greasy black stain on the forest floor and a few hunks of carbonized wood. I pissed all over it and stomped it with both feet just to make sure.

On my way back to my trailer, I stopped at the edge of the woods and looked around. I had a funny feeling that I was being watched and I felt sure that it was Duke. But, try as I might, I couldn't spy another living soul, save for the birds and the squirrels.

Just a few feet from where I stood, I spied the patch of toadflax I'd run through as I fled from the fire we started. A few of the green stalks of the toadflax were still lying crumpled and broken, yellow petals scattered on the ground. But, aside from the few trampled flowers, the patch was a shining pop of color against the woods, the dead grass, and the dying clay.

I decided then to start nurturing that little patch. I'd start up the compost pile my mom was always claiming she was about to start. I'd save up for some Miracle-Gro fertilizer or steal some from the hardware store. I'd bring home some packets of seeds from the seed exchange at the local library.

I became determined that I'd fill up that whole field that stood between the trailers and the woods with flowers and weeds and plants of all kinds. Crimson clover and hairy vetch and toadflax and black-eyed Susans.

It would take years but I would stick to it. I would cover up that whole face of the woods. With enough work and luck, I'd never have to think of those woods or that day or the damned box ever again, and no one else would know what lay behind the thick green tangle of flowers, would never venture behind that curtain, so high and wild.

That was the plan, at any rate. As you and I both know, nothing in the whole, wide damned world is ever easy, simple, or free.

That thicket did grow, in time. My plan, at least the first part of it, succeeded.

Now the thicket and the forest it hid, like the rest of the planet, is a raw and crusted black gash, seeping toxins and bitter oils and spits of smoke from underground fires.

The summer of Duke and Zed and I and the box and what we did are decades behind me. Somehow, I became old during all those years and I do not recall the last time I walked under the sun. I have spent much of my life below ground, with the few others who survived the war and the bombs and the shock troops and the missiles falling from heaven.

All those years ago, I tended my wild patch and I waited for Duke to return. Zed still lived nearby, but he never came by very much, and I didn't blame him then and I don't blame him now. After all, I didn't reach out to him or knock on his door or offer to share stolen beers with him anymore. I mostly kept to myself and watched my weeds grow.

But I heard about Duke.

It was mostly things around town, at first. I'd hear my mom talking on the phone or catch a stray blurb on the television.

Two police officers who had worked together for fifteen years turned their guns on each other, and when the EMTs and other cops arrived to investigate, they found only the two dead cops and spent shell casings. The two sidearms were nowhere to be found.

After that, banks and convenience stores were robbed. Camera footage from the scenes showed tellers and cashiers and bank managers handing wads of cash over to a twelve-year-old boy with a pistol in his hand and another in his belt. The newscasters always asked if anyone could identify the suspect.

I damn sure could.

But I didn't say anything. I knew those pistols weren't for making people turn over their money. He had the tongue for that, after all. The pistols were a message—to me and to Zed. If we breathed a word about what we knew, he'd use the tongue to make the cops or our teachers or someone else bring us to him and he'd waste us without a pause.

Duke didn't stop with robberies.

His power grew with practice.

I caught a news segment one night when the local station had invited him to call in and give himself up or give a message to his friends and family. Duke called in and even over the phone he could hold sway. In seconds the newscasters were stripping off their clothes and barking like dogs or baa-ing like sheep at his command. In the background of all that madness, you could hear Duke laughing over the phone connection.

It went on like that for years. I kept up with it when I could. I dropped out of school. I just couldn't focus anymore, and it's not like anyone was expecting me to graduate. I found odd jobs here and there and eventually got a steady gig slinging sandwiches in a gas station with an attached food counter.

I heard lots more news that way, from customers and cops who stopped in and from the TV in the corner which was constantly blaring.

Duke worked his way around the country. A teenage kid in an armor-plated limousine full of strippers and kegs of beer. He lived on cheeseburgers and pizza and potato chips, all hand delivered to him, along with armloads of cash and bags stuffed with guns and ninja swords.

No one could touch him, let alone stop him. They'd put up roadblocks and he'd turn them away with the tongue. One word was all it took and Duke had never been shy about talking, even before we found the box.

For a while, they kept giving him spots on the local news, thinking he had some list of demands to make and maybe that would appease him or get him to stop or at least slow down.

It just gave him more chances to practice—more targets.

It got to the point that Duke would make a big show of it all. He'd go on the show and make all these demands for body armor and armed guards and all kinds of things. But then he'd just look in the camera and get a twinkle in his eye and start telling everybody watching to burn their own houses down or throw their kids into the lake or drive their cars into the pumps at the nearest gas station.

I knew enough to shut the TV off as soon as he got that look in his eye and started speaking. I'd seen and heard it all before. Millions of others didn't. Millions of others died.

This went on for a while and, sooner or later, it was time for an election. Duke hopped right on that and made the two leading candidates duel to the death with swords on the White House lawn.

That, at least, was entertaining.

But, of course, Duke won out in the end. He was the youngest ever to sit in power in the Oval Office, not even twenty-five years old. Some laws had to be rewritten to make that happen but that was no obstacle. A few words and the entire government was falling over themselves to rewrite the law of the land.

As soon as he was in office, Duke quickly got tired of making everyone jump and dance and strip and kill themselves and their neighbors and families for his amusement. He turned his eyes to other countries.

Not even two full months after assuming power, the missiles started flying and long-range bombers were headed out across the Atlantic and the Pacific.

The sky went black and the planet went cold in a matter of weeks.

I'd had some idea of where things were headed. I had started digging and stocking a shelter while Duke was still rocketing around the country in his armored limousine and turning toy stores and movie theaters and ice cream parlors into machete-riddled nightmares.

I've expanded the place over the years, and taken in a few straggling survivors. Most of the ones I took in died in the end. The ones that lived on weren't right—were hardly human. They don't speak. They scuttle and stare and slobber. They eat the mushrooms and the roots I grow for them. I have enough to live on and some to spare for them. I figure it's the least I can do.

I brought some seeds down here with me, though they can't grow. There's not enough light in here.

I have started to venture out to the surface on occasion. Much of the fallout has dissipated after so many decades. I have no idea if anyone is left out there—if Duke is still riding around in his death car or commanding armies of radioactive ghouls or stockpiling arms to finally kill off the remaining survivors of The Last War.

When I go topside, I scatter seeds.

In one small patch, I found dirt that was still the color of the earth I remembered. I sowed the seeds of the flowers and the weeds and the wildness I collected in my youth.

Maybe one day I will see them sprout. Maybe one day I will see them grow. Maybe they will cover the ugly black scars that grown-up boy dug in the earth with his toys. And I can breathe lungfuls of the poisoned air and, as everything goes black, I will see the green, the wildness, one more time.

Internal Rhyme
Aimee Trask

Downtown Fort Worth was crowded that Saturday night, and we'd parked a long way from the nightspot we were hanging out at. My husband, Curtis, was too drunk to drive and his frat brothers, Brant and Siegel, were shit-faced. I'd had a few drinks, but I was okay. I would drive. We just had to find the Escalade.

This was several years back, and cars—even fancy ones—didn't have key fobs. We didn't even have iPhones yet.

Curtis said we were parked along the west side of Jones St., maybe close to 9th. His buddies were no help. We were walking southeast from Sundance Square on Commerce and turned left on 8th.

"You boys ok?" I asked, addressing Brant and Ziegel.

"Yes, Mrs. Moneypenny," Ziegel half-bellowed.

It was a running joke. My husband's last name was Bond, and Brant and Ziegel jokingly referred to me as Moneypenny all night. It wasn't that funny, even in college. And it was especially stale if you weren't drunk. But I was a good sport. They were some of Curt's oldest friends.

"Five-O," Siegel said, straightening up. "*Five-O*."

"Look sharp," Curt advised unsteadily. "Be cool."

They were cool and the squad car passed us and took a right on Commerce.

"That was sneaky," said Brant. "Fuckers. Where's the truck?"

"I think we're getting close," I replied, spotting what looked like a homeless guy sitting against a brick wall, down a short way. When he saw us, he stood up slowly, like he was using the brick wall for leverage.

As we got closer, it looked like he was holding a drink in one hand and what looked like a wallet or checkbook in his other. He shook the drink and it rattled. It was a Mason jar full of coins and a couple bills.

He shook it again when we reached him, and we stopped.

"Panther City poet," he said, his bloodshot eyes focusing. "Care for a verse?"

We started to turn and walk away, but he shook the jar, again. "Messieurs and Madame, don't be terse. What's the worst result? Knowing or not knowing? Going or knowing?"

"Not knowing what?" Brant managed.

"Not knowing, sir," the poet said. "Isn't that the curse?"

"Curse?" Siegel mumbled.

"That's what they say," the poet replied, but by then he was staring at me. There was something familiar about him. And I think I looked familiar to him, too. It was just a moment.

Curt didn't notice. He retrieved a few dollar bills and some change from his pocket, but the poet stopped him.

"How about something lovely for the lady," the poet said. "And you can reward me afterwards, a pittance or a penance."

"Penance," Curt slurred. "Penance for . . ."

I still don't know why for sure, but I suspect it had something to do with me putting up with his obnoxious friends. The bills and the change remained in Curt's hand. "Ok," Curt continued. "This is my wife, Alice."

"Alice?" The poet's eyes peered into mine. "Alice."

"Yes," Curtis responded. "My wife, Alice. Recite something for the lady."

"Gladly," the poet said, nodding to me, smiling strangely. "And from your strapping lad."

By then I was convinced I knew him from somewhere, and it wasn't the alcohol. He definitely recognized me as well, though I don't think he knew how or why. But by then he had turned squarely toward me. His eyes were light green, maybe hazel. They grew wide, and he began.

fears flung, lungs deep
I breathe you in the curious
half-sleep of our queer young
tongues.
now is this sameness singly ours
the pleasure twinned, the
ages clinging blameless
to begin again.

these are the only wages
the seasons really measure,
*   this is when*
*   we live.*

I was mildly stunned. The poet's dirty hands—the jar in one and what was actually a small black notebook in the other—had gestured in a compact rhythm throughout the poem, expanding near the end, palms up in a semi-graceful bow.

Curt looked at me, pleased. "That was awesome," he said. "*Brav*—"

"Love poems!" Brant interjected, almost sounding sober. "Is that all you got?"

Curtis turned. "That's what I asked him—"

Brant interrupted again. "Knowing or going?! Whatever. It's high school crap. We shoulda went. Panther shitty poet, more like."

"Brant," Curtis cautioned, turning toward his friend. I grabbed his arm and he gave me an unlevel glance. Brant kept going.

"I thought the Shakespeare crowd had retired. I thought it was all about free verse, now. And symbols. Whadda they call it? Symbiosis?"

"Symbology," the poet corrected. "And that piece was written in free verse."

"Yeah, semenology," Brant replied. "That's what I said. But it rhymed. Who's the poet that doesn't know it?"

The poet clasped his hands, almost embarrassed. "It's symbology, good sir. Semenology is the study of sperm. "Fears flung, lungs deep" is one of my scribbles. The rhyme is nonstandard. It's called internal."

Brant's lips thinned. "A real *turdsmith*, are ya?"

The poet slumped and unclasped his hands. They rested at his sides. "It's an honest effort with no guarantee of success, friend. I make no demands."

"Uhhh, I ain't your friend, *broseph*," Brant scoffed. Brant didn't like the way the exchange was going. He was in asshole mode. "Is that all you've got? Did you write that for your fifth-grade sweetheart? Don't you have something that *really* matters?"

Brant's indignance was ridiculous, but the poet straightened, his face red. But calm. "Well, of course, my good man. Of course."

The poet stared at the cracked sidewalk beneath our feet. "Matter," he continued. The poet reassumed his character. "Matter of fact, I do."

"I'm sorry," I said, addressing the poet. "You don't have to. He's drunk."

"That's no excuse, Madame," the poet said. "Your friend is hardly obtuse. He simply dabbles in the bigger questions. I will entertain his suggestion."

Brant crossed his arms, smirking, as if he had proven a point.

I hadn't noticed the poet was wearing a fraying black, pin-striped dress jacket with ragged tails until he turned his back to us. He buttoned it, ran his hands through his greasy hair and then turned back around.

With his hair away from his forehead, I definitely knew him; but it was a recognition without context. A familiar face from a forgotten crowd.

The poet began again, one moment contemplative, one verse flustered, another serene. But when he looked at me directly, I could tell that something behind his eyes was smoldering. He seemed to be on the verge of tears.

a boy sits talking to himself
on a street curb; an old woman with

a piss-pack on her hip lolls by
like she's trying to find the
                    Soylent Green line.

as the light changes and the
walking starts, I can't help thinking
                    that if I had more heart I
would do something,
anything, help the lady across the street
or sit next to the kid on the curb, but I'm
only vaguely disturbed by what I see because
what's happening to them is not happening to me;
besides, J-Lo is singing about
her mac-daddy's bling-bling on a nearby car
stereo, leaving me to trace
the day-glo edges of my own hell,
embrace the normal lies, be all-american and
                    biggie-sized
until this lapse into conscience fails and
thankfully, subsides.

              perhaps
I am the downfall, the drop-off, a
confirmation of our gravest fears; but,
maybe I'm the pinnacle, the be-all
end-all, the hero of a cynical churn that's lasted
thousands of years, a wry, blood-butter
plop that now no one even God can stop, with
no why and no how, just an impulse
to consume and propagate,
defecate and yearn
and burn and repeat as
necessary.

if I'm the boll
weevil that burrowed into
the furrowed fleece brow of this culture's
infantile Santa fantasy, I'm also
it's representative man, clench-fisted but

half awake, standing
at the end of a path that
began with the woeful dilution of
hope and everything at stake or
that mattered—sheesh—if matter only existed

The poem was followed by unexpected silence. Then, the poet smiled grimly. "A little quantum physics humor," he said.

"Fuck you," Brant responded, uncrossing his arms and sucker-punching the poet, striking a blow for who knows what, especially him.

It caught the poet square in the jaw and he fell backward, smacking his head against the brick wall. Brant stood over him. "How's that for free verse, smartass?!"

Curt grabbed Brant and began pulling him away. I heard the dull crack of the poet's head against the brick, but I didn't understand exactly what had happened.

I only registered the aftermath. At first, the poet didn't seem surprised. Then, he gasped and blinked his eyes, finally closing them hard, like he was trying to focus. He dropped his mason jar and it shattered on the concrete beside him. He began sliding down the wall. The spot where the back of his head had struck the masonry now marked his sinking trajectory, a descending, thickening bloodstain. His eyes opened slowly.

Siegel stared in drunken disbelief.

"What the fuck?" Curt hissed, pushing Brant down the sidewalk. "What the fuck is wrong with you?"

"Fuck you!" screamed Brant. "Screw that fucking Nancy ass-wipe, fucking shitting on everything, fucking cracking wise. Homeless faggot! He don't look so smart now, does he?"

Siegel was standing over the poet. "No," Siegel replied. "He looks dead . . . but his lips are still moving." Placing one hand on the brick wall to brace himself, Siegel bent down to listen.

The poet's glance shifted to me. Tears began to run down his checks.

"You're a fucking asshole," I screamed at Brant. "You were being a shit . . . he gave you exactly what you asked for."

The hand holding the black notebook released it, and the poet's sitting posture seemed to slump. His head slowly lolled to one side.

"Dude's out cold," Siegel said. "He may really be dead now. He's sitting funny."

"Let's go," Curt said. "Brant didn't hit him that hard. Let's get the fuck out of here. Now."

"You're all fucking assholes," I said.

"Maybe so," Curt said. "But we're not the kind of assholes who are gonna wait around to see who goes to jail. Give me the keys."

I threw the keys at Curt so hard he dropped them, and I ignored his displeasure. I walked over and knelt in front of the poet. I picked up the black notebook and noticed the poet wasn't moving at all. I stood up abruptly. "He's not breathing!"

"I told you," Siegel said.

"Let's go!" Curt yelled.

We found the Escalade and drove away. I sat in the back seat with Siegel, behind Brant. Siegel yawned and shook his head. "That was weird," he said.

Curt clarified things, giving Brant a sideways glare. "It wasn't weird. It was fucked up. What were you thinking?"

Brant didn't answer. He just stared straight ahead.

I poked Siegel in the shoulder. "What was the poet saying?"

"I'm not sure," Siegel said. "Something about a 'slithy' toll. Maybe a slimy toad. It was hard to make out." He yawned again. "Don't tell me I just heard some homeless guy's last words. I might have to bash Brant's head in with a two-by-four."

I remembered the notepad. I flipped through it. The pages were stained, tattered, and unevenly and intermittently dog-eared. I opened it at one of the largest, dog-eared pages.

> no hope, no hope
> the words stuck in my throat
> i seethe, i seethe
> it's getting hard to breathe

"What the fuck is that?" Curt said, snatching the poet's tattered notebook. *"Is that his?"*

"I forgot I picked it up," I said. "He—"

"Fuck," Curt yelled, taking both hands off the steering wheel and tearing out and tearing at the pages. He lowered his window and began tossing them out. "If something's wrong with that guy, do you know what will happen?"

I sat in frustrated silence.

Curt waited until we were a few miles down the freeway before he threw out the rest of the poet's notebook.

"You're a bunch of fucking assholes," I said, staring out the window.

"You said that already," Siegel noted, yawning. "But, for the record, I may agree."

I suddenly kicked the back of Brant's seat with both feet.

"What the . . ." exclaimed Brant, who was half out of it.

Curt grabbed Brant's shoulder and gave me a look that more than communicated his annoyance. "We hit a bump," he told Brant.

Brant settled back into his seat.

I stewed in silence.

Lionel Burke.

His name was Lionel Burke.

The people they interviewed on the newscast reporting "the death of an unidentified homeless man" the next morning didn't even know his name, but I did. His homeless acquaintances called him "The Busker."

I knew him. I remembered him.

Not at first, though. And I still wasn't sure for a few days. I'd completely forgotten.

I contacted my mom and told her I wanted to drop by and look at some of my old yearbooks. By then Brant was sweating bullets and Curt was alarmingly philosophical. Siegel had returned to Seattle and wouldn't return Brant or Curt's calls.

"Brant was drunk," Curt said. "He wasn't trying to kill the guy. It was an accident. This could ruin his life. Do you really think that homeless guy had much of a life?"

"Is that the point here?" I asked. "Are you trying to justify this?"

"No. Of course not. I'm just trying to be practical. We were there and we didn't offer aid or assistance. We didn't realize."

"You didn't realize."

"And that matters, now? He was probably on his way down already. You think he had a job? You think he had a wife or kids, a mortgage?"

I shook my head. "Seriously? I know he was someone's kid. Maybe even someone's brother. And, yes, maybe even someone's father. Who knows?"

"Alice, really. Are you listening to yourself? He was nobody in particular. Besides, what if you're pregnant?

My jaw clenched and my eyes welled up. I had thrown up the last couple of mornings—and that was something I never did. Even after drinking. It was a premature assumption, but at that moment I knew.

Curt was talking around me. He was talking over me. I knew in that moment that I couldn't stay with him. We were finished. We might get along for a while, maybe even a long while—but I would eventually leave. In that moment I had utter clarity. And complete contempt.

"You were there, Curtis. You saw what happened. Do you remember the poems? You seemed pretty impressed."

"I was drunk."

"So was the poet," I said. "And I was there. Did he sound like a nobody?"

Curtis noticed the edge in my voice.

"We can't do anything about it, now, Alice. Don't you see? It was an accident and he's gone—but we're still here. Brant was the best man at our wedding. That poet was just a homeless street hustler. Please. We have things. You want things. Don't overthink this."

I didn't.

I went straight to the bathroom and did a pregnancy test.

My consternation was met by a blue stripe. I was pregnant, and the asshole I was married to was the father.

I didn't tell him.

We drank a lot. And then we drank more. I decided I would have an abortion.

My hangover was rough, but not guilt-proof. Curt made love to me clumsily, but I couldn't shake the poet.

When I woke up the next morning, Curtis was already out for a jog. He had a good body and he was proud of it. Like he was trying to stay in shape for the big game. It suddenly seemed silly.

Then, it came to me. I didn't need to look at old yearbooks.

I knew it was him. Lionel Burke. We called him "Linus." He was the "Jabberwock" in one of my junior high English classes.

"Twas bry," I said. "Twas bry and." I closed my eyes. "Twas brillig. Twas brillig and the slithy toves . . ."

Linus—Burke—had really poured it on thick. We'd actually read it for homework. Our teacher was a British lady, late twenties or early thirties. She wasn't at the school long. She assigned a special project. Most of us paired up, but Burke did his own thing. I remember him smiling. Especially that day, while he waited his turn. Seventh grade English, before lunch. I can't recall the exact assignment for the project. But I remembered reading "The Jabberwocky" by Lewis Carroll. Carroll was the author of *Alice in Wonderland*—and my name was Alice. And Carroll's "Jabberwocky" was Burke's project.

That's when he knew for sure, I thought. That's when the poet realized who I was that night.

My eyes welled up.

Linus was smiling that day. He was goofy-looking, but he wasn't a goofy kid. And he didn't smile a whole lot. But he smiled at me that day. In fact, he couldn't seem to stop smiling until it was his turn. Then, he got in character. He went up in front of the class and assumed an entirely different demeanor.

He was a tall, skinny boy. Freckle-faced. And he sported a ridiculous mullet that looked like he cut it himself. But that day he smiled like he was the proud squire of a victorious knight-errant. Maybe even the knight, himself, stepped temporarily from his armor. Like he was about to join King Arthur's Round Table or something. He affected a British accent solemnly, but badly. But with unmistakable passion.

Burke recited the entire poem. He had completely memorized the text and delivered it with an enthusiasm and commitment that was as mind-blowing as it was awkward. But he didn't seem to notice. Every time he glanced in my direction, I looked away. When he finished, the rest of us just looked at each other. We knew better than to laugh.

The teacher loved it, but the class just thought Burke was weird. Odd. Incredibly odd.

Now, after all these years, it was also strange to me that he never figured it out. He never realized. He must've never realized you have to keep your head low and fit in, be normal. Here he was, after all this time, and he was still—

"He was still a joke," I said, my eyes welling up again. "He . . ."

I began to sob and bawl.

Later, I realized I got it wrong.

I was the one who hadn't figured it out.

My name. Lewis Carrol's "Jabberwocky".

Burke wasn't doing it for the class. He wasn't doing it for the teacher. He was performing for me. He was speaking to me, directly, mistakenly assuming that I'd get it, that I'd understand. But I was one of the popular kids, and he was new. He was a new, scrawny, lanky, weird kid. And that mullet.

I was a cheerleader. When he went out for the football team, they made fun of him. He looked silly in his jersey and uniform. Like a Jabberwock in a helmet and pads

Burke tried to fit in, but none of us really gave him a chance. He was so different, and we weren't different at all. I wasn't different—so I missed what he was trying to say.

Why had he never learned? How had he gone through life like that, and gotten this far? Or wound up where he was?

He wondered before Curtis spoke my name, and then he knew. He knew.

I wiped my eyes and pulled the comforter up over my nose. I stared at the ceiling for a long time.

Curtis was currently (and successfully) climbing the corporate ladder, a minor local executive. Brant was a regional executive for the same company. He was somebody's nephew and had a corner office over the Dallas skyline. We'd all met in college. I wouldn't have said Brant was Curtis' meal ticket or the only reason we had the Escalade; but I wasn't oblivious to the math. And, like Curtis, I knew how to play the game. I hadn't stumbled onto a rabbit hole and been transported to Wonderland. In almost every conventional sense, I followed the rules and did what I was told. I was taught what it took to win, and I'd married a winner. Curtis and I were from the same social stratus and we both coveted a higher social status. A status which said Burke was a loser. But I'm pretty sure it wasn't that he couldn't compete—he just wouldn't.

The next day, Monday, I went to the clinic. Burke may have been a fool, but Curtis and I were foolish. And Brant was a murderer.

Who would know? Who would notice? Who would even care?

In Carroll's "Jabberwocky" there was no reason given for wanting the Jabberwock dead. They just kill it and everyone celebrates.

O frabjous day! Callooh! Callay!

The Jabberwock never had a chance. They never gave him a chance. They never understood him.

Tears welled up in my eyes, but I wiped them away.

The procedure began.

One, two! One, two! And through and through
The vorpal blade went snicker-snack!

My marriage didn't last long after that.

Fine Leather

Armando Sangre

In the spring of 1969 Howie Kennamer shed his skin for the first time. It had been a restless night full of tossing and turning and dreams of pushing through dense undergrowth in a dark forest. Howie woke to the sound of his mother calling him to breakfast. Groggily pulling himself out from under the sheets and blanket he realized with some chagrin that he must have fallen asleep the night before without getting completely undressed. At that age, just before puberty, when a boy is fighting for all he's worth to cast off the ideas and behaviors of childhood, to be seen by himself and others as a young man, Howie was mortified to think he'd slept the whole night with his pants down around his ankles. No wonder he'd had such fitful dreams.

"Howie, cereal's on the table. Get up or you'll be late for school!" his mother called. Howie could hear the Beatles singing Get Back playing on the transistor radio Julie Kennamer kept on the windowsill above the kitchen sink. He liked the Beatles and wanted to get into the kitchen before the song ended.

Howie kicked the pants off his ankles and hopped out of bed. What the . . ? He was naked. His briefs must have been tangled up with his pants at the foot of the bed. Confused, he dashed to his dresser and slipped into a fresh pair. He hurried down into the breakfast nook where his mother had a bowl, a quart of milk, and a box of Cap'n Crunch waiting for him. The Beatles were still singing and his head bobbed to the music as he poured cereal, then milk, into his bowl.

"Mom, what do they mean when they say, *sweet Loretta Morton thought she was a woman, but she was another man?*"

"I don't know, Howie! I'm not sure it means anything. Could just be nonsense like *John Jacob Jingle Heimer Smith.*" Julie came over and gave her son a morning hug and a kiss on the crown of his burr-cut head.

"Do the Beatles take LSD?"

His mom's face twisted into a comical expression only she could do; her mouth moved over to one side of her face and conveyed shock and dismay, with a touch of humor thrown into the mix. As always, Howie laughed. "How would I know what the Beatles do in their private lives?" she asked.

"You read a lot; I thought maybe you'd read it in a magazine or something. Randy Horton said they do."

"You and I both know Randy Horton has said a lot of ridiculous things over the years."

That was true. Randy had once sworn on a stack of Bibles that President Kennedy had been killed because he was an alien from another planet. The assassination had been a regrettable event but necessary if humans wished to remain free of otherworldly domination. We had LBJ to thank for saving the world, Randy said.

"It's just that I like the Beatles," Howie mumbled, both cheeks full of cereal.

"Don't talk with your mouth full," Julie said, sliding a bologna sandwich into a brown paper bag. "I like the Beatles, too."

"Well, if you found out the Beatles were taking LSD, would I have to stop listening to them?"

Howie's mother laughed. "No, Howie. You can listen to those four lads from Liverpool even if they are tripping on drugs." Julie neatly folded the top of the brown bag containing Howie's lunch and placed it on the table alongside his cereal bowl. Beside the bag she placed a nickel for milk. She gave her son another kiss on the head for good measure. "We're running out of time here. Dress quickly and don't forget to make your bed. I'm going to change for work."

Julie Kennamer hurried off into her own bedroom. Howie raised his bowl and noisily slurped the remaining cereal and milk into his mouth. He put his empty bowl in the sink and returned to his bedroom.

In a minute or two he was in his jeans and T-shirt. Howie slipped on his P.F. Flyer hightops and tied them. Looking at his bed, he wondered if he could get away with just closing his bedroom door and pretending he'd made it. Then he remembered that's not what a mature young man would do. The usual strategy of grabbing both sheet and blanket, shaking them and pulling them taut did not work that morning. There was a big lump at the foot of his bed. Then he remembered. Howie flung the covers back and was appalled by what he saw.

There, in a rumpled tangle, was his skin. Uncertainly, he touched it. The skin was not paper thin but rather thick. It was soft and smooth, like expensive leather.

"Howie, are you ready?" his mom called.

"Almost! Still making my bed!"

"Get a move on!"

"Okay!"

Howie didn't know what else to do so he gathered his skin and tossed it under the bed. Then he spread the covers evenly over the mattress, fluffed the pillow and placed it in the center of the headboard. It wasn't perfect but it was good enough. He'd be home at 3:45, an hour and a half before his mother, then Howie would figure out what was to be done with the skin he had shed during the night.

That day at school, Howie could not shake the sense that something was very wrong. His skin felt abnormally sensitive to every touch, every breeze. He was chilly all day. Naturally, he'd heard of snakes shedding their skins. He had found lots of them over the years in the woods at the edge of their neighborhood. Howie enjoyed Science Class and always listened attentively to the Science teacher Mr. Barnes. He could not recall ever having heard of mammals shedding their skins. Marsupials kept their babies in pouches built into their bodies, and that was weird enough, but mammals did not shed. Humans are mammals, Howie reasoned, and I *did* shed my skin. Therefore at least one mammal has done it. He was vaguely reminded of something he had heard his mother say about one white crow proving all crows are not black.

"What's wrong with you, Howie?" Randy Horton asked at recess. "You're acting weird today."

Howie knew it was true. He had been uncharacteristically withdrawn all day. Even some of his teachers had asked him if he was feeling well. In the eyes of the teachers, the fact that his father was on active duty in Vietnam provided Howie with a lot of leeway when it came to moody behavior. A bubble of uncertainty surrounded him. Still, Howie knew it was best never to agree with Randy concerning one's personal shortcomings. Or anything, for that matter. If you did it was not inconceivable that Randy would soon be accusing you of being an alien, killing a president or worse.

"Screw you!" Howie said, wrinkling the skin on his nose in an expression of defiance. He wasn't exactly comfortable with saying the word 'screw' but he did not believe it was prohibited for young men to use it. He'd heard his father, a Chief Warrant Officer in the army, say much worse.

"Who crapped in your cornflakes?" Randy said.

"I don't eat cornflakes, I eat Cap'n Crunch, and nobody crapped in it!"

That was the end of their exchange. Howie failed to make eye contact and Randy went elsewhere on the playground to find others to annoy. Howie could not shake the feeling that he was in real trouble with this skin shedding business. Worst of all, there was no one he could talk to about it. Who could possibly be an authority on a personal matter like this, a thing for which he had not been prepared?

After school, Howie let himself into the house using the key on a string around his neck. He went straight to his bedroom, no snack, no Kool-Aid, no TV. Before he looked he said a silent prayer, hoping against hope that the whole thing was somehow a dream, that there would be no skin rumpled up among the dust bunnies under his bed.

No such luck.

Howie slid the skin out so he could examine it more thoroughly. Possibly a close inspection would reveal he was mistaken, that it was not at all his skin but something else.

Something yet to be determined. He shook the thing out, making a mental note to sweep the floor of his room before his mom got home. Satisfied that the thing was reasonably clean, Howie spread it out on the bed.

It was his skin. It looked like a deflated version of himself. The mouth gaped in an extraordinarily wide and misshapen manner. That was where it started, Howie realized. Somehow the skin began peeling at his lips, it had rolled back over his head and through the course of the night he had completely wriggled free except for his feet. He sniffed it. Not much of a smell. He touched it. It felt nice. His mother was a seamstress for the Aronson glove factory in town. Howie had seen the expensive thin leather they used to make the trademark Aronson gloves. This skin, his skin, was just like the lambskin and kidskin his mother so carefully stitched into those gloves that everybody wanted to wear. Realizing this, Howie got an idea.

Behind their house was a small storage building. Howie's folks had crammed it full of all sorts of suitcases, boxes, furniture, and whatnot. One quarter of the place was dedicated to material and sewing supplies belonging to his mom. In addition to working at Aronson's, Julie Kennamer also did freelance sewing: prom dresses, wedding dresses, special items of every description.

Howie put his skin on the little table in the storage building and looked around for his mom's shears. First, he'd cut the skin up into sections large enough that they could be used to make something, but with all the identifying features like fingers and toes and face removed. He smiled as he trimmed his cast-off epidermis into squares and rectangles of what, to all appearances, was high quality leather. Shoving the random odd-shaped bits in his pockets, he folded the rest into neat little stacks and placed them on the shelf near some other scraps of fabric. Maybe it would be a while before his mother discovered the leather, maybe she wouldn't question where it came from. Putting the shears back in their place and checking to see that the area did not look disturbed, Howie backed out the door and locked it.

The only thing he could think to do with the odd bits was to bury them in the flower bed, back in a corner under the accumulation of leaves in the shade of the juniper bush. He got the shovel from the garage and had the offensive skin, the incriminating evidence, buried in a matter of minutes. Remembering the dust bunnies strewn around his bedroom floor, he quickly put the shovel away and went to the pantry for the broom and dustpan. Soon he had set the world right. If his mother noticed he'd swept under his bed she'd think he was just growing up, becoming the responsible young man she and Howie's father wanted him to be. He put the broom away, washed his hands, got some Lay's potato chips, and sat down in front of the TV to watch *Speed Racer*, feeling a bit like Racer X after his clandestine maneuvers.

Howie congratulated himself for the way he'd handled the matter. Life had thrown him a curveball. Instead of running around in circles screaming, "The sky is falling!' like Chicken Little in the story, he had stepped up to the plate and hit, if not a home run, at least a base run. One thing still bothered him. Snakes shed their skins periodically. If they kept growing, the shedding process continued. Mr. Barnes had said snakes shed their skins anywhere from four to twelve times a year. Twelve times a year! Was that going to happen to him? Howie knew he was far from being grown. Surely he would shed again. He wondered why he had never shed before. After all, he was much larger than the baby he had once been. Was it possible he had shed before but just did not remember it?

Julie Kennamer came home at the usual time, changed into her casual clothes, and made dinner. They had grilled cheese sandwiches, kosher pickles, and potato chips. The two of them ate together on the sofa in the living room and watched a *Perry Mason* rerun.

"Sorry it's just grilled cheese, kid," Julie said. "I felt too tired to cook."

Howie wasn't sorry at all. Grilled cheese with a kosher pickle was his favorite meal. "Nothing better!" he said.

When Howie went to bed that night he thanked God that everything had worked out. How things might have gone if his mother had found out about the skin he could not guess. He was just very relieved that the whole matter was his little secret. There had never been any real need to involve anyone else.

At breakfast the next morning, the hair stood up on Howie's neck as he heard his mother talking to her friend, Ramona, on the phone. "I had the greatest stroke of good luck last night. I was out in our storage unit looking for something I could use to enter that contest at work. I have no idea where it came from, but I found some really high-quality leather on my shelf next to the gingham. That's just it, I don't remember ever having bought it. And there's a lot of it! That much fine leather would have cost a pretty penny. So, I stayed up late, lost a little sleep over it, but I think I came up with a new glove design that just might win the contest."

When Julie got off the phone and returned to the kitchen to give Howie his customary cranial kiss, he said, "I heard you talking to Ramona. What's this contest?"

"We've had a great year at work and Mr. Aronson, to show his appreciation, is holding a contest. Whoever designs the winning item will get a $100 bonus and their creation will be featured in next year's catalog."

"And you think you may have a winner?" Howie asked, staring down at the stray cereal bits floating on the milk in his bowl.

"Let me show you. You be the judge." Julie left the room and came back shortly with a small white box. It was the same kind of box all the Aronson gloves were sold in at upscale department stores all over the country. Proudly, Julie set the box beside him. Inside was a pair of ladies' gloves. They had some unusual stitching across the knuckles and a little adjustable strap at the base of each glove. "What do you think?"

"Looks great, Mom!" Howie forced a big smile. "I bet you win the contest!"

Julie bent down and gave her son an enthusiastic hug. "Oh, I'm so excited I can hardly wait to get to work. When I discovered that leather last night I could not believe my good fortune! I was so inspired I just stayed up until I was finished. It was worth going without sleep to see my creation come together so quickly! And the best thing is, there's enough leather left to do several more projects! I have no clue where that fine, fine leather came from. It's like that story of the shoemaker and the elves."

"Yeah, I'll bet elves left that leather for you," Howie said.

On the walk to school Howie could think of nothing but the fact that his skin, skin he'd been wearing on his body less than forty-eight hours before, was now a pair of gloves. Ladies' gloves! And his mom was entering his skin in a contest. Howie was glad that Julie was so excited, but he still felt a little queasy when he considered all the circumstances.

There was a moment that day, at the end of Science Class, when Howie found time to ask Mr. Barnes a question. "Mr. Barnes, has it ever happened . . . I mean, is it possible for a human being to shed their skin? Like snakes do?"

"Hmm. That's a new one. Your questions never fail to surprise me, Howie. Humans shed their skin constantly. Every minute of every day bits of our skin flake and fall off our bodies. In fact, if you don't own a pet, most of the accumulated dust in your home is composed of dead human skin cells."

"Gross," Howie said.

Barnes laughed, "Yes, I suppose it is. The facts of life involving biological processes are often off-putting in polite society."

"Are there any examples of humans really shedding their skin? Like, a lot more than dead flakes?"

"There are skin conditions; eczema, seborrhea, psoriasis, these can all cause a dramatic, unattractive, and sometimes painful loss of dermal layers but, as far as I know, no one has ever shed their skin the way a snake does. Except in comic books, pulp novels, or horror movies."

"Thanks," Howie said, thinking, *I may be the first, the only. If I tell anyone I'll end up in the history books. I'll be famous.* Being a famous freak was not at all appealing to Howie. And what would the authorities do to him? Lock him up in a research lab, conduct tests, hold him captive like a lab rat?

That night Julie Kennamer seemed to float, rather than walk, when she breezed through the front door. "Howie! Come on, we're going out to dinner!"

Howie came into the living room from his bedroom where he had been doing homework. "Eating out on a Wednesday night?" Eating out was not a common occurrence in his family, especially when his dad was overseas, but eating out on a Wednesday night had never before happened.

"That's right! Mr. Aronson fell in love with that pair of gloves I designed. He said regardless of the outcome of the contest, he wants to include my design in the new catalog! That means a bonus, recognition in print, and an annual bonus based on sales. I am so happy!"

Howie wrapped his arms around his mom and gave her his best hug. Looking up at her beaming face, he asked, "Where are we going to eat?"

"I thought we'd go to Massey's!"

This was too much. A hamburger and fries would've been great, but Massey's was famous for the best chicken fried steak in town. Howie was beginning to think donating his skin to further his mother's career might not be such a bad thing. Chicken fried steak and mashed potatoes, smothered in gravy!

For the next few months, things went very well in the Kennamer household. Howie got an occasional letter from his father, airmail from Vietnam. Julie was something of a celebrity at the Aronson glove factory. Howie's grades were good and, for the most part, he believed he was becoming the young man he and his parents wanted him to be. Mr. Barnes was already talking to him about the importance of setting his sights on a good university and making admission his most important goal.

About the beginning of summer, Howie shed his skin for the second time. As with all experiences, even the bad ones, the second time never carries the same impact as the first. When he woke in the morning and felt the skin gathered around his feet, he did not imagine he had gone to sleep with his pants on. Since it was summertime and he had the house to himself in the morning, Howie had plenty of time to examine the skin and contemplate the long-term consequences of this strange new biological pattern. He could only assume this would continue for the rest of his life. If he was accepted to university, if he lived in a dorm, he would have to figure out some way to keep the matter private. What if he fell in love and married someday? It would be mighty difficult to keep a secret like this from his wife, sleeping in the same bed and all. These questions were troubling but not overwhelming. He had figured things out once before and he could do it again. Already, he knew he would not be hiding the skin in his mother's sewing area. This time he carefully folded the skin, placed it in a large manila envelope, marked it 'property of Howie Kennamer' and hid it behind a box of Christmas ornaments in the attic. Easy peasey, no muss, no fuss. Howie K was on top of it!

The sense of being in control did not last. One night in June, Julie Kennamer came home looking like she had the flu. Her face was pale and she wore the most defeated facial expression Howie had ever seen. She hadn't contracted a virus. Something much worse had happened at work. The factory was preparing to mass produce Julie's gloves. Neither the lambskin nor kidskin had produced results as sleek, delicate, and fashionable as Julie's prototype. Since Julie had no idea where the leather had come from, one of the other employees suggested having the gloves analyzed. That way there would be no question as to what type of leather to use in the manufacture of the gloves.

"Human!" Howie's mom screamed when he questioned her. "That leather is human! Howie, they're going to send me to prison!"

The next morning both local newspapers were full of the news. An Aronson's employee had used actual human skin to design her award-winning gloves. The repercussions in the Jewish community were without precedent. Was this Julie Kennamer such a hateful antisemite that she took delight in deliberately submitting gloves made of human skin in a contest run by a Jewish businessman—some of whose relatives had died in the holocaust? Outside the papers, in the seedy barbershops on the east side of the city, it was whispered that Aronson himself knew about it. Who could trust a wealthy Jew? Remember the Protocols of the Elders of Zion? The man could be practicing satanic rites right there in the factory. This poor Kennamer woman might be just a Trilby to his Svengali.

That day Julie stayed home from work and Howie sat with her, waiting for the right opportunity and the proper words to come, words that would explain everything, words that would have them both laughing at the whole silly mess. Those words never came into Howie's mind.

"Howie, your father is a good man. No matter what you may hear in coming days. Sure, he's tough. You have to be when you're in the military police. I'm sure he's had to do some . . . difficult things in Vietnam. But he did not kill anyone and hide their skin in my sewing room!"

Until then, Howie had never imagined it could come back on his father in any way. There were a lot of angles to this mess that Howie had simply never anticipated.

"Mom," he said, "I need to show you something."

"What?" Julie asked, lowering her Kleenex and staring with red-rimmed eyes at her boy.

"It's in the attic. I'll be right back."

Julie was dumbstruck when Howie unfolded his second shedding, stunned when she understood and realized what it was. She shook her head, casting off the delirium that was striving to overtake her. "We've got to take this to the authorities. But first, I'm calling Ramona."

That was a long phone call. Howie only heard half of it but it went on for almost an hour. In the end, Ramona had convinced Julie to call a lawyer friend, which is just what Howie's mother did right after hanging up with Ramona. From what Howie could gather, the attorney was ecstatic to be involved in the case. This was the sort of thing lawyers dreamed about, the sort of case that only came once in a lifetime and, even then, only to the exceptionally lucky few.

There was a lot of interrogation after that. Howie was questioned by his mother's attorney, representatives of the District Attorney's office, and a police detective. Lots of reporters wanted to question him, but thank God, the others held the reporters at bay.

"What made you think the way you handled this was appropriate?" an Assistant DA half-shouted at Howie.

To his credit, Howie answered, "Mister, I'm an eleven-year-old boy. Nothing like this ever happened before. What would you have done?"

The Assistant DA had no response, which both Howie and his mother thought was a good thing.

The skin was taken as evidence, analyzed by a police lab using state of the art forensic methods, and eventually everyone was convinced the skin was exactly what Howie had told them it was, his own skin shed through some mysterious hitherto unknown process.

That wasn't the end of the matter but it was the end of its public discussion. Howie's dad was granted emergency leave. He flew home from Vietnam. The family members were glad to be reunited, but they all wished it had been under other circumstances. Authorities came from Washington, D.C. and whisked them all away. No one knew where or exactly which government agencies were involved. Howie was considered a matter of national security. At least that was what was whispered among the neighbors and other people of his hometown. No one knew where the Kennamers had gone or what would be done to the enigmatic skin-shedding boy. Everyone was mystified, flummoxed, clueless. The news had created a hunger for more information but when that was not forthcoming, people eventually quit thinking about Howie. They returned to their safe routines and never again entertained thoughts of the bizarre occurrence. All except for Randy Horton. Randy told anyone who would listen he had always known Howie was an alien from another world and chances were the government had deported him back to his home planet.

The Pumpkin Man
W. R. Theiss

I never wanted to get older. My youthfulness was spectacular, and life could not get any better. Age was my greatest fear.

On a cool West Texas Saturday evening, I pinned up my auburn hair, dabbed a bit more make-up on my face, and slid on my black dress. It was so devilish of me to wear a skirt that exposed not only my ankles, but my knees as well. My parents were already asleep when I slipped out of our house and met Martin around the corner.

A heavy October moon shone so brightly that we almost didn't need the headlights of his imported '23 Alvis. Its sleek torpedo frame rumbled through the vacant countryside toward the Twin Hills west of town. It was Halloween, 1925, and a friend of Martin's was hosting a barn dance outside the city limits. There would be dozens of attendees.

My parents frowned upon anything that was fun, especially on "Satan's Eve" as they called Halloween. I believe that I inherited my spirit from an aunt, who I had always thought to be very pretty and adventurous, despite her bad luck with men. I think that's what always inspired me to do things my folks considered wrongful deeds.

The party was in the middle of a cotton field. The barn was an old building that Martin's great grandfather constructed in the 1860s. It was indeed a very lively festival, with plenty of liquor and spirits of the non-supernatural kind. It was all going well until Martin excused himself from me to fetch a drink.

When he didn't come back after a couple of songs, I decided to look for him, make sure everything was okay. I wish now, even more than then, that I hadn't.

I found Martin with another woman at the side of the barn. The shoulder strap on one side of her blue dress was hanging down her arm, while Martin's vest had already been unfastened. Although I considered myself untamable, infidelity is a line I never crossed.

Before Martin could react, I grabbed a fistful of mud and threw it across both of their faces. To this day, I still hope that there was some sort of farm manure in that mud!

The pitch darkness of the night welcomed me with open arms. I tore away from the dance and went storming through the cotton fields, as far away from the party lanterns as I could run. I heard Martin holler my name a few times, but it was all to no effect. How I wish, now, that I had turned back and just gotten drunk and made out with one of his friends as revenge.

Blinded by tears and furiously mad, I charged headlong through a thick line of trees at the edge of the cotton field. I had no idea where I was going, all I knew was that I wanted to get lost in the woods and find a place to cry.

I crossed a creek and approached the base of a hill. Drifting through the silence, I heard the unmistakable sound of a mandolin being softly plucked on the height of the rise in front of me. I ascended toward the sound.

There was a trail on the crest of the hill. An old one, cut through the woods at least fifty years beforehand. Wagon ruts were still deeply embedded in the surface, and bright beams of moonlight illuminated the scene.

A wooden wagon with a strange shack-like structure covering its back portion, was parked off the shoulder of the trail. The dim glow and soft crackle of a campfire lit up the darkness of the night in front of it all. Warm melodies from the mandolin drew me closer to investigate.

Sitting on a scratched-up stool by the fire, in a vest of dark maroon and a shirt as white as the moon, was an old man, frail strands of gray hair cascading from his head to his broad shoulders. Standing over the waterfall of hair, like a watchtower, was a faded top hat perhaps made of seal skin. Having seen many miles and many years, the hat completed the man's antique appearance.

Laying on the other side of the campfire from the old man, listening to the music, was the gray bulk of a horse that seemed older than the very hill I was standing upon. It saw me from the distance, and immediately lifted its head, neighing threateningly at me.

The mandolin fell silent. The old man spun around and looked in my direction.

"Who's there? Speak or the Devil will have ya before mornin'!"

I inched into the flickering glow of the campfire, noticing a finely painted advertisement on the side of the wagon.

Dr. Thomas F. Driggar
Supplier of the finest medicines
and herbs in North America

"I don't mean to disturb you, sir." I said back to him. "I was lost in the woods and heard your songs."

"What were ya doin' in the forests after nightfall, lass? Ain't ya frightened of banshees or witches?" the man said back to me in a thick Irish accent. He grabbed a faded green frock coat from behind him and slid it on.

"No sir, I'm nearly eighteen. Ghost stories don't frighten me anymore," I replied, stepping into the flickering firelight. He cocked his head at me, one eye sparkling blue, the other a shimmering discolored pupil of gray.

"Not frightened, eh? But we're all scared of somethin'. Even ol' Gunpowder here, though he be over a century old, he's still a blasted coward after sundown."

"A century old?" I exclaimed.

"Ah, older than that even! Got him from a Dutch in a village north of Tarry Town, New York, I did. Ages ago, it seems now. Poor ol' cuss, got chased across the countryside by a headless Hessian with a whimperin' Connecticut schoolmaster on his saddle."

I smiled at him. "You're saying that this horse is the one Ichabod Crane rode upon in Irving's story, Legend of Sleepy Hollow?"

"Legend only to those that don't believe in legends, lass. And what is your name?"

"Shirley, Shirley Lampton. May I join you at the fire? I've had a most difficult evening."

The old man glanced at me with his good eye, not certain of my intentions. Finally, he smiled.

"Ya don't look like a banshee or witch to me, deary, so ya more than welcome here! Care for some Joe?" I glanced at the pot boiling over the fire.

"No, but thank you. Do you have anything stronger than coffee?"

Again, as the campfire crackled and shimmered across his elderly face, he grinned. "I've got a bottle of Scotch. Not as agreeable to womenfolk, but a lass like you, I can tell yer in need of it."

I smiled warmly back at him. "Scotch sounds fine."

In the hours that passed, the old man and I talked and laughed like we were old friends. He was a traveling medicine man, lost in a modern world of automobiles and pharmacy stores. He lived in the wilderness, doing his best to steer clear of highways and property owners. Through our entire conversation, I never once expected him to be anything other than a friend.

At long last, the moon had almost settled into the center of the sky. November was only a few minutes away.

"Shirley, my dear friend," he asked as I finished my third cup of Scotch, "I know I asked ya earlier, lass, but I think I know, now, what it be that you're afraid of."

"Oh, and what do you believe it to be?" I asked.

"Growin' old, like me and Gunpowder over there."

"No, it's not a flattering image. I confess, but please don't be offended."

He laughed. "Me? Ol' Irish Driggar, as the boys called me at Refugio, offended? It takes more than a comment like that to ruffle up my feathers. But why are you so scared of getting older?"

"I don't know," I said, "I think it has to do with my Aunt Charlotte. She was always so fun and full of life when I was a kid. My parents are the complete opposite of my aunt, no life, no fun. They're weighed down by the yoke of hardships, never much even on smiling or joking. I never wanted that."

"And what happened to your aunt?"

I took a deep breath, steadying the beat of my heart, and took the final swig of my last bit of Scotch. "She died. Three years ago, in an automobile accident. She and her boyfriend, at the time, got drunk and drove off a bridge. He lived, but Aunt Charlotte didn't."

"And how did her death affect you?"

"When they learned how she died, my parents blamed Aunt Charlotte for inviting her own demise. They said that Satan had come to collect her dues, that God did not have a place for such improper women in Heaven. That night, I prayed to whichever entity was listening, that I could live forever; so that I could enjoy life any way I wanted."

"And are you enjoying it now?" he asked me.

"Yes. Even though Martin betrayed my trust and love tonight, I'll move on and find someone better."

The old man nodded his head and looked up toward the moon. Gunpowder seemed to have noticed him as well and turned his heavy snout at him.

"I'd like to show you something, lass. Don't move your pretty little self from that chair. I'll be right back."

I watched him, curiously, as he got up from his stool and walked up into his wooden shack. He emerged a few moments later with a rotten pumpkin.

"What is that?" I asked him.

"The secret to living forever, lass. Gunpowder and I have seen a whole century pass because of this."

"A rotten pumpkin?" I said, as he came and sat back on his seat.

"Oh, ah, but it's not just a rotten pumpkin. Do you recall how the story about the schoolmaster and the Headless Horseman ended?"

"Certainly so. The horseman threw a pumpkin at him and struck Ichabod off the horse."

"Right ya are lass, and this pumpkin here," he held the rotten vegetable up to my face, "was grown from one of the seeds of that demon's weapon. They were scattered about Ichabod's hat, and the farmer I purchased Gunpowder from a hundred years ago, had collected the seeds in a bag. He called them the Devil's Roots, because Gunpowder had ate one, but never died."

"You don't actually expect me to believe that do you?" I asked him with a slight grin on my soft lips.

"No," he replied with a grin that was half covered in a slanted shadow, "but if there's a chance that you could live forever, just as you are right now, would you trust me, lass?"

I flashed my eyes at him in disbelief, but also resolution. Firmly, I nodded my head.

"When I turn this pumpkin around, listen to my voice, and stare into its eyes."

He turned the pumpkin around and looking back at me was a black and moldy face that had been carved out of it years ago. Driggar's voice resounded deeply in my mind, deeper with every word he uttered. A strange light, as bright as the pale October moon, grew brighter and brighter from within the pumpkin's hollowed-out shell.

I couldn't take my eyes off it. There was something . . . supernaturally compelling me to keep staring into the rotting face of the Jack-o-Lantern. Even when I noticed bits and pieces of my skin leaving my body and getting sucked into the pumpkin, I couldn't take my eyes off it.

I was startled awake by the sudden screech of a wagon wheel. I had fallen to the cold ground. I woke and looked for a moment, bedazzled at the changing trees of the woods around me. I picked myself up and instantly saw Gunpowder reined and ready to lead the carriage downhill. His fur seemed younger than before, a healthy mass of gray and black.

"Awake are ya, lass?" I heard a young man call out to me in a thick Irish accent.

I stood up and saw a dashing man in a black seal skin top hat and green frock coat sitting on the front bench of the wagon. His features had regressed many years.

"What did you do to me?" I asked.

"I gave ya the best medicine I had, lass. Look at your hands."

I lifted my arms, raising my hands to my face . . . and screamed. The flesh, the bones, the ligaments, the muscles . . . all of it, gone!

"Quiet down, lass, folks'll be thinkin' this trail be haunted by a banshee if they hear you!"

"What did you do to me?" I asked him again through halting, weeping breaths.

"You get to live forever now, lass! Just the way ya were last night."

"You turned me into a ghost! You bastard. You turned me into . . ."

"How ya like that, eh Gunpowder? You do a woman a favor and she gets ruffled by it. A ghost gets to live forever, lass. More so, you've extended mine and Gunpowder's life by a year as well."

I looked at him in disbelief, in agonizing woe. I wasn't sure what to do.

"Where's my body? Where's my skin?"

"I buried ya bones and whatnot over by that tree," he replied, and pointed toward an ancient oak with branches exploding magnificently. "As for your skin, well . . ." I watched him reach into a ripe orange pumpkin that sat beside him, a fresh face gleaming wickedly at me.

He pulled out a pumpkin seed, and with a crooked grin, tossed it into his mouth. His one gray eye sparkled in delight, then transformed to a magnificent blue.

"I say we're square now, lass. Farewell."

He made a clicking sound with his breath, and Gunpowder started trotting away.

That was the last time I saw Dr. Thomas F. Driggar, "the Pumpkin Man," as legends have now nicknamed him. I'm certain he's still out there, somewhere. Turning people like me, who want to live forever, into ghosts in exchange for immortality for himself and Gunpowder.

As for myself, I wish so strongly that I had just stayed at that barn dance. I would have moved along, finding another Martin, getting old until the day I finally passed. But now I shall forever wander these woods, hoping that the Pumpkin Man will return one day and bring to an end this miserable existence. Children have often seen me gliding through the trees, hunters have shot at me to no effect, and outdoorsmen have heard my weeping cries.

They call me "the Lady in the Woods." I am a legend now, embedded into the folklore of this place, as eternal as the bedrock below my transparent feet. A ghost forever young, but as old as an age itself.

One day, perhaps that sly old Irishman will return. But, it's been over a century now, and I have my doubts. I am cursed by the desire I had so eagerly asked for, and for that, I will always weep.

Feral

C. W. Stevenson

"**S**on of a bitch," muttered Jim.

Wiping the mixed beads of sweat and rain from his forehead, he cursed again, realizing he'd done little more than smear mud across his brow.

Ramón's tires were sunk deep in the stuff. Jim, his cousin Todd, and their hunting guide Ramón had spent the last four hours digging around the tires, to no avail. Adding branches in front and behind the tires to gain some traction did little good either. They would need to get it towed. Thanks to another looming storm, Jim knew they wouldn't be going anywhere fast.

Sit it out in the truck. Wait out the storm.

Too dangerous, he decided.

Flash floods were not to be taken lightly. Not here. This part of South Texas was flat—perfect for flooding waters to flow with ease. Uprooted mesquite trees and debris stuck into the fence in several places surrounding the ranch. In some spots, the debris had destroyed the fence entirely, a testament to the power such storms possessed. Lightning, heavy winds, fist-sized hail, floods… all threats that could kill you without the proper shelter.

He wished then they were back in Seattle, not in this snake-infested backcountry. The hunting trip had been inexpensive in comparison to the quotes other outfitters in the region had provided. But on top of divorce attorneys, it was all he could afford at the time.

You get what you pay for, I suppose.

Jim glanced upward. The incoming storm was still a ways off.

The gate was close—their exit from the hunting ranch so close that Jim could see it up ahead, Reeves Station Ranch welded together in large black letters on top.

"Back to camp," Ramón said, flicking out the rest of his cigarette to the wind. "We're done here."

"What about the truck?" asked Todd.

Ramón waved a hand. "The water will take it tonight."

No truck. No cell service.

Jim shook his head. "We're fucked." They hadn't shot more than a few quail. Axis deer, hogs, vermin of all types in the area... some quail were hardly something to boast about. Coming to Texas had been a mistake. Should've seen the Alamo instead, the Fort Worth Stockyards maybe, or driven some scenic routes to see the bluebonnets. Being a tourist wasn't so bad. But the heat? That he hadn't been prepared for, not in May. The only positive thing carried before a storm was a cool breeze.

"Sí, señor," Ramón said. "But we be all right soon. We walk back to camp, okay? In a couple hours, we'll all be drinking some cold beer."

Opening the back left passenger door, Jim grabbed his pack and fit the straps over his back. He tossed Todd's pack to him. The barrel of Ramón's 12-gauge poked out from under the backseat.

"Hand that to me, señor James. Carefully."

Jim grabbed the gun by the barrel at first, making sure it wasn't aimed at anyone as he gently slid it from underneath the seat. He handed the gun to Ramón. "It's just Jim."

"Is that really necessary?" Todd asked.

Jim could see Ramón was a bit pestered, but he smiled regardless. He nodded. "This truck? Is gonna be gone." He waved a hand again. "Se ha ido."

"What?" Todd asked.

Jim breathed deeply, embarrassed by his cousin's ignorance. "The flood is going to wash away the truck and everything in it," he explained.

"Oh," said Todd.

"Precisamente, señor Jim. Now, let's vámonos." Ramón pointed to the sky. "Real bad storm. Gonna be fucked real soon. Real bad. Vámonos." Walking around to the driver's side door, Ramón placed a hand on the top of the steering wheel and bowed his head. "Adiós, muchacho," as if he were saying goodbye to an old friend. And maybe he was. People and cars were the new people and horses. You stick around a thing long enough and it becomes a part of you.

Like Erica had been.

Don't think about her. Don't think about her.

No point anymore.

Off yonder, a squeal of a pig interrupted his thoughts.

They went back the way they came, following the road until it became too muddy to traverse. Three times they had all gotten their snake boots stuck to the point that they had to slip their feet out of their boots to pull themselves free, then they could yank their mud-caked boots loose and back over their soaking wet socks.

So, Ramón led them inland, following old deer trails.

Already, Jim could feel blisters beginning to form on his feet. The others would be in the same shape. Blistered feet, filthy clothes, greasy skin from sweat and rain . . . the sooner they were back at camp, the better.

Some cheap beer didn't sound so bad now—the longnecks of Lonestar beer Ramón had been providing them throughout the trip.

"Texas water," Ramón had called it each time with a chuckle, then he would clank his bottle with theirs and chug.

Nearing a corner, Ramón began to slow his gait. He turned back to Jim and Todd, mouthing a single word:

Hogs.

Jim noticed Ramón's grip tightening around the shotgun.

As they came winding around the bend, Jim watched as several dark shapes scampered off into the brush. Some of them splashed their feet into the slush and muck around a small pond where the sounder had been wallowing.

The pounding of hooves grew faint, their panicked grunts and squeals fading farther and farther away the longer Jim and the others stood in place.

Ramón lit a cigarette, cradling the shotgun with one arm. "Come," he gestured.

They walked on.

Jim spotted scant signs of human life as they continued their hike. A roofless cabin from decades before could be seen off to the east, a broken windmill still standing beside the crumbling ruin. Not too far from the cabin, rusted oil equipment lay scattered about in pieces throughout a clearing.

"No more oil," remarked Ramón.

Coming up on one of the rare oak trees in the area, Ramón gestured upward.

Jim and Todd stepped closer for a better look. Jim stepped around a cactus, noticing small bones littered on the ground.

Coyotes, probably. Or a bobcat.

When Jim and Todd found themselves in the shadow of the tree's branches, they saw it.

"Holy shit," Todd muttered, his eyes wide with as much astonishment as fear.

There in the upper branches hung a yearling, its mangled corpse still dripping blood from a lolling tongue. It was a fresh kill.

"Big cat," said Ramón.

"What—like a mountain lion?" asked Todd.

Ramón held out his arms wide. "*Big* . . . cat," he repeated.

"Dangerous?" Jim asked, his head instinctually turning to see if anything was behind them.

Ramón pursed his lips, shaking his head. "No, no, no. No dangerous to us." Then he chuckled, pointing at the yearling. "Dangerous for her though." He slapped his knees, seemingly unbothered that Jim and Todd did not find it amusing in the least.

While Ramón and Todd wordlessly started on the trail again, Jim stayed a moment longer, taking a last look at the grisly scene. He scanned the area for movement.

Nothing.

He was sure it was out there, hidden amongst the dense growth of weeds and grass, behind some mesquite trees, or behind a bed of prickly pear cacti.

Watching . . . waiting for them to move far enough away to safely retrieve its kill, or to continue feeding.

Shuddering at the thought of such a predator with eyes on them, Jim wasted little time in catching up with the others.

They passed large red harvester ant nests; an insect Jim hadn't even known existed. Huge and red, some of them were half an inch long. Unlike many ant colonies, there was no mound to be seen. No, these ants simply used a single hole in the ground, exiting and entering at their leisure. Four or five trails led away from the entrance of the tunnel like arms, trails used to collect and bring food back to the colony.

A harsh ecosystem. Erica would have hated it out here.

After a few hundred yards, Todd broke the silence. "How far is it?" Todd asked. "Back to camp, that is?"

Ramón clicked his tongue. "Eh, maybe one hour."

It was a large hunting ranch, one of the many in the area, but also one of the cheapest—the biggest bang for your buck. Here, on Reeves Station Ranch, there was no fancy hunting lodge, no personal cook, no fancy this or that. No. Here, there were two-double wide mobile homes that made up camp, and around two-dozen deer blinds scattered on 10,000 acres.

Some years they hunted in Maine for grouse, stopping at the L.L. Bean in Freeport to stock up on designer outdoor gear along the way, making sure to pick up a beanie and some socks for their wives as well.

Not anymore though, not with Erica gone. He suspected it was the only reason Todd had agreed to the trip—a pity trip for his newly divorced cousin. And now, here they were, stuck out in hell.

Maybe Erica had been right, he was a failure.

A failed business. A failed marriage. You miserable bastard.

"Bad luck is all," Todd had told him. "Think of it as a new opportunity. A new beginning. Businessmen fail all the time. Some of the most successful go bankrupt a time or two before making it big."

It was why he loved the guy. He was always there, encouraging him on despite Jim's melancholic state of being. And here he was, wandering the South Texas wilderness before a great storm behind him.

Jim turned to face Todd, who was busy picking at something in his beard. "Hey. I'm glad you came, man. Really."

Todd smirked. "What? And miss all of this?" he asked, gesturing to their surroundings.

They both laughed. Then something caught Jim's eye off to the side of the trail.

He stopped.

"Say, Ramón?" Jim pointed to the gleam of metal not far from the trail. "What's that?"

Ramón furrowed his brow, turning to see what Jim was going on about.

"I see it," Todd said, his words unsure, trying to process what it was he was looking at, like Jim.

"Ah," Ramón said. "Hog trap. Lots of hogs around." Then Ramón's face contorted, and he appeared confused again. Ramón left the trail, heading in the direction of the trap.

From the trail, Jim could hear Ramón. "Oh, *oh Dios mio*."

Jim headed toward Ramón.

Todd stayed put.

He came upon Ramón making the sign of the cross, mouth agape, eyes glued to the wreckage.

The trap . . . was in *pieces*.

"Big cat?" asked Jim.

Ramón shook his head. Clicking the safety off the shotgun, he pumped it once.

"Pinche pendejos," Ramón spat. He turned to face Jim. "Fucking *hogs*."

That surprised him. Before arriving at Reeves Station, he had never taken into consideration that *wild* pigs existed. When he had thought of swine before, he imagined only the domesticated kind who wandered from their sty along with their brethren each morning to feast at the trough. Not the dark shapes he'd glimpsed running off into the brush earlier.

But this . . . this looked like a silverback gorilla had gone berserk. The back of the trap remained intact, but the cage door and much of the side and cage floor had been torn free. Jim could see splotches of blood and bristly black hair stuck to some parts. Whatever had been in there had not been happy.

"How many?" asked Jim, beginning to worry.

There was no trace of anger left in Ramón, just *concern* as he peered through the brush behind the trap. He glanced back at Jim and shrugged. "Don't know. Only one set of tracks." He pointed the barrel of the shotgun to the front of the trap.

Where the ground hadn't been stomped, torn, and dug in, there were tracks. Like Ramón had said, one set, the imprint of hooves revealing the horrifying truth. There was a monster nearby.

"You ever seen the one that made these?"

Ramón began to back away slowly, inching his way back to the trail. "No. Biggest tracks I ever seen. Move back. Quiet. Slow."

Jim did as he was bid, the breeze no longer a comfort but a danger, threatening his hearing as it picked up, blowing stronger with every second that passed.

The creature emerged from the dark cluster of trees behind the trap.

"Do . . . not . . . move," Ramón urged. "*Boar.*"

Jim froze.

Not *just* a boar. A monster.

"*Shoot* it," Jim begged.

"It kill you if I miss. Then kill me. Then Mr. Todd. Stay."

It sauntered over to Jim, showing no sign of aggression at first, appearing merely curious. It was the biggest hog Jim could have ever imagined. He guessed the thing was well over four feet tall, at least ten feet long, maybe longer. Bristly black fur and thick muscle glistened in what rays of light shone down. Jim studied its sharp tusks, then its eyes. Dark, like its fur, they peered back at him. It bared its teeth.

A challenge perhaps.

He waited for this standoff to end with him gored or still breathing, hoping for the latter outcome. He could fix things with Erica. Make things all right between them. A divorce didn't *have* to happen. Didn't near-death experiences put the things most important to you into perspective?

A long line of drool stretched down from its slack jaw. It stomped its hooves, raising a small cloud of dust. Taking a step closer, it sniffed him, then breathed and exhaled. Jim could taste the stench coming from its foul breath. He wanted to run, but fear kept him still, afraid of what this monster was capable of.

Emitting a deep grunt, it walked past him.

Jim wasn't sure how long he stood without moving. He took some time to let it register how close he had come face to face with death. Wiggling his right foot to make sure he was still capable of doing so, he decided then it never felt so good to be alive. He wanted to laugh hysterically. To thank God for allowing him to live another day. Hell, after they made it out of here, he just might start attending church again.

He was so preoccupied with his own brush with danger that he had completely forgotten his cousin waiting for them on the trail. By the time Jim had realized it, it was too late.

"Oh . . . my God! Jim! Ramón!" Todd screamed in bloody terror.

The two of them ran for the trail just in time to see the ginormous black form of the boar ram into Todd with such force that it sent him flying into a bed of cactus.

Jim's eyes darted from the hog to his wailing cousin. His best friend in the world—it made him feel ashamed that he was considering running then, leaving Todd behind in his misery as he screamed at the top of his lungs.

Drizzle began to fall as grey clouds moved in, darker clouds not far behind.

Ramón lifted the gun and aimed as the hog darted across the trail. He fired, the roar of the shotgun echoing across the land.

"Did you hit it?" Jim asked, arriving at Todd's side.

Ramón said nothing as he pumped the shotgun, an empty shotgun shell flying into the grass.

Jim pulled Todd from the cactus bed as Todd continued to cry out in pain. Cactus spines protruded from his forearms, face, and clothes. Above his right knee, a cut gushed out blood. It was beginning to pool onto the ground.

"Is not bad," Ramón assured them. "Pull cactus," he said then, making a plucking gesture with a free hand.

Jim began pulling the thorns from Todd's face to begin with. Todd had calmed some, biting his tongue to keep from crying out. He was shaking uncontrollably. "I'm sorry," Jim kept telling him. "I'm sorry, I'm sorry, I'm sorry," as if it could numb the pain.

Once he had removed all the cactus he could find, he and Ramón lifted Todd to his feet.

Ramón pointed north, toward another trail. "Tower blind, not far. There's a first aid kit inside. One inside all the blinds."

"What about that thing?" Jim asked.

"It's a fucking hog . . ." Todd said, pain leaking through his teeth with each word.

It was one of those animals you never hear tale of reaching such monstrous proportions. But it was obviously possible. He'd seen it up close.

"It's a boar," Ramón told them. "I never," then shook his head in disbelief. "It should not exist. We have to move. Vámonos. To the blind."

Together, Jim and Ramón helped Todd limp along, all the while watching out for the boar, waiting for the bastard to burst onto the trail at every bend.

When they reached the tower blind, Jim noted it was much larger than expected. Climbing up the metal rungs of the ladder, he undid the lock with the combination Ramón provided. He opened the door. Inside, two metal folding chairs faced the main window. On the ground, sandbags for resting one's rifle sat piled on top of each other. In one corner, a first aid kit hung by a nail. He went inside, grabbed the first aid kit, and glanced across the landscape.

In the distance, he could see the white forms of the double-wides.

Jim grinned, relief washing over him. "I can see the camp!" he called down to the others.

From the way they had come, a sea of dead grass and mesquite trees stretched for as far as the eye could see. Through the main window, he spotted a deer feeder about fifty yards away.

Corn kernels painted the ground yellow underneath. There was nothing around. No deer. No birds.

"Sí, señor," Ramón said. "Getting closer."

Light rain began to fall, fat droplets splattering the top of the tin roof of the blind. He heard a grunt then.

Then another.

And another, coming closer.

Jim's eyes grew wide.

It charged before he could scream a clear warning.

An enraged behemoth black mass of muscle and fur burst from the cover of a group of trees to the left of the blind. Hackles erect, it caused the beast to appear larger still. The hog squealed as it pounded its way toward Todd and Ramón.

"Up!" Ramón screamed at Todd, who immediately began to climb, cringing in pain as he planted the foot of his injured leg into the first rung.

Ramón leveled the shotgun.

Droplets turned to heavy rain as the storm hit. Lightning flashed and Ramón fired his weapon. There was a loud grunt, then a *thud* as the boar hit the ground.

"Ah-hah!" Ramón yelled in triumph.

But the boar was back up on its feet a second later, resuming its charge as it bled from the top of its shoulder—a graze, Jim realized. It gained terrible speed, tusks jutting from either side of its snout, aimed at Ramón.

The shotgun clicked empty.

Jim watched in horror as Ramón attempted to use the gun like a club, but it was far too late. The hog barreled into him, using its tusks, hooves, and teeth to tear Ramón apart.

Ramón cried out to God, cried out for names Jim could only assume were family or friends as he tried beating his fists against the giant boar.

The boar snorted, grunted, and squealed as most of Ramón's clothes were ripped away in the chaos, showcasing the awesome power of the animal as it continued its attack. Ramón ceased to move as the giant hooves came down, digging into his skull, smushing his face into a bloody pulp.

Jim screamed at the thing as he helped Todd inside the blind, almost falling as he lost his footing on the top rung. But for all the mindless noise, Jim still attempted to scare it off, doing little good. If anything, it riled the beast into a blind rage.

It shredded Ramón's body to pieces, flinging bits of him around in a violent frenzy. When it had finished, a group of smaller pigs appeared, *normal* sized by the looks of them, followed closely behind by a few litters of piglets. Running up to the area surrounding the tower blind, they commenced to devour what remained of Ramón.

Still . . . the giant boar did not leave.

It glanced up at the blind and grunted, pawing lightly at the muddy, gore splattered ground. Baring its teeth, it flattened its ears and charged.

The boar rammed into the legs of the blind, time and time again.

The smaller hogs had scattered as the storm grew in strength. Flood waters raged on ahead. Jim could see the deer feeder topple over as the current carried it away.

Already, the tower blind was beginning to tilt a bit sideways as the boar rammed into the structure. The thing huffed in exhaustion, yet kept charging.

Relentless.

Unforgiving.

What had driven this beast to madness?

Territorial, perhaps? Or maybe we wandered too close to the young?

Jim hadn't a clue. He wasn't going to pretend he had the answers. Hell, he was just as scared as Todd. Unharmed, but still, he was scared beyond his wits. He had witnessed the horrible things it had done to Ramón in only a few agonizing minutes. Jim was not keen on sharing the same end.

"I threw a stone at it as it passed by," admitted Todd, his voice exceptionally calm for their predicament, not to mention the amount of pain he must still be in.

"When?" asked Jim, taking him a moment to register what Todd had just confessed.

"When it crossed the trail, not long after you and Ramón went to check the trap. It just stood there, staring at me. So, I picked up a rock to . . . to do something! To try and drive it off! It happened so fast. I didn't know it was that big when I first saw it." He shook his head in shame. "I didn't know."

Hail began to fall then, small at first, the size of a quarter, then the size of a golf ball. The noise hitting the tin roof above all but deafened them both to the world around them.

Below, the boar rammed into the legs of the blind, shaking them. The blind tilted more, but the storm blowing in from the opposite direction kept them upright.

"It's alright," Jim said, and repeated, "It's alright," unsure of what else to say, or if Todd had even heard him over the barrage of hail. An accident. That's all it was. But an accident that may mean their lives.

The boar squealed in pain, no doubt the hail finally doing some damage to the creature.

Swinging the blind door open, Todd passed Jim the sacks of sand. Jim heaved the sacks down onto the boar's spine, one at a time. The boar shook its body, as if to do away with a pestering insect.

They would need a weapon. Something. *Anything.*

Jim dug into the first aid kit, retrieving a pair of scissors.

Shit.

There was nothing. Nothing to defend themselves with. Nothing to do except wait for the inevitable.

He reflected on Erica then. Her hair, waving in a breeze, soft, delicate. The smell of the same perfume she sprayed on each morning. Her lips upon his. Her face. Her face. Her face . . .

No.

Thoughts turned to anger as he cursed himself for a weakling.

She had wronged *him*. Always the victim, it was never her fault. Not when she had thrown the roasted duck he had prepared one evening out into the yard, after he had failed to remember she was on one of her sporadic vegan diets. Not when she had trashed his study after he accidentally let the dog leave dirty pawprints on their carpet. Not when she'd grown tired of him, finding another, bringing him into their home . . . into their bed. His fault. Never complimenting her enough. Never holding her enough. Never telling her how much he couldn't live without her.

Never again.

He would never waste another thought on her. As the blind fell sideways, Jim figured that he wouldn't have to wait long.

Jim opened his eyes.

Todd was alive, heaving in deep breaths as he clutched his wounded leg in agony.

Blood trickled down Jim's face from a small cut above his brow. Other than that, he found his limbs still worked. Then, to his horror, he found the snout of the boar a mere two feet away from his face.

The blind must have crashed down on top of it.

It blinked slowly as it came to its senses. Staring back into Jim's terrified gaze, it screeched, long and angry.

The blind moved as the boar began to literally drag it away.

Todd screamed, one hand clinging to a part of the blind, the other holding his leg.

Noticing the scissors still held tight in his hand, Jim thrust the point into the boar's right eye. It twisted its head, tearing more of the blind apart in its fury, removing the door from its hinges in the process.

It tried to leap forward, to bury its tusks into Jim's abdomen, but Jim brought one of the folding chairs up in time to keep the tusks from entering flesh, shielding them for the moment.

The boar used its strength to push Jim back, driving him against Todd. Any longer and the hog would break their frail bodies with brute force as it pushed, pushed, squealing and snapping its jaws at the chair Jim held onto for dear life.

Feeling his energy waning, Jim fought to breathe, to stay alive a second longer. But time was against them. It would not quit. Would not stop until they were like Ramón.

"No . . ." Jim growled.

Jim brought the bloody point of the scissors forward again, stabbing wildly, doing little more than making superficial wounds. So he drove the scissors into the boar's remaining eye, lodging them as deep as they would go.

The boar grunted, blood pouring from both of its eyes. It backed out of the blind, squealing, running blind into the storm.

Jim watched as the flood waters took the injured creature. Its head bobbed up to the surface a final time before sinking beneath the current. Then it was gone.

Hunkered down in what remained of the fallen tower blind, Jim and Todd waited out the duration of the storm in relative silence. Busy using the first aid kit to patch up each other's wounds, Jim only noticed the storm had stopped when bright rays of light reflected off some torn metal and into his eyes.

"Come on," Jim said.

Hobbling out of the blind, Jim regained his balance. He then helped Todd to his feet. They searched the vicinity for *something* to take back of Ramón's—a piece of clothing, a limb, the shotgun even. But there was nothing. All of him . . . washed away with the storm, buried in the mud someplace, and devoured.

"What about the rest of them? The smaller ones?" Todd asked, reluctant to start hiking through the brush once more.

Jim couldn't blame him.

For a while they stood and listened.

No grunts in the brush, no squealing mob of hogs, no hooves thundering toward them. They were safe.

No.

Alive.

"I think we're alright," Jim told him.

Heading in the direction of camp, Jim led them back onto the trail from before. They hadn't walked ten paces before they saw it:

A mountain lion stared at them from the edge of the trail, its body half-hidden in the undergrowth, its tawny coat the perfect camouflage.

Jim stared back. Like his first encounter with the hog, he didn't dare move a muscle. Fortunately, this time, Todd did the same.

The mountain lion turned its head as a dove flew overhead, eventually landing on top of a tree stump farther down the trail. Unconcerned with the dove, Jim, or Todd, it leisurely walked across the trail then, disappearing into the brush.

In the distance, the excited squealing of hogs intensified into a mad crescendo.

Garden Dirt and Hill Country Wine

Jae Mazer

My mom has a difficult time cooking a meal. Maybe she's distracted, absentminded, or sometimes outright disgusted with the food, or the process, or god knows what. But for whatever reason—as she chops, measures, stirs, plates—there's always a pause. And sometimes that pause lingers into an all-out stall that swells into full abandonment.

"Mom?"

Mom stops what she's doing, which isn't chopping the carrots on the cutting board but rather staring at them with her brow scrunched, eyes slits. The sound of my voice does not reignite the chopping, but her gaze moves from the carrots on the cutting board to the window above.

The chicken in the oven is well on its way to being cooked, and the potato water belching steam threatens to soften the root-veg within to absolute mush. Those carrots need to be cut and cooked soon if we want to serve them with dinner.

Mom's dinners were always legendary—good ol' fashioned cook-up with chicken-fried steak, fresh veggies from the garden, topped off with a decadent pecan pie made with the pecans from our very own hickory tree growing at the back of our land. I miss those meals. I miss Mom.

"Earth to Mom," I say, and I set my wine glass down on the island a little too hard.

Outside, a dog barks. Then howls. It matches the bray from the nursery upstairs. My son didn't sleep for long this time. Seems he sleeps less and less these days.

"Remi needs in," Mom says, but she is no longer looking out the window. And she's not looking at the carrots. She is staring at her hands, at the striations there, road maps of her age and experiences.

"Okay," I say. Frustrated. "Do you want me to let him in?"

"Yes."

Her hands are still. The carrots remain half cut.

"Are you busy?" I ask, hoping to spur her into action.

She doesn't answer. Or move.

I get up and go to the back door. Remi, Mom's 12-year-old German Shepherd, is standing in the middle of the yard, hackles raised, staring. Just like Mom is staring at her hands.

"Remi, come!" I call.

Remi hesitates. His back end quavers as bad as his voice. Remi is an old boy, and his hips aren't so good anymore. I think he's holding on because he knows Mom needs him, especially since Dad passed two summers ago. Eventually, Remi trots over and comes inside, then disappears somewhere deeper in the house. Next to Granny Bea in the parlour, I figure. The sound of his nails ticking across the hardwood and Gran's knitting needles colliding are a complementary percussion in the near distance.

I go to Mom and the carrots. Place my hand on hers.

"Mom."

She pulls her hand away.

"I'm okay," she says. "Just tired."

It's not just tired. I worry about dementia, about misfiring synapses, even psychosis. There is fear on her face that I can't explain and that she won't.

"How can I help you if you won't talk to me?" I say.

Mom snaps at me, as she does. "There is nothing wrong with me!"

"I didn't say there was." Even though there is.

"I'm tired," she repeats.

Me, too. That's motherhood, though, right? Permanent exhaustion, compassion fatigue, a dwindling well of saintly patience. But I'm grown and an only child, and Mom has no one left to care for, save the infant grandchild who is still too little to be away from my breast for long. Texas families are big, but ours is so very small. I wonder if Mom longs for more. Like I do.

The click-clack-clicking of Granny Bea's knitting needles in the other room provides a tempo for the crescendoing wail upstairs. My son's cry rings in my ears, a wordless screech that somehow shrieks the word Mom in its own language. Repeating it, over and over again, demanding a response. The front of my shirt soaks as my nipples respond to the sound before I do.

"Fuck." The word sticks in my throat like a lump of cornbread.

I cannot cry anymore. I refuse. My little boy upstairs does enough crying for all of us.

"Cut the carrots."

Mom's voice, so direct and so clear, startles me. She doesn't often make eye contact, but she is now, and the thick grey of her irises transfixes me.

"What?" I say. "I have to . . . He's hungry."

"He won't die," Mom says. "It'll do him good to learn to wait. I will go and read him a story."

Mom doesn't wait for me to agree to this plan. She turns on her blocky heels and clops out of the kitchen, down the hall, and up the stairs—clip, clop, clip—as she moves to the nursery above me. The wailing bounces, jiggles, and softens.

She's holding him. He is safe. He won't die if I take just a moment.

I pick up the knife and start chopping. The sound is so loud, and every time the blade slices through a carrot and makes contact with the heavy wood below, it's like an axe to my brain. I move faster, desperate to arrive at quiet—no more chopping, no more wailing, no more hearing crying in droplets of water or the swish of curtains.

The carrots are done. I plop them in the water, turn the dial, and the burner bursts to life with a whoosh of blue flame.

Do I have a few more minutes?

There is no wailing from upstairs.

I sit at the island, gulp my wine, then put my face in my hands. Granny Bea's needles click, *clack, click, clack*. Her chair rocks, banging on the hardwood floor of the parlour. But no, it's too loud. It doesn't sound like wood on wood. It's tile . . .

A small child giggles like chimes in the wind. Close, right in my ear.

I gasp and fly up from the island, sending my stool crashing to the floor. There is a flicker of movement in the corner of my eye, and a small patter of feet in the other direction.

I try to ignore the children. I always try.

The pipes in the bathroom upstairs groan. The sound rushes over me like water, like the tub filling upstairs.

Mom is bathing him. That's good. Gives me more time.

I pour myself another glass of wine. We love this wine, Mom and I. The wine is there in empty spaces that need filled. We pick up cases every time we visit Fredericksburg. The families there are so large, their vineyards so lush, the wines so bold. Every sip of wine reminds me of road trips through the Hill Country, bluebonnets whispering in the breeze, laughter and cigarette smoke filling the empty expanse of our Oldsmobile Firenza.

Mom and I have already emptied a bottle, and it's only 7 p.m. I should slow down, but the alcohol muffles my endless, nagging responsibilities. The alcohol also heightens the small pleasures still available to me. The aroma of rosemary and sage steaming in the cavity of the fowl in the oven, the solid feel of the stamped concrete tile beneath my feet, the brilliance of the vast and lavish kitchen that spans around me like a cathedral.

I should consider myself lucky to be living in this house, handed down generation after generation. Hard to find old ranch land in the Hill Country now that won't cost you your first-born child. I should consider myself lucky that my husband decided to lube his cock with another woman's mouth so I could move home to my daddy's homestead with its sprawling land, many rooms, and a pool in which my child can swim when he gets older. I try to forget the trauma that lives here, as familiar to me as my own skin. The myriad skeletons in its many closets gave it a price tag befitting a single mother's budget.

My husband's philandering also left me with my pudge, extra wrinkles, and endless parenting responsibilities. He gets to screw, to party, to be a bachelor again, all while my vagina is still healing from the trauma of his spawn. But I guess I have this house, skeletons and all, which I both love and hate.

Steam billows from the pots on the stove. When I stir them, the damp air moistens my face, and I can taste the sweetness of the carrots and the earthy bite of the potatoes. Saliva pools beneath my tongue as I imagine mashing and mixing the veg with gravy. That had always been my favorite food—anything drowning in the gravy made with the secret family recipe. Among other things, that gravy recipe has been passed down for generations. I'll start the gravy while Mom is taking care of the bath, but she'll have to season it and thicken it just right. That art has not been passed down to me yet.

Remi's nails *tick tick tick* on the floor behind me. He's always under my feet when I'm cooking. Always barking when the baby needs to sleep. I love Remi, but sometimes he irritates the shit out of me. I want to not hear or feel anyone or anything, just for a solid half hour. I wait to feel his fur against my leg so I can scream at him to get out, but he must feel my mood. The ticking of his nails stops before he reaches me.

When I open the oven door, a blast of hot air blows my fine hair back from my face—the hair that isn't stuck to my cheeks by wine-induced sweat and vegetable steam, anyway. The scent of the poultry cooking in its juices is more intoxicating than the Cabernet. Donning an oven mitt, I tip the roaster just enough to get a ladle full of bird grease to mix with some flour, but when I bring it into the light, I notice something is wrong.

I pour the liquid into a saucepan. It is too thick. Too red. I tilt the pan back and forth, watching fingers of viscous fluid coat the pan, and I wonder how the chicken is still bleeding.

The pipes overhead groan, and something bangs and crashes. The baby is screeching and thrashing about in the tub like a feral beast. I marvel at how something so small can make such a damn ruckus. And such a mess. Grotesque diapers all day, that curdled yellow vomit after every feeding. And something so small, so soft, so pink, keeping me up night after night. Every minute, every second, wanting, needing, demanding . . .

Knock. Clack-click-clack. Knock. Clack-click-clack.

Granny Bea's incessant rocking and knitting, knitting and rocking is as bad as my boy's crying and shitting, puking, crying, shitting, sleepless hours upon hours.

But the sound is too close. Granny Bea is in the parlor, knitting a jumper for her great-grandson, but the noise is here with me in the kitchen.

Knock. Click-clack-click.

I don't know what I'm expecting when I turn from the chicken-blood gravy on the stove, but it isn't to see Granny Bea sitting in her chair in the corner of the kitchen, rocking and knitting, knitting and rocking. Still, there she is.

"Gran?" Fear squeaks my voice out of my throat—a pinhole in a balloon.

Granny Bea's knitting needles tick together, gleaming like blades in the glare from the naked bulbs in the fixtures above. She is watching me, studying me, her eyes wide and dark. With every rock, she licks her thick, dry tongue over her toothless gums, stretches her thin lips into a grin.

"Gran, how did you . . ."

The entrance, the hall, the parlor . . . it's quite a journey for someone who uses a cane. For a woman who shuffles, not walks. A person with gout, and arthritis, and profound dementia. Someone who can't move a can of soup, let alone an entire rocking chair. But here she is, knitting and rocking, staring and licking.

"Granny Bea, how on Earth did you get in here? You need to be careful!"

I go to her and check her over. I don't know if I expect to find a broken ankle, a laceration, a bruise. But Granny Bea seems perfectly intact and content. She is making exceptional progress on my son's jumper, except it's an absolute mess. She chose white yarn—worst color for anyone, let alone a baby—and it's covered in stains.

"Oh, Granny Bea," I say, as I wipe at the half-constructed jumper with the sleeve of my hoodie.

But it isn't food. It's dark, and crumbly, and smears across the delicate ivory cotton when I rub it, staining it further.

Despite me tugging at the garment, Granny Bea's hands do not slow. She continues working away, pulling through stitch after stitch, her hands moving in robotic rhythm at a steady tempo. They are filthy. Black and mucky, with dirt packed in each wrinkle and fold.

"Gran, what have you been doing?"

I pull her hand to my face and sniff it. I don't know why I do that. Mothers do that, I guess, with unidentified stains and messes. I immediately regret my decision. The Cabernet burns my sinuses as it rushes back up my gorge, coerced out of digestion by the rancid stench of sick and rot.

"Granny Bea!" I shout as I recoil back against the island. "What have you gotten into?"

Granny Bea doesn't answer. She hasn't talked in years, not since she lost my grandfather in the accident. But she does make noise—grunts, giggles, mewls. And now she makes the most raucous, blood-curdling noise I've ever heard. She brays out laughter, thick with mucus, and her folds and lumps jiggle in the chair as her whole body heaves. Remi howls behind me, just out of tune with Granny Bea's voice. He's right behind me, and so loud, and Granny Bea's so gross, and the thrashing in the tub upstairs is getting louder, so loud that I drop to the floor and cover my ears, close my eyes.

The unpleasant noise stops. All of it. No more howling, rocking, no click-clacking of knitting needles, no more laughter thick with the fluids of death. I allow my hands to drop from my ears. The kitchen is filled with the gentle gurgling of boiling water and the soft whir of the oven.

I open my eyes and see shoes. Two pairs of shoes, shiny black. Freshly polished.

I sit up, let my eyes rise to see two pairs of pants, side-by-side, two white button-down shirts with ducks embroidered on the collars. And two sets of milky white eyes buried in pallid, translucent skin.

I've seen these boys before. Always running around my goddamn kitchen. They can't be more than five or six. Twins, towheaded, with black lips and necrotic fingertips. I reach out to them like they are my own sons, and they reach back, their faces contorted in fear, in horror, in pain. When they open their mouths to scream, I hear it, and it is my son's wails. That sound is impossible, though, because no air can pass out of these boys. Wet dirt erupts from their mouths, vomiting down their tidy, pressed clothes. Dirt is coming from everywhere—their ears, their eyes, soiling both the fronts and backs of their trousers. I scream, they scream, and dirt shoots so forcefully from their faces that it splits their heads in two. The four skull halves fall to the floor and masses of worms slither out, chasing me, crawling up my legs, into every orifice, and still, still my son screams in pain from the mouths of these boys.

"Darling?"

The boys are gone.

There were never any boys. Not here, not in this house.

I hate this house.

"What?" I snap at my mom, who is standing in the entrance to the kitchen.

I shoot a glance at the corner where Granny Bea had been rocking. She is still rocking, but not there. I hear her down the hall, the wood of her chair knocking the wood of the parlour floor. I look where the twins had been standing. I wildly scour the kitchen but find only boiling pots on the stove and an empty wine bottle on the island.

"You drink too much," my mom dares to say.

I know this.

"There is nothing wrong with me," I snark, mimicking her.

Mom nods and looks down her nose.

There is so much wrong with both of us.

"I'm sorry about dinner," Mom says, her trembling hand motioning to the pots on the stove. "Again."

"Shit." I forgot the food.

The potatoes and carrots are fine, but the bloody grease is smoldering. I look inside. The liquid, now black and smoking, is full of hair. But not my hair, pale and long. Short, coarse hair. Dog hair.

I pull the saucepan off and toss it in the sink. It clatters, but not like metal on metal. It sounds like someone emptied a sack of bones into the sink. I don't dare look to see if that's true.

"Another wine?" Mom asks.

She's already stabbed the corkscrew into a vintage bottle.

"I thought you said I drink too much."

She nods. "We do what we have to."

Mom is a blank woman. Her face is empty, her mouth a tight, thin line. As her hands turn, pulling out the cork, I try to remember those hands on my body. She was never much of a hugger. She didn't braid my hair or hold my hand. I wonder, as I have many times, if Granny Bea ever brushed Mom's hair, or rubbed her back when she was sick, or kissed her on the forehead. I have never seen affection between the two. But Granny Bea had been sick for quite some time. I only remember cold, silence, rigid indifference. From both of them. From all of us.

Am I cold to my son, too?

I should check the chicken, but I don't want to. I bend, look through the stained, yellowed window of the oven at the meat. It's steaming, the meat bursting and sizzling, Remi's tongue lolling over the side of the roaster.

I gasp. Stumble back and look to my mom as if she's going to help me. She is drinking wine from her perch at the island, with Remi by her side. His head is on her lap, but she is not petting him like she always does. He nudges her with his snout, but she doesn't react. Instead, she reacts to me, her gaze settling on my face.

I turn back around and stand over the top of the stove, steam billowing in my face, my mom's cold stare piercing my back.

"You are tired," she says.

It's more than tired.

"It's hard," I say.

"What's hard?"

Everything.

"I'm tired," I echo.

Something beside the island moves. I steal a peek. It is a little boy, chocolate eyes and hair the color of the peaches in the fruit basket on the counter. Hair not unlike my own, but his isn't thin and scraggly from the hormones of childbirth and breastfeeding. He has time to wash and brush his hair, a luxury I don't have with a babe always pawing at me, screaming, suckling at my teat.

"A mother's work is never done," Mom says behind me, punctuating her wisdom with a sip of her wine.

I cannot take my eyes off the boy child. He is singing a familiar melody, something trapped in the shadows of my brain, words I can't quite understand or remember. He smiles, and I gasp. His teeth are rotted and sharp, and his tongue is a worm, writhing as it's pierced over and over again by the child's sharp incisors as his jaw moves with song.

"Mom?" I ask, without forming an actual question.

Mom peers over the island. Her eyes linger a moment on the boy, then she directs her attention back to the wine, filling the two glasses fuller than a proper wine should be poured. More than we should be having before the dinner is even served. From the other room, I hear Granny Bea's rocking, hear the *click-clack-click* of those knitting needles. I refuse to look at the little ginger boy any longer, and I need a distraction from the noise of Granny Bea, so I direct my attention back to the pots on the stove. The ones that don't need me.

"Sit," Mom says. She is not asking.

And though I do like a good argument with my mother, I choose to be agreeable. Not to appease her but because I am weary. It feels like my legs might give out at any moment.

"Being a mom is hard," she says.

I take one, two, three gulps of my wine. I cannot help but take offense to her burnout. It's the labour of me she's referring to. The young me, who needed to be fed, who refused to go to bed on time. Who bit a girl on a playdate so was uninvited to the rest, leaving her mother isolated and bored. Who pitched fits in stores and slammed doors when she was upset about boundaries and rules.

I wonder if I'll resent my son the way my mom resents me.

"Do you hate it?" I ask.

"Hate what?"

"Being a mom."

Her eyes widen as if she's just received a dagger between the ribs.

"I love you," she says.

I know that. Love was never the question.

"Yes, but, besides me . . . do you love being a mom?"

Mom's mouth moves as if she's chewing on the answer, rolling it around her tongue to find something palatable to swallow.

"No," she says.

The word strikes me like a slap.

"Do you wish you'd never had me?" I ask.

"I wish I'd never lost myself."

Neither of us acknowledge the tears glistening on each other's cheeks. I don't bother to wipe mine away. I let them drip into my wine glass.

Everything is loud again. The gurgling of the boiling on the stove, the knock of Granny Bea's chair. There is movement in the corner, and I try not to look, I try so hard, but I know she's back. Somehow, Granny Bea is back, sitting in that corner, hands covered in rot, knitting and rocking, rotting and knitting.

Something brushes my pant leg. I look down at my feet and find the little ginger boy skittering past, moving like an animal on his hands and feet toward the corner, forcing me to look. Granny Bea is there, in her rocker, in worse shape than she was before. Her hands are black with dirt, and her eye sockets are full of worms. She is naked and splayed out, the sheen of fresh childbirth glistening between her legs. The twin boys are there, too, one attached to each of her breasts, suckling, slurping.

Mom sees, too, but her mouth is not agape in horror. She can breathe, can lift her wineglass without trembling.

"Why are they here?" I ask. "Granny Bea and the twins. This is *my* house."

"Our house," Mom reminds me.

Granny Bea had been haunted. I could tell by the way she used to watch the corners, smile at silent jokes, shield her eyes from unknown terrors.

I never knew the twins. Mom's brothers. They were gone so very young.

"You know, having kids took so much from me," Mom says. "It wasn't your fault, of course. I gave myself willingly. But we only have so much to give, us mothers. Only so much."

Her words sting.

"Was it ever good?"

"Oh yes. Many good moments. But the bad moments encase you in a caul, preventing you from seeing anything but the repetition, the struggle, the isolation. Eventually, all the good moments turn sour because they, too, are encased, all part of the same stew that roils you over and over again, day after day."

Panic starts to take hold. That happens more and more lately. The racing heart, the need to run, to get away, like my organs are splintering, my mind is fracturing, and the sky might compress me into the dirt.

"Please tell me it gets better," I plead.

I am sobbing. She is not. Her head tilts, and I think she's judging me.

"What do I do?" I cry. "I need help. I need . . ."

I don't know what I need. I don't even know what I want. Do I want to be free again? Do I want my husband back, someone to help share the workload? Or do I want to be less broken? The perfect mother who glows, and who enriches their child at every moment and cherishes each and every milestone, hiccup, breath.

The ginger boy crab crawls up onto the island. His legs and arms are bent at odd angles, and his head is propped sideways on his shoulders, not quite squared with the rest of his body. He is broken but smiling a jagged, sharp smile, blissfully unaware of his condition. He plays with the fruit bowl, humming his lullaby, rolling an orange back and forth until Mom picks it up in her hand. He stops, his eyes narrow to slits, and his song ceases, replaced by a feral growl from deep in his belly. He launches at Mom, his sharp teeth bared, but Gran heaves to her feet. She scoops the ginger boy up under her arm and hauls him off into the house as he thrashes and howls. Mom pierces the orange with her nails and juice dribbles onto the counter.

"We mothers have to stick together," she says, looking down the hall that swallowed Granny. "Your grandmother helped me."

Wait …

"What did you say?" I ask.

"Hmmm?"

"Before. You said having kids took so much from you."

"Indeed," Mom says. "As it does all mothers."

I lean forward, forcing her to look in my eyes.

"Kids," I say.

"Kids?"

"You said kids. Not *kid*. Kids."

I stare into her eyes, and she stares into mine. She is trying to see my thoughts. I'm trying to figure out what it is I think I've realized.

Mom stands and goes to the stove. She picks up a spoon and stirs the water. She is disgusted, afraid, something.

"I can help you," Mom says. "Just like Granny Bea helped me."

"Who is the boy?" I ask.

Mom stops stirring. Her eyes are transfixed on the pot and the contents within.

Her voice is a bullet. "Your brother."

My heart clenches. "I don't have a brother."

Mom keeps looking at the pot. Stirring.

"You don't," she agrees. "Anymore."

In the other room, the rocking ignites, and the giggle of children fills the halls.

"You know," Mom says, and the corner of her mouth twitches into a smile. "Your grandmother and I loved gardening. We used to garden so, so much. The fresh vegetables for us to cook every night were glorious. You could just taste the soil churned by our hands. The life we planted there."

The rocking is oh so loud again, and Mom's voice is growing softer. I stand from the island, wobble, my legs weak from wine and fear and exhaustion. I go to Mom, to the stove, because I can't hear her over Granny Bea and the children.

"This house," Mom says. "Such a lavish, grand monster of a thing. Just look at this kitchen! The kitchen was always my favorite. Gran's, too. All the dishes we'd make. When you're cooking, creating, there's no room in the mind for anything else."

The children bound through the kitchen naked, smeared with dirt—the two blond boys with leafy greens staining their hair and the ginger boy with aphids for freckles.

"I had a brother?" I am sobbing, shaking.

Mom nods.

Granny Bea is back, rocking in the corner of the kitchen, the twins latched back onto her pie plate nipples.

"My brothers were needy, squalling things, just like yours was," Mom says.

I don't want to look. But I have to, even though I already know. I go to Mom. Look in the pot. It isn't carrots. It's fingers, an entire pot full, decayed and bloated, maggots writhing under tiny yellowed nails. And in the potato pot, tiny stomachs, heads, hearts.

"I didn't hate your brother, like your grandmother didn't hate mine. We just …"

Granny Bea's jaw drops open, and an awful keen explodes out of her mouth. And the three boys scream, too. It is the sound of lambs at slaughter—pain, desperation, panic.

"Here," Mom says as she hands me a spoon. "Stir. It's soothing."

I stir.

All the crying from all the mouths withers until it is nothing more than the soft sound of boiling water.

I am startled as something falls down the stairs in a dozen heavy thuds. Then movement echoes through the hall—a sliding, dragging sound. Slow, clumsy.

I look away from the fingers in the pot, over the island, to the hall beyond. There is a shape there, a blob, pale and blue and bloated, struggling toward the kitchen.

"Where?" I mumble.

"You are tired," Mom says. "But you don't have to be."

"Where is he?"

"Being a mom doesn't have to be a life sentence, you know."

Mom sits at the island and pours another glass of wine.

"They're never really gone," Mom says. "Every time I peel a potato, cut a stalk of celery, dice an onion … Our babies are dirt beneath our nails that we'll never be rid of. Reminders of what we planted, what we grew."

"Did you leave him in the bath?"

Mom pours wine in my glass.

"You know . . . you have a beautiful garden outside."

Upstairs, my son screams. Gurgles. His voice is becoming slower, weaker . . .

In the kitchen, the twins suckle at Granny Bea's eternally full breasts as my brother steers hot wheels around the grout roads on the tile floor.

Granny Bea rocks and knits. Mom hums the lullaby with my brother, a dissonant duet. I take a long draw of my wine, savoring the taste of road trips and laughter and happiness long passed, as the music of the bathwater upstairs decrescendos to silence.

The Thing on Falling Star Hill

M. E. Splawn

The town they used to call Cottonwood, Texas, in Lampasas County on the Colorado River, is where I met Eugene MacGregor. It was a shithole town, but they had a cantina. I was hungry and thirsty. Riding in on the town's only street, I saw mostly Mexicans. Little brown people. As tired and hungry as I was, I still figured I could whup any number of them if I had to. So, I planned to eat and drink my fill then get back on my horse and ride away without paying. I had nothing to pay. I'd spent my last dollar on a whore in Temple, Texas a few days before.

Soon as I got off my horse, I heard a loud squabble going on and I saw two mestizos with their guns drawn and pointed at a white man with fiery red hair. I'm a quick study most of the time and I'm not one to pass up an opportunity. Took me just a heartbeat to see the red-headed fellow was dressed in the kind of clothes you might see on a man in Kansas City but not out here on the hard-scrabble edge of Texas. The mestizos were filthy, and I didn't doubt one bit they'd lay that overfed dandy in his grave in about two seconds.

I stepped out to the center of the street and by the time the Mestizos realized my intentions, I'd shot one of them. The other mestizo and the redhead were both surprised as hell at what I'd done. I took aim as the second mestizo was swinging his gun toward me and the dandy slapped his arm just as I fired. Long and short of it was, there was two brown-skinned dead men on the main street of Cottonwood, Texas and two white men making their first acquaintance. A few citizens came running out to the street to see what had happened. The women all crossed themselves.

"You look like you could use a good meal," the redhead said, thrusting his hand toward me. "I'm Eugene MacGregor. Let me buy you some dinner."

I took his hand in mine, noticing it was strong, muscled, and rough from work. MacGregor may have worn fancy clothes, but he wasn't a sissy. I was thinking I'd backed the right side of that altercation. "What about them?" I asked, pointing at the two dead men.

"Don't worry about that." MacGregor shouted something in Spanish at one of the old men in the crowd. The old man shouted at two young boys, and they ran off to the church to fetch the Padre. MacGregor patted me on the shoulder and pushed me toward the door of the cantina.

A short while later, my belly was full of beans and corn tortillas, and I had two shots of mescal in me.

"I could use a man like you," MacGregor said. "Don't drink too much of that Mexican rotgut. I've got some fine Kentucky sipping whiskey back at the ranch. Why don't you come out, spend the night and see if it's to your liking. If you've a mind to settle, I'll pay you well. Men who think quick, men with guts, are hard to find out here."

I thanked him and agreed to tag along. At least for a while. That's how I became the foreman for Eugene MacGregor's Falling Star Ranch. The food was good, I had a roof over my head, and I could take a bath once a week if I wanted to. The rest of his hands were a timid lot, mostly little Mexicans, good with horses and cattle but not likely to butt heads with anyone. They did what I told them right from the start, just like I was the boss man himself.

The third night I was there, Mac and I were sitting on the porch, cooling off after a hard day's work. He'd given me a cigar and a small glass of his Kentucky whiskey. The cigar wasn't to my liking, but I puffed at it anyhow just to please the boss man. The whiskey was damn good, and I would've drunk a whole bottle of it if he'd offered. I didn't ask for more because I knew it was in short supply. Besides, Mac was paying me in silver coins. I could buy mescal any time I wanted. The Irishman thought highly of me and I didn't want to make him change his mind by getting stone drunk.

"See that light up there?" Mac asked. He pointed with his chin to a rise, the highest point on his property. A campfire flickered on the hilltop.

"Yeah, what's that?" I figured it was one of his Mexicans keeping watch.

"Squatter. An old woman. People say she's been there for as long as anyone can remember. I've sent my men over there to get rid of her time and again. They say they've run her off but always at night I see her campfire. These damn Mexicans are afraid of their own shadows and that Spanish priest encourages that kind of spineless falderal."

I stood up. "Want me to go take care of her?" I wasn't planning on killing the woman, if it was a woman. I just wanted to scare her off, so she'd stay away permanent.

"No." Mac made a calming gesture with his hand. "She'll see us coming and hide. Let's sleep on it for now. I'll fetch you before dawn and we'll catch her sleeping up there."

His plan sounded reasonable, so I nodded, said good night, and went to the bunkhouse.

There was me and eight Mexicans bunking in that shotgun shack. Most of them bathed more regular than I did, so I couldn't complain of the smell, but such a racket of snoring you never heard under one roof. A young man named Jose bunked next to me and he spoke real good English. "Good night, Jefe," he said as I dropped on my bed.

"Jose, what's the story with this old woman who lives on the hill?"

Jose crossed himself and averted his eyes. "It's no woman."

I waited but Jose said nothing more, so I prodded him. "Well, if it ain't a woman, who's up on that hill lighting a campfire? Mr. MacGregor don't like a squatter on his land. Least of all flaunting it from a hilltop."

"It may look like a woman. Sometimes," Jose said. "But it is not even human. The Comanches tell of a star that fell from the sky. Long, long ago. Hundreds of years before the white man came. They say it happened at the beginning of time. That thing fell from the sky."

"Jose, you surprise me," I said. "Big fellow like you believing those stories."

"Señor, they say the great Geronimo got his power on that hill. A very bad kind of power to have. The less said of the hill the better. Let us speak no more of the *enemiga*. Señor MacGregor was wrong to name this ranch the Falling Star. It can bring only trouble."

Jose turned his back to me and said no more. I didn't press him. If he had nothing to say but a bunch of boogey man hogwash, I didn't want to hear it anyhow. Mac was right, I thought, these Mexicans are like scared kids. It was a good thing he'd found me. I wasn't no high-brained professor, but I damn sure knew how to deal with squatters.

It was dark when Jose shook me awake. "Señor MacGregor waits for you outside," he said quietly.

I would've welcomed another hour of sleep. Mac's whiskey could pack a wallop on the morning after. I knew this was my chance to show the boss what I was made of. I went to the well and splashed some water on my face and met Mac in the barn. He'd already saddled both our horses. That struck me as odd that a landowner like MacGregor would saddle my horse. I flattered myself that I thought he was beginning to think of me as a friend as well as a hired hand.

As I swung up on my mount, Mac said, "We'll take care of the bitch on the hill, then we'll come back and have a fine breakfast. How's that sound?"

"Suits me right down to the ground," I answered, touching the brim of my hat. That made him smile and we rode off.

That squatter must have gathered a bunch of wood and brung it up the hill because the campfire was still burning bright before sunrise. That was hard to figure because the hill was too steep for our horses. We tied them off and climbed on foot to the top. And it was no easy climb.

As we topped the rim of the hill, I saw a dark figure crouched near the fire. Looked like it was wearing a buffalo hide with the horns still attached, just like the getup I'd seen on an old Lakota Sioux Medicine Man once when I was way up north. I looked at Mac. In the flickering light of the fire I swore his face was filled with uncertainty. In the short time I'd known him, I'd never seen that expression on Mac's face. When I looked back toward the fire there was no buffalo hide. No horns. Just a frail little woman with long gray hair. I'd have swore she was expecting us from the peaceful way she looked up.

Mac didn't waste no time getting to the meat of the matter. "You're on my land!" he near shouted, taking a stance opposite the fire from the old woman.

She laughed. A big gaping toothless laugh. Her mouth looked to me like it could have swallowed the world. I'd be lying if I said a chill didn't overcome me. I'd be lying if I didn't admit that laugh nearly made me lose my piss. It wasn't human. It was like a sound I heard once when a locomotive derailed outside St. Louis and the metal twisted so it shrieked like a dying animal.

Mac cleared his throat. When he did that, I knew he was rattled just like me. And that gave me a bit more confidence. "Are you going to leave of your own accord, or do we have to force you away?" Mac shouted, trying to sound more certain than he was.

When the woman spoke, her voice didn't sound like a voice at all. At first I would have swore I was listening to a mountain lion fighting with a coyote. The sounds rising up from that shriveled old throat and gathering in the toothless hole in the woman's face made the hairs stand up on my neck. I heard Mac groan. Almost like a band launching into real music after tuning up, the sound shifted into words. But it still didn't sound like any woman. It sounded like an echo from hell.

"Your land?" the voice said. "I have lived here a hundred thousand winters."

"Who . . . who are you?" Mac asked.

It laughed. And that laugh is not a thing a man can forget even though right away he wishes he could.

"Now you ask. I am the falling star, Lucifer. I am the master of men. I am enemiga."

"Now, listen here . . ." Mac started.

I pulled my gun and drew a bead on the thing. At that moment, the thing resembled most a sun-dried mummy that maybe had been rotting on that hilltop longer than I'd been alive. I was ready to believe I'd only imagined everything that had just happened. I started to put my gun away, then it spoke.

"I see," it said to Mac, "that you are a hungry man."

"Hungry? To hell with you! I've never been hungry a day in my life!" Mac said.

"Not so," the thing replied. "You hunger for power, land, and gold. You hunger for the adulation of others. If such were possible, you would be king." It laughed.

I lowered my gun. Somehow, I knew it would do me no good, just as I knew everything it said about my boss man was true.

"Shall I satisfy your hunger?"

Mac looked like a man sweating in a fever dream. He wasn't himself. His eyes looked at the bag of bones, but I thought he was seeing something else. "You . . . you can do that?" he asked, licking his lips.

"Yes. More than you imagine. First you must do something for me."

"What? Anything!" Mac was like a drunk or an opium eater. His eyes darted all around him like he was watching a parade or one of those dancing girl shows they have in Kansas City. Whatever he was seeing, he wanted it.

"Of your own free will, step off that cliff." The thing raised a boney finger and pointed at the other side of the hill. It was a sheer drop down about a hundred feet or more. The thing reached into the blanket it was wrapped in and took out a small wooden flute. It played and, so help me God, Mac danced right off into the air.

It laughed and this time I couldn't hold my water.

I looked down over the edge and saw Mac all twisted up like a dishrag. I ran down the hill the way we'd come up and made my way around to the other side. As I rounded a boulder, I saw

Mac walking toward me as clean and happy as you please. Not a scratch on him. And I knew, just a short while before, a lot of his bones were broke and his neck had been turned the wrong way.

"Mac . . ." I said. God as my witness I couldn't say another word.

"Yes?" He acted like he had no idea why I might be all worried. He patted me on the shoulder. "Let's go back up there and talk some more with the little lady." He grinned.

His grin and that word 'lady' just done something to my insides. I threw up whatever was in my stomach and did my best to spit out the bitter taste in my mouth.

"Easy, there, my friend," Mac said, as affable and gentle as if we were in a church meeting. "Come on."

I didn't want to, but I followed Eugene MacGregor back up that hill. He made that climb like a man half his age, skittered over those rocks with the ease of a mountain goat.

The thing was sitting there by the fire. When it spoke, it sounded like a woman, and I saw it was younger. The skin didn't have so many wrinkles. It wasn't like a mummy at all. It just looked like some Mexican grandmother. I think it may have had a few teeth in its mouth. "Welcome."

"I wish to include my friend in the bargain," Mac said. "He's not as outspoken as myself, but he's a loyal employee and a capable sort."

"Now, Mac . . ." I started.

"You are hungry to serve this powerful man," the woman said. "You want comfort, wealth. Is this not so?"

God help me, I could not say no. I wanted to say no. I wanted to run as fast as I could away from there, get on my horse and gallop as far from Lampasas County and the Colorado River as I could get. But I guess you'd say the woman's words were true. Deep down in my soul, I wanted what she said I wanted. In spite of all my fear, I nodded.

She grinned happily and began to play her flute.

Mac shouted, "Hoorah!" He took my hands in his and began dancing. Together we danced off the cliff. I hit a jutting rock and broke my shoulder. The impact spun me, and my skull shattered on a boulder a little farther down. The pain was unlike anything

I'd ever known. Through the agony, on the edge of my awareness, I could hear Mac screaming.

Next thing I knew we were climbing back up the hill.

This time the thing wasn't a thing at all. It was a woman. A fine-looking woman. She smiled and gestured for us to sit with her. None of us spoke. There was just a knowing that fell over us. Like my mind was no longer mine. Like something bigger and smarter and unbeatable had chosen to take the reins and all I could do was go along. The pain was part of it. The breaking I'd experienced on the fall off the cliff was just the beginning. There would be much more pain. That was understood. Just as the thing had been cast out of heaven, we were cast down and would never be permitted to enter heaven. But there would be pleasures I never knew existed, more money than I could ever hope to spend. Mac and me were going to be kings among men. Not really kings. That was an idea that had outlived its time. The world was too scientific, too industrial, too democratic now for kings and such. He would always be my boss, on account of his desire being so much grander than mine. I didn't mind that one bit. He wanted it the most and deserved to have it. And the pain, well, we both deserved that, too.

When the sun came up, we saw we were alone by the remains of the fire. Where she'd gone or how she went we couldn't recollect.

We went back to the ranch house. Just like he'd promised, we had a fine breakfast. As we were finishing up, Mac said, "Take the day off. You and the boys do some fishing or something. Let's consider this a holiday. April 21, 1876. A day to remember. I think I'll go upstairs and write an entry in my journal to commemorate this day!"

That thing—I don't want to call it a woman because I know damn well it was no woman – was true to its word. Right away, things fell into Mac's lap. He didn't even have to work at it. Before we knew it, he owned most of Lampasas County. We had everything we wanted, anything we could dream of, no matter how depraved our longings might be. A thought would flit through my mind and the next thing I knew I'd be acting it out. I couldn't even stop it if I wanted to. I killed more men than you could count. Always in self-defense, it turned out. I had every woman I fancied and did things with them I'd be ashamed to put into words.

Every year on April 21st, before dawn, we climb as high as we can and just jump. Sometimes off buildings, other times off cliffs, once right into the Grand Canyon. During the oil boom we crashed down off the tallest oil derrick in Beaumont, another time off that Empire State Building in New York City. It hurts. The pain gets worse every time and we know in our hearts we're headed for a time when eventually there will be nothing but pain. We make the best of it. Just a couple of high-living chums making the most of life. We've changed names more times than I can remember because most folks can't just get up and walk away after they've broken every bone in their body, you understand.

After midnight tonight it will be April 21, 2024. We're in Dubai.

Ever heard of the Burj Khalifa?

Tallest building in the world. 163 floors. Over 2700 feet high. Now that'll be a doozy. It's going to be hard to top that once we've done it. I suppose we'll think of something.

Last of the Kilgore Boohags

Kathleen Kent

"See, this here's what your problem is."

The plumber rocks back on his heels and points to the curved elbow of the pipe beneath the kitchen sink.

"There's something clogging up the P trap. Probably a big ol' grease ball. You been emptyin' your fat can down the drain again, Mrs. Conroe?"

Donny Conroe gives a bleat of laughter while eyeing his mother's ponderous weight, but does a quick sidestep before she can backhand him. Jerri Dean Conroe looks at the brackish, foul smelling water pooling in the stainless-steel sink and shakes her head doubtfully.

"Why does it smell so bad?" she asks.

To illustrate the point, Donny pinches his nostrils shut with a forefinger and thumb and pulls his mouth down into a grimace. "It stinks," he says. "Smells like a dead cat."

Ellis Hinton has done much of the plumbing fixes in Kilgore for the past fifteen years, and often the common denominator in many of the dwellings in the southerly part of town is a careless indifference to house cleaning. If cleanliness is next to Godliness, then most of the inhabitants of Live Oaks Trailer Park in south Kilgore are going straight to hell. Surprisingly, for all the jumble of broken toys and car parts in the front yard, the inside of Jerri Dean's trailer doesn't look too bad. Kitchen floor clean, dishes put away, not a lot of empty Frito bags lying around.

"Well, how long has the water been standing?" Ellis asks.

"Just since last night," Jerri Dean answers. "It just sort of leeched up out of the pipes."

Ellis sticks his head beneath the sink again to hide any expressions of disbelief. *More like four or five days that water's been standing*, he thinks. From the bubbles forming at the surface, it seems as though whatever's in the sink is starting to foster an impressive well of fermenting microbes.

"I'll take the pipe apart, clear out the mess, and have you good to go in about ten."

"Okay," she says. "I'll be outside for a bit."

Jerri Dean goes to sit in her lawn chair to smoke. Donny stays for a bit to ask questions—*"Ever find any money down in there? What about rings and jewelry and stuff?"*—until he gets bored and goes outside to pester his mom.

The only jewelry Donny's ever going to lay claim to in this place, Ellis thinks, *will be a plastic decoder ring, unless the retrieved item had been stolen out of some pawnshop.*

Ellis had also, on occasion, done plumbing work for the local middle school where some of the pipes were fifty years old. He'd heard some unsettling rumors from the janitor of Donny Conroe torturing animals too small to bite or claw their way out of his grubby hands. If the bruises on the boy's arms were any clue, the last thing he'd been learning at home was a gentle touch.

It takes Ellis longer than expected to loosen the collar nuts, but as soon as he gets some movement with his wrench, he positions the bucket beneath the trap to catch whatever water will be draining from the sink, as well as from the vertical drain behind the wall.

As soon as the first nut disconnects, the rush of liquid from the sink splashes into the bucket, and Ellis rears back from the stench so quickly that he lands hard on his ass, his hands struggling to find purchase on the linoleum tile. The fluid is viscous, black, with clots of solid material that plop into the bucket with a meaty slap. He turns his face away, eyes watering, struggling to suppress his gag reflexes. He's unclogged some unholy messes in his time, but never anything this noxious.

What in the Good-God-Almighty has that woman been throwing into her sink?

He must have made a sound of protest because Jerri Dean sticks her head into the trailer and says, "You alright in there?"

She wrinkles her nose at the toxic smell and quickly moves to close the door again.

"Hey," Ellis calls, "can you keep that door propped open? I can't work in here without some clean air."

She props the door open with a laundry basket and moves her chair farther away from the trailer.

Holding a cloth over his nose, Ellis pulls the bucket from under the sink, walks quickly out to the small yard behind the trailer where he dumps the foul mess onto the grass. It glistens in a dark, bubbling stew under the late afternoon sun before seeping into the dirt.

Donny has come to stand next to Ellis, one hand over his mouth and nose, and pointing with the other. He asks in a muffled tone, "What's that?"

Between the thick runners of the Bermuda grass a whole bunch of . . . *somethings* are squirming. Pale, gelatinous forms—each about as big as a grub worm—are writhing actively around the blades of grass. Donny has picked up a stick and begins to stab at the thrashing worm-like creatures. On close inspection, they look to have tiny suckers along one side, and ridged orifices at each end, opening and closing hungrily.

Jerri Dean has come to stand next to Donny, and she pulls him back, away from the things on her lawn.

"What are they? Hookworms?" she asks.

"No, I don't believe they are," Ellis says. "They're too short and fat."

"Mealworms?"

Ellis shakes his head doubtfully.

Before she can stop the boy, Donny has started stomping them with his bare feet.

"Uh, uh, uh," he grunts with each heel strike. "Die, fuckers."

Jerri Dean slaps his head hard with the flat of her palm, knocking him off balance.

"Get in the house right now before I really hit you," she yells.

Donny charges off toward the trailer, and throws himself into the lawn chair, pouting, his arms crossed defensively over his chest.

Jerri Dean's sizeable bulk is blocking the rays of the lowering sun, shadowing the still-writhing patch of grass. "I'm gonna kill that old bitch," she murmurs.

"'Scuse me?" Ellis says.

"That old lady I hired to tend my house. This morning when I told her to clear out the mess in the sink, she told me I was the one caused it, so I had to clean it up myself. I fired her on the spot. I see her again, I'm going to shove her nose into this mess and make her tell me what she did to plug up my *God damn sink!*"

Ellis wonders how in the world Jerri Dean Conroe can afford a cleaning lady, but it does explain the reasonably tidy state of her trailer. She rushes in the direction of the trailer and returns a minute later with an empty jelly jar. With difficulty, she leans over to scoop up some of the worms. When they don't cooperate she uses her finger to prod a few toward the container. One latches on to the tip of her finger and she squeals as she shakes it into the jar. She then screws the lid on and watches the captured things through the glass, absentmindedly wiping the hand that touched the worms on her pants leg.

"See if the old bitch likes these crawling through her hair," Jerri Dean says triumphantly.

Ellis spends another hour snaking the vertical drain and flushing out the kitchen sink and pipes with bleach.By the time he's packed up his tools the stench in the trailer has been reduced to a near tolerable level. He loses another ten minutes arguing with Jerri Dean about the money he's owed for the work he's done. Nearly an hour and a half to complete a job Jerri Dean thought would be completed in less than half an hour. She finally relents and pays him for the time.

When he gets into his truck to leave, he notices Donny sitting on a rusted tricycle, scratching frantically at one of his bare feet.

The Conroe trailer was his last job of the day, and he calls his boss to say he's headed home. After a few miles of narrow farm to market roads he turns north on Route 259. He keeps all the windows in his truck rolled down, but the smell from the trailer seems to cling to his clothes, and the inside of his nostrils, like smoke from a burning cesspit. He wishes he had captured a sample of one of the worm-like creatures in one of Jerri Dean's jelly jars. He would have taken it to his cousin, who owned the Yellow Rose Garden Shop, to ask her if she'd ever seen, or smelled, anything like it.

The sun is setting to his left, turning the soil a coppery red, the soft afternoon light casting a forgiving mantle over the sparse yards and meager houses fronting the road.

Just before the turnoff for the business spur of 259, he spots a woman walking alone on the shoulder of the road. She's walking very slowly, with a limping gait, dragging what appears to be a shopping cart behind her. When he passes her, he sees she's quite old, her face contorted in pain or weariness. He pulls over onto the shoulder and gets out of the truck.

"Ma'am, you okay?" he calls. "You need help?"

The woman continues her slow and steady progress.

"Your car break down?" he asks.

He walks toward her and sees that, not only is she old, she's positively ancient. Her face is deeply lined, the sections of hair escaping from under her hat are white and as wispy as corn silk.

She looks up, her eyes focusing with some difficulty on Ellis, and says, "Haven't got a car."

"Where are you headed?" he asks. "Can I give you a ride?"

"Oh, bless you," she says, patting his arm. She leans in, as though revealing a deep confidence. "I'm going to Longview."

"Ma'am, that's over twelve miles away. Were you thinking you could walk there?"

The woman is not only aged, she's tiny. Less than five feet tall, her back bent, her hands twisted with arthritis.

"Well," she says, looking around as though seeing the downtrodden landscape for the first time. "It's closer than Tyler."

She smiles at him in a self-deprecating and humble way, and he finds he's smiling back at her. She's what his own grandmother would have called True People. Brought low by adversity, but not hardened. Beleaguered by the passage of years, but not embittered. Misshapen by physical trials, but still able to laugh at misfortune.

But it's possible that she's in a state of forgetful dementia. Maybe she'd wandered away from her home and, even now, has family looking for her. As slow as she was moving, she could have walked out of a house only a few hundred yards away.

"You have any people around here?" he asks.

As though reading his thoughts, she says, "There's nothing left for me to do in Kilgore. But I've got connections in Longview. They'll take care of me."

He gently takes the cart from her with one hand and gives her his other hand to hold on to. Her fingers are dry, the skin as thin as parchment, but the grip surprisingly strong. They make their way to his truck, and he helps her into the cab after placing her shopping cart in the back. It's filled with plastic bags bulging with what may be the sum total of her belongings.

He gets into the driver's seat and, after making sure she's safely fastened her seatbelt, he continues his drive north.

"I'm Ellis Hinton," he says.

"And I'm Mathilda Belle Johnson. Pleased to meet you."

She holds out her hand to shake his, and he sees with some amusement that the old girl's wearing what looks to be a dozen small bangle bracelets that rattle together pleasantly.

She takes off her hat and her hair springs free like a gauzy corona around her head, her pink scalp visible beneath the thinning curls. "I have to say, it feels good to be off my feet."

"Where were you coming from?" he asks.

"From my last job."

He looks at her skeptically, and her smile widens.

"I had a job as a housekeeper. But I got fired this morning." The grin broadens further. She squints her eyes coyly at him, as though the firing was a source of great delight. "The lady of the house had some unwholesome habits, so I was only happy to leave."

He remembers Jerri Dean telling him she'd just fired a housekeeper that morning. "*I'm going to kill that old bitch*," she had said. But the trailer park was miles away. It didn't seem possible someone this aged and frail could have walked that far. Or even be fit enough to efficiently clean a doublewide trailer. Beyond that, how could a sweet old lady fill a sink with the horrible stinking mess he'd found in the Dean's kitchen?

Especially a mess she'd probably have to clean up herself.

And yet . . . the part of his brain that had been working overtime to forget the foul-smelling worms gives way, and the memory of Donny smashing their glistening bodies with his bare feet, the wet popping sounds as the wiggling forms exploded, fills his head. The lingering stink seems to swell again inside the cab of the truck, despite the air circulating through the windows, and he cautiously sniffs at his shirt to see if he's the source.

He thinks to ask her the name of the lady who had fired her but doesn't want to unduly embarrass her. "You live in Kilgore?"

"Until this morning I did."

Her accent is softer, more languorous than East Texas speech.

"Where are you from?" he asks. "I mean, originally?"

"My people were from Charleston, South Carolina. But we moved to New London, just south of here, when I was three years old. We were a big family. I was one of eleven girls. The youngest of eleven sisters, with no brothers, if you can imagine."

"That is a big family."

"We moved to Kilgore from New London after the big gas explosion at the school."

A vague memory of Texas history and oilfield disasters tugs at Ellis' consciousness.

"But that was a long time ago," she says. "And what about you?"

"Oh, I've lived in Kilgore my whole life."

"You're married," she says.

She says it as a certainty. But Ellis doesn't wear his wedding ring while on the job. It's the quickest way to dislocate, or even lose, a finger messing with unstable pipes with sharp edges.

"I can just tell when a good man is married. There's a settled quality about him. It changes the contours of the face, the way he carries himself." She looks at him, her eyes alert and searching. He notices for the first time her necklace—long, ivory-colored pendants, carved with indiscernible patterns and strung on a cord. Her knobby fingers stroke the worn surfaces in an intimate, and vaguely disturbing, way. The shape of the pendants is somehow familiar . . .

She laughs then. Not an old lady giggle, but the deep-throated laugh of a much younger woman. Her posture seems less bowed, the deep furrows across her forehead diminished. A trick of the softening light, Ellis thinks.

And the sunset is flaring to its final show of crimson and purple. It will be full on dark by the time he gets back to Kilgore after dropping his passenger off in Longview. He makes a mental note to call his wife soon, letting her know to hold up dinner for half an hour or so.

"You can call your wife," she says, turning her head to look out the passenger side window. "Let her know you'll be late."

Ellis startles with the idea that she's been catching his thoughts. He stares at the back of her head. He can't see her face, but he gets the feeling that she's grinning at some hidden joke.

He takes out his phone and calls his wife, telling her he's carrying a lady he found stranded on the highway up to Longview. When he disconnects the call, Mathilda Belle Johnson is staring past him, taking in the last few moments of the sunset, her face bathed in its red light.

"You didn't touch them, did you?" she asks, without looking at him.

"Touch what?"

"The things at Jerri Dean Conroe's place."

Now her eyes have found his, and a chill, as when he was stricken with scarlet fever as a boy, ripples through his body.

"No," he says. He remembers Donny decimating the worms with his bare feet, and Jerri Dean scooping them into the jelly jar with her fingers. He also remembers the boy scratching at the bottom of one foot, a look of concern etched into his face.

"Yes," she says softly, stretching out the sibilant 's'. "It's dangerous to walk around this part of the country in your bare feet."

In that moment, Ellis Hinton does not want to look at the old woman. He keeps his eyes pointed to the road. She's caught his thoughts again, and a sour tightening of his stomach that is nothing like indigestion cramps his middle. As a boy he did spend most of the year traipsing around the Piney Woods in his bare feet. And he'd had his share of encounters with scorpions, spiders and red ants, as well as near misses with copperheads. But he'd never in his life seen the likes of those thrusting, searching worms in the Conroes' back yard.

He increases the pressure on the gas pedal. The less time Mathilda Belle spends in his truck, the better. The March evening air has begun to cool, but he's loath to close the windows. There's still that smell of something foul in the cab, and he's pretty sure at this point that it's not him.

How's the saying go, he wonders? No good deed goes unpunished.

"But how much more satisfying it is to punish the *bad* deed."

She must have moved in her seat because her voice sounds closer. Almost as though she's talking right into his ear. For the briefest moment, he wonders if he's been speaking his thoughts out loud. But he doesn't think so. All his limbs, his jaw, and even his eyes seem nearly fixed and rigid. He can see the road ahead, and his right foot maintains pressure on the gas pedal, his hands gently correcting the wheel. But he might as well be a crash test dummy, controlled by the engineer sitting behind the observation window.

"'Vengeance is mine,' thus sayeth the Lord. At least that's what the faithful believers always say in the South, isn't it?" she asks.

"But us Southerners have also been known to say less charitable things when we've been greatly wronged like, 'I'll skin you alive', or 'I'll tear your arm off and beat you to death with it'."

Mathilda Belle chuckles, her breath hot in his ear. "Echoes and echoes of a darker, more ancient past. When women exacted their own vengeance."

She goes quiet for a moment, and Ellis begins to count the broken white lines on the shadowed highway to distract him from the certainty that she's going to elaborate on just what that vengeance looks like.

"You're too young to remember the New London School tragedy of 1937. But I was there when a gas explosion ripped apart almost three hundred students, some as young as eleven years old. I lost eight of my sisters on that day. I probably would have died, too; except I was only ten and the first through fourth graders had already been excused for the day."

She was ten years old in 1937, which meant she was ninety-two. He wanted to sneak another look at her but was unable to turn his head.

"Eighty-two years ago, today, I sat in the playground waiting for my older sisters to be released so we could all walk home together. It was a beautiful day on that 17th of March. We'd had lots of rainfall over the winter, so spring had already arrived in East Texas. At seventeen minutes past three in the afternoon, a sound like the end of the world broke across Rusk County, carrying for five miles in all directions. The walls of the school first bulged out like an overblown balloon. Then slabs of concrete, some the size of washing machines, were hurled into the air; one of them smashed onto a brand-new Chevy, crushing it flatter than a biscuit. The roof went off like a rocket.

"Roughnecks, many of them kin to the students, came from all over to help dig through the rubble with their bare hands. What they found under the tons of debris made even the most hardened of those oil field workers cry for their own mothers. Of my eight sisters lost, we had to identify all of them in pieces. Martha, my next oldest sister, had colored her toenails with a pink crayon the night before. We were too poor to buy nail polish, you see. My father identified her by her left foot. It was all that was left intact."

She pauses for a moment and wraps her fingers tightly around Ellis' arm.

"Can you imagine it?" she asks.

And he can imagine it. It's as though her touch is transmitting through his skin her own memories of the event. He sees the devastated building, the smashed cars, the roughnecks sweating and sobbing, their clothes covered in soot and ash and blood as they pull lumps of cement and steel away from small, pale bodies looking like so many broken dolls.

"I show you all this so you'll understand why we did what we did. My two sisters and I."

She removes her hand, and he's suddenly aware that his face is wet from tears. His breath is hitched and jagged, as though he'd been crying for a good long while.

"The explosion was caused by waste gas accumulating for who knows how long within the basement and walls of the building. The gas was odorless, so the teacher who started up the electric wood-shop sander didn't know that any spark was sure to ignite the conflagration.

"The whole winter before, the school had been heated with good, commercial-grade gas. But come spring, the school trustees decided to save some money, so they had workers tap into a pipeline carrying waste gas produced by another, smaller refinery. Imagine that. The best-endowed school in three counties, constructed at a cost of over a million dollars—which was a fortune in those days—was built from the wealth pumped out of the ground by oil barons. And the school trustees, millionaires all, wanted to save a few hundred dollars a month.

"Jefferson, Miller, LeBeaux, Warner, and Lawson. The names of the five trustees of the New London School. Any of those names sound familiar?"

The names did sound familiar to Ellis. The businesses, schools, and cemeteries in Kilgore, and close neighboring towns like Overton and Gladewater, were filled people with those surnames. His best friend in high school, Bill Miller, had gotten into some trouble after graduation with drinking and drugs, and had died in a fiery car crash. One of his cousins had married a girl from the wealthy Lawson family. She'd taken a lethal overdose of pills after her affair with her fitness coach was made public.

If he really thought about it, he could probably lay claim to knowing lots of people who'd been born into those families. He'd gone to church with them. Had worked in their homes, attended their funerals, which, now that he thought about it some more, seemed disproportionate to other East Texas families.

Those five families were the First Families of East Texas and had all been made unimaginably rich from the oil and gas they sucked out of the red clay dirt. Their names were on buildings, large and small. And they were stricken with the usual curses of the overly wealthy: addiction, infidelity, mendacity and a seemingly tireless drive toward self-annihilation in general.

Ellis suddenly remembers when he was called to clear some pipes in the big LeBeaux mansion in Laird's Hill, a three-story, Victorian-style monstrosity, still owned and occupied by the aging daughter of the LeBeaux patriarch. After being greeted cordially by Priscilla LeBeaux, and given some lemonade and a moon pie, she excused herself, climbed up onto the roof, and jumped off.

Ellis held her hand, comforting her, until the ambulance arrived.

Her last words to him before she died were, "They *made* me do it, Ellis—"

They made me do it.

Finally, he's able to turn his head and he sees Mathilda Belle gazing peacefully into his eyes, but she hasn't moved closer to him at all. She strokes the pendants around her neck, and he counts ten of them.

I was one of eleven sisters, she had said.

"An inquest after the school explosion found that no one was to blame," she explains. "It was simply an accident of nature. An Act of God, if you will. My sisters and I didn't see that as justice. No justice at all. Eighty-two years it's taken to even the scales. My sisters and I, working together for decades, until Florence died, and then there were two. Then Anna died, leaving one sister to finish our life's work. Mathilda Belle Johnson.

"We brought more with us from Charleston than suitcases, Mr. Hinton. We brought with us the Venus glass and haints and spells that were old when the pyramids were built."

Ellis stares at the ivory pendants again, the recognition of what they are refusing to coalesce inside his waking mind.

"Do you know what Jerri Dean Conroe's name was before she married?"

Ellis shakes his head.

"Jerri Dean Jefferson. She and her son were the last of the Jefferson line."

He's looking at the road again. "Were," he croaks. "You said *were* the last."

In response, she exhales a long-satisfied sigh, as one will do after a particularly trying task is completed.

"But he's just a boy," Ellis says. In his mind's eye he sees Donny's frenzied scratching at the place on his foot where the worms had touched.

"He's a twelve-year old with a killer's heart, and with a mother who pedals poison to children. The world will be a better place without them."

"What was that in the Conroe's sink?" he asks.

"Re-tri-bu-tion." She pulls out each syllable the way a preacher does when he shows his congregants the edges of the Fiery Pit.

His head feels like it's filled with helium, his chest tight, his left arm tingling as well. Ellis Hinton thinks that he may be heading for an imminent heart attack. He thinks of all of his shortcomings, his defects of character, the many mean-spirited thoughts he had over the years, directed at friends and family. Toward his own mother, especially after she had told him that his father was not his father. But, rather, he was the son of a Warner family heir with whom his mother had had an affair.

"Who are you?" he asks, his voice breathy with fear.

She pats him on his thigh in a friendly way. "You're safe with me, Mr. Hinton. You're a good man helping out a little old lady."

At her touch the tightness under his ribs dissipates, his vision sharpens again.

"We saved them where we could, my two sisters and I. The selfless, the kind, the compassionate, like yourself." She gives a short bark of laughter. "But they were in the woeful minority . . . Mr. Hinton turn left just here."

He realizes with a jolt that he has negotiated his way through the streets of Longview without being consciously aware that he had even entered the town limits.

She directs him to pull up to one of the modest houses facing the Grace Hill Cemetery, and, as though they'd been waiting for her to arrive, a group of young women and girls exit the house and stand on the porch in an expectant cluster.

"Mr. Hinton," she says, giving him a maternal smile. "Your profession has allowed you to see the worst of human excrescence. The hidden things that were never meant to see the light of day again, but which, like a bloated corpse, often rise to the surface again. I'm of a mind to see you as a sort of sentinel to the Underworld. One who illuminates to the living that the sins of the father can come back to infect the child.That you have not been infected is a testament to your goodness. And why you'll go home to your wife tonight."

The women and girls approach only after Ellis has helped Mathilda Belle out of her seat. They gather around her, welcoming her, and then lead her carefully into the house. The youngest of the group, a girl of about eight or so, stays behind to take charge of the shopping cart that Ellis has lifted from the back of the truck. She thanks him, smiles, and wheels the cart into the house behind her sisters.

Ellis had counted eleven of them. He checks the name on the mailbox. The Baileys. Eleven Bailey sisters, each one a mirrored image of the one who'd come before.

After calling in sick for a week, Ellis Hinton's first call back on the job is at the local middle school. A pipe in one of the science lab's sinks had backed up. Ellis completes the job quickly with the drain snake—some bright bulb had tried to flush bits of paper down into the pipes—and he gathers up his tools, spending a few moments talking to the school's janitor who, as usual, gives him the gossip of the past few days: which kids have been arrested for mischief, which teachers are reportedly fooling around with which students, and so forth.

He also tells Ellis that after Donny Conroe's failure to show up for school for a few days, the sheriff stopped by their trailer and found both he and his mother dead from some as-yet-unknown disease. Evidently, according to the janitor, their bodies were swollen almost past recognition, and they had to be identified by their dental records. The smell, he said, had been unbelievable.

As the janitor relates in lurid detail the state of the Conroes' remains, Ellis seeks to hide his growing horror at the news by turning away, pretending to check once more the counters and floor, as though he's making doubly sure he's not leaving anything behind. His gaze rests on the replica of the anatomy skeleton in one corner, its skull rakishly adorned with a sombrero. He follows the attachments down, from the collarbone to the *humerus*, to the double bones of the forearm whose names he has forgotten, to the . . . *phalanges*. He's remembered the Latin name for the finger bones.

He now knows what the ninety-two-year-old Kilgore woman had been wearing around her neck. Ten cylindrical bones, a few yellowed with age, more blackened as though with a terrible heat, but all inscribed with mystic symbols. A bone taken from the hand of each one of the deceased and strung together as a necklace to adorn the last remaining sister—Mathilda Belle Johnson.

The Man Becomes the Door

Andrew Kozma

What I need you to know right now is that my cousin's apartment is haunted. Nothing like the movies. I mean, there's no demonic presence pushing its face through the walls, but I can feel it. You could feel it, too, if you were here. Everyone who has visited the house comments on it, directly or indirectly. My cousin, when he showed me the place, said he thought there were rats in the walls. My ex was convinced someone was watching her and couldn't stop glancing over her shoulder at the strangest times. When we had sex, for example, she couldn't help peering around into the dark corners of my bedroom.

"You'd tell me if someone was there," she said, and I'd say, "Yes, yes, of course," because what else was I supposed to say? There was only the one entrance to the bedroom, and we were several stories up. Once, she'd threatened she was going to climb out the window because she was so freaked out, but I explained there was no fire escape, not even a tree tall enough for an enterprising thief. Or murderer.

That's actually why we broke up. She was positive we were going to get murdered, and when I didn't show the same concern, then she decided *she* was going to get murdered. She didn't say she thought I'd murder her, but, really, would you say that to someone you thought was going to murder you?

The thing is, I've lived here longer than anyone else ever has. My cousin bought the apartment when the building was the shell of an old bank, taking one whole floor of the rotting building. He's an architect. Started his own firm and called it Ghosts and Co. He thought it'd be funny because our family's name is Goss, with a long o, and he sold himself as someone who "removed the old ghosts from a home so you could make your own." He gutted the floor, rebuilt it from floor to ceiling into an amazing model home, though he left the bank vault door as a clever entryway to the bedroom.

But he only ever used the place to crash when stuck in the city for work or after partying too hard downtown. He spent most of his time in his self-designed suburban home when not traveling the world. Which is to say, this place has only ever been *my* apartment, as I'm the one who's given it personality. I know what scars on the walls are from the furniture I moved in. The art giving the walls character is mine. The litter spilled into the cracks in the faux-aged wooden floor are from the cats I've fostered. I can mimic how the place creaks during a hurricane and point out those spots on the ceiling where I had to repair the leaks myself because I couldn't afford to pay for repairs, just as I couldn't afford to live downtown if I didn't have this place.

How can the apartment be haunted if no one else has ever lived there? That's what Zariya asked me when she invited herself over and I said, really, no, you don't want to come. Zariya is a friend, and a co-worker, and a love interest. Or she was. Or still might be.

Let me explain.

Both Zariya and I are freelance writers. We will write whatever you want as long as you pay us. We'll edit what you write, too, and evaluate it if you want. We'll tell you it's shit or it's the best thing since sliced Shakespeare, if you pay us to. Zariya is tall and beautiful and dark, with a sharp nose that seemed almost too much until she fixed her eyes on you. She specialized in cover letters for job applications as well as grants, anything that would get you money and requires selling yourself as someone you're not. I worked in fiction, by which I mean advertising. We met online through sharing leads and that led to work brunches and just a general friendship, the first I'd really had in the city since my girlfriend left.

Not that I was looking for Zariya to be my girlfriend.

Nor would I be disappointed if that happened.

Look, none of that is the point here. The point is that Zariya and I met up at The Watch Company, she'd had too many drinks to drive home safely, we walked back to the apartment, and now she's gone.

At first, I'd recommended a rideshare. I'd told her, "You don't want to come over."

She'd smiled in a way I couldn't parse. "You don't know what I want to do."

"You don't understand," I argued. "My place is haunted."

For a second, she looked offended. "You told me you're the only one who's lived there. How can a place be haunted if no one's lived there before?"

After that, she wouldn't take no for an answer, and I was lonely, and, frankly, sometimes I was scared about going back to my apartment alone, and it was one of those times. I shouldn't have done it. I regret it. That's what I'm going to tell Zariya when I see her again.

How is the place haunted if no one has lived here before? Zariya suggested a number of possibilities on the way to my apartment, taking full pleasure in devil's advocating herself.

"Maybe it's the angry ghost of a bank manager. No, a bank accountant! One who has to account for every missing penny in every incomplete roll of change!" She laughed, stumbled a bit, and steadied herself with my arm. "Or maybe spirits choose where they go after they die, wandering around like cats, searching for the best place in the sun?"

We were both drunk. My brain was fixated on her touch on my arm. I said, "What if the ghost isn't a person at all?"

Her hand let go as she turned to look at me, face a puzzle of confusion. "What else would it be?"

I hadn't thought that far ahead.

"I don't know. An emotion? A ghost of a place? An idea, even?"

Zariya shrugged. "An idea of a person?"

I nodded. "A ghost of an idea."

She frowned thoughtfully. "Maybe it's a future ghost? The haunting of who will one day haunt the place? Like a blank page, you know, that could be a drawing, a story, or a grocery list, but until it's anything it's just a blank page. It's still there, and it's not really anything, but it's still something. Right?"

"I live there, though, so it can't be a blank page." I smiled. "I'm not a blank page, am I?"

"The metaphor's not perfect. You know what I mean. Besides, blank pages can be quite handsome."

She didn't touch me again, but for the rest of the way to my apartment we were shoulder to shoulder, close as confidantes.

The apartment isn't big, but somehow being haunted makes it seem larger. This isn't helped by the fact that, built from the bones of a bank, the thick walls absorb sound like a sponge. Those rooms on the edge of the apartment have large windows, but the light never fills the place, so it always feels like twilight, that liminal space between sleeping and waking.

That's one of the things I loved about the apartment when I first moved in. I love those moments before sunset and just after sunrise. I enjoy dimly-lit bars where lamps make the darkness outside of their soft glow all the more defined: a warmth to sit inside, a mystery to step out into.

The wooden apartment floor is a blessing to bare feet on hot summer days, but not the most comfortable. My cousin covered it in rugs of various sizes and colors and textures, and I left them there, adding my own I'd occasionally find for cheap or free.

All of which is to say that, even haunted, there was something homey about the place. And when Zariya went missing in my apartment, the hominess shifted from comforting to stifling, from warm hugs and nostalgia to a past I could never escape, no matter how fast I ran.

I made tea for her. It's still steaming on the table. The smell of it suffuses the house. Zariya went to the bathroom and never came back. It's been fifteen minutes. My place isn't that big. I didn't hear the toilet flush.

At twenty minutes, I walk over to the hallway bathroom. It's down the hall and around a corner, and at each step I feel I'm just about to intrude on someone else's privacy. Not just Zariya in the bathroom, but someone, anyone, just another presence in the apartment that has claimed it for its own. There is a pressure of silence weighing down on my lungs. I have to make every breath deliberate to keep myself calm, to stop myself from a quick, desperate wheezing.

The bathroom, when I reach it, is empty and dark, door open and everything inside untouched and clean, almost blank, as if never used. I blink, and now I see all the dirt, grime, and hairs I'd missed in my last attempt to keep a tidy apartment. Dried water stains dot the mirror. I resist the urge to wipe them away with a towel. A shape flickers in the mirror, movement in the hall outside, and I jump, whipping my head around.

"Zariya?" I say, but it comes out a whisper.

On my own, the haunting of the apartment doesn't really bother me. I've never been unable to sleep or terrified or felt that I had to just *get out right now*. At most, I felt crowded, a little discomfort, a niggling in the back of my brain like I was forgetting something.

That's alone.

But with other people in the apartment, their fear sticks to me like a leech. They twitch at a creak in the walls, the building settling and shrinking after a day in the heat, and the hairs on the back of my neck rise. Zariya is here, and suddenly I am terrified.

My apartment isn't big, but darkness makes it huge. Every room has a closet that looks like it leads into another room, even if each room is individual, separate, the layout of the place a labyrinth of dead-ends. When I flip on lights, the rooms are stark in the illumination, laid out like bodies in a morgue, and everything familiar becomes strange. In the living room, I stare for minutes at a picture of two men who stare back with awkward, tired smiles, eventually recognizing them as my cousin and myself. That picture is surrounded by other pictures, all filled with equally blank-eyed strangers.

My heart pounds and my body shakes with a sudden weakness, as if I'm about to faint. I scan the room, pointedly avoiding the pictures, but can't find Zariya among the crowd of furniture, couches pushed up against loveseats bordered with side tables propping up decorative lamps. The TV is a dark mirror on the wall, looking like a still pool at night, the scum and trash so obvious during the day hidden by the shadows, but still there, waiting. I stumble back into the hallway, and my heart slows.

There's nothing here. There's no one around. I'm alone. I have no reason to be afraid.

Except that someone is *supposed* to be here.

"Zariya?" I say again, loudly. My voice disappears into the emptiness.

She can't be gone. I didn't hear the door, and I would have seen her pass back by the kitchen on the way from the bathroom. There isn't any other exit, unless she climbed out a window. But we're three stories up. Why would she do that?

But maybe Zariya didn't come back to the apartment with me at all?

That's the only explanation that makes sense. I was too drunk. I didn't notice she left me at the door to the building as she took the rideshare I'd suggested at first, just wanting to make sure I got home okay. Or maybe I just completely imagined walking back with her.

I don't have a history of hallucinations. My family is all sane and well-adjusted and has been as far back as I can remember. We've never been prescribed brain drugs. We've always been the people you call when you want someone to tell you that you're imagining things, that you're worrying over nothing. And if my parents were still alive, maybe I'd call them right now, huddled in the linen closet only a few steps away from me, and wait for their calm voices to let me know that I don't need to be afraid of the dark. There's no point in being afraid of the dark. All you need to do, son, is turn the light on.

The light is on in the hallway. It's not helping.

Down the hallway, I can see a bit of my bedroom. The hallway zigs and zags, I suppose to avoid necessary struts and pillars holding the building up, so I can see just a sliver of the dark entry to my room. I always leave the door open. Having a bank vault door for the entryway is cool, but heavy and, frankly, when it's closed it's as if I've sealed myself in.

But the door is closed. Light glints off it as I take a step forward.

"Zariya?" I ask, but I can't even hear my own voice. I'm almost as afraid of her answering as I am she never will.

I'm spotlit. All the other lights in the apartment are off. I don't remember turning them off. I don't remember a lot of things. I don't remember what Zariya's voice sounds like. I don't even remember what she looks like. Tall or short? Black hair or dyed blonde? Long fingernails or short, lipstick or not, the color of her eyes, what she was wearing, how it fit her body, that I can't picture.

I could leave right now. I could run. I have my wallet in my pocket and I could stay at a hotel and come back in the morning—no, send someone in the morning to get my things. I could get out of here. And I turn to face the door out and walk towards it. I don't need to be here. I can call the police, if I need to, and they'll deal with this shit. I'm careful to keep my footsteps quiet, as if the very apartment will hear me if I'm not careful, sliding my shoes gently along the floor.

I follow the turns of the twisting hallway and end up only a few feet away from my bedroom, the opposite side of the apartment from the front door. I'm scared. I'm terrified. But I don't try to run away again. The apartment won't let me go. More importantly, I tell myself, there is someone here, someone who I can't remember, and their being here is my fault. If I walk away, if I manage to leave the apartment, what happens to them? They need a witness. I need to witness.

The bank vault door hangs heavy in the doorway, cracked open.

With a slight push, it opens all the way.

There is a woman in the room, on the bed. She is facing away from me. The hall light behind me goes out, leaving only the ambient light of the city filtering through the room's high windows. It bathes her in a glow which outlines her head like an eclipse.

My heart is pounding in a steady rhythm, like someone angrily knocking on the door. I'm afraid she's going to turn her head. I'm afraid to see who she is. I'm afraid I won't know who she is.

"Please let me go," the woman says.

I tell her, "You can leave whenever you want."

I'm blocking the doorway. I could move from it, but I don't, because I know if I do that she'll leave. She'll leave and I'll never know who she is or who she was. There's something missing in this apartment. I can feel it. There's something hungry that wants to be filled. Did I fill it? Or was it me all along? I'm afraid that what I'm afraid of is me, just me, a me I never knew, wanting things I never admitted to before, and will not admit to even now.

"Please just open the door," the woman says.

There is no door.

Valentine

Julie Aaron

T he road into Marfa, Texas, was a long one. Faded white and yellow lines stretched until the mirages glimmered them away. The small Prada store installed a few years ago would be up on the right eventually. I just had to make it there first.

This time of year, there would always be an influx of tourists flocking to the art piece. Vehicles pulled over on the shoulder; cameras pointed with purpose, the air conditioning trapped between four doors as families stopped to stretch their legs at the middle-of-nowhere luxury pit stop. Their sweaty, sunburned hands would pull on the locked door handle, smudge the windows with fingerprints, and let their road-trip weary kids climb all over the iron fence behind it. All that to say, there would be help. There would be someone with an extra seat out of town in their van or RV, maybe even someone with a cell phone. There might even be some tech boom yuppy from Austin, on the scenic route back to LA, with a palm pilot tucked into their cup holder. Maybe even one with internet service way out here among the dry mountains and hot asphalt.

The bullet wound in my right thigh gushed thick wetness down my leg into the opening of my combat boot, turning everything it touched a deep blackish red, but it would not slow me down. Running for my life now. The machete in my left hand gripped so hard that I flex my fingers to avoid a cramp. With the midday West Texas sun beating down my brow, the sweat accumulated at the base of my back rolled and soaked my already yellowed work shirt. My boots struck the roughness of the road, clapping over and over as I moved forward, fast. I intended to kill him, even if it killed me.

Windless heat weighed me down. The blood loss did not help. I took a moment to turn my head and squint my swollen eyes, both blackened by him. Behind me I saw the Toyota Camry sitting cockeyed, one tire haphazardly lying in the middle of the road. Blood, both his and mine, created a clear trail along the shoulder, keeping me from ever being too far from him.

I remembered the feeling of my tire iron sinking into the side of his head. His once neat dark hair was now disheveled from sudden impact. The sounds around me at that moment were like an orchestra: the quiet of isolation, the sizzle of sun on asphalt, the metal on bone, and the crescendo—a beautifully pained whine that escaped his busted, blood-red lips.

Music to my ears.

Again, I felt the laugh I had released bubble out from my raw throat. The screams of elation chafed my vocal cords. In our solitude, parked on the right side of the highway where anyone could see us but no one did, I had raised the tire iron above my head, eager to land another blow. My eyes were locked onto the blood pouring from his perfect wound, enamored by the thought of scalp and hair being dug out entirely and flung into the ditch for a stray coyote to feast on after sunset.

My vision blurred and pain spiked through my face. His foot had risen, kicking with might against my jaw, making me clack my teeth and bite straight through the fatty muscle of my tongue. I was set off balance, and from there he was on top of me, tackling me to the ground. Hot small rocks embedded in my back, tearing against my skin. I thrashed, trying to get away. He managed to pin my arms beneath his knees, immobilizing me while his large pale hands gripped painfully tight around my small, tanned ones and ripped the tire iron from me, throwing it before he began to move away. It was too late. I had locked my legs around his waist, holding him to me and squeezing with my thighs as I unsheathed the Bowie knife that is always strapped to the waistband of my jeans. Without him even realizing what had happened, I had buried it to the hilt between his fourth and fifth rib before withdrawing and slicing across his stomach and stabbing into the sinewy fat there. Adrenaline must have coursed through his six-foot-tall frame, because he jolted out from my grip and scrambled away from me clumsily. His stuttered plea, *"Stay away. I'm warning you,"* fell on unsympathetic ears. I walked toward him. I was going to end this. The motherfucker had broken my nose. My playful mood was over.

When I heard the distinct click of a hammer, rage overcame me. I lurched forward, knife brandished, ready once again to deal the final blow, but his trigger finger was fast. He fired a warning shot toward the ground beside me and took the time that bought him to create more distance between us. He had come prepared. He must have shoved the small caliber pistol into the back of his jeans before exiting the cab of his truck to help a poor woman, me, seemingly stranded on the side of the road.

"I'm serious. I will shoot you and leave you here," he said as he made his way to his white Ford Ranger. Anxiety exaggerated his movements. Fear bled from him, mixed with all of his own precious blood. The front end of his truck had angled off the edge of the road when he first pulled over. The weeds growing in the ditch now reached for the ankles of his pants as he swung the driver's side door open to slide in. He tapped his pants pockets, digging his right hand into each of them, front and back, before frantically turning his breast pocket inside out.

To no avail.

His shoulders slumped knowingly, and his head shook once. When his eyes rose to meet mine, he saw his blood painting my wrist all the way down to the middle finger, where his purple key ring now dangled tauntingly. With my knife still in my hand, I waved gently, a slow smile overtaking my face.

"Don't. Please," he begged as I raised my knife to my cracked lip and ran my bloodied tongue against the flat edge of it. It turned my mouth maroon with the strong taste of iron; the visceral fluid sat heavily on my tongue, stained my teeth. I couldn't wipe the smile off my face, even as my nose sat crooked and jammed. It just added to his horror. I stalked him, getting a running start before launching his keys into the tumbleweed-infested fence line as far as I could throw. Panic set into his deep brown eyes.

He realized there was no escaping now, except on foot. To him, my car was out of commission. Idiot. All he needed to do was remount the tire I had cleverly removed, pull my keys from the sunglasses compartment above the rearview mirror, and be on his way. He was stronger than me, taller; hell, he had a gun. He should've killed me. He'd never walk away from this now.

It happened something like this every time. It really wasn't his fault. Like so many others, he was simply in the wrong place at the wrong time. Men would see me on the side of the deserted highway with my car jacked up and the tire off, the same driver's side rear tire, and pull over to help. After that, it was fairly easy to debilitate them. Sometimes, like today, it was a tire iron to the head. Others, a slit throat while they tightened my lug nuts. Once, I drove a screwdriver through a tow truck driver's eye. The sound it made was like popping packing bubbles. When I pulled the tool out, the gray eye, still impaled, came with it. I kept that eye in my glove box for months. As for the bodies, the heat and animals took care of them for me. A murder of curious crows, circling turkey vultures, and a pig farm within walking distance of that stretch of road where I hunted, all became my unknowing but willing accomplices.

Today should've been no different, but as I approached him, ready to slide my knife into his tight skin once more, he raised his trembling hands around the heavy, silver metal in his grasp and gracelessly pulled the trigger. The hot bullet dug through the meat of my thigh, burrowing and splitting through layers of skin, tissue, veins and cells before exiting in fragments out the backside, just under my buttock. I doubled over in quiet pain, refusing to grant him a whisper of discomfort. He took this moment of vulnerability to tie a dirty t-shirt from the floorboard of his truck around his waist tightly and take off toward Marfa in a dead sprint. I was worried he was overworking himself, and I hoped to God he didn't bleed out and collapse before I could catch up. I had a plan that involved digging his tongue out of his mouth and using it as vulture bait.

Sighing and turning back toward the barely dried blood trail on the asphalt, I jammed my index finger into the pulsating bullet hole to take a break from the bleeding. The feeling of the tip of my finger being swallowed and held to the beat of my pumping heart calmed me. I had exchanged my Bowie knife for a more intimidating machete back at the car.

Empty fields of dead grass passed by as I jogged after him, the sun cooking his blood into the road under my feet. If I squinted my sore eyes, I could see him up ahead. His tired body slumping and slowing as his head wound intensified in the heat with his exertion. Not a single car had passed us, and even if they had, a woman chasing after a man just wasn't something a vacationing family or tired farmer was going to stop for.

I remove the finger from my wound before bringing it to my waiting mouth to suck it clean, letting the coppery taste fuel me with one final push. Between the heat waves and delirium, I see the white and black outline of the art fixture. No cars around. I knew I had to hurry before it became the site of an engagement photoshoot or Myspace status update. I scanned the void, looking for him. I searched the brown expanse around us, hoping to see his staggering gait, his head lolled to the right, and one arm clutched tight around his midsection to keep his guts inside his shirt. Instead, I see him on his knees, facing the door of the Prada store. He has made this really inconvenient for me.

I approached, I let the tip of my machete drag against the ground for him to hear. I wanted him to be scared. He whimpered, with one hand outstretched as if in prayer, his palm up, the other putting weakening pressure on his torso wounds. Before he has the idea to move, I swing my machete down into him, slicing four of five fingers off his hand. They land quietly in the gritty sand. He released a quick shriek, startled at the sudden pain, before returning to quietly whining. I bent at the waist to retrieve the smallest finger, sizing it against my index before deciding the fit is good enough and jamming it into the bullet hole in my thigh. Hoping to stop the bleeding long enough to wrap this up, put my wheel back on, and get the hell out of West Texas for a few weeks.

One last time, I raised my weapon above my head, grinning, my teeth still smeared with both his and my own blood. As the length of the blade descended toward him, he shifted slightly, and moved the hand clutching his innards. Too late, as I saw the barrel of his gun poking out against his side as he hugged himself tightly. His arm cradled his wound along his stained clothing and makeshift bandage as he pointed the pistol at me for the third time today. The smoke curling around us alerted me to the pain in my midsection. The deafness of my ears told me he had fired again. This time, it was straight through my intestines. My guts rushed to exit through the wound, forward, as the bullet tears them, shredding my insides. Bile, blood, and tissue escaped me, and, before I knew it, I toppled over, and the point of my machete drove straight into his spine. He made no noise besides the grinding sound of metal on bone as the blade wedged against his vertebrae and slid down his back. I slid against him. Eventually, our breathing synced, slowing, slowing. Heavy on his back, I bled.

The seconds agonize by. And he, with his skull and spine exposed, grew more and more haggard. Our lungs rattled in our ribcages, our bowels crawled toward each other, pooled into the sand, leaking from us, mixing together, and turning the steps of the Prada Marfa art installation bright red. Our bodies rapidly empty out around us.

The Moon, the Fields and the Mysteries of the Eternal Grove

Robert Stahl

They run out of things to talk about a hundred miles out of Dallas, so Rick sits in the passenger seat watching the piney woods go by. The campsite is still another hour down I-45, but he secretly wishes it were farther away. It's his first time visiting the LGBTQ-themed park, which has a reputation for the promiscuous clientele it attracts. Deep down, he's been putting off dealing with this trip ever since last month's Big Fight, when Jeremy announced he wanted to explore new sexual experiences—with or without Rick. Reluctantly, Rick agreed. What else could he do? It was either that or lose Jeremy. Now he's so conflicted about the whole thing, it catches him off guard when he sees a figure standing in the dusky shadows near the woods.

"The hell?" Rick says, sitting bolt upright in his seat. He flicks the volume down, muting Lana Del Rey to a whimper.

"What are you doing?" Jeremy says, a twinge of agitation in his voice. "That's the best part of the song."

Rick cranes his neck to get another look at the mysterious shape lurking in the grove. They're moving too fast, though; the area is already shrinking away in the waning afternoon light. "There's a man out there."

Jeremy's eyes never leave the road. "A hitchhiker?"

"Don't think so. He was way over by the trees."

Jeremy glances his way, a sly twinkle in his eyes. "Was he hot?"

The question ignites a pang of jealousy inside Rick—he's still getting used to this idea of free love. He'd thought Jeremy wanted a monogamous relationship when he'd moved in with him last year—a move which had spurred the wrath of Rick's disapproving Baptist family. So, Jeremy's change of direction is a bitter pill to swallow. But he loves Jeremy, will do anything for him, so now so he's doing his best to navigate this strange new world of casual sex. He takes a deep breath, exhales, hoping to quell some of the tension raging in his anxious mind. "Well, he was shirtless," he offers, in as pleasant a voice as he can. "Probably kinky, too, with those horns on his head."

There's a slight stiffening in Jeremy's posture. He glances into the rearview again, as if to get a look. "What do you mean *horns?*'"

"Like, animal horns. On his head."

"A headpiece?"

Rick's annoyed at Jeremy's sudden interest in a half-naked stranger who may or may not be homeless. "Hell if I know, Jeremy," he fires back. "I'm just telling you what I saw. It was creepy, honestly. He was looking straight at me."

When Jeremy speaks again, his tone is tempered, as if he's deliberately dialing it back. "A camper, probably. Told you some of the guys were into some weird shit."

"A camper?" Rick asks. "This far out? We've got to be sixty miles from the campground." He glances at his phone where he's been minding the navigation app. Up until five minutes ago it had been working perfectly. Now the red pathway was jumping and twitching across an ocean of digital green. "Damn. Signal's dropped.".

"Dwain said that would happen when we got close." Jeremy runs his fingers through his dark hair. "We're out in the middle of nowhere, so it's not surprising."

Rick says nothing, turns to stare out the window, feeling numb.

Jeremy shuts the music all the way off. "I'm sorry. You sound tense is all."

"I'm fine," Rick says, surprised at how easily the lie floats across his lips.

"I hope so. It's going to be a fun weekend." Jeremy turns the music back up, and Lana croons about looking for love in all the wrong places. "But you've got to learn to relax."

Despite the warm May evening, the hairs on Rick's arms bristle as Jeremy steers the Mustang down a gravel road. Above them, interconnected tree branches blot out the fading sunlight, casting long, mournful shadows. As the car's tires crunch beneath them, Rick realizes he's holding his breath a little. He doesn't breathe easily again until they pull into a driveway and stop in front of a closed iron gate. Jeremy enters a code into a keypad, and the gate creaks slowly open.

"Buck's Acres?'" Rick says, reading from a crudely hand-painted sign depicting a cartoonish goat in a pink shirt smashing its way out of the forest. "Remind me why we're here and not on the couch binging Netflix?"

"You'll see," Jeremy says, with a hungry look that Rick's never seen before. "It's a special party, one Dwain only throws every few years." When he grins, Rick's heart melts. With Jeremy's thick, wavy hair and chiseled features, Rick would follow him into a minefield. Always. "And because I'd have to deal with him pouting at work if we didn't."

"Alright, let's do it," Rick says.

Jeremy steers the Mustang down a narrow dirt lane that leads into the woods. Rick pulls out his phone, his nervous hands needing something to fiddle with. "Signal's out, remember?" Jeremy says. "For three days, it's just you, me and the wilderness." He reaches over and playfully squeezes Rick's knee. "Oh, and about fifty horny old goats."

As they pull into a clearing, Rick sees the campsite for the first time. "Look, there are your goats now."

The campground is alive with activity. Men gather in small groups in front of a couple dozen Airstreams and Winnebagos. Some of the men are playing cards or drinking beer, but all of them stop to check out the occupants of the Mustang as it cruises slowly by. Despite what Jeremy said, not all of them are old; it looks like a mix of guys from every walk of life, from older to younger and everything in between. Some, but not all, are very handsome. Jeremy waves casually as they drive past. Many of them smile and wave back.

They drive past a long, covered pavilion to an area dotted with a handful of tents. Before long, they're both hard at work pitching their own tent on a patch of ground alongside the others. The task complete, they crawl inside to rest. Rick's tired from the trip, so he yawns and stretches out on his back. Jeremy sidles up next to him, drapes his arm across Rick's chest.

"You feel that?" Jeremy says. His head is cocked, like he's listening to something Rick can't quite hear.

"Feel what?"

"The vibe out here. There's an energy in the air or something." Jeremy's got a faraway look in his eyes and a ruddy color in his cheeks that Rick knows all too well. He reaches inside Rick's shorts. "It feels good out here. Sexy."

Rick's nowhere close to being in the mood. He needs a shower first, and there are people close by who might overhear. "Jeremy, I'm not really in the—"

But Jeremy is already undressed, and whatever hesitation Rick offers doesn't last long. In the closed air of the tent, the scent of their afternoon musk commingles, triggering a primal need. Their lovemaking is brisk and vigorous, building in intensity with every stroke and flick of the tongue. Jeremy is more aggressive than usual, handling Rick in a way that borders on the animalistic: tugging Rick's nipples, pulling his hair, using his full weight to pin Rick to the tent floor, so that by the time they finish, Rick's moans are borne more out of pain than pleasure.

They walk to the showers in silence, and Rick feels that numbness return. He's thankful for the water that quickly covers his sudden tears. He thinks about how closed off Jeremy has seemed for the past few months, and about how awkward their new arrangement feels. He thinks about the Big Fight, about how both of them seemed to know on that day, dabbing at their hot bruised flesh on the cold bathroom floor, that their relationship might not survive another.

It's night and Rick's using his phone to light his way on the dark path winding from the tents to the campgrounds. Jeremy is just ahead, bobbing his own light to the disco beat thudding in the distance. The sky is full of stars, and Rick's craning his neck to take them in when he hears a snorting sound off to his right.

Something is shuffling around in the underbrush.

He raises his light to get a better look, and when he does, his foot catches on an obstacle. He trips and falls, his hand still clutched tightly around his phone. Cursing his stupid luck, he lays there a moment before lifting the phone in Jeremy's direction. In the light, he sees Jeremy stop and turn. A flash of some ugly emotion passes over his lover's face—irritation? annoyance?—but it's only there a second. Then Jeremy puts on his boyfriend face and walks over to lend a hand. "You hurt?"

"Just my pride," Rick says. The light reveals the reason he tripped: a gnarled tree root curling across the dirt path. "I heard something following us. Like, an animal."

"A hog, maybe?" Jeremy glances up the trail ahead. "They've got wild hogs out in places like these."

"Don't know, but scared the hell out of me." Rick finds a fallen tree branch nearby, picks it up and wields it like a club. "Just in case."

"Hold on, Superman." Jeremy eases the branch out of his hands and tosses it into the underbrush. "Dwain would have mentioned dangerous animals. I'm sure it's nothing. We can ask our friends about it when we get there."

Our friends? Rick can't help but think. *More like your friends*.

Three minutes later, they crest a hill that overlooks another camping site. "This is the residents' area," Jeremy says.

Rick gazes in awe at the trailers he sees. He's never been into camping, has always thought of camping trailers as drab eyesores, but the trailers here are impressive indeed. Boasting modern designs, they glisten and gleam in their parking bays as if brand-new. Their owners' attention to detail extends to the surroundings, too. The grounds around each trailer are decorated beyond what one would expect at an ordinary campsite: tropical plant beds, sturdy oak picnic tables, the latest stainless-steel grills, and rainbow flags everywhere. Each one seems to be flashier than the last.

"It's like a pissing contest," Rick says.

"Boys and their toys."

They arrive at Dwain's trailer, the largest and flashiest of all. Sparkling LED lights illuminate the perimeter of the space, giving it a nightclub feel. A long beverage bar runs the length of the small yard and a few men lean against it, sipping, chatting. Others sit at wooden benches or gather around a concrete dance floor, drinking from paper cups, talking and laughing. A handful of partiers sway to the music from the live DJ. Light from a mirror ball streaks off their shirtless, sweating bodies. Jeremy scans the crowd, his green eyes eager and ready.

Rick shifts about awkwardly. He's always felt a degree of social anxiety and the sexually charged atmosphere at Buck's Acres exacerbates it. He picks at some potato chips in a bowl on a picnic table before checking out the spoils of Dwain's luxurious lifestyle: the palm trees that surround the space, the shirtless young waiter offering shots to the crowd, the water fountain topped with a flute-playing figure splashing water out of its engorged phallus. It's part man, part fawn; like something out of mythology.

"The Great God Pan," a voice says from behind. Rick turns to find a man standing there, holding a drink in each hand. He's a little funny looking. Short, ruddy complexion, buggy brown eyes, a pink boa draped around his shoulders. "Once worshipped as the god of the pastures and woodland but also celebrated as one of the lords of lust and sex."

"Dwain," Jeremy says. "You devil. How about a kiss?"

The two embrace, but Dwain quickly turns his attention back to Rick. "Did you know that ancient man once made sacrifices to Pan? They believed this would summon him, and that his presence would bring them many wonderful things." He stands rigid, like a garden gnome, with a smile on his face that's thin and brittle.

"What kinds of things?" Rick says, feeling his guard go up.

"Oh, awesome things," Dwain says, his pouty lips dramatically enunciating every syllable. "Virility. Fertility. Abundance."

Rick shifts on his feet, uncomfortable under Dwain's penetrating gaze. It's obvious Dwain's one of those pretentious, bitchy queens, but Rick's determined to stand his ground. "Sounds just lovely," he says. "I'm Rick, by the way."

"Dwain, this is the guy I'm always talking about," Jeremy says.

Rick winces when he hears this, as if he's a minor part of Jeremy's life.

"Of *course* it is," Dwain says, matter-of-factly. He hands Jeremy one of the drinks, offers Rick a jellyfish handshake with the other.

"Nice to meet you," Rick says, another necessary lie.

Dwain responds by taking Jeremy by the arm. "We've been waiting on you all night, darling. Come, meet some of these fabulous people." They make their way into the crowd, leaving Rick standing alone.

Rick tries to keep a polite face on as he watches Dwain introduce Jeremy to a group of men, but it's difficult. Feeling awkward and uncomfortable, he reaches for his phone again, then remembers there's no signal. With a frustrated sigh, he heads over to the bar.

The bartender is a shirtless energetic youth with a charming Spanish accent. When Rick reaches for his wallet to pay, the bartender doesn't let him. "Dwain takes care of everything," he says.

Of course, he does, Rick thinks.

Rick thanks him and then leans on the bar to watch the action on the dance floor. Jeremy's swaying with the rhythm, chatting and smiling with everyone, making it look so easy. Rick knows he's lucky they're together. Jeremy has always had the edge on him in the relationship: the better-adjusted one, the one with more friends, the guy with the better job, the better body. Rick knows he's got some work to do on himself. Now he's wondering if Jeremy has figured it out, too.

"You okay?" the bartender asks.

Rick realizes he's been staring. "Sure."

The bartender gestures at the dance floor, where Jeremy is now twirling to the beat. "That's your boyfriend?"

Rick takes a giant gulp of his drink. "Apparently."

The bartender pops open a beer bottle, slides it down the bar and into the waiting hands of one of the guests. "Yeah, this group moves pretty fast," he continues. "You okay with that?"

"I think so. I mean, I want to be . . ."

The bartender smiles. "I'm Manuel, but everyone here calls me Manny."

Rick shakes his hand and orders another drink. Manny's perky and easy to talk to and it's not until Rick's third drink that Jeremy shows back up. He holds a silver object to his nose and takes a giant snort.

"Sharing?" Rick asks.

"You sure?" Jeremy says, glancing for the quickest moment at Rick's wrist. Rick instinctively flips his arm over to hide the scar.

Rick can't keep the edge out of his voice. "That was a long time ago, Jeremy. Give me the bumper, will you?" Jeremy relents and hands over the ketamine. Rick lifts it to his nose, inhales it deeply. The drug stings as it coats his sinus passages, leaves a bitter chalky taste in his throat which he washes down with his cocktail.

And then Jeremy's off to the dance floor, peeling off his shirt, swinging it above his head, being Jeremy. A couple of men spot him and make their move. Their hands paw at his smooth, muscular chest, trace greedily over the tattoo on his right arm, and make their way down to his hairless belly.

His guts knotting up with envy, Rick watches as long as he can until he starts to see tracers of light. A tickling sensation rises up inside his stomach. His legs go rubbery, and when he looks down at his feet, the floor looks like a giant sinkhole, the edges collapsing on themselves. Instantly, he knows the drug was a bad idea, that it hasn't been enough time since rehab. The music is pounding now, pounding so, so loud. Dwain has jumped up on a raised platform, glow-sticks in hand, and he's dancing like a lunatic. Below him, the men are grooving on the dance floor, some of them are coupled up, gyrating against each other. And then everything goes slow motion, the music, too, the bass line blaring like a freight train, and suddenly Rick can't make out Jeremy anymore, can't make out anyone's face. Everyone seems to be shrouded in darkness, and all he sees is a group of half-dressed demons pumping their arms up and down like they're summoning some powerful force out of thin air.

It's all he can do to get away from the crowd, to get some air. He staggers away, doesn't stop until he's ducked behind the trailer. There, he drops to his knees to gulp cool air into his lungs. It feels great, until he catches a whiff of animal dung.

That's when he hears a snuffling sound, the bleating of an animal.

He turns to find a bearded, horned beast glaring back at him with awful yellow eyes. He gets up to run, but his feet are jelly and won't go where he wants. He ends up stumbling back to the dance floor. The last thing he remembers is the bartender—Marcos?—Manny? jumping over the bar, running toward him, but by then it's too late. He's falling, arms pinwheeling, careening into one of the picnic tables, sending chips and dips flying everywhere, and then everything goes black.

"I should have told you about the goat," Jeremy whispers to Rick the next night, over a mouthful of meat.

Rick's still nauseous from the night before, and irritable—he spent most of day in the tent nursing a hangover—but he can't stop staring at the poor beast stretched out on the buffet table, steam rising from its charred hide. He pushes away his plate of potato salad and cold macaroni and gawks at the crowd. The men are lined up with their plates, pulling meat from the goat's ribcage with tongs.

"Don't stare," Jeremy says. "It's rude. And eat something, for God's sake."

"I'm not eating goat," Rick says, eyeing a corner of the serving table, where a slow drip of grease is pooling on the pavilion floor. A fly buzzes on the goat's charred neck.

"It's tradition for Dwain. His family carried it over from Greece when they settled here a long time ago. Anyway, how is it different from eating a burger?"

"I'm not eating a fucking goat, Jeremy."

Their argument is interrupted by Dwain, who makes his way to the front of the pavilion, clinking his wine glass. "A toast," he says, lifting the glass high. The men put down their forks and give him their attention. "To the meat which sustains us. To the moon and to the fields and to the great mysteries of the eternal grove. Salut."

"Salut," comes the response, and the men clink their plastic cups.

"Look, eat, or don't. I don't really care," Jeremy whispers, popping the last piece of goat into his mouth. "I'm going to mingle. You good?"

Rick nods, but he doesn't mean it. Jeremy could obviously care less how he feels. He flits over to the next table to talk to a group of guys.

Rick doesn't blame him, wouldn't want to be hanging out with himself either. Shit, what a waste of a day. He had vague memories of being carried to the tent, where he slept fitfully the rest of the night, and woke up feeling lousy. Jeremy came every few hours to check in, bringing him water and wet washcloths for his face before running off again to hike with his new friends, or whatever. Around noon, the smell of the cooking goat spread across the campground, and Rick had to step out of the tent to puke.

At the table, Rick's pushing food around his plate when someone plops down next to him. It's Manny.

"You should eat something," Manny says. "A man needs his strength."

Rick's face flushes with embarrassment. "Jeremy said you were the one who helped me to the tent. Thank you."

"No worries," Manny says. "This crowd, right? Work hard, play hard."

"I didn't mean to ruin your night," Rick says.

"You did not," Manny says. Under the table, he grabs Rick's hand and gives it a squeeze.

It feels strange, holding hands with another guy with Jeremy so close nearby. But it's nice, too. Rick's starting to smile when Manny's thumb caresses his forearm, glides up onto his wrist, rolls across the scar. Instantly, Manny's expression changes.

Rick jerks his hand away. "I think I need to go."

"Wait," Manny says, but Rick is already butting into the crowd Jeremy is talking to. Jeremy's chugging back a shot of Fireball when Rick puts his arm around him, pulls him away from the crowd.

"I'm sitting this one out," Rick says.

"Jesus, Rick. Tonight's the big party—"

"Look, I'm just not up to it. I'm sorry," Rick says, walking away.

"You always do this!" Jeremy shouts after him.

Rick knows, yeah, he does. It's all he can think about as he crawls into the tent, where he stays until he drifts off to sleep.

In the tent, Rick is dreaming.

He wakes Jeremy with a kiss, a caress on his face. Still a little drunk from the dinner, Jeremy is slow to wake.

"I want you," Rick says.

"Now?" Jeremy asks. "What time is it?"

"Doesn't matter. Let's do it. Out in the woods."

Jeremy, dog that he is, can't resist. He smiles in assent.

Rick slings his backpack onto his shoulder and leads Jeremy along one of the trails. They find a clearing near a copse of bushes and begin to kiss. Jeremy is slow to warm up, but within minutes he's eager, ready, naked and sprawling in the cool, soft grass.

"Close your eyes," Rick says.

"Rick Sloane, you devil," Jeremy says. But the wry smile on his face tells Rick he's into it. He shuts his eyes, and Rick reaches into the backpack for a knife.

"Lord Pan," Rick calls out into the night. "For your loyalty, I offer this payment of blood."

The knife enters near Jeremy's navel and his scream splits the calm of the night. Rick stuffs his shirt into Jeremy's mouth and works quickly, slicing the knife up to the hollow of Jeremy's chest. Rick tosses the knife aside and plunges his fingers into the wet sticky mess, digging them deeper and deeper into the warmth. He feels no emotion: not sadness, or remorse, only a surge of adrenaline as Jeremy's ribcage cracks under his knuckles and viscera and tissue snap away under his unyielding assault. There, his penetrating fingers find what they seek. He tightens his grip around the slick orb of Jeremy's heart and lifts it up, gleaming, throbbing, squirting, as an offering to the moon.

From the darkness, something catches his eyes: a dark figure crouched in the shadows. It's up on a tree limb, watching him with glowing red eyes.

Rick feels no fear, only a sense of awe, of wonder, of excitement.

Rick wakes with a gasp, his heart thudding in his chest. Through the opening of the tent, he can see the moon shining bright and full. He rummages for his watch. It's past midnight, and Jeremy's not there.

He lays his head down, takes a few deep breaths, tries to forget the dream he'd just had. He turns his thoughts to Jeremy. He remembers the day they moved in together, when they'd picked up the keys to their new apartment, how they'd rushed out to Target immediately after to pick out décor, how they'd cuddled so tightly after making love in their starchy new bedsheets, staring into each other's eyes for hours in silence, their hands exploring their bodies. It had been true love, something Rick had never experienced before. Jeremy made him feel like it was all possible.

So what if Jeremy wanted to have a little fun? That *was* why they'd come out here this weekend, right? Rick had agreed to go on the trip, so could anyone really blame Jeremy for acting like he was? At least Jeremy had said what he wanted out loud. And what did Rick want?

He wants Jeremy, more than anything. And if he has to share him with others every once in a while to keep him, so be it.

Being with Jeremy is better than being alone.

Rick groans out loud. Christ, what an ass he'd made of himself today. Was it too late to turn things around?

He sets his jaw and steps out into the night with a renewed sense of purpose. The tents are quiet, the flaps left open, empty. He makes his way to the pavilion. The food is put away. The men are gone, but they were here recently. Melting ice clinks in a paper cup.

There's music in the distance, some kind of flute.

He finds a trail, creeps along in the moonlight, following the sound. It's several minutes before he smells the torches. Ahead, there's a clearing and movement.

The flutist comes into view first. He's wiry and naked except for a black rabbit mask that covers his head.

And then Rick sees the mass of writhing bodies. The campers are all naked except for their masks. Each seems to be wearing the visage of a different animal: a fox, a raccoon, a skunk. They dance together in a tight circle, their arms and legs interconnected, their bodies swaying. When the flute dips to a low note, they all crouch, and Rick sees they're dancing around a stone table.

It's what's on the table that makes him shudder.

Two of the men are fucking, their bodies glistening with sweat. One of them is on his back, his knees spread out wide to receive the other. His face is obscured by a pig mask. But the tattoo on his arm gives him away.

It's Jeremy.

The man pumping between Jeremy's knees is bare-chested, and his head is thrown back in ecstasy. His lower limbs are covered in thick hairy leggings and he's got large, curling horns affixed to his head. There's no mistaking it's Dwain. With his potbelly jutting out over his thrashing pelvis, he'd look comical if not for the ornate knife he clutches in one hand and the butchered rabbit lying next to them, dripping red with blood. Dwain rubs his hand on the rabbit and smears red all over his chest, his nipples, his belly. Another stroke of his hand anoints Jeremy as well, his shoulders, his crotch, his face.

This is no ordinary orgy.

It's a goddam sex cult.

Rick stifles a scream. He wants to look away but can't. In his chest, his heart is pounding, pounding. He takes a step back to recoil into the shadows, and a twig cracks under his feet.

He may as well have fired a pistol.

The men turn in his direction and the music stops. Jeremy's blue eyes stare coldly out from the eyeholes of the pig mask.

Then Rick does scream, flinging himself into the woods and back down the shadowy trail. Tears blur his vision, and he turns back to see if he's been followed, which is why he doesn't see the person in front of him until he's smacked into them.

It's Manny. He grabs Rick in a bear hug and holds him tightly.

"Shh," he says, over and over. "Calm down."

Rick struggles, but Manny is too strong, and anyway, Rick doesn't sense any malice. It's a moment before Rick stops shaking, and another before he's able to catch his breath again. Already, he can feel the sense of shock subsiding.

"You need to face this," Manny says. "It's now or never."

Rick nods, wipes the tears away from his eyes.

Together, they walk back to the clearing.

With Manny at his side, Rick stands before the men, who are all naked except for their animal masks. The torches crackle in the night, heightening the tension. Inside the pig mask, Jeremy's eyes lock onto Rick's with a mix of frustration and confusion. Everything's awkward and quiet until Rick takes a deep breath and finds the nerve to speak. "What is this, Jeremy?"

Jeremy removes his mask, takes a step toward Rick.

"I'm sorry," he says. "I thought you were asleep."

Rick's no longer capable of concealing his anger, nor is he trying to. "You're sorry? For what, Jeremy? For doing this? Or sorry that I caught you?"

"Rick—"

"No, I'm going to say what's on my mind, like I should have a long time ago. You said you wanted an open relationship. Fine. I came out here to give it the old college try. So sue me if I'm having a hard time watching the man I love fuck other guys. But this, Jeremy, this isn't some random kink. This is some perverted, twisted shit. Look at you. The masks, the blood, what the hell?"

"Not hell," Dwain says. "This has nothing to do with Christian beliefs like heaven and hell. We do this in honor of the Great God Pan, who dwelled on the earth long before."

"Shut up, Dwain!" Rick shouts. "You're the reason for this insanity, the spider at the center of this sick, twisted web. What's the point of all this? You think your little sex party is going to summon Pan?"

"Not summon. He is already here. He has always been here. The sex ritual only aligns us with the things he represents."

"And what is that, pray tell?"

"Pleasure. Power. Unfettered freedom."

"God, listen to this bullshit . . ."

"Rick, that's enough." Jeremy steps between them, obviously trying to deescalate the tension. In his voice, there's an earnestness that catches Rick off guard. "Now that you know about this, you have a choice. You can expose us to the world, tell everyone what you've seen here."

Dwain leans in, inserting himself into the conversation. "Though why anyone would believe a recovering drug addict is beyond me."

"Dwain!" Jeremy scolds. "Knock it off."

Rick fixes his eyes coldly on Dwain. "I doubt I'd do that, even if it would serve you all right. What's the other choice?"

"You could join us. You'll get used to it. You may even end up liking it."

Rick shrugs his shoulders. "This isn't me. I'm sorry, it never will be." He turns on his heels, begins to head back to the tents.

Manny runs after him. "Rick, wait."

Rick turns on him with a fury that surprises even him. "Leave me the hell alone," he says, snarling. "You twisted fucks."

The moon above glows like a spotlight, so bright it almost hurts Rick's eyes. It's an expected side-effect from the drugs, Rick knows; he's been through it many times in the past. His thoughts turn to Jeremy. Besides Jeremy's penchant for ritualistic sex parties, he'd never been good at hiding things. Like his secret stash of Molly, tucked away in his backpack. About an hour ago, Rick had stolen two pills, popped them into his mouth, and washed them down with a few quick beers. Now he's feeling no pain at all. The way he sees it, Jeremy owes him for this fucked up weekend. In the morning, Jeremy or one of the campers will give him a ride back to Dallas. If they don't, he'll hitchhike. If that doesn't work . . . well, then he doesn't know what he'll do. It's not like he has anyone he can call to come pick him up.

"Oh, well," he says. "Fuck it." Until then, he's going to trip his balls off in this clearing he's found. All by himself, like it was meant to be.

He remembers a saying he learned in Narcotics Anonymous: *Insanity is doing the same thing over and over again but expecting different results.*

"I'll tell ya what insanity is," he says, aware that he's slurring his words but also not giving a shit. "Grown ass adults fucking each other in animal masks."

The thought cracks him up, and he doubles over with laughter. A flood of dopamine surges in his brain, making him feel wonderful. It's the best he's felt in days. Hell, weeks. A year?

"Child," a deep voice says. "Why do you torment yourself so?"

Rick looks up to find he's not alone. On the other side of the clearing, a few yards away, there's a man sitting on the stump of a fallen tree. How had he snuck up on Rick like that? He should have made some kind of sound with the underbrush surrounding the clearing. From somewhere deep in the woods, a coyote howls in the night.

Moonbeams filter through holes in the treetops, hitting Rick directly in the eyes, making it difficult to focus. He staggers to his feet, squinting to make out his newfound observer.

The stranger isn't any of the campers he's seen so far. He's a wiry bastard, sinewy and muscular. A mane of thick, wavy hair curls around his face, and—is it the drugs, or is he wearing a headpiece that makes it look like he has horns? The man has a striking, boxy face, with a long beard jutting from his chin. His complexion is dark like melted caramel and his body is covered in dark, curly hair. A scarlet kilt made of crushed velvet is wrapped around his waist. He watches Rick with one foot propped up on the stump and an elbow resting casually on his knee.

"I saw you," Rick says, grinning so hard his teeth grind together. "In the woods, on the drive out here. Are you supposed to be Pan or something?"

The stranger stares at him with eyes as wild as the untamed wilderness. "You refuse to give in," he says. His voice is unlike anything Rick's ever heard. Deep, throaty, and dripping with masculinity and vigor. "I like that."

That's when Rick realizes the woods have grown quiet. No crickets chirp. No owls hoot. Even the coyotes are silent. The air, too, has grown still. It's like the entire scene is encased in amber, like one of those paperweights with bugs trapped in them. Rick finds he's unable to move.

The stranger rises from the stump. "This way, child." He turns and makes his way into the woods.

Rick feels hypnotized watching him. There's something strong about his movement, the way his muscles flex under his skin. Stealthy. Majestic. Animal. Every step exudes confidence, purpose.

Rick begins to move, or rather, he watches his feet moving. He feels . . . well, he doesn't know what he's feeling. Strange. Different. And not just because of the drugs. He looks out past his feet, to the footprints the stranger leaves behind. Rick doesn't see footprints, though. What he sees are the cloven prints of a wild hooved animal.

He puts his foot into one of those prints, and then another, following the stranger deep into the trees, and deeper still.

Civilized Homes
William Jensen

No one wanted the house. It was old and falling apart with rotten floorboards and a sinking roof. Mold, like bruises, wide and violet and deep, smeared the walls. There was no electricity. No water. Outside, the brush had grown wild, thick, and ropey, stabbing through the porch and strangling the posts and beams. The place had stood vacant for a hundred years, unclaimed, decayed, and alone.

Nash had forgotten about the house until a small-town lawyer told him he'd inherited it. The place had been passed down from one descendant to another but ignored. No one cared to fix it. The repairs would take too long, be too costly. No one had managed to sell it or hadn't bothered to try. Now a distant uncle had died, and Nash had been named as the beneficiary. The last time he'd seen the house, Nash was six and with his grandfather who wanted to check how much damage occurred after a storm. That had been his only visit.

"This could really change things," he said. He drove southwest from Austin through the hill country with his girlfriend, Laura Dell, who gazed out the window as they sped down the highway.

"I can't believe we're homeowners, at least technically," she said.

"I bet we can flip it," said Nash. "It's a big Victorian. Lots of rooms. We'll put in modern conveniences, a fresh coat of paint, and sell it to some Californians or to retired boomers."

"How much work will that take?"

"I don't know. If it's really bad, we'll tear down the structure and sell off the land. Somebody will want to build a McDonalds there."

The lawyer, Mr. Blackwood, had agreed to meet them at the property, which stood at the end of a pink gravel road, guarded by a small hill and groves of cedar, live oak, and mesquite. He was already pacing in front of the porch when Nash and Laura Dell arrived. He was short and balding with plucks of silver hair at the sides of his skull, and he wore an orange bow tie. He didn't look either of them in the eye when he shook their hands.

"I'll need you to sign a few things," said Mr. Blackwood producing a series of papers, "but generally it's straight forward and done. I have the keys in my pocket."

Nash used the hood of his car as a desk to sign the documents while Laura Dell gawked at the house. The walls, brittle and gray, reminded her of bones, like an excavated grave. The roof slanted dark and crooked and sharp. The windows were all boarded except for one at the top center, and this had a baseball-size hole in its corner. Nothing made any noise. There wasn't even a breeze.

"So we're allowed to do whatever we want?" said Nash.

"I suppose so," said Mr. Blackwood. "But I have no say in those matters."

They followed Mr. Blackwood onto the porch. Laura Dell noticed Mr. Blackwood wore large cowboy boots, as if they were two-sizes too big. The boots were black, but she observed they were snakeskin. He stopped by the door, jangling the keys from his coat.

"When was this built?" said Laura Dell.

"At the end of the nineteenth century," said Mr. Blackwood. "It was constructed by Captain Rice, a Texas Ranger who fought in the U.S.-Mexico War and then with the Confederacy. He is the man this county is named after. He died upstairs not long after completion when he was seventy-five. When his wife passed a decade later, their oldest son inherited it, but he was killed in the trenches of the first world war. After that it fell into a limbo of siblings, cousins, children and spouses."

"Captain Rice?" said Nash.

"I believe he would be your great-great-grandfather. There's a historical society in town that could tell you more if you're interested."

"Nah," said Nash. "I think we're good."

"As you wish."

Mr. Blackwood unlocked the door. A dense musk of soil and clay, rancid and spoiled, clawed at Laura Dell's eyes and nose. She nearly gagged. Knox covered his mouth. Mr. Blackwood stood patiently by the jam with clasped hands. His face stayed unmoved and wrinkled and leathery and pale. Laura Dell peered inside. Leaves and dirt cloaked the floor. A broken chair lay spewed in pieces to the left. She heard something scurry away and into the walls, which made her gasp but not scream.

"Gross," she said.

"I will now depart you," said Mr. Blackwood. He handed the keys to Nash. "You have my number if you have any questions. Apologies for not staying longer. I do not like to be here after sunset."

Laura Dell watched Mr. Blackwood creak down the steps and toward his Buick. He walked neither slowly nor quickly but straight forward and with his head low, his shoulders hunched. The sky, blurred and overcast, mirrored the drab earth.

"Let's check it out," said Nash.

Dusk dripped like a halved peach in the west. Laura Dell sensed the temperature cooling, too. Though she'd been excited on the drive down, now that she saw the house in its deteriorating isolation, she was left with a stone of hesitation and worry in her stomach. Nash took out his phone as a flashlight and went in first, smiling and snickering. Laura Dell paused but soon followed.

The first-floor sprawled dim and decayed. Cobwebs caked the walls. Dust scattered over everything. The parlor reeked of animal feces and mud. Grains of glass dusted the floor. The kitchen in the back was slick with grime. Cockroaches scuttled on the counters and in the sink. When Nash suggested going upstairs, Laura Dell said she wanted to leave.

"It's a dump," she said. "There's no way we'll get this shaped up to sell to anyone. It needs to be condemned. It's a health hazard."

"Where's your sense of adventure? This is ours, this is for us. Let's explore the other rooms. Maybe we'll find gold."

Before she could protest, Nash jogged ahead. He leapt up the staircase only for the third step to break. Nash braced against the rail, saving himself. He cursed a little and progressed. He made it to the top and waited for Laura Dell who navigated her way carefully while staying close to the wall. The landing stretched into a long hallway, reaching into darkness. Laura Dell held her breath.

To the left was one door, which Laura Dell assumed led to the attic. They tried this door first, but it was locked.

"Don't you have the keys," she said.

Nash fumbled with the ring of keys Mr. Blackwood had given him, but none of them fit. He rattled the doorknob. He pulled and pushed. The door never shifted. He shrugged and said they should look at the other rooms and then they could leave. The first one opened to only dust and a filthy rug, sour and stained. The second room contained an antique desk, still solid and standing. Nash went and opened the drawers but found nothing. The last room, which must have been the master bedroom, was large with several windows but contained only a rocking chair, rickety and frail.

"Okay," said Laura Dell, "we've seen everything. Can we go?"

Nash panned his phone across the room. The light shined into one corner and slowly illuminated the walls inch by inch. Nash aimed it carefully and steadily. The beam fell upon the rocking chair.

A hot breath blew through Laura Dell's hair.

She shrieked and turned around, swatting at her neck.

"What are you doing?" said Nash.

"Something… I felt something," she said.

"What?"

"I'm going to wait in the car."

"Fine. I'll be out in a bit. I'm going to look around some more."

Laura Dell was halfway down the stairs, her hands against the wall to guide her through the dark, when she heard a woman's voice, soft but stern, like a scolding mother's whisper, say, "Look at what you've done."

Laura Dell turned around; her breath caught in her throat. She saw only blackness. She called out to Nash but heard no response. She called again.

"Nash, did you hear that?"

Nash didn't reply.

The air in her lungs froze, and her mouth turned dry. She didn't want to move. She didn't want to stay, but she didn't want to leave. She made her way back to the top of the stairs. The door to the master bedroom remained open. Slowly, she stepped forward. She took out her phone to light her path. Nash wasn't there. She scanned the floors and the walls, finding only the rocking chair.

Laura Dell stared at the chair, halfway expecting it to rock on its own, when she heard a door creak. She turned and saw that the locked door to the attic had opened. Her breath came heavy and deep. She didn't call for Nash. She tried to stay soundless and still. Maybe Nash had fiddled with the lock, gotten it loose somehow. If he was up there, she'd tell him to hurry up. She wanted to be back home and with all the lights on. She didn't care how much the house was worth.

She stepped cautiously forward. The pathway into the attic was narrow. She shined her phone with an outstretched hand. She thought she heard breathing but not her own. The attic lay dusty, the air thick and stale. Nash wasn't there. By the one window, which she'd noticed outside earlier as the one with the baseball-sized hole, sat a large chest. She didn't know why, but she felt compelled to open it, so she went and kneeled and pried open the lid.

At first she thought it was a rug, bearskin perhaps. It looked black and thick and like fur. But when she reached in, she realized it wasn't one item but dozens. Hair. Black hair. And attached to the hair were leathery patches, tan and red. She didn't comprehend at first. But then her thoughts focused.

Scalps.

It was full of human scalps. Mexican and Comanche and Apache. Women and Children, and warriors of indigenous tribes. Taken over a century ago, cut from the dead and the dying.

Laura Dell gagged and thought she was about to retch. She stared at her hands in terror knowing what she'd just been touching.

In the dark corners of the attic, she saw legs, naked and blue in the gloom start to walk forward. Then she heard the woman's voice again, this time hissing, "Look at what you've done."

The pale legs began to emerge from the shadows. Walking toward her. She bolted down the stairs, her screams so loud she heard nothing else.

She found Nash in the master bedroom, sitting in the rocking chair, swaying back and forth, forward and back. She couldn't see him well, but she rushed to him, her face wet with tears and spittle. She pawed at his shoulders to stir him, to make him run with her far away. Her eyes quickly adjusted and saw the top of his hair was gone. His blood slathered skull was exposed like a horrible halo. Nash stared straight ahead, wide-eyed but lifeless. Laura Dell stepped back in repulsion.

A breath fluttered across her neck again.

"Your turn," said the voice.

Weeks later, Laura Dell's parents drove down from Dallas and visited Mr. Blackwood's office near the small town's square. No one had heard from Laura Dell or her boyfriend in over a month. Mr. Blackwood sat at his desk and wouldn't make eye contact with either Laura Dell's father or mother.

"Our daughter said her boyfriend inherited a house around here," said the father.

"Yes, it's off Farm Road 1126."

"Can you take us there?" said the mother.

"Not at the moment," said Mr. Blackwood.

"And why not?" said the father.

Mr. Blackwood sighed and kept his sight down.

"It's getting late," he said, "and I do not like to be there after sunset."

Gold of the Ancianos
Todd Elliott

Thunderclouds flickered like great Chinese lanterns floating in the night as they rolled over the prairie outside Gethsemane, Texas. Inside the dark bunkhouse that faced the road, Carlito Navarro lay on his bunk and stared through the screen door, savoring the spring breeze that passed through the building. It was cool now, but the prairie would be an inferno in late summer when he returned to harvest the cotton he and the others had sowed today.

Out in the night, lightning illuminated a shape on the road that meandered back to town. Squinting, Carlito tried to make it out, but it was too dark. He rose from the bunk and leaned against the door, peering through the torn screen.

"What is it?" Martinez asked, looking up from his rough hands as he whittled on a piece of wood.

Carlito squinted into the rain, finally making out the shape. "It is a *viejo*—like you. A *viejo* with a burro."

"*Viejo?*" Martinez cocked an eyebrow. He set aside his wood carving and stood up to go to the door.

There on the road an elderly man dressed in a sombrero and a poncho guided a gray burro laden with a heavy chest. Rain poured upon him, but he paid no attention. He looked like something from the revolutionary days of old, back when musket and cannon fire echoed across the prairie.

To Martinez, Carlito said. "The rain will wash him away." And then he pushed open the screen door and called out into the night, "*¡Abuelito, venga aquí!*"

Martinez shushed him and pulled him back in the shadows of their shelter. "We don't want him to see us, *muchacho*."

"Why?" Carlito asked.

"Because, my young and naïve friend," Martinez pointed out into the darkness, "*that* is the ghost of *El Peón*."

"So," Carlito scoffed. "We are also *peones*. Why should we fear him?"

Martinez tucked his chin into his neck and gazed at him under hooded eyebrows. "Because, if he sees us, we will die."

"What's all the yelling about?" a twangy Anglo voice said, startling them. Bob McIntyre shone his lantern into the bunkhouse as he stepped through the rear door with rain dripping from his straw cowboy hat.

The two Mexicanos peered at him, gauging his expression. Even though McIntyre was a good man, as good as any they had worked for in years, neither of them wanted to lose their job on the farm. McIntyre was not rich—he was only a sharecropper. The land belonged to a man who lived in downtown Gethsemane and drank iced tea on his front porch as his black maid cleaned the house and cooked his supper. McIntyre could not afford to pay them money.He hired them for seasonal jobs and paid them in livestock—chickens, hogs, or goats—which they carted down to Los Gatos, the shantytown on Wailing Woman Creek.

Martinez nodded at Carlito. "My amigo saw the ghost of *El Peón*." His eyebrows danced as he said it.

"El Pee-on?" McIntyre laughed. He set the lantern down on the rough-hewn wooden table, unwrapped a plug of tobacco, and cut a piece.

"Who is *El Peón*?" Carlito asked. "And why is he a ghost?"

"I heard of that one," McIntyre mumbled as he shoved the tobacco into his mouth. Pulling up a chair, he nodded to Martinez. "I think you better tell it, compadre. That story belongs to your people."

Taking one last look to see if the *viejo* had heard him cry out, Carlito saw nothing but the relentless rain and sporadic flashes of lightning. He stepped away from the door and sat down on his bunk.

Martinez smiled and returned to his chair where he had been carving. "Back when Texas belonged to us—"

Twisting the corner of his lip, McIntyre spat tobacco juice on the floor. "Don't you mean back when Texas fought for its independence from that tyrant, Santa Anna?"

"*Ay, pinche gringo*," Martinez chuckled, then winked at Carlito. "That malicious murdering pig, Santa Anna." He also spat on the floor and continued. "During the Texas Revolution, when General Cós was garrisoned at the Alamo in San Antonio, he received a large shipment of gold from Mexico to pay all the troops in Texas. Shortly after it arrived, an army of mercenaries—"

"Patriots," McIntyre insisted.

Martinez smiled and cast another glance at Carlito. "Yes, yes. Those *patriots* assaulted the Alamo, took the gold, and—"

"And they allowed General Cós to leave with his life, like true gentlemen in combat," McIntyre finished for him. "Not like what Santa Anna did later, by the way."

"Señor, would you like to tell the story?"

McIntyre shook his head. "I'm sure you'll tell him your version after I leave anyway. Go ahead. I'll stop interrupting."

Martinez turned to Carlito, smiling now. "So, the gringos had the Alamo *and* the gold, you see. But that is just the beginning of the story. General Santa Anna came north with nothing to pay his troops, so he promised them a fortune to be found in the Alamo. As you know, Santa Anna defeated the pirates—"

McIntyre harrumphed and rolled his eyes.

Martinez ignored him and continued, "They retrieved the gold, but instead of paying his troops immediately, Santa Anna carried it along in his wagon train. If he was to hold on to Texas, he had to destroy the Anglo settlements near *San Felipe de Austín*—where Houston is now—but if he paid his troops first, they would all leave and go back home."

"His own soldiers tried to steal the gold, so Santa Anna decided to bury it on the way to San Felipe so that he could maintain his command until the war was over. He picked an old *peón*—a farmhand—from the countryside, with his burro packed with the gold, and marched him out in the middle of the night to a spot between Wailing Woman Creek and where Gethsemane lies today. *El Peón* found a good spot and started digging. When he was done, he put the gold within—and Santa Anna shot him in the gut. He fell into the hole and Santa Anna buried him alive with the treasure. After that, *el general* pressed his troops towards *San Felipe*, where they were defeated by the gringo mercenaries."

"*Patriots*," McIntyre interjected.

Martinez rose an eyebrow and pointed toward the door. "And on dark nights in March, sometimes the ghost of *El Peón* walks with his gold-laden burro up to the very site where that treasure still lies."

"What are we waiting for?" Carlito said as he jumped out of his bed.

"The catch is," McIntyre said, "that though you can see *El Peón*, and follow him to the treasure, if he turns around and sees you, you will die."

"No," Carlito said. A look of disbelief washed across his face.

"It's true, it's true," McIntyre said. "Why, last year, I hired two men from Los Gatos just like y'all. You might remember them, Sancho and Miguel Rodriquez."

"But they vanished—"

McIntyre nodded. "It was a night like tonight, and we had the same discussion. Sancho had seen *El Peón*, and we told the same story. The next morning, I found their beds empty. They had left all their clothes and belongings behind. I took everything back to their widows, and they said that the old witch down on Wailing Woman Creek told them that El Peón had taken them away."

"*Dios mío,*" Carlito said as he crossed himself. "I remember that."

"So, you boys don't go making the same mistake, you hear?"

"Yes, señor," Martinez said.

McIntyre bid them good night and went back to the main house where he lived, which sat back farther from the road. The front door slammed shut as he left.

Lightning flickered across the sky, painting the white building in stark contrast to the bare grey dirt of the yard.

Martinez turned back to Carlito. "So, what do you think?"

Carlito scowled. "I think it's a story gringos tell us."

"About *El Peón*?"

"No. About the Rodriquez brothers." Carlito pulled on his boots. "If there is a ghost headed to a treasure, I want to follow it and find it for myself. Maybe then, one day, I'll have my own land to rent to gringo sharecroppers while *I* live in a house in Gethsemane and drink cervezas while my own *peones* cook and clean for me." He stomped his boot heels on the planks of the bunkhouse floor to firmly seat his feet within, slapped on his sombrero, and strode out into the night.

Lightning snaked across the sky, leaving in its wake peals of thunder that shook the road beneath them. The winds drove rain into their faces and torrents poured down the hilly incline of blacktop, visible in the flashing night only as a rippling ribbon that writhed at their feet.

Ahead, the gray blur bobbed in the darkness with the steady gait of a burro.

"Perhaps he will kill us with pneumonia," Martinez said. "Or send lightning down for a quicker death."

"*Jajaja*," Carlito laughed, his voice carrying on the wind. "I look forward to seeing how the *abuelito viejo* will kill us." Raising his arms to the sky, he challenged the night, "If he has the power to bring down lightning, let him do so!"

Martinez shushed him. "We must remain quiet so that *El Peón* doesn't hear us."

"But he is a hundred yards away," Carlito scoffed with a wave of his hand. But he fell silent anyway, paying heed to the warning.

For another mile, they followed and gained ground. The gray shape in the darkness became clearer—the burro with a wooden chest on its back. A shadow of white walked along its side—*El Peón* with his white wool trousers and white shirt—the tail hanging wet down to his knees. His brown poncho cut a V-shape into his outline, and the wide-brimmed straw sombrero canted down to shield his face from the rain.

"Why do you think he will kill us if he sees us?" Carlito whispered, barely audible over the wind.

"I don't know. Perhaps he thinks that whoever follows is Santa Anna, and he wants revenge."

Stepping off the road, *El Peón* led the burro into a trail that rose up a gentle slope. He disappeared into the cover of the wet brush, but the burro stood out like a beacon in the darkness, as if the gold it carried emanated a haunted glow visible through the aged wooden chest.

"Just as I thought," Martinez said. "He is headed to the old Payaya burial site."

"Payaya?"

"Yes," Martinez cocked his eyebrow. "The legend says that *El Peón* was a Payaya half-breed who lived near Wailing Woman Creek. It would make sense that he would bring it here."

"Por qué?"

"*Porque está* in the middle of nowhere, and most people are too scared to come here."

"Why?"

"What do you think, *tonto*?" Martinez glared at him. "Ghosts and vampires live here."

Carlito shook his head and took the lead.

The old trail climbed up the slope that rose up from the prairie. The terrain grew steeper as they ventured farther to the peak of the last hill, where they viewed the entire area. The hill where they stood was one of a ring of hills that encircled a massive depression, at least five-square miles in area. Within the brush-choked bowl, mounds rose in ornate patterns that ran together in spirals and paisleys of earth.

The men stood in awe at the sight of the Payaya burial lands. None had trespassed here for a hundred years, not since *El Peón* had died upon a bed of gold.

Behind them, thunder boomed and lightning illuminated the prairie to the west as the next volley rumbled forward. Below, a pinprick of light marked the tiny window of McIntyre's house, and miles beyond that, a few newly electrified streetlights shone in downtown Gethsemane.

El Peón continued on the trail as it eased down the side of the hill in a series of switchbacks. His burro glowed in the stormy night.

"What will you do with your share of the gold?" Carlito asked.

"My share?" Martinez shrugged. "What else, but take it home to my family? Why else would I be here? I can buy a nice home for my wife, and pay for my mother's medicine, and keep my *hija* in school."

Carlito laughed out loud. "You are so sentimental!"

Martinez cupped his hand over Carlito's mouth. "For the love of God, *cállete tu boca*," he hissed.

Carlito shuffled away from him and complained, "Shut your own mouth, you're talking as well."

El Peón climbed the side of a mound, following the trail that spiraled around it until, finally, he and his burro climbed inside the crater at its peak.

Fighting the stiffening winds, and increasing downpour, Carlito and Martinez avoided torrents and waterfalls of cascading water as they made their ascent. Creeping to the top of the ridge, they watched as *El Peón* retrieved a shovel from his burro's pack. It looked more like a pickaxe than a modern shovel—battered and pitted like a lost relic from an ancient war. With a feeble swing, he sunk its spoon-shaped blade into the sodden earth.

Lightning flashed, painting his bent body in brilliant white light and casting his shadow across the crater—a scrawny, tattered revenant clutching the aged wooden spade. He released the handle and gazed up.

For a full minute he stood, peering into the roiling night sky as if hypnotized by the flickering cavalcade of clouds.

"What is wrong with him?" Carlito asked.

Martinez shushed.

El Peón cocked his ear and glanced around.

"He heard us," Martinez said through clenched teeth. "Whatever you do, do not look at him." He ducked back behind the ridge and closed his eyes. Carlito did the same.

On the other side of the crater, a sound rose through the trees. At first it whined and hissed like the approach of a million angry bees out of the wild brush. Crescendoing in ferocity to a roar, it barreled toward them, casting forth an accelerating wind as it advanced.

Carlito could stand it no longer. Eyes wide open, he peered over the ridge.

El Peón turned toward him—the weathered brim of the sombrero unveiled a fleshless skull face stained brown from a hundred years of burial under rich, fertile soil. Lacking a jawbone, the mouth hung open in an eternal cry, and weeping bloodshot eyes filled the sockets like poached eggs. *El Peón* stared at Carlito cowering there just beyond the lip of the crater.

Lashing at the mesquite trees, the winds shook their limbs back and forth and pressed the grass flat against the ground. The cacophony of angry bees transformed into a raging freight train roaring on phantom tracks straight through the heart of this holy ground.

Reacting to the crashing coming toward them, Martinez gazed up, ready to flee, but, in doing so, revealed himself behind the ridge of the crater so that he, too, was visible. He found *El Peón*'s gaze upon him, but it was the least of his worries now. A terrific volley of lightning exploded the night sky. In its brilliant white glare, an evil black coil descended from the roiling skies and touched the earth with a deadly kiss. Backlit among the crackling display of light on the horizon, more funnels reached down as if some cyclopean arachnid descended from the stars.

Martinez screamed "Tornadoes!" Paying no heed to *El Peón*, he flung himself forward into the crater, pulling Carlito with him. The raging winds swept darkness over them.

A moist spring sun broke over the summit of the burial grounds, bringing with it the lively chattering of mockingbirds. A gentle vernal warmth spread across the hills, chasing away the sepulchral chill of the previous night's storm.

Carlito sat up. He had sunken into the wet earth and it now squelched beneath him. Martinez rolled over onto his back. His clothes had been embedded into the ground and were covered with a sticky layer of watery mud.

A path of destruction lay before them. The nearest tornado's approach into the Payaya netherworld had sliced a bald path through the age-old brush, across the tops of several other mounds to the one where they sat. *El Peón*'s crater had sheltered them from its wrath. Once the tornado had crested the treasure mound, it had continued on and followed the path they had taken from McIntyre's farm.

"McIntyre," Martinez said. "It must have hit him."

Carlito rubbed a hand across his face. "Aye, aye, aye." He stood up.

"We'd better go back there. He might need our help."

"What happened to *El Peón*?"

"The tornado got him, I guess."

"What about his burro?"

"The same."

"Are you sure?" Carlito pointed up to the crater's edge

Martinez planted a hand into the soggy earth and hoisted himself up. He glanced up to where Carlito pointed. From where they had watched *El Peón* the night before, a gray burro stood on the slope of the mound, dipping its white muzzle down to graze on clumps of grass. Its back was bare, without a rope or bridle. Or treasure.

"Unless you want to dig in that spot with your bare hands, I suggest we go back to McIntyre's and get shovels," Martinez said. "And at least check on the *pinche gringo*."

The burro followed them as they hiked back.

Carlito threw rocks at it to make it go away, but it persisted. "What is this?" he asked.

"It is a curse," Martinez said. "Instead of killing us, *El Peón* sent his phantom burro to bother us."

"Perhaps we should put it to work, if it insists on following us." Carlito walked toward it, but it snorted in avoidant retreat. "Now it does not like me."

"Perhaps he doesn't like the way you smell."

Carlito laughed. "I smell like dirt. I thought burros liked dirt."

"No, my friend," Martinez smiled. "You smell like a *pendejo*."

Before they reached the farm, the destruction was apparent. The tornado had descended the hills and furrowed a path through the trees toward the house It had hit the barn and reduced it to splinters. Naked chickens clucked and giggled as they pecked their way through the front yard. A dead cow lay on its back with its legs in the air. The bunkhouse had vanished completely, but McIntyre's house was untouched, except for a broken windowpane in the kitchen.

There was no sign of the farmer at all. However, his pickup truck was gone.

"Where is he?" Carlito asked. "Did he go into town?"

Ignoring him, Martinez shook his head at the destruction. "This *is* a curse," Martinez said.

"Our things are gone," Carlito pointed out. "Yet McIntyre's house still stands."

Martinez dipped his head and gazed under hooded brows. "That proves the truth of the curse of El *Peón*."

"But we are not dead," Carlito smiled.

Martinez shrugged. "No."

"And if we had not gone for *El Peón*, then we would have surely died," Carlito said. "Perhaps this is a sign from God? Maybe we are chosen to find the gold?"

Martinez shook his head. "I don't know what this all means. Perhaps we *should* see the bruja."

"The bruja?" Carlito rolled his eyes. "Down in Weeping Woman Creek? Just like McIntyre's story?"

Martinez sighed and shook his head. "Yes, just like that story."

Los Gatos had stood on the edge of Wailing Woman Creek for over a hundred and fifty years, when the creek was called *Arroyo del Duelo*. The village had been a ferry landing for El Camino Real, the wide meandering path that led up from Guerrero, on the Rio Grande, through San Antonio, and farther east beyond the Sabine to Natchitoches. Now it was a wide spot in the road where the new Works Progress Administration bridge stretched over the swollen creek, the construction an anachronism among the wooden row houses that lined the fresh highway that bypassed the village, much like society had bypassed its inhabitants.

When they reached the bridge, they stepped off the highway and followed a dual rut path forged by wagon wheels. Weeping Woman Creek gurgled as water from the hills above collected within her arms and flowed down toward the Brazos River valley. A dead horse—a victim of the tornado—was perched, impaled in the top of an ancient oak tree as a black cloud of flies swarmed around it.

The trail led away from the rest of the town and off into the woods. Beyond that, separated from the others, a crooked house stood on the slope that led down to the creek. Made of a wide variety of wood collected from surplus lumber and storm salvage, the shack appeared as waterproof as a sieve. The door—a recycled window shutter with louvers—hung open on a single rusty hinge, and a column of smoke rose from a twisted chimney made of pipe. A spiderweb of a variety of fence wire lined a rudimentary yard with an open gate made of a headboard. Chickens pecked at the bare ground while being harassed by a red and black rooster, and a trio of goats inspected the bushes at the edge of the fence.

Martinez stepped through the gate—a deep rut was worn into the mud where the makeshift headboard door had been opened and closed many times. He knocked on the door. "¿Señora Galvan?" He waved Carlito forward and they stepped into the house. The burro stopped at the porch and grazed on stunted forest growth with the goats.

The bruja sat at her table and rummaged through a box. Sunbeams pierced through the innards of her lair, illuminating dust motes and casting twisted shadows on the walls and floor. As they watched her, she froze and turned her face toward them.

Despite her reputation as the old bruja on the creek, Señora Galvan was beautiful. Her luscious red lips stood out against her smooth olive skin and accentuated the plump roundness of her face. Her luxurious, raven hair had a streak of white at her crown that flowed as it fell like water down her shoulders and back. Her beauty belied her age, which some *viejos* said was over a hundred years.

"*Ay, hermosa*," Carlito whispered, licking his lips at the sight of her.

"*Chingón*," Martinez hissed at him and furrowed his eyebrows.

The bruja smiled. Her perfect teeth gleamed in the morning light. "Step into my parlor, *amigos*. I've been expecting you." Shadows gathered on the wall behind her head in eight crooked lines, making it appear as if an enormous spider hung behind her.

"Expecting us?" Carlito asked. "Why would you expect us? We haven't even met before."

Cocking her head to let her hair shimmer in the light, Senora Galvan winked. "I wouldn't be a very good bruja if I didn't know you were coming. Don't you think?"

"Señora Galvan," Martinez started, "we have had much trouble last night. We followed *El Peón*." He told her the story up until they found the burro that followed them.

"That burro?" she asked, pointing through a window in her lair.

"*Sí, señora*."

"And this all happened on the old Payaya burial site?"

They nodded.

The bruja smirked and started digging through her box once again. "This site is *not* a Payaya site as they have always thought. My father was a Payaya and he knew this to be true. That site was a city built by *Los Ancianos*." She cocked an eyebrow. "The Ancient Ones—before the time of Payaya or Apache or Karankawa. *Los Ancianos* were dust before our people came, but their powers remain. What happened to you had nothing to do with *El Peón*, for once he entered that land, his powers ceased and *Los Ancianos* prevailed. They sent down tornadoes to punish your trespassing, just as they had sent defeat for Santa Anna years ago. As for that burro, I suspect that he is also a victim of the tornado and his presence is a coincidence." She lifted two charms from her box and gave them to Martinez.

"What are *these*?"

"Pretty things for you to wear when you return back to there," she said cryptically.

Martinez placed a charm over his neck and gave the other to Carlito. Both were a small golden coin with the image of a fly stamped into it. Neither knew what to say.

"Until I see you again, amigos," the bruja said, smiling—her teeth glistening in the odd morning light.

"We are getting so close to the gold, I can taste it," Carlito smiled as they once again climbed the treasure mound in the old necropolis.

"You wouldn't know what gold tastes like," Martinez said. It was his turn to scoff, this time at his young friend's naïveté.

For at least the third time, Carlito lifted the charm from his neck and bit it, sinking a tooth into the soft metal. "I suspect that it tastes like this," he laughed.

They had stopped at the farm on the way back, recovering a shovel and pick from all the tools amidst the wreckage. Employing the burro this time, they strapped the equipment— along with rope and burlap sacks—to its back; and returned to the city of *Los Ancianos*.

As they crested the ridge into the crater atop the hill, they froze.

A crucifix, fashioned from a jagged two-by-four, bound with coarse jute twine to a shovel, pierced the mound of freshly turned earth where *El Peón* had dug the night before. Martinez placed his hand upon the shovel. It was not the ancient one wielded by the ghost, but a modern one with a familiar scoop and long oak handle. He knew the curve of the smooth wood as well as he knew the curve of his wife's body.

Two burned letters etched the dirt-stained handle: RM.

Robert McIntyre.

"That gringo beat us to it!" Carlito cried out in anguish as he dropped to his knees and clawed at the mud with his bare fingers.

With a gentle hand, Martinez placed his fingers in Carlito's tousled hair and squeezed his shoulder. Their bright future— their freedom as men in a land full of Anglo oppressors—died in a single instant. There was no escape from Los Gatos and no salvation from migrant work. No sharecropping *gringos*. No maids with supper and iced tea. And no houses in Gethsemane nor Monterrey.

Martinez's eyes soaked in the burial site of *El Peón* as his blood started to boil. "*Hijo de puta!* He will pay for this."

Tire tracks led from the crater. McIntyre's missing pickup truck. While they had been at the bruja's shack, McIntyre had come directly across the open country from the other side of the ring of hills that lined the city of *Los Ancianos*. The burro brayed as if it read his thoughts. It stepped into the buggy tracks and started to trace them.

Martinez pulled Carlito up to his feet and started dragging him after the burro. "*Chingale!* Let's go get our treasure back."

In the darkness of the stormy night before, and in their haste to leave that morning, they had not seen the path that snaked up the other side of the depression. Avoiding the highway, it led in a circuitous route back down through wild brush filled with mesquite and rattlesnakes until it made a final curve back west. As the trees fell away to tilled soil, they recognized it immediately—the east forty acres of McIntyre's farm.

"I've seen this trail a thousand times," Carlito said. "I thought it was just a deer run."

"Who would have thought where it led," Martinez shook his head. "We were busy following *El Peón*, who haunts the road between Los Gatos and the burial land, while a shortcut was here the whole time."

McIntyre's pickup—an old 1926 Ford Model TT pickup—sat behind the farmhouse. In its bed lay an impressive bulge beneath an old tarp. As they picked their way over the debris-strewn field, McIntyre rounded the corner of the house with a burlap sack perched on his shoulder, as if he were hefting a bag of feed. Without seeing them, he stepped to the wooden slat tailgate of the pickup.

Martinez and Carlito both realized what they must do to save their dreams. Martinez picked up a board from the wreckage of the barn, and Carlito took the pick from the burro's back. Without a word, they knew the plan. It was simple—kill McIntyre, get the gold, and head back to Mexico. They came to claim their inheritance—their heritage—raised from the earth by their forefathers, stolen by Cortés, and lost by Santa Anna.

McIntyre pulled back the tarp. Bulging mud-encrusted burlap sacks lay stacked three high—much more gold than that old man's burro could have ever carried on that night a hundred years ago. With a groan, he dropped his bag into the bed of the pickup with the others. It crashed with the song of coins, and its weight made the truck bob up and down.

The burro brayed—its dumb voice echoing off the outer wall of the farmhouse.

McIntyre turned around slowly. As he saw the gray burro, he groaned again. "Oh, no." Horror filled his wide eyes as they locked on them. His pupils dilated as he lifted his hands to his face. "It can't be," he whimpered.Shaking his head now, he cupped his hands over his mouth as if to stifle a scream.

Martinez jabbed his finger in the air. "I should have known you followed us. We were too scared of *El Peón* to worry about you. That is our treasure and we will take it as easily as we will take your life."

Writhing now, McIntyre dropped to his knees and clutched his chest. Glistening beads of sweat erupted on his forehead, and his skin blanched. Twisting his eyes shut and grimacing in pain, he yelled out, "Dear God, it's true!"

"We will kill your gringo ass," Carlito said as he stepped forward with the pick.

Realizing something was not right, Martinez caught his shirtsleeve and asked, "*What's true?*"

McIntyre did not respond, but continued to writhe in pain. With a violent spasm, his eyes rolled up and he fell face first into the soil as his limbs shook violently.

Reaching down, Martinez hoisted him over sideways, onto his back. "What's true?" he repeated, desperation soaking his words now.

Foamy spittle oozed out of one corner of McIntyre's mouth. His eyes opened again and scanned Martinez's face with stoic finality, as if it was the most unbelievable thing he had ever seen. "The curse," he groaned. "It's true." Dry-heaving the air from his lungs with a hiss, he arched his spine backwards as he died— his arms and legs curling in on themselves like a dead spider's.

What did he mean?" Carlito asked as they drove away from McIntyre's farm. Nine burlap sacks—full of gold coins minted in the Republic of Mexico onc hundred years before—lay in the back of the truck. The burro trundled after them, but fell behind as they sped away.

"I don't know," Martinez said. His first thought was to flee to Mexico, where they could live as rich men, outside the reach of the Texas Rangers, who would pin McIntyre's death on them. But something bothered him.

The curse is true.

If *El Peón* saw the people who tried to follow him to the lost treasure, they would die. *El Peón* had definitely seen Martinez and Carlito. That jawless skull face, with sockets filled with weeping, bloodshot eyes, was burned into Martinez's mind.

But they had survived. Hadn't they?

Martinez pulled the truck to a stop in the shell driveway just before it ended at the highway that ran between Los Gatos and Gethsemane.

Martinez looked down at his hands. They were just as soiled and dirty as he would expect after a night out in the woods, and his fingertips and palms were as calloused as they had been since—well, since he was a child. He had meaty, strong hands. Hands that moved mountains and plucked entire fields of produce. Hands that had caressed the flesh of his fair share of women. He flexed his fingers, noting the grime under his fingernails, the hair on the backs of his hands. He pinched the web of skin between his left thumb and forefinger, and it ached.

I am alive, he thought.

"The curse said that we would die, but here we are," Martinez said.

"What are you doing?" Carlito cried out. "Just go! That burro is still following us!"

Martinez glanced back in the rear-view mirror to see the burro clip-clopping behind them, but instead of the comic dumb look on its gray face with its snow-white snout, rotten empty sockets stared after them. And as it brayed an infernal noise that sounded like the cyclonic cacophony from the night before, its skin ruptured open with a swarm of black spiders that scurried across its fur and fell away with writhing rafts.

Tearing down the highway that led away from McIntyre's Farm, the shanty village of Los Gatos and the white-picket fences of Gethsemane, Martinez drove, trying to shake the image of the burro from his mind.

"I didn't see anything like that," Carlito said. "It just looked like a stupid burro to me."

Martinez shook his head. "I know what I saw."

"You must have hit your head last night. You're acting loco. You're driving too fast and those gringo police will pull you over. Or you'll miss the turn to Highway 35."

"I know how to get back to Monterrey," Martinez replied. The rural highway would take them through San Antonio then Laredo, where the bridge over the Rio Grande would welcome them into Nueva Laredo and beyond. It was a long drive for sure, but it was a journey Martinez had made many times over the years. He just hoped this was his last.

"What is that ahead?" Carlito asked. "Did you miss the turn?"

Before them, the asphalt road wound through the prairie, but gradually narrowed. This had been a stretch of road that had been a WPA project, connecting the interior rural areas like Gethsemane with the larger cities like San Antonio and Austin. It had two lanes that were evenly painted with yellow stripes, unlike anything that he had seen outside of major cities.

"We haven't reached the turn yet," Martinez said as he slowed down. "This is the road from Gethsemane, no?"

The asphalt ended and the surface was just dirt, as primordial as that of the hills beyond. The trees rose up around them, gnarly mesquite that the farmers complained about because of their ugly, chaotic branches.

"Go back," Carlito said. "You took the wrong road."

"There is no place to turn around," Martinez replied, slowing down and sizing up the width of the road. It narrowed further and the mesquite branches scratched at the truck's sides, digging furrows in its paint. "We'll have to continue on until we find a clearing."

But instead of clearing, the trees pressed in and the ground rose, quickly becoming hilly as the path snaked around. Soon, the truck was chugging up a sharp incline, the trail tracing a familiar switchback that made the back of Martinez's head tickle with fear.

"I don't like this," Carlito said.

"It's like—" Martinez didn't finish his sentence, because just as the truck heaved its way to the summit of the hill, the only clearing they had yet to see came into view. Just beyond the ridge lay a crater in the earth, ringed by trees that had been torn asunder, and in its center lay the heap of freshly turned dirt with the makeshift cross made of a two by four and McIntyre's shovel wedged into the earth—the treasure mound of *El Peón*.

"Martinez, what have you done? Why did you bring us back here?" Carlito lurched across the cab of the truck and grabbed at his clothes.

Shielding himself with his elbows, Martinez slammed the truck to a halt. "I did nothing! I don't know how we got here. You saw where we were going with your own eyes!"

He shoved Carlito back across the cab and scowled. "But I intend to find out why," he growled. After wrenching the parking brake tight, Martinez jumped out of the truck. Down in the crater where they had left it just hours before, stood McIntyre's makeshift cross, piercing the heap of freshly turned dirt.

Carlito followed him and cried out, "What are you doing?"

"We have to see what is buried here," Martinez replied.

"No, we don't," Carlito insisted. "Nothing is buried here."

"Then why put a *cross* here, eh?" Martinez pointed. "Why would he do that? Unless a body is buried here."

"Perhaps it is *El Peón*," Carlito replied. "Besides, who cares? We have the gold."

"I care," Martinez said. "There is something off here. Why would McIntyre mark this grave? He already had the gold. Why did he die when he saw us? And why does that damned burro still follow us?" He nodded back up toward the truck.

Their old friend—its body intact again—brayed a loud, squeaking hee-haw that resounded over the hills of the necropolis.

Carlito chuckled. "That is what you sound like, amigo. Like a burro. Braying your nonsense like a fool. While we were seeking answers from the bruja, McIntyre was stealing our gold. And now that we have it, you bring us here instead of fleeing. Those gringos will kill us if they find out we have it."

"You are the fool, Carlito. I didn't bring us here," Martinez insisted. "We *are* cursed."

"There is one thing for sure," Carlito shook his head. "I'm a fool for listening to you. Now, go on and dig, fool. I just hope that it's more gold."

Huffing, Martinez pulled the shovel out of the dirt. He glanced back, scowling as he tore loose the twine that held the makeshift cross together, tossed the board into the bushes, and started digging.

Just inches beneath the surface, Martinez hit something in the dirt. It was soft and pliant, like a root beneath the soil. He tossed the shovel out of the way. "*Ayudame,*" he said. Then Carlito eased into the crater and they dug with their bare hands until they uncovered it.

An arm lay buried in the soggy earth. Perhaps it was El Peón himself, preserved for a hundred years by the magic of *Los Ancianos.*

"Look at this." Tracing an outline in the moist earth, Carlito revealed another body.

The makeshift crucifix had marked two dead bodies. They cleared them with haste and staggered back in shock. Storm-torn and caked with mud, the bodies of the two men down in the shallow grave gazed up at them with open, clouded eyes.

Staring back in disbelief, Martinez and Carlito drank in the revelation in gasping gulps. Two men, who looked like them, lay dead in the same hole Santa Anna had murdered *El Peón* amidst Mexican gold. They were perfect copies, down to the clothes and boots. It was like they were looking down on a clear pool of water, reflecting their image up from the murky depths. They were so perfect that it could only be magic.

A cackling pierced the heavy air like the mocking cry of a crow.

Cringing with dread, Martinez recognized that voice. He backed away, instinctively throwing an arm out in front of

Carlito like a cautious father, while Carlito gawked, his mouth hanging open.

Señora Galvan stepped from the thick bushes dressed in black, her raven hair cascading down her shoulders like blades of obsidian. She gazed down upon them from the edge of the crater.

"Bruja!" Martinez hissed. "You brought us back here."

She smiled as she taunted them, her teeth gleaming in the sun. "Congratulations! You found the gold. You almost lost it to that gringo, but you recovered. Nice job. I'm so proud of you." Her tittering pierced the air as she tossed her head back.

"But what of this?" Martinez yelled as he pointed to the bodies in the hole.

The bruja placed her hands on her ample hips and turned her face into the breeze to smooth her black hair. "That is the work of *El Peón*. You said that he saw you, so, therefore; you must be dead. So the story goes. Am I right?"

"But here we are," Carlito said as he held his hands up in front of him.

"So what of it?" She snarled.

A wave of understanding washed thought Martinez. "We've been dead this whole time, haven't we, and you didn't tell us."

A chuckle erupted in her throat and rose up to her lips. "You poor fools. You have no idea." She shook her head. "But what else is to be expected from simple farmers." She sneered at them. "You've been stuck in my web since you first saw him. And I just used you lead me here. The others, like Sancho and Miguel, only made it as far as the first hill." She flashed her eyebrows and cocked her chin.

Hair prickled on the back of Martinez's neck at the sound of those names. He had worked with them. Even McIntyre had mentioned they vanished. Everyone had assumed they were back in Mexico, but nobody knew for sure.

"This is *our* gold," Carlito cried.

"*Your* gold? When I was a girl, a man came to my father's house on *Arroyo del Duelo* and insisted he show him a good hiding spot. My *father* took him to the best place he knew—the necropolis of *Los Ancianos*. That man—*Santa Anna*—killed my father. I couldn't give a damn about the gold. It's my father's bones I've been searching for since that night."

"That was a *hundred* years ago," Martinez said with disbelief.

"A hundred years of picking through these ancient ruins for *one grave* among the necropolis of an entire civilization. The ghost of my father could not lead me here, like you might think. He could only cry at me—not tell me where he was buried. After a hundred years of his ghostly tears, all I could do was follow you greedy bastards, but *papá* always saw them before they tracked him to the exact spot."

"That *mortal* man had a name, and it was Valentín Galvan, and he was born in San Antonio de Valero, the son of a Payaya woman and a *soldado* from Saltillo. He was descended from a long line of Payaya medicine men and women who had passed down the teachings of *los Ancianos* by word of mouth."

"When Santa Anna found him, he looked like another farmer from the hills, trying to scrape an existence from this land, but he was a wise man educated in the lost ways. I watched as they took him away, following as he led them here to this holy place of our ancestors. Not just to find a hole to bury a treasure, but to meet my mother." A sinister grin spread across her face.

"I, too, am just a Payaya *half*-breed, but the *other* half is even older." She scowled. "As old as the proverbial hills." She raised her arms and gestured to the necropolis complex. "We are still here, the children of *los Ancianos*. And so are our mothers."

Carlito charged toward her. "We will kill you like we killed that gringo McIntyre. With our eyes."

The ground trembled.

Carlito stopped in his tracks—ripples of fear spreading across his face like the surface of a disturbed pond.

Her own eyes glittered bright green—not that of a human nor usual beast, but that emerald sparkle of spider eyes caught by lantern light. The bruja lifted an amulet from her breast. Unlike the ones she had given them and said would protect them from angry spirits, it was a gold medallion as large as a tea saucer, carved with a hideous bass-relief of an eight-legged arachnoid creature. Cocking her head up to the sky, she spoke aloud words that were neither Spanish nor English, or even Nahuatl or any of the Indio languages they were familiar with. Her voice made harsh sounds full of glottal clicks contrasted by sibilant susurrations.

Grabbing at the amulet that she had given them that morning, Martinez found that, instead of a simple carved fly, the image was now a pill-shaped carcass wrapped with countless threads of web so exquisitely crafted he thought he could see individual strands. He tore it from his neck. "This was all a trap?"

"Like I said," the bruja replied as she cocked her eyebrow. "You have been caught in my web all this time."

From somewhere beyond the crater's ridge, stones crackled and crunched, shaking the earth more, and sending up a plume of dust. The sound of it made the burro flee, leaving behind only a series of high-pitched squeaks.

Smiling, the bruja stepped around to the driver's side of the truck. "Thank you for showing me the site of my father's final resting place," she said as she slid into the seat. "As for the gold, it might buy an elegant gravestone. Or at least a nice house down in Gethsemane where I can sit on my front porch and have my servants work for *me*." She slammed the door shut.

The sound of tree limbs cracking and tearing emanated through the woods as if the ghost of the tornado had returned to mark its path from the night before.

"But what about us?" Martinez said, shaking. "What do we do now?"

The earth thudded now, in rhythm—cyclopean footfalls sending tremors through the woods and shaking every branch. A fetid stench soiled the atmosphere, as if every grave in the mound complex had fallen open.

"Say hello to my dear mother." Señora Galvan ground the truck into gear and eased away. Her cackle filled the air above the city of the dead—a necropolis of a lost people with two new inhabitants.

From out of the quivering mesquite rose the God of *Los Ancianos* on eight bristling legs that clambered over the crater's ridge with predatory precision. With teeth like cutlasses and the hot sulfurous breath of a thousand *escopetas*, it descended upon them with the relished vengeance of a conquered and forgotten race.

What Was It?

Lewis B. Smith

"**W**hat was it, Dan??"

Those were the last words my best friend Roger ever spoke to me. His vital signs crashing, blood streaming from multiple wounds, one hand gone, eyes bulging, his face twisted by fear and shock, he grabbed my arm as the paramedics lifted the stretcher into the ambulance and rasped those words out with a desperate intensity. By the time they got him to the hospital, he was dead.

That agonized question played over and over in my head as I answered the sheriff's questions that night, and later on, as I made the heartbreaking phone call to Amanda, his beautiful wife—widow, I mean! What an ocean of suffering that simple transition of nouns conceals—I could still hear them echoing in my head. Even as I helped carry his coffin to the grave that had been dug in the small cemetery near the church he and his family attended, that question played in my mind over and over again, those frantic eyes seared into my memory, his voice mustering up the last of his dying body's energy to demand an answer from me.

The truth is, I didn't know. I still don't. Even though I was only ten feet from him when he sustained the injuries that ended his life, I cannot say with any certainty what the creature was—

if, indeed, it was a living thing. The fleeting glimpses I caught in the moments leading up to the final horror were of a being that had no place in a rational world, and the memory of them still haunts my dreams, waking me in the middle of the night, screaming out the same question that my friend asked me before he perished. Because I have no idea what it was, and even now, I'm not sure I want to know.

This all sounds confusing to me, staring at what I've just written, and I'm sure it must be even more so to you, whoever you are, as you try to figure out what on earth I am talking about. I guess I should start at the beginning and do my best to explain what happened. Maybe writing it down will help me make sense of it all—if such a word can even be applied to what we experienced!

It started as a routine trip to South Texas. Roger had gotten permission for us to go digging for arrowheads on a large ranch near Bandera. Such permission had been easy to get years before, when he and I started collecting Indian relics as a hobby in the 1990's. In the decades since, however, ranchers had discovered that collectors would pay fifty bucks a pop to hand dig on a good camp for a day, and upwards of two hundred dollars a day each for a "screen dig"—where a large table with an iron mesh top was set up, and a small bulldozer would scoop out a load of undug soil and dump it on each screen table for the hunters to sift by hand. Two hunters per table, six to eight tables per camp, until the whole site was destroyed, and all the artifacts went home with the customers. A large campsite, rich with points, could mean tens of thousands of dollars to the property owner. With that kind of money to be made, few ranchers were willing to let people come dig for free anymore.

So when Roger told me his dad's cousin Jimmy had a big ranch near Bandera—prime artifact country!—that had never been dug, and that he was willing to let us come down and spend a weekend exploring and digging all we wanted, I was excited at the prospect. I talked to my wife Priscilla and asked her if she'd made any plans for us that weekend, and when she said we were free, I bribed her with a day pass at her favorite beauty spa. Not that she needed it; I know that's what a husband is supposed to say, but in my case it's the plain truth. I married about six floors above my level and I know it. Roger's wife was ten years younger than him and had always been happy to let him sneak off for a weekend with me; she and Pris were close friends and often hung out together when he and I were out digging. Pris occasionally joined us, though—she liked artifacts and wasn't afraid to get her hands dirty or break a nail. I thank God she stayed home that weekend—it was hard enough seeing my best friend ripped up before my eyes; I can't imagine seeing the love of my life die like that.

Friday afternoon at two, Roger and I met up after leaving work early. Since he'd secured the spot, I provided the vehicle and gas. It was about six hours from our neighborhood in Lancaster, on the south side of Dallas, to the small town of Bandera, west of San Antonio, and that was if Austin traffic wasn't hopelessly congested, as it often was. We debated swinging west and going through a series of small towns instead of taking the interstate, but the latter part of our drive would be in the dark, and even with cell phone navigation, assuming we had a clear signal, the odds of a wrong turn seemed rather high. So onward we hammered, down I-35, getting through Waco ahead of the afternoon rush, and then sat and sweltered for the better part of an hour as the stop-and-start traffic of the state capital rendered my truck's AC useless. We finally got free of Austin by about half past six in the evening, and the last hour and a half or so were cross-country, free of the interstate, watching the sun set about an hour before we finally arrived at the small town of Bandera around 9 p.m.

We didn't want to bother our host so late in the evening, so after a quick text to let Jimmy know we were nearby, we checked into the smallest of Bandera's three hotels, and managed to grab some fast food at Sonic—the steak house where we'd hoped to dine was already closed—and then turned in for the night. Neither of us slept well, of course—we were too excited at the prospect of the next day's dig! For those unfamiliar with our hobby, northeast Texas, where we lived and normally hunted artifacts, is a flint-poor region, and most points we find are small and made of rough quartzite or petrified wood. Southwest Texas is loaded with slick, glossy Edwards plateau chert, which comes out of the limestone in huge tabs and could be made into large, beautiful points, much nicer than what we normally found at home.

By 7 a.m. we were both wide awake, and we had a hearty breakfast at the town's diner before heading out along the farm-to-market road that led to Jimmy's ranch. Our host was waiting for us—a crusty, seventy-five-year-old West Texas rancher who could have stepped straight out of a 1960's Western. Greeting us both with a handshake that could have crushed concrete, he told us a little bit about the place we'd be searching.

"I never was that fascinated by Indian rocks," he said, "but as a kid I found a bunch of them on that slope below the cliffs yonder. They'd wash down from the overhangs into the crick, and after the spring rains they'd be scattered down the slope. If you go north, round the shoulder of that bluff, there's a spring comes out of the rocks and trickles down into the creek. There was always a bunch of them there, too. You fellers can dig all you want. All I ask is fill in your holes and don't destroy any of my trees—except the cedars. You can take out all of those nuisances you want."

"Thanks, Jimmy," Roger said. "This really means a lot to us—not many folks are willing to let us come dig anymore in these parts."

"Too many folks got dollar signs in their eyes," he said. "I don't want them dang dirt rapers coming on my place! I saw what was left of the Holloway's ranch when they were done, and it was pitiful. I mean, they filled in their holes, but they also destroyed everything that made that place so beautiful. I don't mind friends and family coming here and digging up a few arryheads, and as long as I'm careful about who I let in, and how many, there'll be Indian rocks to be found by my grandkids' grandkids!"

"It's a huge place," I said. "I imagine we'll find enough to go home happy and leave plenty for those who come after us."

The old man laughed and clapped me on the shoulder.

"That's exactly what I thought when Roger asked me if y'all could come," he said. "He also vouched for you, or I wouldn't let you near the place. No offense, I just don't know you yet."

"Understandable," I said. "Well, my students have rated me 'mostly harmless,' my dad has conceded that I'm not a disappointment, and my mom is happy that I married what she called 'a nice girl'. Anything else you want to know?"

"You a Cowboys fan?" he asked.

"I bleed silver and blue," I replied.

"Reckon you'll do, then," he said. "Now, there's an old foreman's cabin out back; I put fresh linens on the bed so you fellers don't have to worry about a hotel. Shower in the cabin is busted, but you're welcome to come up to the house and use the guest shower there. Supper's at six; I got some ribeyes on sale at the meat market yesterday – if you're late, I may finish all three of them myself!"

"I imagine by six we'll be ready for them," Roger said. "Digging's hungry work; we packed sandwiches and drinks for lunch, but by supper I imagine they will have worn off."

"One other thing," the old rancher said. He seemed to choose his words very carefully. "I've had some cows come up missing lately, so if you find a carcass or some sign of predators, let me know. I want to find out what's killing them, or if I have a thief to contend with." He broke eye contact as he spoke and I remember thinking he seemed uncomfortable about something more than just missing cattle.

"Sure thing," Roger said. "I think we're both ready to get out and start searching! Anything else we should know?"

"Nothing I can think of. Watch out for rattlesnakes; they're not as active now as they will be in a few months, but they still come out to sun on warm days. They'll avoid you if you give them a chance."

"I don't kill snakes unless it's unavoidable," I said. "Plenty of room out here for us and them."

"Yup," Jimmy said. "As long as they stay out of my house and yard, I leave them alone."

With that, we bid each other good day, and Roger and I headed to the base of the big hill he'd pointed out. Sure enough, the slope between the bluff and the creek was littered with flint, and we found several broken points and two nice whole ones within the first hour as we slowly worked our way toward the spring Jimmy had mentioned to us. We talked about many things that fine morning, but one of the first things I said after we got out of earshot regarded Jimmy's missing cows.

"Do you really think there are cattle rustlers out here? I mean, this is the 2020s, not the 1890s!" I asked.

"Not a chance," he said. "More likely a pack of coyotes, or maybe a mountain lion."

Of course, it turned out to be neither of those things, nor cattle rustlers either. In retrospect, I think I would rather have faced all of them at once instead of the thing we found—or, I suppose it would be more accurate to say, the thing that found us. But I'm getting ahead of myself. I'm trying to explain this whole thing in order, and the horror didn't really begin till the next day— although there was a sign that first day that I wish we hadn't ignored.

It had taken us all morning to search the slope between the bluff and the creek, from the place behind the ranch house where we started until we came to the curve of the hill where the clear, fresh spring flowed from a cleft in the rock. Just as Jimmy said, the signs of ancient occupation grew thicker and thicker close to the spring, and we were each avidly searching the ground, flipping over every exposed bit of worked flint we saw, and crying out when we found a complete point or tool.

Then the breeze shifted and I caught the unmistakable smell of rotting flesh nearby. I swiveled my head, trying to locate the source, and saw a large spatter of dried, blackened blood on the ground next to a post oak tree. There was a trail of drops on the tree's trunk as well, and as my eyes followed it upward, I found the source.

Ten feet off the ground, leaning against the bole of the tree where a sturdy branch emerged from the trunk, was the head of a cow. It had been dead for several days, and flies were buzzing around it.

"Something reeks!" Roger said at that moment.

"Look up there," I told him, pointing.

"How in the Sam Hill did a cow's head get way up there?" he said.

"I think we can rule out coyotes," I replied. "Only predator I can think of that climbs trees would be a mountain lion."

"I want a closer look," he said. "Can you reach it with your walking stick?"

I had to stand on a rock, but I managed to poke the thing hard enough to knock it loose. It hit the ground with a sickening wet thud and the smell of rot wafted up so strongly I nearly gagged. Roger held his nose and bent over the severed head, grabbing one of its horns to turn it over.

"This is odd," he said.

"Oddly disgusting!" I replied.

"Well, duh," he said. "It's pretty ripe, but look here, at where it was severed. This wasn't a wild animal. That's a clean cut, not a bite or claw mark!"

I had stepped upwind to get a breath of clean air, but I circled back and saw that he was correct. The head had been cleanly cut off, about six inches down from the ears, and even the vertebrae were cleanly sliced, with no jagged edges protruding. Interested despite the stench, I looked closer and noticed something else.

"Roger, both its eyes are gone," I said.

"Don't birds always go for the eyes first?" he said.

"Have you seen a bird out here all morning?" I replied, for I had noticed how silent the woods had been around us for some time.

"Come to think of it, I haven't," he said. "And normally a chunk of carrion this big would have a dozen buzzards fighting over it!"

"I'm all in for a mystery," I said, "but this thing really stinks. Let's snap a couple of pictures for Jimmy and move on!"

We photographed the head from several angles, turning it over with our walking sticks, and then resumed our search. Still, I found the grisly image floating in my thoughts—who would neatly decapitate a fully grown cow and leave its head up in a tree? And where was the rest of the beast?

By the end of the day we had each found a half dozen or more whole points, including a beautifully worked corner tang knife that I flipped out of the dirt after only seeing one corner of the base exposed. We'd also picked a spot to dig the next day, an ancient midden just on the other side of the spring that looked very promising. We made it back to the ranch house a few minutes before dinner, and the smell of grilled steaks drove the day's odd discovery out of our heads for the half hour it took us to devour them.

"Looks like you boys had a fine day hunting rocks," Jimmy said. "Did you see any sign of my missing cows?"

"Dang, that reminds me," said Roger. "We found the weirdest thing. There was a severed cow's head in the fork of a tree, near the spring, about ten feet up! We knocked it down and took some pictures. Crazy thing, the head wasn't bitten or torn off, it was cut clean as a whistle!"

The old rancher paled, and then silently took Roger's proffered phone, scrolling through the pictures of our grisly find. He handed the phone back, his face set in a grim line, and the room grew deathly quiet—until Jimmy slammed his hand down on the table so loudly we both jumped.

"Damn it all, it's come back!" he snarled, and then let loose with a string of profanity that my old Navy buddies would have been proud of. He finally wound down after a couple of minutes and let out a long sigh.

"I was hoping it was gone for good, or at least that it wouldn't come back in my lifetime," he said softly.

"What is 'it'?" Dan asked, unconsciously foreshadowing the final question he would rasp out to me in about twenty-four hours.

"No one rightly knows," Jimmy said. "Only a few people ever caught a glimpse of it, and none of them in broad daylight. Last time it came around was in the nineties, around the time they impeached Slick Willie.Before that, it was when Reagan was President. Once during Vietnam, and before that, not long after Pearl Harbor. There's stories going back further still, to the days of the Indian Wars, but I can't vouch for them."

"Stories about what?" I asked. I was incredulous but still fascinated—I've always loved a good real-life mystery, from the Bermuda Triangle to Oak Island.

"It always starts with cattle," he said. "They go missing, and then parts are found—always neatly severed, never torn up. Scavengers won't touch them. Some say that, if found soon enough, they're covered with some sticky green, snot-like fluid, but it melts away when the sun hits it. It goes on for a few weeks, and there's stories—I don't know if they're true or not, but my Pop swore at least one of them was—of people being taken, too. During the war they found a boy's head in a tree over in Johnson

County, right after a string of cattle were found cut up, and both his eyes gone neat as you please. Then, for whatever reason, it stops. Cattle quit disappearing, people quit seeing strange things, and we persuade ourselves that it's gone for good this time. But it always comes back."

He shifted uncomfortably in his chair, and then stared at Roger.

"Look," he said. "I gave you two permission to come out here . . . but if you wanted to go home and come back in a month or two, when this is all over, it'd ease my mind a bit. If something happened to you out here, it'd weigh on me mighty heavy."

How I wish we'd packed our gear and headed home that night. But Roger shook his head slowly.

"We won't have another chance to come down for a couple months," he said, "and by then it'll be a hundred ten in the shade, and the ground will be like concrete. We found a sweet-looking midden across from the spring, and I'd really like to get in just one day of digging. Tell you what—if it's OK, we'll cut out at sunset tomorrow; we'd be back in Bandera by dark and drive home Sunday morning, early. But I'd really like to get in one more day of hunting, since we drove all this way."

Jimmy nodded slowly, and then stood up, gathering our plates.

"I reckon as long as you're out by dark, it'll be all right," he said. "But stay in your cabin tonight! And take this with you tomorrow, just in case."

He reached into a nearby cabinet and pulled out a huge, gleaming silver pistol, a .44 hogleg that looked like something out of a war movie.

"I don't expect you'll need it, but I'd feel better if you had it," he said.

"Thanks, Jim," said Roger. "We'll be careful."

After we retired to our cabin, I looked at my friend closely.

"Do you believe any of that tall tale?" I said.

"I remember seeing something about cattle mutilations in the news back in the 90s," he said, "and I remember my dad talking about finding a huge bull sliced clean in half on their ranch, one county over, when he was a boy. I always thought he was spinning one, kind of like you thought Jimmy was tonight. But I tell you, west Texas ranchers don't scare easy, and that old man looked scared to me. I don't know if this whole thing is real or not, but I'll guarantee you HE thinks it's real. As for me, I'm going to take a long shower, climb into that bed, and not think about it til tomorrow."

I nodded, and as he trudged back to the ranch house for a shower, I looked out the window at the dark bulk of the limestone hill rising behind us. As majestic as it had looked under the warm springtime sun, by the faint light of the waning crescent moon it took on a more sinister aspect, like some enormous beast buried deep in slumber, dreaming of its prey. Then I noticed a small but very bright red star gleaming just above the tree line. It shone brighter than Mars or Venus, and as I watched, it seemed to split into two for just a moment—and then it winked out. Must have been an airplane or a drone, I thought.

I got my own shower when Roger came back, and as I padded back to the cabin in my shorts and t-shirt, I thought I heard the screaming bellow of a wounded cow far off in the distance. I shivered involuntarily, but then reminded myself it was calving season, and decided all I'd heard was a new calf being born. With that rather positive image in my mind, I quickly faded off to sleep.

The next day, as soon as we'd wolfed down breakfast, Roger and I headed straight to the midden we'd found the day before and started digging. The rich black soil was full of snail shells and charcoal, and within a half hour Roger pulled out a nice Pedernales spearpoint nearly four inches long. A few minutes after that I found a Marshall point with flared, delicate barbs, and from that point on we forgot about mutilated cattle, missing children, and mysterious disappearances. I will say this about that day—it was the best dig Roger and I ever had together. Between the two of us, we found fifteen points that day, several of them large and perfect examples, nearly all of types that rarely, if ever, were to be found in North Texas.

We hung the .44 in its holster from the limb of a tree that overhung our dig, but neither of us ever really thought about it after that. The sun was shining, the soil was soft and damp, and the artifacts abundant and beautiful. We talked about our friends in the hobby, some still around and others long gone, and about how much fun we'd have showing off our finds at the big show in Temple in a couple months' time. The sun seemed to fairly leap across the spring sky that day, and long before we tired of digging the shadows started to lengthen.

We filled our holes back in and gathered our things, rescued the .44 from its perch, and headed back down to the ranch house as we'd promised. Jimmy seemed relieved to see us and told us to go ahead and take a quick shower while he grilled us some cheeseburgers as a parting meal. We'd barely stopped digging to eat our sandwiches at lunchtime, and those burgers were delicious. Our bellies full and our flint craving satisfied, we thanked Jimmy many times over for his hospitality and climbed into my truck to head to town just as the sun dipped over the horizon.

It was a bumpy mile down a rock and gravel road to the nearest pavement, and as we neared the farm to market road, I noticed that the wheel was thumping a lot harder than it should have, rough road notwithstanding.

"Well, crap," I commented to Roger. "I think we have a flat!"

"Here's a level spot," he said. "Pull over and let's get her changed before it's full dark."

We were within sight of the paved road that led back to Bandera, and there was perhaps a half hours' worth of twilight left. I jacked the truck up quickly, and Roger got the spare out from under the bed of the truck, where it was held in place by a cable and winch. I was just loosening the lug nuts when I first heard the sound that still haunts my dreams. First there was a whistling, whooshing sound from somewhere overhead, not too close, but not far either. And the sound that followed—God, I have taught English for nearly thirty years, and I have two master's degrees, but I'm not sure our language has any words that convey the horror of that awful noise. It seemed to combine the worst elements of mechanical sound—the screeching of an engine on the brink of shredding itself—with the most haunting ululations a predatory animal can make. Screeching, warbling, roaring, and whistling, all at the same time, and still I can't convey the horrible other-ness of it. It was a sound that had no place in this world, or in any other world created by a sane God.

"What the hell was that?" Roger gasped, straightening up, and then a dark shadow came between us and the fading light in the western sky. I looked up too late to catch more than a glimpse of something huge swooping above us. Its wings were somewhere between those of a bat, a giant insect, and a biplane. Three long, forked tails twisted and curled in its wake, and as it banked and swooped back toward us, I saw the same red lights I'd glimpsed in the distance the night before, blazing through the dark in our direction.

"Get back in the truck!" I shrieked at Roger, even as I dove for the door myself. He was right behind me when two whiplike appendages came lashing out from an orifice beneath those blazing red—eyes? Headlights? Portholes? *Portals?*—and wrapped around his waist and neck.

I didn't have a gun of my own with me, but I had packed along a razor-sharp machete to help clear the stubborn mesquite roots and branches while digging. I reached into the bed of the truck and grabbed it as Roger was dragged helplessly along the ground behind that winged monstrosity.

"Hold on, buddy!" I cried, and then managed to catch up with him after a short sprint. I swung with all my strength, and the cord or tentacle or whip around his neck was cleanly severed. The monster retracted the damaged appendage quickly, and as it shot past my face some greenish fluid struck my cheek and burned on contact. A second time that horrific sound assaulted my ears, much closer and more discordant than ever. Aware of nothing except my desperate need to make it stop, I hurled the machete at the giant shadow that filled the sky over our heads. One of the glowing red orbs suddenly winked out, and the horrible screeching doubled in volume, so loud that I fell backward with my hands over my ears, trying to blot it out. But I'd injured whatever it was, and the cord around Roger's waist released him as the shadow retreated upwards, the awful shriek falling silent for a moment. I crawled to my friend and helped him to his feet, staggering back to the truck while trying to keep him upright.

But whatever it was, it had not given up. Just a few feet short of the open door, we were struck in the back and knocked flat as the thing swooped even lower than before. I felt a sharp pain across my shoulder blades, and later that evening the doctor at the local hospital would stitch up six parallel gashes, about an inch apart, that had cut clean through my tough denim jacket and flannel shirt.

For some reason, the flying entity was focused on Roger. The huge bulk settled to the ground on top of him, and I saw multiple legs and tentacles and some sort of tubular proboscis that was descending upon his body. He jerked and shrieked as they penetrated his flesh.

The closest thing to a weapon I had at hand was the long, curved "wiggle pick" I'd used to dig for points earlier in the day. I staggered to my feet and grabbed it, lurching forward toward the nightmare shape that was trying to devour my friend. I swung as hard as I could and buried the pick in one of its limbs, which was covered with prickly black fur but jointed, like a spider's. A second limb swatted at me and knocked me flat, and then the nightmare creature dropped Roger and advanced toward me. I scrambled away, unable to get to my feet. In the gathering darkness, I saw the winged shape lift its four front legs off the ground as it prepared to spring.

A flash of blinding light and a report like a thunderclap sounded from behind the creature, and I felt droplets of that burning liquid strike my face and hands. The monster shrieked again, and I detected a note of pain and anger in its roar this time.

"Get off them boys, you bastid!!" Jimmy's voice came roaring out of the darkness. "Get back to whatever hell you came from!"

Three more deafening shots were fired, and by the muzzle flash I could see Jimmy standing there, legs apart, the .44 leveled at the creature that had been trying to kill us. I heard that awful cry for the last time, and then the thing launched itself into the air, hurling itself at the sturdy West Texas rancher as he squeezed the trigger for the last time. The thing angled upward, passing a few feet over his head, but as it did, a narrow, whiplike appendage lashed out, wrapping around Jimmy's neck. The old man barely had time to let out a choking scream before the creature tightened its grip and his head was severed from his body, dropping to the ground between his feet. Jimmy's headless corpse remained on its feet for what seemed like an impossibly long time before slowly toppling backward, the gun still gripped in his hands. Then, with no more sound save the rush of air over its four wings, the creature flew back toward the dark mountain in the distance.

I struggled to sit up and pull my phone out of my pocket. My skin was burning in a dozen places where the creature's blood—or was it oil?—there was something in the way the thing moved that was more mechanical than biological – had spattered on me. I dialed 911 and then crawled over to Roger. He was bleeding profusely, and one of his hands was neatly severed just above the wrist where the thing had wrapped one of its appendages around him. Of the missing hand there was no sign, and I shuddered as I thought of whatever foul gullet was digesting it.

The paramedics were there in less than a half hour; an impressive response time considering how remote the old man's ranch was. I sat there, holding Roger, trying to stem the flow of blood, as we waited. He barely spoke, whimpering in pain as the life drained from him, but after they arrived and placed him on the stretcher, he reached out to me with his remaining hand, grabbing my sleeve and pulling me close.

"What was it, Dan?" he rasped out.

God help me, I still don't know.

Cuckoo Cocoon
Derek Austin Johnson

"I can't find my mom," the child said, his voice cracking.

Melinda looked between the sparsely populated cereal aisle and the rows of cash registers jammed with disinterested shoppers, but didn't notice anyone looking for their missing child. She leaned down to speak with him face-to-face, but her chin lined up with the top of his head. Hair the color and texture of cornsilk capped his head in a bowl cut. It ruffled, possibly from the store's air conditioning.

"I'm sorry. We'll find your mother. What does she look like?"

The boy said nothing but dropped his gaze to the bright tiled floor, his arms straight but tense. His pale skin was only slightly darker than his white short-sleeved shirt, which contrasted with his black polyester slacks. He looked like he was dressed for a formal birthday party, or Sunday school.

Wincing, Melinda squatted to get a better look at him but he turned his face away. She had to spread her feet widely apart.

"It's okay. You don't need to be scared. She can't have gone far. What's your name?"

His mouth pinched shut, hollowing his cheeks.

"Not supposed to speak to strangers, huh?" Melinda asked. At the continued silence, she offered a reassuring smile. "I get it. When I was little, I wasn't allowed to talk to anybody I didn't know. Or people my mom didn't approve of. Which was a lot of people." Her smile widened. "It'll be different when I have children."

Still nothing. It was impossible to tell how old he was; he might have been a large four-year-old or a very small eight. Melinda was never able to tell anyone's age, let alone kids. To her, they all were the same age.

Melinda realized this, too, was something she needed to change.

She asked more questions. Did he know his mother's name? Where had he last seen her?

No answer, not even a shake of the head.

Customers swarmed the registers and self-checkout kiosks. Anxiety surged through her. She'd come to this Central Austin HEB because the web advised it was almost never busy during the afternoon. Everyone else must have read that post, too. If she could leave before rush-hour traffic clogged Burnet Road, she would consider herself lucky.

"Why don't we go to the customer service center?" Using a shelf as leverage, she managed to stand. A groan escaped her lips and she laughed. "They can call your mom from there."

The boy took her hand and walked with her to the front of the store. Despite his size, his grip was tight. As she explained the situation to a bored clerk, she flexed her fingers so blood could flow back into her hand.

The checkout lines had grown longer by the time she waddled back from the vitamin shelves. As she waited, she listened for an announcement concerning the boy, but nothing interrupted Michael Jackson's "Human Nature" on the PA system. Probably a fan, she thought, while passing the clerk her debit card, maybe they will make an announcement after the song finishes.

The boy stood near the customer service counter, his head turning to track her position as she stepped through the sliding glass doors. Melinda smiled at him. His eyes were wide and round and completely black. Melinda's smile vanished.

Averting her eyes and quickening her pace, she fished her keys from her purse and the prenatal vitamins sank to its bottom.

When she got home, her husband Daniel sat on the sofa, his laptop open. "You'll never guess what happened today."

"Probably not," he said, his attention never wavering from the spreadsheet on his screen. "Brenda and Alex called to confirm dinner on Thursday. Oh, and I haven't fed your cat yet. Been putting out fires all day."

In the kitchen, the cat, Nina, sat on the cool tile floor waiting for her evening meal. Melinda relayed the story of the boy as she stirred wet food in a neon pink dish. Nina watched with interest and contempt.

"You wanted the store to call this kid's mother?" The criticism was overt in Daniel's question "Do you know how much trafficking is going on? Anybody could have said they were the kid's parent. Especially if he wasn't talking to anybody. I mean, considering your condition . . . Can you bring me some wine? I think there's some in the Bota Box."

Merlot splashed into a stemless glass. "I had to do something," she said as she set the glass on top of a wicker coaster on the coffee table. "Nobody else was stepping up. I'm certain he wouldn't go with anybody but his mother. Besides, I think he was a special needs child. His voice was, I don't know, off. Like he was speaking through Autotune, or maybe like ChatGPT imitating a person's voice."

"He was on the spectrum?"

"Maybe."

Daniel closed his laptop and swirled the wine in its glass. "It's still a bad idea. You know how parents can get when it comes to their children. Hey!" he shouted at Nina, who had jumped on the coffee table to sniff the laptop. The cat leapt away and ran to the bedroom.

"It seemed important to help," she said, following Nina. The cat sprawled on the bed and licked a space beneath her dew claw. Her own belly was large, and Melinda envied her ability to move with speed. Daniel often joked Nina was having a sympathetic pregnancy.

"In a world full of crazy people?" A dismissive noise. He set his bare feet on the coffee table. "What should we make for dinner?"

Nina's hiss woke Melinda. The cat lay on Melinda's legs. Her legs tingled from Nina's weight. Even when Melinda moved, Nina didn't budge from the foot of the bed. She growled at the moonlight shining through the gossamer curtains draped across the bedroom window, the fur on her back spiked like porcupine quills.

Melinda cooed at Nina and rose.

A peek through the window revealed nothing but the overgrown back yard, weeds towering above ragged grass.

The cat snarled and raised her tail, ready to pounce. Melinda stroked Nina's head, but the cat remained focused on the window.

"You want out, don't you?" She yawned and opened the window.

A shadow moved across the tall grass.

With a yowl, Nina leapt from the bed and darted through the open window. She let out a high-pitched scream, which was followed by an answering wail. Melinda couldn't tell if it was a sound made by another cat or a human. Still, the question occurred to her—was there someone in her yard? She grabbed her robe, cinching it closed over her swollen belly. She rushed to the back porch outside the kitchen. The gate clapped against the cedar fence, the faint sound of running footsteps slapped the sidewalk. Houses up and down the Brentwood neighborhood lay quiet. The pecan tree in their front yard broke the moonlight into abstract patterns on the lawn.

She closed the gate.

On the back porch, Nina sat next to one of the potted ferns, licking her paws, before hopping back into the house.

Daniel went into the office the next morning. After pouring kibble in Nina's dish, Melinda splashed water in their coffee cups and sat on the couch with her laptop, searching for a job. She'd been laid off from her previous employer a couple of months before. Not exactly the best timing, but Daniel assured her they could make it all work, especially when the baby came.

When the watch chimed its reminder for her to stand, she walked to the kitchen, her hand pressed against her stomach to feel the baby kick, and frowned.

Nina's morning kibble remained untouched.

Calling the cat's name, Melinda searched the living room and master bedroom, but didn't find her. Her usual hiding spaces in Melinda's shoe closet and beneath Daniel's suits were empty. Had she slipped outside when Daniel left? Melinda couldn't remember, though it was within the realm of possibility.

The doorbell rang.

Melinda opened the front door and stepped back in shock.

It was the little boy from the supermarket. He stood still and straight, arms at his sides, wearing the same clothes as yesterday, though a portion next to the chest pocket appeared ridged and puckered, as if his mother had rushed through the ironing. Despite the humid August morning, sweat neither beaded on his nose nor spread beneath his arms.

"Um, hello," she said, stammering. "Can I help you? Is your mother here?"

The boy looked up at her with bright red irises devoid of pupils. Blue veins webbed his alabaster skin. His hair rippled, as if tossed in a light breeze, though there was none.

"I can't find my mom," the child said.

Melinda understood the words, but they sounded odd, almost as if he was speaking backwards, like someone playing an old tape recording in reverse.

Inside her, the baby kicked.

From the bedroom came a high-pitched screech. Without thinking, Melinda rushed to investigate, leaving the child at her door.

Nina writhed on the floor in front of the bed. She yowled in pain and fear, the screeching so loud it put Melinda's nerves on edge.

On Nina's prodigious stomach was a large swelling sac, like a tumor.

Melinda leaned down to pick her up, but the cat swiped at her, thick claws missing her by an inch. She backed away and pulled her phone from the pocket of her dress. By the time she pressed the last digit of the vet's phone number, Nina gave a final screech and stopped moving.

For a moment, Melinda thought Nina was dead, then she saw the faint rise and fall of her chest.

"It's okay, it's okay," she said, retrieving the carrier from the closet and opening the small wire door. "We'll get you taken care of." With her pale pink blanket, she scooped Nina up and placed her in the carrier. The cat was limp, her breath shallow. "It'll be all right," Melinda said in the garage as she fastened the seatbelt around the carrier and pushed her car's ignition button.

By the time the vet's assistant led her to the Greater Austin Animal Hospital examination room, Melinda realized she had left the front door open. What became of the strange child? Had the bizarre child really been at her door? Was it possible she had imagined the encounter?

The vet sent her home. Though he promised to do what he could for Nina, he offered no reassurance. During her drive back, Melinda fought the urge to pull over and cry.

There was no time.

Tires screeched as she stopped at the curb. The front door stood open, its stopper bent in an L-shape, making the knob thump against the foyer wall. The hinges creaked as she shut the door.

Melinda checked the living room and bedroom. Everything seemed in place. Though the garage was open, no one had taken the mower or power drill. The drill still had its bit inserted, wooden shavings stuck in the grooves.

Sighing in relief, she moved the car into the garage and glanced at her phone. No call from the vet. She texted Daniel about Nina. His concise response stated he would come home early.

She went to the kitchen for a glass of water. As she drank, a realization dawned on her. The plate of frozen hamburger she had left out thawing for dinner was gone.

She heard smacking sounds in the dining room.

When she went to investigate, her glass slipped from her hand and smashed on the tile floor, splashing water over her bare legs.

The boy sat at the table, the plate of raw hamburger in front of him. He squeezed a handful and pushed it in his mouth, thin blood dribbling from his lips.

"Hey!" Her shout reverberated in the dining room, startling her. The boy did not jump or even respond.

Melinda stormed to him and slapped her hands on the table. Her baby kicked in response.

"What the hell are you doing here?" Anger flushed her skin. "You need to get out. Right now."

The boy opened his mouth. Out came hisses, chitters, and the whir of an old audio tape being rewound.

She reached for him, intending to squeeze his chin and look into his eyes.

He screamed.

Melinda clapped her hands over her ears. The scream pierced the padding of her palms, an excruciating shriek, rising in pitch the longer it went. The sonic assault crumpled her into the China cabinet. Cracks webbed the panes, which shattered and showered her with glass.

A long shard landed at her feet.

The boy's face contorted, his black eyes a pair of bottomless pits. His jaw elongated revealing a long, pointed onyx tongue.

Frantically, she snatched the long shard at her feet and with a yell she rushed the boy. The jagged shard came down and down and down and didn't stop until Melinda was covered in foul-smelling yellow ichor and the child no longer resembled anything human. Her palms bled freely where the glass had made contact with her unprotected flesh.

She carried the makeshift glass dagger with her as she half-waddled, half-stumbled to the bathroom. There she dropped the shard with a sharp tinkling sound on the tile floor and vomited into the toilet.

"What happened in here?" Daniel asked.

Melinda hunched over the dining room floor. She wore rubber gloves and sponged up as much of the dark amber fluid as she could with their kitchen towels. Her mouth was open, and she huffed as she dropped the towels in the garbage bag sitting next to her. On the table, paper towels soaked up more of the fluid. The dining room reeked of rotten meat and cleaning products. Light from the chandelier glinted on the fragments of glass littering the tile floor.

"Seriously, what's going on? Was all of this because of your cat?"

"Her name is Nina, Daniel. And yes, she's at the vet. But that's not what this is." Cinching closed the garbage bag, she pulled herself up using the table ledge, then dragged the garbage bag to the garage and tossed it in the trash can. The trash can's wheels rumbled as she rolled it to the curb. She stripped off her gloves and tossed them in the trash can as well. The gauze on her hands was spotted with blood.

When she returned, Daniel sat in the living room, his face a mixture of confusion and concern. He opened his mouth, then closed it, unsure of what to say.

She told him about the boy, and what happened to Nina, and what she'd done when she found the boy in the house.

"He wasn't wearing clothes," she continued. "It's like the shirt and pants and shoes were part of his body."

As she spoke, Daniel's face was an expressionless mask.

Finally, he stood.

"I have no idea what to say to this."

"It's true."

"I didn't see any blood in the dining room. It looked like you spilled that cheap dish soap."

"It wasn't blood. But it was some kind of body fluid."

Daniel sighed. "Let me see what you took outside."

Melinda led him to the curb and he lifted the trash can's lid. The trash can had been outside for ten minutes and already the mix of trash and garbage stank. Daniel opened the garbage bag and peeked inside. Amid the sopping kitchen towels lay chunks of meat slick with what looked like black jelly. He tightened the bag's draw strings and cursed as one of the shards of glass nicked his finger. He sucked at the blood welling from the cut.

Melinda swatted his shoulder. "Don't do that! You'll get infected!"

Daniel wrapped his finger with a handkerchief, then closed the trash can lid and went back inside.

"I'm not making this up," she said as he wrapped gauze around his wounded finger.

"I didn't say you were," Daniel said. "But come on, it looks like you tossed out the brisket we were supposed to cook for Brenda and Alex, and let the veggies go bad. Didn't you go to the store yesterday?"

Her lips tightened. "I was picking up my vitamins."

"Right." A nod.

"And that's not the brisket or any of the vegetables. Why don't you check the refrigerator? The only thing you'll find missing is the ground beef."

"That he ate."

She said nothing. He nodded again.

"Look, you told me once the vitamins make you loopy. They're probably having an effect. I'd be seeing scary children, too, if I was in your condition and worried about my pet."

As if on cue, Melinda's phone buzzed. The vet's office.

"I'm very sorry," said the veterinarian's assistant, then explained what had happened to Nina.

She'd had her kittens but died giving birth.

The kittens were gone.

"That little boy came by to pick them up," the vet said.

She locked herself in the bedroom and refused to come out. As she latched closed the bedroom window, Daniel knocked on the door and offered what sympathy he could. The knocks seemed to coincide perfectly with the blood rushing in her ears.

"I know you loved her," he said. "But you can always get another cat. You can take your pick. I'm sure there's one that looks exactly like her. It's not like she was our kid."

"That's not the point!" she shouted at the door as she paced in front of the bed and fished the vitamins from her purse. She put her strength into opening it but the cap refused to budge. "It's not just about Nina. That was her name. We've been married for three years, and you never learned that. No, something is coming here. Nina scratched it, and I'm pretty sure when she cleaned her claws whatever that thing used for blood also carried something that allowed it to reproduce. It probably absorbed her kittens, then left when she gave birth."

"I thought you said the vet didn't know what happened."

"He doesn't. Whatever that creature is, it used Nina as a vessel. A cocoon." She huffed in disbelief. "They're similar to cuckoos, those birds that kick other birds out of their nests. They look like boys from some other time. It's like an alien studied human beings from an earlier period and dropped them here."

Silence from the other side of the door. "When was the last time you talked to your doctor?"

Melinda barked out a laugh. "I don't need my doctor. I'm not hallucinating and I'm not paranoid."

When Daniel spoke again, it was as if speaking to a child.

"Melinda, I know this hasn't been the easiest time. I read that pregnancy book with you. But you're scaring me. You need to see someone. I'll call Alex. He has a good therapist. And I'll tell him we need to postpone dinner tomorrow. They know you're due soon, so they'll understand. Now, will you let me in?"

Outside, wind rustled the leaves of the pecan tree in the back yard.

"Fine," he said after a time. "I'll sleep in the baby's room. But I need you to think about your behavior. This can't go on. It's not healthy for you or the baby."

Through the door came the stomp of feet on the carpet.

Melinda sat on the edge of the bed, listening to Daniel stomping away and staring at herself in the dresser mirror. Her eyes were as puffy as her belly and felt heavier. In one of her bandaged hands was the long shard of glass from the China cabinet, a kitchen towel wrapped around the bottom like a makeshift hilt.

A sudden gust rattled the bedroom window.

A door's creaking hinge startled her awake.

The clock on the end table told her it was three in the morning. Moonlight cast the bedroom in silver, sharpening the edges of shadows.

The door stood ajar. Blue light from the television in the living room shone along the hallway.

From the living room came a squelch.

Slowly, Melinda crept down the hall, her grip on the shard so tight she worried it would break in her hand.

At the hall's opening, she peeked around the corner.

Daniel lay on the floor in a pool of blood, black in the light from the television's blue screen. His chest was torn open, exposing the cavity of his torso.

Next to him stood the boy.

The cuckoo.

It was smaller than the one she had killed, but otherwise identical.

Melinda hid behind the corner and squeezed her hand over her mouth to keep from screaming. As terror surged through her body, she forced herself not to run or be sick. Slowly she exhaled and peered around the corner again.

This couldn't happen, she told herself. She wouldn't let it.

She let herself into the guest bathroom and pushed toilet paper into her ears, then went back into the hallway and turned the corner, glass shard held ready.

In front of Daniel's body, the cuckoo stood, waiting. It chittered and whirred.

Inside her, the baby wouldn't stop kicking.

She rushed the cuckoo.

Even with toilet paper padding her ears, she winced at the sound of its scream. It backed away but remained close enough for Melinda to grab its cornsilk hair. The strands of hair curled around her wrist and bit into her skin. The cuckoo's scream drowned her own. She swiped at the cuckoo, gouging a large wound through its fake clothing and into its chest. She released her grip on its hair, the embedded strands slipping from her wrist. As the cuckoo fled to the kitchen, Melinda examined the bleeding puncture wounds in her wrist.

Beyond the kitchen, the door to the garage opened, its hinges creaking.

Melinda leaned into the garage and turned on the light. Yellow fluorescent light bounced off the hoods of her car and Daniel's. She could trap the thing here, she thought, but she had no idea how smart the cuckoo was. Could it learn how to get out of the garage and escape—maybe back to the grocery store. Or some other populated area, where it could be taken in and reproduce.

She rubbed her wrist. The area punctured by the cornsilk hair grew numb. Frantically, she flexed her fingers and moved her hand. It still worked. She would need medical care after she was done with the cuckoo.

Melinda shuddered at the thought of what exposure to this alien creature might do to her baby.

The fingers of her other hand ached. How long had she been holding this shard? Walking back to the kitchen, she placed it on the counter and stretched her fingers, then slid a butcher's knife from a drawer.

She entered the garage, closing the door behind her.

Other than the squeak of the utility locker's open door next to Daniel's car, it was quiet.

In front of her car, and between the washing machine and dryer, sat their plastic clothes hamper, the metal flap still. She leaned over and, with the tip of the knife, she pushed open the flap. Daniel's t-shirts lay wadded at the bottom.

When she stood, something crashed into her legs, spinning her onto the hood of Daniel's car. She slid off, landing on her back, her breath rushing out of her lungs. The blade of the butcher's knife had become caught between the hood and fender of the car.

The cuckoo towered over her. Chattering and whirring, it straddled her chest and opened its mouth, the jaw distending, its pointed tongue protruding. She tried rocking her body, but the cuckoo weighed more than she expected. Twisting her head away from the cuckoo's face, she glanced at the hilt of the knife sticking up from between the hood and fender. Melinda's hands scrabbled over the fender of Daniel's car, but she couldn't quite reach it.

The chittering stopped, replaced by the scream.

Melinda thrashed, tears streaming from her eyes. She squeezed them shut and when they opened she saw the utility cabinet. Where the drill sat, its bit in place.

She reached for the drill as the cuckoo's scream rose in pitch. Her other hand pressed against the cuckoo's chest and managed to lift it just enough to gain some movement. Enough to reach the drill.

She clutched it and pressed the bit against the cuckoo's head, hoping the drill's battery still contained a charge.

It did.

The cuckoo stopped screaming as the bit sank into its head, the pits of his black eyes filling with gray as it ceased moving.

Melinda pushed the cuckoo off her chest, rose, and stumbled back into the kitchen, setting the drill on the counter next to the glass shard. She collapsed on the floor, exhausted. Her eyes fell to the puncture wounds on her wrist. She wondered if the cornsilk was like a rattlesnake's fangs, meant to poison her, or if they contained the same sort of fluid that allowed them to reproduce.

She wondered if the baby would be okay, which made her think of Daniel, and she choked back a sob.

Exhaustion overtook her. Sleepily, she lay on the floor and scratched her wrist. Then her stomach. As her consciousness slid away from her she realized the baby didn't respond.

Not immediately.

Not with a kick.

But her stomach began swelling.

A car parked in the driveway. Two people got out, a man and a woman. The man wrinkled his nose at the stench coming from the garbage can on the curb. They walked to the front door and the man pressed the doorbell.

No answer.

"They said seven, right?" Alex said.

Next to him, Brenda tapped her phone. "That's what the calendar says. 'Dinner with Daniel and Melinda. Bring the baby gift.' Maybe they're running late."

Alex frowned. "They couldn't be. Melinda has been staying home." A sad look crossed his face. "Daniel told me she's exhausted most of the time."

"Pregnancy can take it out of you." Brenda tapped Melinda's phone number and held the phone to her ear.

A phone rang behind the door.

They looked at each other.

Cupping his eyes, Alex pressed his face against the door's frosted glass window.

The door swung open.

"Oh god," he said, and gagged. The coppery smell of blood was overpowering "Call the police."

As she dialed the number, a figure appeared. A small boy in white shirt and black slacks. His black eyes studied them, then it chittered and leapt at Alex's chest. Alex fell backward, smacking his head on the walkway. Stunned, his eyes blinked, then turned glassy.

Dropping her phone, Brenda screamed and ran to the car.

The boy hopped off Alex and ran after her.

It got her before she reached the driveway.

Another cocoon. Another cuckoo.

The bodies were dragged into the living room, the blue television screen shining on them. Each took turns ingesting the former hosts and their mates until everything was gone.

They wandered the house. Their whirrs and chitters began to resemble human speech.

In time, they both left, heading in opposite directions.

One finally made it to a place that seemed familiar.

The cuckoo entered the grocery store. Cool air ruffled the cornsilk hair. Nostrils flared at the smell of human beings strolling aisles of cereal and canned goods, detergent and paper products. Ears took in the rattle of shopping carts, the babble of human voices, the speaker system playing a song about human nature.

A bump.

"Oops, sorry," a young girl said. She was eight or nine years old and wearing a t-shirt displaying a pair of men in dark glasses and black suits. "I didn't see you. Hey, are you okay? You look scared. Are you lost?"

Mouth opened—not wide enough to let the girl see inside, but to form words. Speech was still new, but the words came.

"I can't find my mom," the cuckoo said.

Noche De El Chupacabras

Juan Perez

Somewhere near the American-Mexican border, 1941

I
Among stories of Mexican Indians
lives a spirit, so wild and uncanny
    one dangerous creature without restraint
without purpose for mayhem or malice
one that won't be summoned but just appears
all on its very own without notice
one that can change a man to a monster
and then back again if it so wills it
one that can't be reasoned within ethos
nor understood under its influence
one that mostly demands to stay in form
regardless of the rules that govern it
yet that simply won't work for those who live
in the careless, lit hours of the night

II
Among every dark corner of this land

it wrestles with hunger, waiting for food
this is a blood-eater that's for certain
but not as one would think as a vampire
this is a shape-shifter, this is confirmed
derived from the myth of Kokopelli
this lost cousin of coyotes built with
something more by its very creator
this thing, this green-grayish aberration
with one row of spikes upon skull and spine
this old and terrible experiment
let loose from labs of ancient visitors
yet where are they to be found for advice
or to rescue humankind from their curse

III

Among the steady heartbeats of worn drums
Meshica priests chant into the long night
see there by the prickly pear cactus patch
near the cover of ancient, mesquite trees
see them sweat blood with extreme inciting
in the dead language of incantations
see the sharp darkness of obsidian
as their prayers rise up with an urgent plea
see the obscure creature percolating
through the thin skin of the unsuspecting
see how his face trembles violently so
distorting whatever was once a man
yet there he just stood, spouting strange sonnets
to a now stunned crowd, growling at the sky

IV

Among the spreading chaos of humans
running everywhere in the name of fear
hear the ripping of fresh flesh by the stage
a paralyzed front that never felt chance
hear the loud shriek of disembodiment
as arms and legs rocket into the sky
hear the pleas for peace and dear appeasement

begging for continuation of life
hear the horror of a swift denial
as decapitations become décor
hear the widening silence in the air
as many fall prey to this mystery
yet its real lust is nowhere around here
except in the pens of some nearby farms

Among the bodies of beaten chickens
deep in the quiet pens of sucked-dried goats
feel the senseless slaughter of innocence
born for the kill much earlier than planned
feel the serenity of morning peace
and the awkwardness of a naked man
feel the grogginess of some drunken bliss
measured by questions of wide-opened eyes
feel the anger of vigilante mobs
coming to exact their peasant justice
feel the rough noose around the neck tighten
as the man-beast swings in the air just once
yet transforming again at the gallows
tearing life and limb, laying waste to all

V
Among the woods, hiding from the others
hiding from this thing that now becomes him
smell the rancid rotting of humanness
worn upon a harsh, transformative skin
smell the fear of exiting normalcy
for things he can never ever explain
smell the scent of death's guide, the xolo dog
used now to track down the hellish monster
smell the tension in the electric air
as the dogs draw near and heartbeats beat strong
smell the desperation of hunted man
looking for a way out of this dark mess
yet once again, the man-beast will escape
live to be transformed on another day

VI
Among the arms of his dear beloved
he finds his much-needed rest and rescue
taste the sweet, luscious lips of a woman
the soft, slim extremities of passion
taste the drug that put him under, to sleep
as the drums and chanting begin again
taste the iron grip of ropes that hold him
awakening upon a stone altar
taste the deep confusion of the man-beast
as the sacrifice signals solutions
taste the bitterness of the betrayal
soft hands of a priestess disguised as love
yet this time there is no escape from death
as she holds his still-beating heart skyward

Hank and the Scorpion
Bev Vincent

Hank didn't think he'd ever look at the world the same way again after he found a scorpion on the floor of the upstairs bathroom in his house. A goddamned scorpion. How the hell did it get here? he wondered. He had been living in Texas for over thirty years and had never seen one of these poisonous arachnids before.

Anywhere. To find one inside his house—upstairs, no less—shook him to the core.

It wasn't dead—its tail curled and uncurled lazily—but it was clearly on its way out. He threw a towel over it and stomped on it. Several times. His slippers had thick rubber soles, so he felt protected from the creature's stinger. When he was done, he carefully bundled up the towel and carried it downstairs and outside to the garbage can. He could have flushed it, but he wanted to make sure it was gone from the house for good.

He was only mildly comforted by the fact the scorpion had seemed to be dying. It had been nearly two months since the pest control service last came by. That indicated that the noxious chemicals the technician—a big man named Roger, who carried on a nonstop conversation with someone via Bluetooth while he worked—had sprayed around the house were still working. That was comforting but also a little worrisome when he thought about it.

It wasn't the biggest pest the poison had brought down over the years. That honor fell to a number of Palmetto bugs, a somewhat palatable sobriquet for what were actually big-ass cockroaches. He'd been flabbergasted the first time he'd seen one of them racing up the wall of his first apartment in Texas, and then mortified when it had taken flight. Jesus Christ Almighty, those things could fly.

Scorpions couldn't, though, so how had it gotten upstairs? A search on his phone gave him all the information he never wanted to know about the striped bark scorpion, which was apparently what he had just encountered, including the two facts that their sting was painful but rarely fatal, and they could climb walls. One website gave helpful hints on how to position your bed to keep them from falling into it from the ceiling and Hank didn't think he'd ever go to sleep again.

Another webpage claimed scorpions were solitary, so the interloper who'd showed up in the upstairs bathroom might have been a one-off. Of course, he didn't stop there, digging into pages about scorpion lore like a sick person Googling symptoms on WebMD. He was fascinated to learn there were people in Asia who smoked scorpion venom by inhaling the smoke as the creatures were burned alive over hot coals. The high could last from ten hours to three days, although the first six hours were incredibly painful as their bodies adapted to the poison.

The next link was the true stuff of nightmares—a picture of a female scorpion carrying some two-dozen offspring on her back. He imagined all those creepy little scorplings finding hiding places among his clothes or in the pantry or . . . anywhere.

When he moved to Texas from the northeast, people had warned him there were four kinds of poisonous snakes in the area. In all the time he'd lived here, he'd never seen a single living snake, just one dead snake on the side of the road when he'd been out biking several years ago. His backyard was wild, and home to some critter that lived under the back deck—a possum, most likely—but no snakes. He had convinced himself he'd never encounter anything dangerous. No one had said a word about scorpions.

Hank briefly considered torching the house and moving somewhere with glass or metal walls. Apparently, scorpions could only climb rough surfaces. He poured a glass of bourbon, even though it wasn't yet 9:00 in the morning. After a few sips of the aromatic liquid, he found himself a little calmer. The little bastard had been dying, after all, and it was the first one to ever breach the confines of his home. True, global warming meant all manner of changes to the ecosystem, but he wasn't going to be like Flitcraft, the guy in Hammett's novel who abruptly abandoned his comfortable life after a close encounter with a falling construction beam. Hank could pack up and relocate somewhere that didn't have scorpions—he could work anywhere that had good internet—but that would mean the scorpion won, wouldn't it? And he couldn't have that.

After he finished his drink, he went upstairs to his office. As he toiled away at his workstation, he kept watch on his surroundings. Several times he thought he detected motion out of the corner of his eye but there was never anything there when he turned to look.

At the end of the afternoon, after he signed off, he felt the need to get out of the house. He'd never before felt so uncomfortable within those four walls, not even during the strained days after Margo, his ex-wife, announced she was leaving him to join a commune in the middle of the state. The middle of nowhere.

He walked to the local Mexican restaurant and found an empty two-top in a corner of the bar, where he ate a plate of tacos and downed Negra Modelos. Eventually, though, he had to return home. Once there, he settled into his recliner and found a hockey game in the third period. He thought he heard the announcer call one of the teams the Scorpions, but they turned out to be the Krakens.

When the game was over, he started watching the second episode of a Netflix series that had caught his interest. There was a guy buried in a barrel in the Australian Outback and the main character, who had amnesia, was trying to retrace his steps to find him. It was all going well enough until the scene changed to show a huge scorpion—several times larger than the one he'd found in the bathroom—climbing through the pipe the bad guy had installed to supply air to the buried victim. When it dropped on the man's chest, his light blinked out. Then there were screams. Hank clicked the TV off so fast the imprint of the remote button stayed on his thumb for several seconds. It felt like the universe was conspiring against him.

Still rattled, he decided to turn in. First, he moved the bed two feet from every wall to make it less likely a scorpion would fall on him during the night, and confirmed that the bedclothes weren't touching the floor. He read until he was drowsy, convinced he was going to have nightmares, especially one inspired by that photo of the mama scorpion and its slew of offspring, but instead he dreamed about his ex-wife. It wasn't an unpleasant dream, although he didn't know why he was thinking about her.

When he woke up in the morning, his mouth felt like he'd gargled smoke. For one panicked moment, he imagined himself like Gregor Samsa, except he'd turned into a scorpion instead of a cockroach, or a Palmetto bug, or whatever. He clamped his eyes shut again, then opened them one at a time, slowly. He had not metamorphosized overnight, nor was he sharing the bed with a scorpion that had fallen from the ceiling, so far as he could tell. Once that thought was lodged in his mind, though, he sprang from bed and threw back the covers, searching between each layer for unwanted guests.

Then he realized he was standing barefoot on the carpeted floor at the edge of the bed, beneath which a striped bark scorpion could be waiting to plunge its stinger into his big toe. He stepped back a couple of paces, colliding with the bedroom wall, and retreated to the bathroom. He showered—after making sure nothing was lurking in or above the shower stall—and shaved, then got dressed, shaking his shoes before sticking his feet in them, because he'd read scorpions liked to lurk in dark places like empty shoes.

Since he was going to be stuck working indoors all day, he decided to go out for breakfast. He didn't linger in the garage— there were too many dark corners—and even gave his car a cursory checkout before getting behind the wheel. The windows had been rolled up all the way, so it wasn't likely any critters had gotten into his vehicle, but still.

When he backed into the driveway and paused to be sure the garage door closed, he cast a suspicious eye over the front yard. There was a tangle of vines in the landscaping box where flowers once grew among the trees, and the lawn was a little longer than he liked. He craned his neck to look up into the leafy crowns of the trees. His unwanted visitor had been a tree scorpion, after all. How many others were lurking up there among the squirrels and birds? He made a mental note to wear protective clothing the next time he mowed. There were worse things than mosquitoes out here.

He wasn't exactly a regular at the neighborhood cafe, but he went often enough to be nodding acquaintances with several patrons. He ordered his usual, filled his travel mug with coffee, and found a quiet corner. While waiting for his food to arrive, he pulled out his phone. The first image that greeted him when he opened the browser was the picture of the female scorpion with her brood. He quickly closed that window and pulled up a news site. As usual, it was all doom and gloom—the war in the Middle East, a new strain of coronavirus, the war in Eastern Europe, a mass shooting at a compound west of Austin, the discovery of a missing child's body. None of it was useful information, and he wondered—not for the first time—why he insisted on being well-informed. Knowing how many people died in a landslide in a country he'd never visited, and probably couldn't find on a map, wouldn't turn him into a brilliant conversationalist.

He pulled up the entertainment section and distracted himself with the comics and sudoku. He noticed the link to the horoscopes and paused. He had no interest in such folderal, but Margo had been obsessed by them, reading aloud both of their forecasts every day. He'd listened patiently, having given up trying to convince her they were rubbish a long time before.

Hank was a Gemini. Margo's birthday, he recalled, was November 10th. That made her . . . a Scorpio.

He shook his head at the coincidence and went to the daily Wordle, which he got in four tries, then put his phone down on the table when his food arrived.

He'd just finished eating and was contemplating a third cup of coffee when his phone started vibrating. Glancing at the display, he saw it was his younger brother, Gord. Rather than suffer the withering gazes of the other café patrons, he softly told his brother to hang on a sec, delivered his dirty dishes to the counter, added a splash of coffee to his mug, and went outside where he found an unoccupied bench. He needed to head home soon to sign on for work, but he knew the call wouldn't last long. Gord liked to call to tell him some tidbit of news he'd gleaned— usually bad and often something Hank already knew.

"OK, Gord, I'm here."

"Have you heard about . . ."

Hank rolled his eyes. Eighty percent of Gord's calls started with those same four words. There was no way, though, that he could have anticipated the next one.

". . .Margo?"

"What? What about her?"

"She's dead."

Hank was stunned into silence. Finally, he choked out a single syllable. "How?"

"Apparently things at that Alacrán place weren't as harmonious as they wanted people to believe."

"I'm not following you."

"The mass shooting. Didn't you hear about it?"

Hank thought back to the headlines he'd scanned a few minutes earlier. "When?" Even in the moment, Hank was struck by how terse his responses to his brother were, like a journalist trying to tease out the 5Ws of a story.

"*Dude*, it's all online."

Hank hated being called "dude" and Gord knew it.

When Hank didn't react, Gord continued, "Apparently the shooting happened yesterday morning, but no one called the cops until sometime last night. A delivery guy found the... umm, well..."

"The scene," Hank supplied.

"Yeah, right."

"And the shooter?"

"The leader of the commune. He offed himself, too, so no one knows what bug crawled up his ass. Probably never will know."

Hank felt surprisingly relieved when his brother referred to the shooter as "he" For a moment he'd been concerned that it might have been Margo, as crazy as that sounded in his head now. Gord's reference to a bug crawling up the cult leader's ass led him to imagine . . .

"I have to go," Hank said suddenly. Usually, it was Gord who abruptly ended their calls. He pulled up his daughter's number. She was married and living in Tacoma with her husband and their two children. Margo had waited until Sarah graduated high school before going down an internet rabbit hole that led her to a wackadoodle commune, giving up all her earthly goods and abandoning her family. At least she hadn't emptied the bank accounts, as sometimes happened with cases like this. Hank had been able to help pay for Sarah's college education and remained as close to her as possible, given the distance. As far as he knew, Margo never even contacted their daughter once she decamped, which was the cruelest part of the entire debacle, as far as he was concerned. She'd never even met her grandchildren. Might not even have known they existed.

And now this.

He was tempted to take a moment to read the news accounts so he'd be better informed when he spoke to Sarah, but decided against it. He checked the time—it was still quite early on the West Coast. He decided to text her husband first. "Are you awake?"

Brandon responded almost immediately. "yep / what's up"

"Stand by. I have some bad news for Sarah and she might need your support."

"gotcha / standing by"

Hank was always amused by Brandon's chaotic approach to punctuation. He punched the icon to call his daughter.

"Daddy? Are you OK? What happened?"

"It's your mom," Hank said. "I'm afraid she's gone."

There was a long silence before Sarah responded. "She's been gone a long time."

It hurt Hank to hear her the bitter coldness in his daughter's voice. "This is the big gone, sweetie."

Another silence. Then, "What happened?"

"A mass shooting. At that place. It's in the news."

Hank heard some muffled conversation between Sarah and her husband. "I see it now," she said.

"I'm terribly sorry, Sarah."

"Thanks, Daddy. I . . . I need a moment to process. Can we talk later?"

"Of course. Love you."

"Love you, too, Daddy. What about you?"

"What?"

"Are you okay?"

Hank paused. "I guess so. It's a shock for sure, but, like you said, she's been gone a long time."

"Yeah. I'll call later. We have to get the kids ready for school."

"Okay. Talk later."

Hank hung up and took a sip of coffee. It was cold, but he didn't care. Now he pulled up the articles and read the few details that were known and the endless speculation that followed. He didn't feel particularly enlightened, but one piece of information stood out. The current estimate was that the shooting had taken place the previous morning between 8:00 and 9:00.

Around the same time as he'd found the scorpion on the upstairs bathroom floor, the bathroom that had been Sarah's when she lived at home. Margo the Scorpio had been killed while he was stomping on a striped bark scorpion. And he had been plagued by thoughts of and references to scorpions ever since.

Margo would have said it was a sign. She had told countless stories about being visited by people at the moment of their deaths. Relatives, friends, casual acquaintances, no matter. Hank had always scoffed—internally, as he had no desire to rob his then-wife of these notions, comforting as they were to her. He'd never had a similar experience, though.

Until now, perhaps. He took another drink of cold coffee. Time to go home.

After parking in the garage, Hank put his travel mug on the trunk and went around the corner of the house to the garbage can. The towel was sitting on top of a few trash bags. He thought about going back to the garage for a pair of gloves but shook that off. He plucked the towel off the pile and tossed it on the driveway. He gingerly unfolded it, expecting to find the smashed corpse, but there was nothing. No scorpion guts, even, and he'd heard that thing crunch under his foot. He was sure of it.

He picked the towel up and examined it closely. It was as clean as if freshly laundered. Baffled, he pulled the garbage bin around to the driveway and spilled its contents on the pavement. Other than the three well-sealed bags, the bin was empty.

It could have survived and crawled out of the bin, he thought, but how likely was that? What other mental gymnastics would he need to perform to convince himself the scorpion had never really been there? That it had been a . . . what? A sign? An apology? A farewell?

Hank tossed the bags back into the bin, returned it to its storage place, then took the towel into the house and deposited it in the washing machine. Before heading upstairs, he sat in his recliner for a few moments and stared at the ceiling. He no longer worried about what he might see up there.

But he thought he might look at the world a little differently from now on.

House of Hearts
Lawrence Buentello

On the seventh day of his trip into the Texas wilderness, Keith Burrows found the house again.

He had been camping in the oak and mesquite off the road leading toward the small town of Traveler's Pass, wandering the hidden pathways during the day in search of a house that didn't exist except in his childhood memories. He'd begun to doubt his own recollections by the end of the sixth day—when the storm swept in from the south, borne on warm Gulf winds blown back into an early autumn cold front, he scarcely had time to carry his gear into his tent, secure the door and close the vents before rain dropped from the sky like violent ocean waves. Lying in darkness, unable to locate his lantern, he could only watch the tent lighting up brilliantly every time another shaft punished the nearby trees.

Camping out alone had proven unnecessarily risky, but who would have accompanied him given his reasons for doing so?

The storm had lingered over the tent for hours. After its passing later in the night, he fell asleep to the sound of water dripping from the limbs of trees. Before falling asleep, though, and frustrated by his lack of success, he'd decided to leave for home come morning. At sunrise he collected his gear, rolled his sleeping bag, deconstructed the tent and prepared to load his old pickup truck which, he hoped, could achieve traction enough to drive out through the mud fields left by the storm. But before leaving, he'd strung the tent across low tree branches to dry in the morning air, which hung cool and humid, in order to prevent mold from ruining its fabric.

And while the tent dried in the anemic morning breeze, he'd taken a final walk among the oak and mesquite, feeling his childhood obsession had finally come to an inevitable conclusion.

But in the mists of a clearing he *swore* he'd trespassed several times over the previous days, the house had inexplicably risen—

For a moment, Burrows stood wondering if he might be dreaming—the morning fog covered the wilderness in a gauze, blurred the porch and windows of the house sufficiently to cause him to doubt his senses. From a distance, the house seemed like any other old country dwelling, neglected and in need of repair. But then he breathed deeply, tasting ozone from the moist air, and knew the same house now stood before him as he remembered from twenty-five years before. No, he felt *certain* no house had stood in the clearing the previous day; the structure had simply manifested, as the old people of the county once told him, from a place in the world inaccessible on common days.

Burrows knew he should run back to his truck to retrieve the camera he'd left in its leather bag—but would the house still be standing in the clearing when he returned? As much as he'd planned to record his experiences, were he to ever find the house again, he knew he couldn't risk losing an opportunity that might vanish once he turned his back.

He stared down at his boots briefly, uncertain, and, if he were being honest with himself, frightened. Then he gazed up at the house in the mists again, slipped his fists into the pockets of his denim jacket and began walking into the clearing.

Strangely, he noted nothing else in the clearing *but* the house, no fencing, no worn pathways, no rusting equipment in the grass, no debris indicative of past habitation. Only the house. A small front porch, shaded by a narrow wooden awning, faced away from a front window clouded over by untold years of grime. The porch railing turned an angle to the side of the house and stopped sharply. A three-paned gabled window stood to the left of the front door, its glass panes also obscured. Above the gabled window sat another steepled window staring out on the trees, and then another window above the front door. Raw shingles framed the gable like gray fish scales, while the roof seemed constructed of rusted corrugated steel. As he approached, he felt the structure's age in his bones, its antiquity weighing on him as if he were walking toward an old graveyard.

Instead of immediately climbing the stoop, and because a subtle fear still tensed the muscles of his back, Burrows quietly began walking around the left side of the building, studying every inch of feathered wood, every rusted nail head protruding from the boards. He noted the odd absence of windows on the side of the house, and then, glancing down to where his boots sank into the wild grass, he noticed a small window half-buried in the ground indicating a cellar. Cellars in houses in that part of Texas were uncommon, given the density of the soil, particularly caliche; he bent to peer through the glass, but again years of filth had left its surface completely opaque. Around the back of the building he found a small flight of wooden steps leading up to a back door and a single small window, and then the same curious lack of windows on the opposite side.

Now he stood before the front of the house again, the chill of the morning causing him to shiver despite his jacket. And then he became aware of the complete silence surrounding him, not a lack of urban noises experienced in the country, but an utter absence of any sounds at all, no bird calls, no rustling tree branches, no insects calling from the weeds. He turned to glance back at the trees, noting their unmoving branches and leaves, then out past the house to the static fields of grass, which vanished into low fog. An irrational sensation of suspended time overcame him, one he had to fight to throw off superstitious fears. If he weren't alone—

But he was alone.

Burrows inhaled deeply, exhaled, then walked up the porch and knocked on the door. Of course, no one answered, nor had he expected an answer. His knocking had been an act of courtesy, should he have been mistaken—

In the wilder places of Texas, away from large cities and the hypnotic social architecture of myopic people, enigmatic things existed and had existed since native cultures walked alongside their spiritual ancestors thousands of years before. His grandfather had told him stories of these things when he was a child, though his father only scoffed at the old man's clinging to supernatural folklore. According to his grandfather, spirits walked through the trees and across farmed fields, all the way from the frozen Northern Territories of Canada to the warm Gulf beaches, leaving their mystical influence across the land. Sometimes, perhaps only at the right time, a person might see, hear, or experience these mystical expressions in a way people would be incapable of doing so in the streets of Dallas, or Austin, or San Antonio. And then that person might know the truth of the universe, instead of the narrow fiction embraced by those afraid to live in any other but a sterile environment.

The old people in the farmlands where they'd lived, where Burrows had spent his childhood, talked of a house which only occasionally manifested, along spiritual ley lines known to ancient cultures, an incorporeal house with a life which vibrated with the beating of many hearts. Only a very few people had ever glimpsed it, and no one ever claimed to have passed through its front door.

Twenty-five years before, Burrows had managed to lose his way while happily exploring in the trees off the main road; only six years old, he became deathly afraid of being lost forever and ran in circles through the oaks and mesquites. But then he found a house in a clearing and felt heartened. Hoping to find a kind face, he ran up to the front door and knocked, and knocked, and knocked. But no one ever opened the door. He'd sat on the porch waiting for someone, anyone to come back to the house to help him find his way home, but no one came. He thought at the time that someone must be inside, because he felt a low, rhythmic drumming vibrating through the boards on which he sat. But then, why hadn't anyone come to the door? Eventually, he became drowsy and fought to stay awake; he may have actually fallen asleep for a moment, but then came wide awake when he noticed that the sun had fallen dangerously close to the horizon. Certain no one was coming to help him, he jumped from the porch of the old house and ran through the trees again, eventually finding his way to the main road where a neighbor in a sputtering old Buick stopped to rescue him from the deepening night. His father insisted no house had ever stood where the boy claimed he'd encountered one. No, his father never believed him, insisting instead the boy had lied to excuse his recklessness. But his grandfather believed him, instructing him to never search for the house again. *Keith, it only looks like a house.*

After his grandfather died, Burrow's father sold the small ranch on which they'd lived and relocated his family to Fort Worth, but Burrows never forgot the house, nor did he lose his desire to one day find it again and solve its mystery.

Burrows touched the old glass doorknob, its faux crystalline clarity whitened by age. If his instincts were mistaken, if the house actually belonged to some county resident living far off the main road, he'd certainly be trespassing. And, perhaps, justifiably shot. His fingertips lingered on the knob a moment, and then he felt a subtle vibration; he quickly pulled his hand away, turned to stare behind himself self-consciously, then touched the doorknob again. The knob trembled in its lock, steadily vibrating, so he wasn't mistaken—

I've spent a week of my life searching for this place. I can't run away from it now. I've waited my entire life to find it again.

Certainly, longer than he'd ever wished to. His memory of the house had stayed alive in his mind over the years, haunted him through his adolescence, through college, through two relationships he'd failed to nurture more than his own obsession. He'd studied esoteric volumes more closely than his own textbooks, searching for meaning in his past experiences but never finding satisfaction. His mediocre grades were evidence of his inability to concentrate on the prosaic world. But now he'd finally found a stable job, saved enough to buy a reliable truck, earned his vacation days and executed a plan he'd drafted only after his father died.

Now I'll have my own story to tell the old people, Dad. And you won't have to listen.

Burrows turned the doorknob, feeling the hesitation of corrosion in his hand, hearing years of rust grinding in the mechanism. Then he pushed the door open and stepped inside.

As a clouded light filled the vestibule with resurrected dust motes, Burrow's boots fell still on a splintered wooden floor. He let his eyes focus through the shadows—but the sight confronting him wasn't one he'd expected. He stood within a short entryway breathing warm, stale air, the walls and ceiling around him strangely bent inward, the walls also striped by unusual protrusions beneath yellowed wallpaper, as if they'd been formed around a slightly curving lattice. Of course, he found no signs of supernatural entities, no levitating ghosts—the deathly silence unnerved him, though, the inrush of air from behind him chilling his neck.

Before him, beyond the end of the shallow vestibule, a mantle stood in the distance bearing a small pendulum clock, its counterweight hanging like a silent tongue, its face displaying an incorrect time: 6:30. The silence in the house meant the clock wasn't running, perhaps hadn't been running for a generation. But if the house had been abandoned long ago, why did it still hold any possessions? Surely the clock, as an antique, and even if no longer functioning, should have been confiscated long ago. The air kept pushing steadily at his back, insisting he step further inside.

Now Burrows felt his resolve fracture minutely. He felt himself swallowing involuntarily, but then chastised his reticence. No, he would examine every inch of the place, satisfy his superstitious beliefs, or prove his beliefs unfounded. No shadowy rooms would stop him.

He stepped forward, his footsteps echoing loudly in the absence of other sounds. *I shouldn't expect to hear anything else this far into the wilderness.* The short hallway opened into a living room, dully lit by sunlight struggling through the clouded front windows. He'd left the front door open, the morning air following him into the room and rippling the filthy linen tarps covering an old sofa to his right and an old table and chairs to his left. The air seemed to swirl beneath these coverings, ballooning their fabric up and down to the rhythm of the breeze pouring through the narrow vestibule, and for a moment Burrows stood breathing deeply in time to these displays, until he recognized his mimicry and suddenly held his breath. *Why does this room seem familiar?* But most old country houses were similarly designed, and he'd visited so many with his father and grandfather in his childhood.

Then he turned toward the clock on the mantle and leaned close to study its age. Yes, the glass and the tarnished mechanism found life in another century, though he felt curiously disappointed the clock wasn't functional. He stared at the hour and minute hands behind the glass face for a long moment, attempting to understand why they'd ceased moving at that exact time, forming a perfect vertical line. But the time at which the hands were stopped needn't have significance.

The linen tarps continued their rising and falling, feigning moving bellows in the shadows, and he now wished he'd shut the front door; but he still had several rooms to explore. To his left stood a stairway leading up to the next floor, completely hidden in dense shadows; to the right of the mantle, a doorway leading on to another room, perhaps a kitchen. He knew he'd eventually have to challenge the dark passage of the stairway, but for now he chose to walk through the doorway and into the adjacent room.

The room indeed proved to be a kitchen, or a large pantry, though he had difficulty seeing in the feeble light forcing its way through the accumulated filth on the only window, the same window he'd seen from the back of the house. A splintering wooden door—the back door he'd seen next to the window—faced him, so he immediately tried to open it to let in more light, but the mechanism seemed locked, or perhaps rusted shut, leaving him to peer through darkness. A rusted basin stood on iron feet beneath the sill, while a pair of standing cupboards, undoubtedly once beautiful antiques, stood decaying in the gloom, their doors hanging open on broken hinges, their shelves empty except for cobwebs spun up from the dirty floor. Burrows refrained from touching any of these accouterments, blaming a consideration for hygiene, though he'd never previously obsessed over cleanliness. An impression of filthiness kept his hands down at his sides, as well as a stale, almost nauseating scent of rotten food not actually in evidence. *What am I sensing?*

Again, a terrible feeling of familiarity overcame him, as if he were trying to conjure an inaccessible memory, and failing. His mother had died when Burrows was only an infant, but his father and grandfather kept an immaculate house, and so he possessed no childhood memories of squalor. Why? He leaned in to study the basin in the impoverished light, seeing nothing but a rusted drain and patterns of corrosion oddly frightening in their design, as if delineating black veins branching across the partially enameled metal. Then, surprisingly, a faint sound seemed to emerge from the drain—

Burrows leaned even closer, careful to keep from touching the basin, definitely hearing a soft whistling noise emitting from the open drain. He pulled back and bent to examine the dark space between the basin's iron legs, finding a long pipe connected to the bottom of the basin and stabbing down through the wooden floor. He stood up again and leaned in once more, listening carefully; a gentle burping of air definitely rose from the drain, coming from—where?

Burrows instantly regretted sniffing at the drain to see if he could detect a definable aroma—the stench assaulting his senses caused him to jerk backward violently. He stood coughing and spitting between curses, wiping his face on the sleeve of his jacket, still trying to define the odor. Sewage? No, it seemed more like bile, or vomit. *The damned thing must be attached to an old septic tank.*

This seemed a logical assumption, though he'd never heard of a kitchen drain being directly joined to a conduit for sewage. Still, country people often built their homes in creative ways, given their financial limitations, and he found himself wanting to accept a prosaic explanation.

As he stood in the shadows of the kitchen, still trying to wipe the ugly odor from his nose and failing, he noticed a door near the corner of the wall he hadn't noticed on entering the room. *Why didn't I see it?* But his eyes were only now adjusting to the darkness of the house. With insight he didn't understand—*why does this house seem so goddam familiar*—he instinctively knew the door belonged to the stairs leading down to the cellar.

Now the sound of burping air became more discernible in the room, but Burrows only glanced back at the basin in disgust, forgetting its mysteries in lieu of approaching the cellar door. When he reached to touch the doorknob—the same series of faux crystal hardware as the front door—he felt the house's vibrations suddenly transferring through his boot heels. His hand fell away as he stood listening. But had he actually *heard* the strange beating, or only *felt* it in his body? Was he actually hearing it now? Yes, it seemed more intense, stronger, very strong, and when he finally touched the door knob the vibration flowed through the glass straight up his arm. *It's going to be dark down there. Damned dark. I'll save the cellar for last.*

Abruptly, he dropped his hand, turned away from the door and stepped quickly from the kitchen into the living room again. The brighter light heartened him, though why he couldn't fathom. He really hadn't experienced phenomena bizarre enough to frighten him; certainly, his isolation had to be to blame for his impressions. *This is just an old house.*

But as he approached the staircase leading to the second floor, the realization fell over him that his perception of the interior of the house didn't quite match his examination of its exterior. The dimensions seemed incongruent—the interior of the house presented differently than the exterior suggested. He felt another room should exist adjacent to the kitchen, and yet the space appeared finite, indicating either a misjudgment on his part, or— or what? He stood by the foot of the stairs studying the light from the open doorway, a light seemingly more subdued than bright sunshine might provide, stifling an urge to turn and run from the place, leaving its incongruities for other eyes. *No, I've waited too long. I won't be scared away.*

Burrows turned from the light and began climbing the stairs, buried in black shadows. His weight strained the risers, raising muffled groans with every step; his ascent felt as if he were rising through an inky black tunnel, its shadows unrelieved by the looming hallway. The staircase possessed no handrail, so climbing through the darkness left him with slight vertigo, and a fear he might fall off into—what? An infinite blackness? He struggled to focus, failing. When he reached the top of the stairs he nearly stumbled, expecting the staircase to continue; he cursed, told himself to be more careful, then turned to his left.

Only two thin lines of light lit the floor of the hallway beneath two doors, the closed doors to the house's bedrooms, no doubt; no other doors, pantries, or shelves shone in the insufficient light.

Burrows stepped forward, listening, and this time heard a faint sound coming from one of the rooms, perhaps the nearest to him. He reached out and found another crystal doorknob in his hand. He turned the knob, still listening intently to the sound—a chattering noise, perhaps of swarming insects, though not bees or wasps—and pushed open the door. A wave of subdued light stung his eyes, sunlight filtering through the single window. He stood in a small bedroom without a bed, only a dirty, web-strewn white wicker chair dormant near the window, its caned backing splintered and clattering from a stiff breeze blowing in from a jagged hole in the lowest glass pane.

The room lay empty except for the chair and a thick layer of dust on the floor. An old house, of course, wouldn't possess inlaid closets, but he'd expected an old bureau or standing wardrobe. Now the chattering noise seemed to intensify, so he crossed the room to investigate it. He hadn't seen the broken pane from outside the house, though felt certain he would've noticed. In fact, he'd marveled that a house so old had kept all the glass in its windows intact.

Now he stood staring at a clearly broken glass pane while an unaccountably consistent burst of air poured in strongly enough to flutter the broken cane backing of the chair, robust enough to raise the chattering he'd heard from behind a closed door. The lengths of cane flicked against one another, creating an almost intelligible fount of words. *What am I hearing?* He bent closer, but not close enough to touch the chair, closed his eyes and heard—

Language? No, not from a chair. But the more intently he listened, the more he became convinced he heard something other than incidental sounds, as if someone who spoke a foreign language were whispering just strongly enough to be heard by an uninformed listener. The longer Burrows stood listening, the more he seemed to perceive the *intent* of the words being interpreted through an analogue of speech—imprecations, angry curses, forebodings spat with vehemence into the room. Images began coming into his mind, shadowy shapes, inhuman, animal. *Damn it, it's just my imagination.*

He straightened away from the chair and rubbed his mouth with his fingers. No, he *couldn't* be hearing actual words. His mind had begun conjuring eidolons where none existed, his superstitious expectations creating atrocities from his subconscious.

Burrows turned to leave, but then felt an overwhelming desire to sit in the wicker chair. Why? He turned again to stare at the chair and its fluttering cane backing, still perplexed at the constancy of the current of air pouring in through the break in the window glass. *Why in the world would I want to sit in an old broken chair?* Had he seen a similar chair before in his childhood? Sat in one? But no memory of such a chair came to mind. Still, the desire remained, nearly intolerable, so he turned and walked from the room into the hallway again.

When he began moving down the hallway, he couldn't help feeling that its length didn't correspond to his estimated width of the house. He'd taken too many steps, or perhaps only a couple feet more than he should have taken, but the interior of the upper floor definitely seemed larger than its exterior implied. He felt absolutely certain, now. And when he stood before the second closed door, thin reddish light at its threshold marking its location in the hallway, his grandfather's words flared up in his conscious thoughts like a stern warning—*Keith, it only looks like a house.*

His confidence waning, he turned the doorknob and pushed open the door of the second bedroom.

The cause of the reddish light met his eyes as he stepped into the room—a single window, absent of any damage, appeared smeared over with a film of red, yellow, and brown matter, unidentifiable fluids long dried on the glass, which gave the incoming sunlight a strange, multihued glow, as if through a multicolored membrane. The bloody light fell over the floor and walls of the room to bathe Burrows in its colors, and when he stared at his hands, his fingers, they seemed to undulate with a bloody wash.

The room lay as empty as the previous room, except, like the previous room, for one object, an antique standing mirror, full-length, oval, and kept prisoner by a splintering wooden frame from another century. The mirror stood directly across the room from the window and lay filled with its strange light, a cast of dust over its glass obscuring fine details in its reflection, rendering its images oddly opaque. The mirror gave Burrows an impression of a sunny sky reflected in a pond inundated by algae, though the bloody colors it contained spoke of the dead rather than the living.

The chatter from the adjacent room no longer seemed audible; silence held him, as well as the close air of a room which hadn't been ventilated in decades. He turned from the window to the mirror, finding a disturbing kinship between the two, as if the mirror had been intentionally positioned to reflect the grotesque light. Again, why? The house obviously hadn't been lived in for many, many years, why leave only a few furnishings behind, and positioned so peculiarly? *There must be some meaning in this.* But nothing he'd experienced seemed to make sense, no rational sense.

Suddenly, the intensity of the light changed, as if clouds were moving over the sun above the house. Burrows watched the window a moment, studying the random alteration of colors as the light shifted and played over the filth covering the glass; then he turned to watch this display reflected in the large, oval mirror, stepping closer as his curiosity deflected his apprehension. The merging of colors in the dust layer created an artist's palette on the glass, and, as he stood watching, his vision, assisted by a momentary trance, blurred in his perceptions until he began seeing definite shapes, forms moving beneath the crimson veil, writhing, perhaps, or pulsing—yes, pulsing to the rhythm of the vibrations he'd felt coming from the doorknob leading down to the cellar. *What am I seeing?* He could almost discern a dreadful, curved shape pulsing—

Burrows abruptly shook himself from his trance and turned away from the mirror. It seemed as if the house were trying to leave him paralyzed, or, at least, caught in a trance so deep he'd never be able to break away. Or was this only his imagination again?

Then an unsolicited thought came into his mind—*in the cellar.*

Where had this thought come from? From himself? Was he only talking to himself?

All the years of his life since that day in his childhood had been a slow building to that morning. Nothing in his life had ever seemed as meaningful as the mystery of that single afternoon, and now he felt too afraid to complete that impossibly long journey to some revelation. *I should leave. Go home, find satisfaction in the life I've made for myself.* But he knew that unless he finally solved the mystery of that day, he'd never find satisfaction. His life would remain an open question, a life without purpose.

Burrows left the room, walked down the long hallway and down the stairs.

A long moment passed before he realized the deadened light now falling on the living room hadn't originated from a cloudy sky, but because the front door now stood shut. He waited, listening for any sign of another person in the house, but heard nothing. The door must have slowly closed itself owing to a shifted foundation—but even though this seemed a reasonable explanation, would the angle prove steep enough to allow gravity to succeed against rusted hinges? *I should leave.* Despite his reservations, he turned and walked into the kitchen again.

As soon as he entered the room the regurgitations from the basin sink resumed, raising a putrid smell, turning his stomach. He ignored this distraction and stepped to the cellar door, his fingers hovering over the faux crystal doorknob. Though his hand wasn't touching the knob, he still felt the vibrations, the heavy pulsing which had given the voluble old men an impression of a beating heart. He knew the darkness awaiting him would feel intolerable, he knew his nerves were nearly wrecked by his circumstances; still, he *had* to know. He grasped the doorknob, turned it, pushed back the door.

A percussive wave rolled through Burrows' body as if he were standing in front of powerful amplifiers—but no music swept through him, only the incessant drumming beat, now obnoxious and painful. The flight of stairs began in subdued light and terminated in complete darkness. He tried listening for any sounds beneath the powerful vibrations but heard nothing distinct. *I wish I had a flashlight, a lantern. Any damned thing.* Now he held his breath and began his descent, again without the benefit of a handrail to steady himself, falling deeper and deeper into shadows.

By the time he reached the cellar floor he stood blanketed in blackness, blind to anything except a thin sliver of light from the window he'd seen half-buried on the side of the house. The beating continued, stronger now, as if rising in intensity in his presence, buffeting his chest and face, electrifying his spine. He moved closer toward the middle of the room, then stopped, dissuaded by his blindness. He gazed up over his shoulder toward the cellar door, but couldn't see any light. *This isn't an illusion.*

Then Burrows' body cringed under the assault of a new level of sound; he thought he might lose his hearing to the relentless beating. No matter where he turned, he perceived nothing in the darkness except for the horrible drumming, and then he covered his ears with his palms, a searing pain erupting in his skull. His entire body now shuddered with the force of the vibrations, as if he were standing at the center of an earthquake, strange images flashing in his mind, things moving in shadows, large shapes, limbs swimming through the air. Then, overwhelmed by the forces threatening to break his bones by the sheer violence of their sound, he screamed out, loud enough to be heard over the cacophony, "God damn you! What are you!"

The beating stopped. For a moment Burrows stood in complete silence, still drowning in black shadows, but finding relief from the brutality of the noise. He dropped his hands from his ears and turned in the cellar, still trying to see *something*, anything that might explain the sound. Then something—a large, black shape in a far corner—caught his attention, and he stood trying to focus on its movement. This shape seemed to undulate through the retinal flashes of his eyes as they struggled to see in nearly complete darkness, a large, round mass, lying on—a table, a bed perhaps, rising, falling, its surface smooth enough, or wet enough, to catch minute flashes of light from the buried window; then the beating began again, softly at first, and then rising in volume, stronger, in concert with the expansion and contraction of the massive thing on the table. Burrows watched this exhibition, eyes wide, his lungs struggling to find enough air in the close space of the cellar, his hands cupping his ears again, until, through the dense shadows, he believed he caught sight of the emergence of two tiny white spots on the surface of the object. Eyes?

Then Burrows shut his own eyes in agony as he felt his heart beating violently in his chest, stronger, and with so much pain he fell to his knees expecting his heart might rupture from the strain. His heart beat with a ferocity of an animal trying to escape its cage, pounding against his sternum, while the forsaken beating sound rose again in intensity and deafened him. He opened his eyes long enough to see the black thing in the corner of the cellar pulsing with orgiastic power, its white eyes flashing, as if, within its beating lay laughter unheard by human beings except in supernatural dimensions. *You've been to this house before, haven't you? You found the ley lines known to ancient cultures, you opened the door on a house that wasn't a house, but only appeared to be a house to a frightened little boy, to an obsessed young man, and you had to know, you had to walk into the mists of inhuman energies, you had to know that a house is the sum of its parts, just like the body, just like the spirit—*

Burrows felt his chest heave again and thought he would die, fall dead in the shadows of the old cellar. His pain flared again, and he screamed, holding his torso with his arms and bending over far enough for his forehead to touch the moist cellar floor. A vision of himself as a little boy rose in his thoughts, superimposed over recent memories of him moving from room to room, the two series of memories merging in time and becoming one new memory, one expression of his life. Then he thought he heard a voice—

Welcome home.

Bright light rushed in, blinding him again, but the brutal pain ceased, his heart ceased trying to beat through his chest and the ugly, persistent, deafening vibrations ceased as well. Exhausted, he straightened on his knees, his eyes slowly adjusting to bright sunlight, his hand still pressed against his sternum as if to hold his heart inside himself. But he felt no pain, and when he stared around himself he realized he knelt in an open field of grass, the sunlight of noonday having burned the mists away. He no longer knelt in the cellar of a house   the house had vanished around him.

Burrows rose to his feet in the clearing, trying to rescue his senses from the nightmare he'd endured. Then he turned in a circle, trying to find the old house again. Several sparrows flew overhead in the direction of a standing grove of oak trees; birds sang in the distance, too, and he heard the annoying sound of horseflies darting past his ears. No, the house had vanished back into the mists, which hadn't found their origin in the quiet Texas countryside. He stood for a very long time trying to understand his experiences, trying to weave together some meaning from seemingly disparate incidents. He *couldn't* have been hallucinating.

Slowly, and wondering if the house would manifest before him again, he began walking back toward his pickup truck, contemplating his observations in the relative silence of the wilderness, knowing he had so much more to learn, to study. If he returned to the clearing later in the year, if he adequately prepared himself for the house again, he might finally find the answer to its mysteries. *I'll draft my notes, I'll write up my theories, come back to the same location. I'll be much better prepared.*

But as the days passed, and the weeks, and then years, Keith Burrows never seemed to collect his notes or form any theories; and no matter the times he woke in the middle of a dark, dark night, fighting off nightmares that were only memories, he couldn't resurrect the obsession that once held him, or form any conclusion to his experiences. Nor did Burrows feel any true desire to find the house again, and for a very long time he couldn't understand why this should be the case, until he recognized a complete absence of caring in himself, not only for the house and its mysteries, but for much of anything else. He'd lost his heart for life.

Railroad Bill Rides the Bus

Bret McCormick

Last spring my mama called and said she wanted me to promise I'd come home for Easter. Mama lives in Houston County, outside Crockett a few miles. Easter's a big thing to Mama and I knew she wanted to cook a big meal and have me go to that little Baptist Church with her to honor the resurrection of our Lord. I tried to find a graceful way out, an excuse she might take at face value without asking too many questions. But Mama is nothing if not a persistent woman. She would not take no for an answer. And I didn't want to outright lie to her. Not with her going on about Jesus and my obligation as a Christian to remember the price he paid on the cross. She knows how to make me feel just plain shameful sometimes. I suppose that may be what the good Lord had in mind as a mother's primary purpose on Earth.

I told her I'd try to get time off from work. She knew I'd sold my beat-up Toyota at the first of the year. It truly was falling apart. I hadn't lied to her about that. The whole truth, the part I didn't tell her, was I'd been laid off my UPS job after the Christmas rush. The money I got from selling the car was the only thing that was keeping me going. My rent was cheap. I was paying $245 a month for a spare room in the home owned by a convicted sex offender. The guy never did me any real harm, said he'd been set up by his ex-wife, but that's another story.

Mama said she'd send me bus fare. I told her that wasn't necessary, that I'd be there on Good Friday and we'd have a fine Easter together. I called in a few favors and bought a roundtrip bus ticket to Crockett. My bus would leave at 1:40 a.m. on Good Friday and arrive in Crockett at the Exxon Station that doubles as a depot at 7:45 a.m. I figured I'd just sleep most of the way. That way the trip wouldn't seem so long.

I took everything of value from my room and left it over at my friend Sal's place. James, the sex offender, wasn't above snooping through my stuff, especially if I was going to be away the whole weekend. I'd never caught him red-handed but I'd seen signs he had been in my room when I was gone. I'd been down and out before but I'd never ridden a bus other than the school buses when I was a kid. At thirty-five, I wasn't a kid anymore. The days of wangling rides from willing friends were long gone. Truth is, I felt like the biggest kind of loser when I arrived at the Greyhound Station in downtown Fort Worth in the middle of the night.

The stark environment, stained by years of grit and grime, harshly illuminated by the overhead fluorescents, one of which was flickering, reminded me of nothing more than a passive trap for lost souls. No smiling faces at the Greyhound in the middle of the night, I can tell you that for sure. I stepped through those automatic doors and felt like I'd crossed over into the *Twilight Zone*. At least it was a little warmer getting out of the nip of that early morning chill.

An old man with a battered suitcase looked up at me. I didn't make eye contact. I was afraid he'd try to panhandle me and, after I'd bought my bus ticket, I only had thirty dollars to my name. That thirty would have to last me until I got back in town, until I found some kind of paying job. There was a young couple snuggled together, talking softly to one another. Maybe students going somewhere on their spring break, I thought. Then I revised my thinking. Students who had money to pay a university probably had enough to get a cheap fare on one of the discount airlines. If they didn't have the cash, their parents probably did.

These two might just be free spirits who were running away to start a new life together, hoping the world wouldn't be so hard, so demanding, in some other town. I knew about that, I'd been there. A janitor in a gray uniform swept the floor. That was a losing battle.

I sat down in a corner, away from the others, and waited for the announcement of my bus's departure. I needed to keep my distance, felt like I was in danger of being swallowed up by something Christianity has no name for, a force more personal than the devil, a process more nuanced than heaven or hell. When the announcement came, it blasted me out of my skin, working my last nerve. I guess they had the volume turned up extra loud so even folks in the restroom could hear it. I went back out into the chilly night. Even in the heart of the city I could smell the awakening life of spring on the breeze. I wished I wasn't leaving town. Don't get me wrong, I love my mama, she's a dear soul. I truly love her, wanted to hug her, and smell the goodness of her kitchen. I was just sick of being the failure, the black sheep, the ne'er do well son who couldn't win for losing.

I climbed the steps up into that bus feeling lower than a snake's belly. I picked a spot toward the back and rested my head on my backpack. I just wanted to sleep. I wanted to dream of being anywhere else. Even a nightmare was welcome so long as it wasn't about me riding a bus to see my mama for Easter. I was already living that nightmare. I wanted escape, even sweaty, fearful, running from the devil escape. Thank God, he gave me the escape I was craving.

In the dream, I am on the bus and we're whizzing along the highway, not in the middle of the night but in bright daylight. I look out the windows and see a brilliantly lit, Easter-egg colored world flying past. Inside the bus everyone is happy. People are talking and they're all dressed in bright colors. There's a glow around everyone and everything and nobody has to explain this is lifeforce energy, the sacred blood of Jesus running through everything, or the om the Hindus speak about. The thought occurs to me that this bus is one of the many mansions Christ talked about, a special little niche created for souls like me, folks who had a hard time in the real world. A woman cries out, "Watch out for that dog!" The driver slams on his brakes, but not quick enough. I hear a yelp and the woman covers her eyes and begins to cry. I get out of my seat and walk toward the front to get a look at whatever it is that has happened. As I pass the crying woman, she opens her hands enough for me to see she looks like my mother. Not now, not my old mother, but the way she looked when she was in her twenties. "Oh, no!" I hear someone shout. I step down off the bus and see it's the driver. He has his hat off as a sign of respect and he's looking down at a black dog lying dead in the center of the crossroads. The driver looks up at me and says, "What are we going to do now?" In the background, behind the driver, on one side of the road, I see a swarm of dark, ill-defined creatures, all antsy and eager to snatch up that dog. On the other side of the street I see some calm, flowing, human-shaped beings, just watching. I look down at the dog with blood flowing out of its nose. I say, "I guess we gotta bury him." The driver nods.

"No!" someone shouts. The voice comes from above. I look up and see an old black man, taller than a two-story house, staring down at us. The black man is leaning on a gnarly staff with a snake wrapped around it. "Don't touch my dog," he says, "That dog belongs to me." Then the old man shrinks down til he's a normal sized man, about the same height as me and the bus driver, but skinny under his loose, thrift store clothes.

The driver looks scared, even though the old black man is smiling and doesn't seem upset at all that we've run over his dog. "You again," the driver says, having trouble getting the words out because he's so frightened. He's real scared, you might say terrified. The old black man stoops down and touches the dog. The snake on his walking stick slithers off and right into the dog's open mouth. Softly, the old man says, "Come to Papa Legba." That name seems familiar but I can't say why. Next, the old man is climbing up into the bus. The driver looks at me and says, "Not again. I can't take much more of this!" I follow the old man. He carries the dog to the seat where I'd been sitting before the bus came to a stop. As he passes down the aisle, all the colorful passengers reach out and touch him, like he's their favorite uncle or something. The old man lays the dog down on my seat. I see the blood collecting in a small puddle on the floor. The old man grins at me. "What now?" I ask. "Sit down," he says, "talk to Papa Legba." He pushes me down right on top of the dog.

I woke up with a jump. There were no bright colors, no dead dog, no happy passengers, just a bunch of depressed shadows of humanity, people like me, riding the bus because they couldn't afford to do otherwise. People winding their way into another Good Friday with no joy in their hearts, no sense of belonging, nothing to look forward to. Right away I wished I was still in the dream. In that other world strange shit happened but my soul seemed lighter, stronger.

"You still in the dream."

I looked across the aisle and saw a slender, tall, muscular black man dressed in very old-fashioned looking clothes. On his head was a wide-brimmed hat, something like you might see in a western movie. Nobody had to explain that the black man had read my thoughts. That's why he'd said I was still in the dream. I didn't recognize him. He had not been on the bus before. I imagined the bus had made a stop somewhere while I was asleep, that the black man had come onboard while I was dreaming.

"This bus didn't make no stop. This bus don't stop til I say so." He grinned at me.

Without asking permission, he slipped across the aisle and seated himself next to me. I pulled away toward the window, letting my backpack drop to the floor. I suddenly remembered the dog's blood and glanced down to see if I'd dropped the pack into a puddle of blood.

"That blood was ceremonial, just to open the door," he said, as if that explained everything.

"Who are you?" I asked the question, but just like I'd believed I'd heard the name Papa Legba before in my dream, I believed I already knew this black stranger's name. His eyes were deep, like a vertical shaft in one of those abandoned Colorado silver mines. Deep they were and filled with treasure, not played out like those old mines. Treasure. But was he here to share that treasure or just to taunt me with it? Crazy thoughts. I knew those thoughts were crazy even as I was thinking them. Then I wondered if I really knew who was doing the thinking.

Like I say—crazy.

"My name is Morris Slater. Some folks call me Railroad Bill." He looked at me with a sideways tilt of his head, almost like he was saying he really shouldn't have to explain this to me.

The name rang a bell. But it was a bell that hadn't been rung since sometime deep in my childhood. It was an old vinyl record, an LP from my grandfather's collection that my mother used to play every now and then. Ramblin' Jack Elliott singing about Railroad Bill.

The man on the bench seat beside me grinned and nodded. He knew I was picking up the thread. Softly, he sang the words, "Railroad Bill, Railroad Bill. He never worked and he says he never will. Ride, ride, ride."

I started to say, 'How do you do that?' But for an instant I saw Papa Legba's face grinning at me and I knew it was a foolish question. Old Papa Legba could do anything he damn well pleased, couldn't he? Like hijacking a man's dream and riding shotgun on his reality. I said nothing. I knew thinking was just as good as shouting where Railroad Bill was concerned.

"That bit about me never working, it wasn't the crackers said that about me. That was my own people added that line to the song. They didn't want to work hard and they imagined I never had. They was wrong, though. I worked in three different turpentine camps. Course, a soft white boy like you wouldn't know nothing about that kind of hard work. Turpentine gets in your skin, in your eyes, down in your chest. It can make a man miserable."

I felt like I needed to sort of apologize. "I can imagine," I said.

"Yes!" He laughed out loud. I looked around the bus, thinking his laughter was sure to draw some looks from the other passengers, but no one paid a bit of attention. "Yes, you can imagine. That's why you seen Papa Legba. He don't waste his time on people with no imagination. It's a gift. Without it, you a slave to whatever the dream of the world throws at you."

The dream of the world.

From deep within my mind, like a gusher erupting up from a black pool in my subterranean consciousness, I remembered the words, 'A dream is always dreaming us.' Now, I couldn't tell you where I'd heard those words, or if I'd read them in a book. I just knew they were familiar and that they were important.

"Yes," said Railroad Bill, Morris Slater, the ghost in the seat next to me. "It's all dreams." He brought his hands together, intertwining his fingers. "Dreams all tangled together with other dreams, wove up tighter than the threads in your mama's bed sheets."

I was interested. I wanted to hear what Bill had to say, though I wasn't sure he even was Bill and not Papa Legba. I knew that everything he was telling me was knowledge already buried deep in my own mind, that his mind and my mind were woven together like his bony fingers. I knew he was a dream and he was waking me up from another dream I'd been caught up in for a long time. Bill, Papa Legba, me, all of us, just one big ongoing, never-ending process that proceeded through time and space, dreaming itself in and out of being. It was like being outside myself, still I retained enough of an individual identity to wonder why he'd chosen me.

"I didn't choose you," he said. "You chose me."

"I did?"

"Yes, sir. You chose me cause you were tired of your weak little, whiny ass, poor me, peckerwood dream you been living."

Okay, so that made me angry. And Bill laughed. He laughed hard.

"You a whiny little no account bitch, wallowing in a hog trough of self-pity."

And then he went right on laughing. I wondered what would happen if I tried to smack him with my fist right in his self-righteous, scornful face.

"You can try," he said. "Don't think it'll accomplish anything for you, though. But I will tell you this. Anger might be just what you need. You get angry enough, you might just punch your way into a new world, might just stop being a whipped pup with your tail all curled up around your pecker."

"I'm listening," I said.

"You think you got it hard. Son, you don't know what hard is. Try being a nigger, see how that suits you."

At the sound of the N-word I looked around the bus. I already knew nobody could see Railroad Bill except for me. All I knew was I didn't want anyone on the bus to think I'd blurted that word out. Everybody just rocked along on the gently swaying bus, dreaming their own dreams, dreams that didn't include me or Railroad Bill.

"My mama taught me never to use that word," I said.

"And for that, I say she's a good woman. Feisty, strong-willed, too. Not a little whipped dog like her boy."

I drew a deep breath like I was gonna give him what for, I wanted to rail at him for insulting me that way, but by the time I looked in his eyes the wind just left my sails. My resolve deflated like a balloon the morning after a party. I knew he was telling the truth, even if it was rude as hell and not the sort of thing you should ever say to a stranger.

"We ain't strangers," Bill said. He wove his fingers together again to illustrate his point. I nodded. He flung his arm over my shoulder. His arm had weight, no different from a real flesh-and-blood man. It occurred to me maybe he would actually feel a swift punch in the nose. He shook his head. "I wouldn't try it. A ghost that can feel a punch can make you feel one, too. And I've had a lot more practice hitting folks than you have."

"Just so I understand; you're like the ghosts in that story about Scrooge. You come here to set me on a better path, except there's only one of you and this is Easter instead of Christmas."

He gave a sardonic little laugh, not big and loud like before. "You know what hubris is, white boy?"

"Yeah, I think so."

"Well, you should. You white folks are so damn full of it you hardly ever see the elephant."

"See the elephant?"

"The way things really are. Figure of speech. No. I am not here for your benefit. I'm here doing my own work, weaving my own dream. It's just you were lucky enough to come along. Papa Legba want to help you out. But if you can't see you're needing help, if you unable to accept help, if you are so full of hubris you can't turn the corner … well, if that's the case, you deserve what you get."

"Papa Legba," I said, thinking about my other dream, "is he mad at us for hitting his dog?"

Bill grinned real big. "Come on, now, you know better than that."

"I do?"

"Damn, son! You are the dog!"

When he said those words it was like I was there sitting on a seat with Bill and at the same time I was falling into a black abyss, falling and falling, and then I hit the rocky bottom. A jolt of realization, a painful awakening swept through me.

"Now. That's better. Ever hear of rock bottom? That's where you are. Now that you've arrived, you can set your course for wherever you wanna go."

"I can?"

"Yes. And you already know you can. Got nothing to do with me saying it. You saying it to yourself. You standing under the half-moon at the crossroads, boy. Half-moon's a good sign for you to stand under. Which way you gonna go?"

"Up."

He grinned. "That's right."

We rode on in silence for a minute or two.

"They call you Railroad Bill. What are you doing on this bus?"

"Reckon they ought to call me Greyhound Bill?" He laughed and showed those white teeth.

"Well, yeah. Besides, I heard you were buried in Florida. I think that's what my granddaddy said."

"I'm here because of him." Bill nodded toward the driver.

"The driver?"

"Yep. And that business about my grave in Florida; just more of the white man's lies."

"Why'd they lie about that?"

"They sent my body to Birmingham, Alabama where some greedy ass bastards done what they called a petrification. They made my body sos it would never rot away, not for a long time, not like a dead man's supposed to. They wanted to show me on exhibit. Folks was ready to pay good money to see the remains of the famous Railroad Bill. See, I was the most outrageous uppity nigger any white folks ever heard tell of. White man shot at me, I shot right back. Killed a few of them. I outran their fat white asses every time they chased after me. Took a ambush in

Atmore, Alabama to bring me down. Even then, every one of those cornpone, peckerwood sumbitches lied about everything that happened. J. L. McGowan was the telegraph operator. When he saw I was dead, he ran over to the telegraph office and right away laid claim to the reward money. Twelve hunnerd dollars was a lot of money for a dead nigger back then. White men had got used to killing us just for the fun of it. But that's because they was killing little scared whipped pups like you. They didn't figure on old Railroad Bill fighting back. The man who shot me in the back wasn't J.L. McGowan. It was a bounty hunter name of Dick Johns, from Texas."

"So you came to Texas because the man who killed you was from here?"

"Only a living man would see it that way. Truth is, I can be anywhere I want, as many places as I like, and all at the same time."

"You're here for the driver?"

Bill nodded. "He's the great great grandson of Dick Johns. But I'm not here just to mess with Harold. That's his name, Harold Johns. I'm here because they didn't bury me in Florida. After they petrified my old body in Birmingham they brought it out west. The towns back east made it illegal to show my corpse for money. So they just brought my petrified body out here and went right on showing me around at fairs and carnivals until 1931."

"Really?"

"Gospel righteous truth."

"Where's your body now?"

"Prominent family, a family you've heard of, paid two thousand dollars for me after it got illegal to show a dead nigger's body around for money. They got me down in the cellar on one of their ranches in McLennan County."

"Really?"

"Sure enough. Course I spend a good deal of time messing with them, too. They kind of sickly. In the mind, I mean. For a few generations that family collected body parts from any famous renegades, anyone who stood up against their white authority. They dark people—dark in the soul, white in the skin. They go places in the dream I'd never dare to go. Too dark, too wicked. They know all about hell. Things you and me'll never know."

"Man, I don't know what to say."

"Sun's coming up soon. Not much time left to say anything. But I do need you to say something to the driver when you get off the bus."

"What's that?"

"Tell him Railroad Bill was here and sends his regards. Promise me now."

I promised.

The sun rose over the dense pines to the east and soon the bus was pulling up at the big Exxon station in Crockett. Bill was gone. I didn't see him leave. Just like I hadn't seen him come. I stopped by the driver before disembarking.

"Sir," I said.

"Yes?"

"I have a message for you."

The driver's eyes narrowed. "What's that?"

"The black man back there says to give you his regards. Said his name's Bill."

The color drained out of the driver's face.

"Who told you to say that? Who put you up to this?" He stood up and leaned into my face angrily, his sour breath filling my nostrils. I didn't budge, despite the man's sickening breath.

"Bill. Railroad Bill. He told me about your great great granddaddy. Sucks to be you."

Shouldering my pack, I climbed down from the bus and started walking. It was a good two and a half miles to Mama's place but I welcomed the exercise in the fresh morning air. The world around me was green, alive, vibrant, reemerging into a new phase of life. Just like me. I was doing that, too. I knew I could be a little more like Railroad Bill and a little less like a terrified mongrel.

Before I knew it, I was at Mama's back door, rattling the screen. A beautiful smile lit up her face as she responded to my knock, coming out of the kitchen, drying her hands on her apron. Already I could smell delicious food she'd been cooking for our Easter celebration. Born again, that's what I was. I hugged my mama and said a silent prayer of gratitude to God, Jesus, Papa

Legba, Railroad Bill, and any other gods or spirits that were woven into the big dream of which I was a slender thread.

That was one Easter I'll never forget.

Contributors

Julie Aaron, small town lesbian and published author previously featured in *Terrorcore's Doors of Darkness* anthology, currently lives in Houston with her awe-inspiring wife and their lazy German shepherd. Outside of her career at a children's hospital, she finds time to create stories about women that kill, survive, and deal with the devil. She has a passion for reading, desserts, and shining a light on queer stories. You can find her day-to-day life on Instagram @julierubixxcube

E. R. Bills
Known more for his non-fiction than fiction, E. R. Bills is an award-winning journalist and author from Fort Worth, Texas. He has over a dozen nonfiction titles with four publishers, and has written for the *Austin American-Statesman*, the *Fort Worth Star-Telegram*, *Texas Co-Op Power* magazine, *Fort Worth Magazine* and *Fort Worth Weekly*. His speculative fiction has been compared to the writings of Ray Bradbury, Richard Mattheson, Stephen King, and Theodore Sturgeon. His fiction titles include *Pendulum Grim*, *Nature Calls*, *The Amulet*, *A Dark White Postscript*, and *Tarry Tornado*. A *Kirkus* reviewer recently called his work "first-rate, thinking person's horror writing."

Lawrence Buentello is a prolific short story writer and poet from San Antonio, Texas. His fiction has been nominated for the Edgar Award and the Pushcart Prize, and he is a past winner of the Short Story America Prize. Buentello has published fiction in multiple genres, including literary fiction, science fiction, fantasy, mystery, humor, and the supernatural. His contact info is hesanantoniowriter@gmail.com.

T. Frazer Eliot was raised by smugglers and bootleggers in the Galveston Bay area. He spends his days pushing paper at The Spaceship Factory TM and his nights thinking about writing. His fiction and poetry have appeared in *Space and Time*, *Dark Planet*, *Lovecraft's Weird Mysteries*, and *Big Pulp*. He is currently working on a sci-fi zombie rom-com.

William Jensen is the author of the novel *Cities of Men*, and he served as the editor for *Road Kill: Texas Horror by Texas Writers, Vol. 7*. His short fiction has appeared in *Mystery Tribune*, *North Dakota Quarterly*, *The Texas Review,* and elsewhere. Mr. Jensen is the editor of *Southwestern American Literature* and *Texas Books in Review*.

Kathleen Kent is a *New York Times* bestselling author and an Edgar Award Nominee for her contemporary crime trilogy, *The Dime*, *The Burn*, and *The Pledge*. Ms. Kent is also the author of three award-winning historical novels, *The Heretic's Daughter*, *The Traitor's Wife*, and *The Outcasts*. Her seventh novel, *Black Wolf*, an international spy thriller, was published February 2023 and has received glowing reviews in both the US and the UK. She has written short stories and essays for *D Magazine*, *Texas Monthly* and *LitHub*, and has been published in the crime anthology *Dallas Noir*. In March 2020 she was inducted into the Texas Institute of Letters.

Andrew Kozma's fiction appears in *Apex*, *Factor Four* and *Analog*, while his poems appear in *Strange Horizons*, *The Deadlands*, and *Contemporary Verse 2*. His first book of poems, *City of Regret*, won the *Zone 3* First Book Award, and his second book, *Orphanotrophia*, was published in 2021 by Cobalt Press. You can find him on Bluesky at @thedrellum.bsky.social and visit his website at www.andrewkozma.net.

Bret McCormick is an author, artist, and filmmaker who resides with his wife in Bedford, Texas. His short stories can be found in *Road Kill*, *Weirdbook*, and various other anthologies. His movies can be seen on TUBI and his art can be viewed at BAMart.studio

Mario E. Martinez is the author of *San Casimiro, Texas: Short Stories*, *A Pig Named Orrenius & Other Strange Tales*, *Ashtree*, *NEO-Laredo*, and *The Glowing Pigs of El Cenizo*. He lives somewhere in South Texas. His works are available at marioemartinez.

Jae Mazer is a Canadian who was born in Victoria, British Columbia, and grew up in the prairies of Northern Alberta. After spending the majority of her life battling Sasquatches in the Great White North, she migrated south to Texas to have a go at the armadillos. She is a connoisseur and creator of gothic horror, splatterfolk, splatter westerns and folk horror. She is degreed, won awards, been in anthologies, has chameleon hair, and lots of skin ink. Mazer enjoys mustard and alcohol, and, these days, lets very little thing phase her.

Juan Manuel Pérez, a Mexican-American poet of Indigenous descent and the Poet Laureate for Corpus Christi, Texas (2019-2020), is the author of numerous poetry books including the award-winning, poetic-memoir, *THIRTY YEARS AGO: LIFE AND THE FIRST GULF WAR* (2023) and the Mexican-American Barrio Horror Novel-In-Verse, *LA SANTA MADRE TAMALERA* (2023). Juan, a former migrant worker, is also the 2021 Horror Authors Guild's Inaugural Lifetime Achievement Award winner and a recipient of a 2021 Horror Writer's Association Diversity Grant. This poet's credits also include a Regal Summit Book Award (2024), two Pushcart Prize Nominations (2017, 2023), three Elgin Book Award Nominations (2021, 2022, 2023), four Rhysling Award Nominations (2011, 2012, 2013, 2020), four Dwarf Star Award Nominations (2012, 2020, 2021, 2022) with one Honorable Mention win in 2022, and one H.E.R.O.I.C. People's Choice Award Nomination (2024). To learn more about this award-winning poet, combat vet, history teacher, and Native American Gourd Dancer, please check out his official website at: juanmperez.com.

L. H. Phillips is a retired molecular biologist with a life-long love of speculative fiction. She lives in San Antonio with her husband and cat.

Armando Sangre is a pseudonym used by an author and elementary school teacher from San Antonio.

Mary Elizabeth Splawn is a homemaker who discovered her passion for writing late. She published her first horror story, "Exorcist Camera," in *Road Kill, Vol. 5*.

Robert Stahl grew up in Texarkana, Texas. He based the campground in this story on a real-life campground in Central Texas, which is far less lascivious than the one depicted here. However, while sitting around the warm glow of the campfire at night, he couldn't help but wonder what hidden evils might be lurking in the darkness of those deep piney woods. He currently resides in Dallas with his husband and a rotating cast of rescue pets.

C. W. "Clint" Stevenson is a San Antonio native and he still resides there with his wife, son, and their retinue of furry companions. When Clint isn't working, he's spending time with his family, traveling, eating Mexican food, and collecting too many books to read in one lifetime. In 2023, Clint won the National Fantasy Fan Federation Short Story Contest. His work can be found in *Alien Dimensions*, *Illustrated Worlds Magazine*, *Creepy Pod*, and various other magazines and anthologies.

Lucas Strough is a writer, musician, podcaster, and journalist living in East Texas. He enjoys weird fiction, tabletop role-playing games, fermenting his own hot sauce, and befriending animals. "Toadflax" is his first published short story.

W. R. Theiss was raised in Kingsland, Texas, and started writing creatively at an early age. Always a horror fan, he got his earliest inspirations from the *Goosebumps* series and Texas ghost stories. He currently resides in Palacios, Texas with his wife and two sons and writes both fiction and non-fiction.

Aimee Trask is the pen name for an educator who resides in the Houston area. She loves books, film, and travel. "Tommy" is her first published piece of writing.

Bev Vincent is the author of *The Road to the Dark Tower* and *The Stephen King Illustrated Companion*, as well as over one hundred short stories published in *Ellery Queen's*, Alfred Hitchcock's and *Black Cat Mystery Magazines*, and *Cemetery Dance* magazine. In 2018, he co-edited the *Fight or Fright* anthology with Stephen King. To learn more, visit bevcincent.com.

OTHER HELLBOUND BOOKS
www.hellboundbooks.com

ROAD KILL: TEXAS HORROR BY TEXAS WRITERS - VOL 8

For four years now, Bret McCormick and E. R. Bills have been beating the bushes and peering into abandoned wells to seek out the most terrifying tales the Lone Star State has to offer. They have left no stone unturned, no attic unexplored, and no grave undesecrated.

And boy howdy, their diligence has paid off! Road Kill Volume 4 is the best and grimmest yet!

You hold in your hands a grand collection of 16 goose-flesh-inducing prose. But, don't just take our word for it; these sixteen stories speak – or perhaps scream – for themselves.

Featuring tales of Texas terror from:

Corey Lamb, E. R. Bills, James H Longmore, William Jensen, Patrick C. Harrison III, W. H. Gilbert, Jeremy Hepler, Dan Fields, Thomas Kearnes, Sylvia Ney, Mark A. Nobles, Russell C. Connor, Elliott Baxter, Ralph Robert Moore, Carmen Gray, and Andrew Kozma

ROAD KILL: TEXAS HORROR BY TEXAS WRITERS - VOL 7

Everything is bigger in Texas - including the horror!

A Piney woods meth dealer clones Adolph Hitler. A nightmare exorcist meets an inexorable fined. An eyeball collector gets collected. The apparition of a lynching victim tracks down his executioners. A Texas lawman is undone by shades of his past. A Baphomet recruits converts as a local summer camp. The tales of the baker's dozen who appear in this anthology demonstrate why everything is scarier in Texas…

Including tales of terror from

Jeremy Hepler

Madison Estes

Bret McCormick

James H Longmore

ER Bills

Shawna Borman

And many more...

Flanagan

"Straw Dogs meets Fifty Shades - heart pounding, gut-wrenching, sexy as all hell and with a twist you'll never see coming!"

Meet the Sewells, your typical, all-American couple; happily married for ten years, respected high school teachers, still crazy about one another and with a secret, shared dark side.

During their annual Spring Break vacation to recharge their batteries and reconnect as a couple, they are waylaid by a perverse gang of misfits in the one horse, North Texas town of Flanagan.

Taken hostage as the focus of the gang's twisted games, the Sewells are brutalized into performing increasingly vicious physical, sexual and emotional acts upon one another, until events take an unexpected turn - triggered by an unintentional death.

As their circumstance descends into the worse nightmare imaginable, the Sewells find themselves involved in an altogether different situation...

The Gentleman's Choice

"A clever twist on the age-old adage, Art imitates reality, drives this terrifying possibility into the deepest places of your imagination." Andrew Neiderman, author of *The Devil's Advocate* and the V.C. Andrews novels.

A sleazy internet dating show blamed for a viewer's death, a host with a dark, secret past, and a killer with a sadistic grudge…

Someone is kidnapping and murdering previous contestants from the popular streaming show *The Gentleman's Choice* – a strictly adult hybrid of *The Bachelor and Love Island.* Private Investigator, Vanessa Young, is hired by a victim's family to infiltrate the show as a contestant to expose and capture the killer.

Vanessa and Cole Gianni, the show's charismatic star, begin to fall romantically for each other, until Vanessa's plan goes terribly awry when they're drugged and taken to a remote location to take part in their captor's own brutal, ultimately fatal, version of *The Gentleman's Choice.* With the clock ticking toward their fateful final night, Vanessa and Cole are forced into a battle of wills to survive their tormentor and escape with their lives before it's too late…

**A HellBound Books LLC
Publication**

www.hellboundbookspublishing.com

Made in the USA
Middletown, DE
30 October 2024